# Sandel

Angus Stewart was born in 1936, the son of John Innes Mackintosh Stewart, the novelist and Oxford academic who wrote bestselling crime fiction as Michael Innes.

He was educated at Bryanston School in Dorset, and later at Christ Church Oxford, loosely disguised as St Cecilia's in *Sandel*.

His first published work was 'The Stile', which appeared in the 1964 Faber anthology and won the Richard Hillary Memorial Prize in 1965. His breakthrough came with *Sandel*, his first novel, written in 1966–7 in the wake of the Wolfenden Report on Homosexual Offences and Prostitution, when homosexuals were routinely put in prison. In recent years, when the novel fell out of print, it developed a cult following and commanded a price of over a thousand pounds a copy on Amazon.

It is now known that Stewart filtered the human drama of the novel through the perspective of autobiography. He wrote pseudonymously about the central affair as his own in *Underdogs: Eighteen Victims of Society*, edited by Philip Toynbee in 1961.

In 1968 Stewart moved to Tangier in Morocco. His experiences there resulted in a second novel, *Snow in Harvest* (1969), and a travel diary entitled *Tangier: A Writer's Notebook* (1977). A third novel, *The Wind Cries All Ways*, which includes a startling description of the author's incarceration in a Tangier mental asylum, has never been published.

After his mother's death in 1979 he returned to live in England, and died in Oxfordshire twenty years later. A play based on *Sandel*, written, produced and directed by Glenn Chandler, was first performed at the Edinburgh Festival, 2013.

# SANDEL

## ANGUS STEWART

PILOT PRODUCTIONS

Published by Pilot Productions 2013
Grove Farm Sawdon, North Yorkshire YO13 9DY

2 4 6 8 10 9 7 5 3 1

A catalogue record for this book is available
from the British Library

ISBN 978-1-900064-08-8

First published in Great Britain in 1968
by Hutchinson & Co (Publishers) Ltd

Jacket design by Berni Stevens
Design Assistance by William Vokes-Dudgeon

Typeset in Life by Mark Heslington Ltd,
Scarborough, North Yorkshire
Printed and bound by Short Run Press Limited, Exeter, Devon

Other books by Angus Stewart

*Snow in Harvest*
*Tangier: A Writer's Notebook*

*Book One*

## 1

T HE satchel gave him a *bias*. That was the word. His
father's bowls had them. It meant a weight on one side.
When the bus dropped him, and he started up the long drive
to their house, he ended in the bushes on the right. Then he
had to put the satchel on the other shoulder, and after a bit
he was in the bushes on the left. Sometimes he didn't get that
far. Today he would have hit the lodge if he hadn't changed
shoulders quickly. Now he was in the laurel bush. Gregory was
there, playing with sticks and the ambulance.

'I've got a good swop,' David said.

Gregory stopped pushing the sticks in through the window
of the ambulance, and held it tightly. None of the paint was
chipped. It had a red cross and a silver bumper-bar. Gregory
gave him the broken tip-up. David pushed it away.

'What you got, then?' Gregory asked.

David took out his jeep. He still looked at the ambulance.

Gregory wrinkled his nose, and pushed the ambulance
round behind his back. 'Your mum went in one, didn't she?'
he said.

David didn't say anything. He couldn't remember. 'Well,
she did, my mum says. It was just after you was born.'

'You ought to swop,' David said, 'because it's my birthday
tomorrow. I'm eight and I'm having eight candles.'

'Can I come to the party?'

'You're not allowed,' said David. 'You only live in our lodge
and you're too young.' Gregory had a flap instead of proper
fly-buttons.

'Can I come next time, then?'

David squatted down so he could see the ambulance better.
'I'm not having any more birthdays. I'm going to boarding
school in the south.' He wasn't sure what the south was.

Gregory put the ambulance up his jumper. David held up

the jeep in front of his nose so that it was driving straight into his eyes. He closed one of them.

'Will you swop just those white tyres for the black ones off this jeep?' David changed eyes and tried to reach the front wheels with his tongue. It wouldn't stretch. He wondered if his mouth was big enough to make a garage for the jeep. But he only drove it up to his lips.

Gregory hugged the ambulance against his tummy. David knew they were too near the lodge for him to grab it. Anyway, when Gregory howled he felt frightened. He shoved him with his knee, so that he rolled on his side in a ball still hugging the ambulance.

'Your mother spanks you, doesn't she,' he said. He bent over Gregory and patted his behind. Really it was only pretending. 'She does, doesn't she?' He thought of kneeling on Gregory but was afraid he might squash.

Gregory snatched a handful of earth and threw it in his face. David turned away spitting.

'You don't scare me, see, an' you're not having my things!' Gregory shouted.

David stepped backwards, swinging his satchel by the strap like a battle-axe. 'I'm going to have a real car faster than the lawn-mower. Your father's going to build a road for it round the lake so I can race.'

'When are you having one?'

'Next year,' David said. I'm going to have a gun too. I might shoot you.

'My dad's got a gun.' Gregory was holding his wee. He still had the ambulance up his jumper, the way a boy at school kept a mouse.

'That's only an old one of ours,' David said. He put his hands in his pockets to show he didn't have to keep things up his jumper. 'I'm having a new one from London. It'll kill you better.'

'Why's your mum got no legs?' Gregory asked.

David picked up the satchel again and swung it round his head. 'She has. It's just they don't work.'

He swung the satchel faster and faster, wondering if it would lift him off the ground like a helicopter. Soon his arms began to ache. 'I don't want even the white tyres,' he said, stopping, and looking at Gregory. The ground under him seemed to be rocking as if he'd suddenly stood up in the boat on the lake.

Gregory was quite still though. He just sat on the ground, holding the tip-up now as if he might throw that, and watching him.

David started up the drive again, thinking about the words 'late' and 'legs'. In the break they'd been talking about him. He'd been in the playground under the window. 'Of course, they had him very *late*, I believe,' Miss Perry said. Then there was Miss Gardiner's voice, 'Isn't David an only child as well?' After that they'd made sort of clucking noises. 'It was a terrible beginning,' Miss Perry said. David didn't hear much more because he was watching a bee over the flower-bed. But then Miss Perry's voice suddenly said, very slowly, 'Poor woman!' It was shivery and sad like the whistle of a train before it goes into a tunnel. David wondered whether he should call it out aloud, now, to the bright park, to see whether it would sound the same here, and when he said it. He decided not to try.

Without watching where he was going he found he had hit the bushes again. If he wanted to go straight he could put the satchel on his back. He supposed he didn't because it was more fun to go in curves. Anyway, after the next twist in the drive, he used the bias to pass the place where he'd killed the blackbird. When the stone hit it he couldn't believe that he'd thrown it. You could never catch birds because they always flew away. But this one fell over, quite still. He hadn't been able to move either. Then he did go up to it, although his whole body was trembling. Its eye was half closed and crinkled like a squashed raisin that was split a bit and shiny inside. Its feet seemed to have withered away.

He was past the place and could see the house. From outside it looked heavy and dark. Inside it felt heavy and dark. In the music room he sometimes got under the piano because he thought the ceiling might slip down the walls. The windows seemed to be watching him as he turned the last corner in the drive, and he looked at the ground.

He opened the door very carefully; listening for the wheel-chair. The house was quite still. When he didn't know which room his mother was in, then she was somehow in all of them. There was none he could go into without the chair turning round. It was a square shape blocking the doorways and windows. When she was only talking she was shouting.

David put his satchel down beside the thin basket that was

full of guns and golf clubs. He took his spear. As soon as he was outside again he ran down the path to the lake, jumping into the air over the caterpillars because they were ten-foot high. Once or twice he looked back over his shoulder, but soon the windows were hidden behind trees. There was no sound by the lake. Far out the water was gold and bumpy in the sunshine, like pineapple skin. Near the bank it was clear and green. There were fish as thin as pencil-lead. They lay quite still in groups, then suddenly went wild, and seemed to be biting and chasing each other.

David went to the boat-house where the lawn-mower was kept now. He unscrewed the cap and smelled the petrol. He tasted some on the tip of his finger. It was cold and sour. Coming out he found a cobweb on the back of the door. He scooped it up and it rolled into a sticky rope in his hand. The sun was bright after the darkness of the shed. David turned back inside to poison the tip of his spear with petrol. There was a swarm of midges like gold dust over the landing-stage. They were far too small.

He set out to walk right round the lake. The flowers in this part of the park were nearly all daffodils, but he often got down on all fours to see if he could smell any difference between the yellow and the white ones. Sometimes he threw his spear at a bunch, though always so as to miss it on purpose.

By the time he got round the lake the sky had turned white and seemed to have grown larger. All at once birds began singing as if they'd been asleep before. In the kitchen-garden Gregory's father was throwing something on to a bonfire. David watched through the tall iron gate. The smoke rose up in a thick yellow pillar, then turned brown, and spread out against the sky like fine strands of hair. Screwing up his eyes, David tried to see how high they got before they disappeared.

The cook was calling him.

'Coming!' he yelled at the top of his voice.

As he raced up the path he shouted again. It would be terrible if they thought he'd got lost.


'We were *prisoners,*' Cole said witheringly. 'We were helpless, man! When the Japs seized our plantations it was useless to resist.'

Cole sprawled in the big armchair in the prefects' room. He always bagged the best one. He wriggled down lower in it. The seat of his shorts seemed to have stuck to the cushion so that almost the full length of his legs were bare.

'It was torture,' he said. 'Oh boy!' He looked up at the expectant faces and took a bite from a two-ounce bar of Cadbury's blended. It had just been tuck shop. Cole always got four ounces because he had his mother's sweet coupons too.

'What happened when all the boys were lined up?' someone asked.

'Our hands were tied behind our backs – with *wire*,' Cole said. He forced his wrists under the small of his back, and David watched, fascinated, as he writhed into the position. His knees lolled apart and then slapped together again. They were the colour of new pennies.

Cole rolled his eyes. '*Then* – then we put them out or they pulled them out. They came along the row touching them with their swords and shouting, "Go stiffer!"'

'In Japanese?'

'Of course they said it in Japanese.'

'How often did they do it?'

'Five times a day,' Cole said.

'Did *all* the men do this to the boys?' Mudd asked. He was serious and borrowed books from the staff Common room.

Cole twisted his head to look at him. 'Yes.'

'Shut up, Mudd, we want to hear,' someone else said.

'Odd,' Mudd muttered, turning away. 'A few might. Or rather more, if they were hysterical.' He looked almost as if he didn't believe Cole. Then he seemed to have an idea, and turned back. 'Is that *all* they did? Didn't they sort of hug you?'

'They were being dirty, man!' Cole shouted angrily. 'Whatever would they want to hug us for?'

'So rats, Bookworm!' said Fielding, who was Cole's best friend.

'Go on, Coley. What happened when you'd put them out?'

'When they'd pulled them out, you mean,' another boy said. 'His hands were tied behind his back.'

Cole looked at him dangerously.

'There's something else,' Mudd said, coming back into the circle. 'What about the captured girls? There must have been some.'

Everyone stared at him. Cole blushed.

'Girls don't have them, bookworm squirt, so they didn't do anything to the girls.'

Mudd had taken a book out of his locker and was running his finger down a page. 'You're revolting, Cole,' he said slowly, without looking up.

'Not *me*, man. *Them!*' Cole shouted.

Mudd stopped moving his finger down the page of the book. 'I make it that when the Japanese were in Malaya you were four,' he said.

'Oh, chuck him out, someone!' Cole snorted.

Fielding pushed Mudd out of the room and carefully closed the door. Cole arched his body off the seat of the chair, and then settled back more limply than before. David watched his lolling knees. His head felt light and he didn't think he could stand up much longer. Suddenly he left the room, shutting the door behind him. The southern English were very strange.

He crossed the hall slowly with his hands plunged in his pockets; putting his feet carefully in front of each other, and trying to walk on only one of the brightly polished floorboards. Half-way across he stopped, balanced, listening to the tick of the clock that hung there. Through the window the winter evening had hardly any colour, like water paints spread on grey sugar-paper. David wished the evening was colder, and that the coldness would cool his body. His clothes felt warm and heavy. They clung to him almost as if he had fallen into a pond. He looked at his chest, half expecting to see steam seeping out from beneath his pullover. He thought perhaps he might melt completely away; overflow his shoes, and then go to fill the cracks between the shiny floor-boards that were loosely packed with dust. He shuddered, stood on one leg, and then lifted his whole weight on to his toes. It was no way for a senior to behave, but there was no one about. The exercise made him feel no better. If anything he felt worse.

David kicked the lavatory door so fiercely that it hit the adjacent wall and bounced shut again. He kicked it several more times until the banging seemed to fill the building. Only when the increasing echo began to alarm him did he go into the lavatory and lock it. Then he had a better idea.

He came out and went into the squits' playroom. There was Ping-Pong and fights and an awful row. He saw Gray, hobbling across the room on the sides of his shoes, and felt embarrassed. Even when he was pretending to be a crab or something Gray was as beautiful as a doll. He had on a white cricket pullover with a floppy collar. Just then he got down on his hands and knees, *so* perhaps he was being a polar bear.

David walked slowly round the room, keeping his step very casual, and trying to will Gray to go away. When he turned round Gray had gone. David suddenly felt excited because he could do what he liked now. Almost, anyway.

Hawkes was sitting on the window-seat watching the Ping-Pong. He had his fists in his pullover, making breasts, but no one was watching. David went up to him.

'Your sister's got red hair,' he said.

Hawkes pulled the breasts out and looked up.

'I said she's got *red hair.*'

Hawkes kicked at him suddenly. David moved closer so he could hardly miss next time.

'Peregrine!' David whispered. Really, he was being exceedingly unpleasant. It didn't do to think about that, though.

Hawkes' next kick caught him on the thigh.

'It's a fight, is it?' David said. He took the squit's wrists gently, and rolled back on to the floor, pulling him down on top of him. Hawkes tried to free his wrists and began thumping David's chest.

'Always get shoved to the back of the tuck queue, don't you?' David said, settling himself more comfortably.

Hawkes' knees dug into his ribs, and he clawed at David's pullover. He was beginning to lose his temper. 'You always *barge*! All the seniors barge!'

David still held the squit's wrists, but pretended to be nearly beaten. He groaned. 'What you mustn't do is *bounce* . . . bounce on my stomach . . . that's not fair fighting . . .'

Hawkes began to bounce on his stomach, and David easily slid the weight lower down his body. He watched Hawkes' tight mouth through half-closed eyes. It curved downwards like a bow. Suddenly he pressed the back of his hand against the lips because he couldn't kiss them.

David knew that he must split open. Perhaps his whole stomach might. It wouldn't matter now if the headmaster's wife and all the matrons came in in a file. Even if Gray came in he wouldn't care. He released the squit's wrists and locked his arms round his chest. He began pulling him down, waiting for their chests to touch . . .

David pushed Hawkes away. He drew up his knees and screwed up his eyes. A minute later he found saliva had trickled out of his mouth and turned cold on his chin. He rolled over on his stomach and felt like a jelly-fish. He was staying there till the prep, bell went. The plop of Ping-Pong balls, and the row the squits made, were far away.

'Are you all right, Rogers? . . . Rogers?'

David didn't need to look up. He turned his head quickly so that Gray couldn't see the tears that suddenly soaked the cuff of his pullover. He wondered how long he'd been in the room, and his tears seemed to come faster. Opening his eyes a bit he could see Gray's feet. He was standing on the sides of his shoes again.

'What's the matter? Did you trip or something?'

David didn't answer. The blubbing began to shake his whole body but he couldn't stop it. He locked his head in both arms and licked the dust on the floor for something to do with his tongue. His blubs turned to hiccups, and then giggles. They were a mixture of all three because if he stood up Gray would probably think he'd wet his pants and was really a squit. But he didn't care. He knelt upright suddenly. Then he couldn't look at Gray higher than his nose. He tried to raise his eyes but they wouldn't go. He looked round instead. There was nobody near.

'D'you want my tuck?'

'Why? Don't you want it?' Gray asked.

'It's only blended and Smarties . . . in my locker. I don't like them much. I don't really like them at all.' David still couldn't look higher than Gray's nose. Gray had brown eyes like a stuffed deer. David realised he had never known anyone with brown eyes before.

'Gosh! Thanks then, Rogers!' Gray said. He ran away, properly on his feet this time.

Outside the clouds had blown apart. There were only two squits left in the room. Where the light lay across a corner of the Ping-Pong table it was a brilliant emerald like the lawns at home in sunshine. David turned his face towards the window, and promptly sneezed. He groaned dramatically and let his forehead crash to the floor to see how much pain he could stand. He deserved it.

Bruce Lang put down his pencil with a crack. 'If it's the price of peace in here, then take it!' He opened the drawer of his desk and handed the tightly furled scroll to Parker over his shoulder. 'And for God's sake don't cut holes in it. I can't think why you never order your own.' He bent over his textbook again, which was all glass tubes and electrical wires.

Parker opened the photo across his own desk, spreading out his arms to stop the ends springing together again. A couple of times he said, 'Wow!'

'It's an optical illusion,' Lang said. 'The school sits in a semicircle in front of the building, and the camera pans from a fixed point. Subsequently, we all appear to be in a straight line, and the building behind appears convex.'

Parker looked up in horror. 'Building? We, Bruce?'

In the armchair David went on reading Beethoven. The study was full of sunshine. It seemed to expand the walls, but the room remained too small. The mess irked him. No one cleaned the milk pan and the slop tin stank. If you picked up a cup the saucer came with it. As often as not even the teaspoons were Siamese twins.

'What do you think of the new boys?' Parker asked neither of them in particular.

'We can only hope they're settling down happily,' Lang said, consulting a slide-rule.

Parker tossed the photo on to his desk in disgust. It had curled up into two cylinders like binoculars. 'By the way, that flat-footed Greaves has been hopping around Henderson like a pet flea – but Henderson couldn't be more bored by Little Boys.'

David's eye stopped in the middle of a bar. His body pounded as if he'd been playing rugger when he still had only his holiday wind. Strangely, the insult implicit in Parker's casual remark was of no consequence. He didn't feel jealousy or anger. As far as he knew the idea of having a Little Boy was wishful and empty; a nervous drivel with which people like Parker bemused themselves. It had nothing to do with his feelings for Peter Greaves. What shattered him was the mention of

Peter's name. In any context his reaction to it must have been similar. He thanked God that the school was four hundred strong, and that Peter had avoided the tag Little Boy. Even in Parker's school list he'd escaped the red circle that apparently meant 'beautiful', and the black one that meant 'pretty'. Of course lately he'd been slack about keeping his records but, either way, it was an insult best suffered in silence.

'Fill the kettle!' David said, heaving his chest and yawning to disguise his trembling.

'From the *cold* tap,' Lang said.

Parker left, but put his head in again to kiss the pin-up girl on the back of the door which he'd cut from *Paris Match*.

'I'd give a lot to see Alan confronted by a live girl or a live Little Boy,' Lang said when he'd gone again.

David said nothing. Increasingly his sense of isolation silenced him even among his friends. For nearly a year Peter's image had lived in his mind. It was a pastel-coloured ghost that haunted the periphery of his conscious thoughts. Sometimes it gained solidity, becoming a bright, startling reflection whose wonder overwhelmed him. When that happened it seemed as if needles had been thrust into his eyes, his face creased, and he cried like a child. That was how it had been last night. Or rather, there'd been more self-pity than wonder. Perhaps his depression reflected his shame. He looked at Lang, bent over his desk, and wondered what he must have told the Chaplain. Probably it had been: 'Sir, David Rogers has started to cry in our study. He won't go to bed, or do anything.' Then he must have said something about his being upset over a Little Boy. Of course, he wouldn't have used that term. Hellish-Holy Bruce. He'd only brought it on himself.

David scowled furiously in his embarrassment, remembering how, after that, everything had been madness. The Chaplain had come down and led him away to his room like a sulky offering. He made tea and put saccharine tablets in his own. He called them depth charges because of the way they erupted on the surface a few seconds after you'd dropped them into the tea. David watched them exploding one after the other. Then the Chaplain was talking. Sometimes his chin fell downwards and sideways so that he looked like one of those saints in medieval paintings whose necks seem to be broken. The attitude gave him a humility that moved David. There was no contact between them. When the Chaplain tried to reach him he only felt more guilty. The failure to communicate was his own.

'Bruce tells me that you've been very upset, and he thinks it may be over some small boy,' the Chaplain said. 'Is that the trouble, David?' The sad tone embarrassed David. It made him remote, and remoteness was the last thing he needed.

'More or less . . . There is someone . . . I love.'

He was silent after that, staring at the carpet which seemed a strange thing after the bareness of schoolrooms, so that his eyes examined it minutely. Then the nightmare began. He could watch it building up slowly. But it was like one of those nightmares in which you know you are dreaming, and whose incidents cause no apprehension.

As the Chaplain talked, it became clear that he thought David had had some sexual contact with the unnamed boy. It was the only way in which he could interpret his remorse. Like the sleeper, David shook his head and said, 'no'. He didn't make any violent protest because the Chaplain's thoughts no longer concerned him. The suggestion was fantastic. In its remoteness it failed to disgust him; while, having no meaning, it became almost funny. But David didn't laugh. The scene was being conducted without relevance to himself, and was a part of the dream.

His isolation was a trance. He knew it was a defence he had built about himself, and that it was fatal to remain in it. Yet he hadn't the power to break out. He sat, half listening, and was only dimly resentful of the man's inability to see that it was the weight of love alone with which he couldn't cope. He was silent because he had to be. You couldn't talk of love. Its size made it inexpressible. It couldn't come out through the mouth. Hints of it might, but you could only show it all if you could somehow hand over your brain. Now he was seeing the effects of releasing those hints. Their inadequacy tortured him, baring his loneliness.

'You're a pretty remarkable lad, you know,' the Chaplain was saying. 'Let's see, you're not yet seventeen but you were already playing for the First XV last year, weren't you?'

'Yes, sir,' David said.

'Then wouldn't it be a good idea to forget about these things, old chap?'

'Yes, sir,' David repeated. The man must have had his brain destroyed with a pin like one of the frogs in the lab. How could he think that David had somehow elected to be possessed by Peter, or forget him because he chose to do so?

The Chaplain directed him to kneel on the hearthrug. He pronounced a long prayer, calling David 'this child'. Told to his friends it should have been terribly funny. David didn't think he ever would tell them.

'Where the hell's the lid of this thing?' Parker stood over David with the kettle.

'Try next door,' Lang suggested.

'Or the bottom of the bin,' David said. 'You can count me out, Alan, I'm going for a walk. Anyway, I don't think we've any tea left.'

'Christ!' Parker exploded; then looked non-plussed. 'No one put it on the list.'

'I won't drink cocoa at four o'clock in the afternoon,' Lang said, without turning.

David put his feet up on his desk. It was brand new and had a transparent yellow glaze like barley sugar. 'Incidentally, Bruce finished the sherry before lunch.'

'Put sherry on the shopping list as well,' Lang ordered.

'And who effing well pays, comrade? I suppose you know the wine merchants have stopped our credit?'

'Only because you rolled in there in school uniform,' Lang said. 'Get grocers'. But not *British* Brown.'


David perched on a gate in the beech woods. It was what must be meant by a five-barred one. He'd never thought of it before, but there they were: four horizontals and a diagonal. He lit a cigarette. They didn't taste so good in the open air, but unless one were to squat on a bog seat in the middle of prep, it was the only place to smoke them. After a moment he put it out. Autumn had its own smoky taste that tingled in your nose and at the back of your throat. Perhaps the decaying of leaves was really, some process of burning.

David looked at his hand. There were two pale crescent moons of skin where his nails had cut into the palm. Peter was reducing him to a nervous wreck. The wounds, though, were his own fault. He should cut his nails shorter. Love had made him clairvoyant, but the discovery was no surprise. Moreover, his premonitions afforded him no protection. Before coming out of a classroom, or turning a corner in a corridor, he would suddenly know that Peter would be there. Invariably he was; yet the foreknowledge somehow never prepared him for the shock. He had taken to carrying a pencil, and holding it with his hand. When he met Peter like that it broke. Last time he hadn't been holding the pencil, and it was his own nails which had cut his hand. David looked at the crescent marks again. Really the whole thing was absurd. He seemed to see himself from the outside, but was powerless to revise what he saw. He had to go on living in the present, aware of the futility while he participated in it, and the awareness made him cynical. The horror of the third piano sonata was proof of that. Of course, he took himself too seriously. He could only assume it was the fate of his age, but, again, the assumption wasn't comforting. What irked him most was that the power of his love had turned inwards. There being no possible contact with Peter it consumed himself. Self-pity was never far away. The third sonata showed that too. Its burden lay beneath the threshold of articulateness; lacking the transformation that could make it malleable in his own hands, or accessible to anyone else.

David heaved two lungsful of air, perched precariously on the gate. He took his fourth sonata from its impertinent hiding place in the Beethoven folio and began to read the slow movement. After a moment he puckered up his face and swore. It was little better than the third. He put it away and turned to Beethoven. It was the only experience where he found peace. The revelation of genius amazed him equally with Peter's beauty, and, by virtue of this, Peter's beauty lost some of its power to torture him. He'd discovered that there was other beauty, different, though as potent as Peter's, and the relief was immeasurable. But the music provided something more by making his unhappiness irrelevant. He felt his significance dwindle to a point where he was scarcely responsible to anything at all. Yet at the same time he himself was giving something of the music's greatness.

Reading on, it occurred to David that the desert he inhabited was acting as a forcing house where greater intellectual comprehension was being made available to him. Exile in the wilderness had driven him more quickly to discover, and to dwell in a world without words or physical symbols.

The thought came back as insistently as a fly making for the eyes of a horse. David laid the folio on his knees and the orchestra shrank in his head. What, after all, was Peter *for*?

He faced the wildest possibility squarely. It wasn't sex. He could find none in his most cynical introspection. There was no connection between Peter and the happy animality of his behaviour at prep school. Of course that had been neither happy nor animal, though it might seem so now: it had filled him with shame, and been furtive to a degree of lunacy. David smiled, remembering. It hadn't even had the alleged charm of innocence. There was nothing prelapsarian about orgasms enjoyed fully clothed. Yet innocence there had been. He felt far more shame and confusion now at the barest thought of Peter than he had done when caught with wet pants by Gray.

It could only be that Peter possessed him entirely, filling an emotional need that hadn't existed before. The emotion precluded sex. It was centred in a hypnotic magic whose focal point was obscure. Peter's neatness and fragility seemed to be threatened in their stone-bound, rowdy world. Then there was the inconsequence. The image of his sitting beside another, ordinary person on a bench using a knife and fork. David's mind couldn't grapple with things like that. Here was where the danger began. Where the mind refused its responsibility; backing out from a reality it couldn't cope with, even had it been identifiable. No wonder he stagnated! He didn't attempt to know Peter. Any fact he did learn was sufficient to fill him; its magic so enormous as to leave room for nothing else. The sum of fragments was catastrophic. He couldn't order it. If he were enabled to reduce it to coherence it wouldn't be in real terms at all.

'I wish I could kiss him,' David murmured aloud. As he spoke, involuntarily, his embarrassment nearly made him fall off the gate.

He regained balance only to realise he was unsure of it once more. Twenty yards away Peter Greaves was regarding him through a telescope. He stood quite still in the beech wood with a case shaped like a quiver slung over his shoulder. He couldn't have been there a moment ago. David's nails went into

the spongy wood of the gate. He felt dizzy as if he'd inhaled a
cigarette after weeks of abstinence.

'Pretty funny bird!' the small boy called out clearly.

David couldn't have said whether it was self-conscious or
not. But now Peter Greaves had dropped the telescope into its
case and started towards him. As he came up David was chiefly
aware of the wet leaves sticking to the soles of his shoes. This
was because his eyes kept slipping down to the ground.

'Ostrich, I think,' Greaves said, stopping a yard away. He
must have become aware of David's apparent preoccupation
with his feet for he began scraping his shoes on the bottom of
the gate. David vibrated with it. 'Actually you won't do because
I'm looking for magpies.'

David looked at him now. His slight figure was ludicrously
incapacitated by the dangling telescope case. The warm, hay
shade of his skin, and soft sheath of his clothes, were familiar
in every detail, but remained a mystery almost beyond endur-
ance. The vision drew his eyes and yet threatened to burn
them. They had constantly to leap away and cool down.

'You a bird watcher?' he asked.

'Yes.' Greaves nodded. 'At least, on alternate free days I am.
On the others I do train timetables.'

David nodded too, but more heavily. The new information
was beginning to saturate him. 'There must be a lot of birds
here.' The inadequacy mocked him before his mouth had
closed.

'Yes, there are,' Greaves said. He gave a gasp. 'Aren't you a
monitor!' He'd fallen on the cigarette-end and was looking at
David with wild joy. He jumped backwards and began wrapping the muddy butt in his handkerchief. 'Blackmail! Just in
case of impositions! There'll be finger-prints.' His lips moved
in a strange way. The words had no meaning on them David
felt foolish.

Greaves seemed promptly to have forgotten the butt-end.
He stooped again. This time it was a frail leaf-skeleton that
he picked up. The skeleton was complete, with the flesh fallen
cleanly away from the frame, so that it was like a web worked
in fine copper wire. As he looked at it he said, 'Goodness!'
The remark was so unlike a normal school exclamation that,
instantly, it rarefied him still more. Then he came towards

David, holding it out, and he took it by its delicately fluted stem.

He examined it on the palm of his hand, but was aware only of the dream-like approach of the boy, which was an unfocused memory of motion, because he had been steadying his hand and eye to receive the brittle gift safely. Now, sensing Peter still unfocused beside him, and with the moment of intense concentration past, he began to shake all over.

'I think it's going to rain,' Greaves said.

David gave him the leaf back. He held it in front of his eyes and looked at David through it. Then he looked up at the trees, and back at David. There was nothing coquettish in the gesture. His curiosity simply wanted to employ the fine mesh. Keeping the leaf flat, he lowered it into his jacket pocket, and adjusted the heavy telescope case so as not to disturb it. He turned round.

'I'm off.'

'Goodbye, then.' For some moments David had been looking at Greaves squarely. Now he watched him retreating. As the distance increased the challenge became more unbearable. Suddenly he didn't care how his voice shook. '*Peter!*' he called. 'I'll tell you if I see any magpies.'

The boy looked back. It seemed certain to David that he must ask how he knew his name, but he only smiled, and called, 'Thanks!'

David found the gate vibrating beneath him. Peter went on a few paces, then, without turning, he took out his bunched handkerchief and shook it at arm's length. David could just make out the cigarette-butt as it fell to the ground.


'The thought-police are going to arrest *Greaves* tonight!' Parker announced excitedly. 'I knew it . . . I always *knew* it!'

Lang was drinking cocoa after all, though the humiliation didn't register with David.

Parker, perhaps because David didn't normally seize people by the throat, now looked very frightened. 'Only the *thought-police,* David,' he said uneasily. 'Routine admonishing, you know, comrade . . .'

*Book Two*

## 2

D AVID Rogers rested his head against the sharp gravel. His arms were spread and floating like the tissue-weight wings of a gull. Now they were limbs stolen from Madame Tussaud's melting on a hotplate. New metaphysical game. He was sprawled on his back in what, making allowance for the fish-pond, was the geometrical centre of the Great Quad.

Peering under the opaque jewel, that must be the tortoise-shell rim of his spectacles, David let his eyes stray along the south wall of the quad and muttered 'St Cecilia's' to himself incredulously.

They were re-facing the Hall, but even from here he could see that the monstrous Portland stone gargoyles represented neither porters nor dons but were simply the vestigial night-mare promptings of a forgotten craftsmanship. The twentieth century no longer knew fear with horns. These faces were empty parodies of evil, and might have been coloured transfers on the S.A.C. bombers at Brize Norton.

There were very few people in the quad. It was Sunday, and the vacuum hour. David's eyes wandered along the east face of the quad. The façade was rust-stained like the teeth of a smoker. One of the teeth was missing, and the gaping hole led into the Temple. Any second now the first of the suede-shoed Anglicans would emerge. They would cluster together outside with their white surplices vainly brushing the rust-stains like so many magical dentifrice fairies. Their conversation would be tingling fresh.

David decided to watch for the appearance of either the first surpliced youth with a hunting gait, or the first North Oxford lady who was a card-holding friend of St Cecilia, and then to close his eyes and rely upon his ears to describe the gradual dispersal as, inevitably as it must, it drifted away around him over the huge quadrangle.

North Oxford won. In fact it was David's moral tutor's wife

who first emerged. She was clutching an infant, who in turn clutched a soft-toy whose broken neck rendered the particular species uncertain.

David settled himself finally in the gravel and closed his eyes. For perhaps five minutes he lay back dimly sensing the dispersal of the worshippers. Though feet of fifty different weights constantly tramped past his ears they made less noise than he'd imagined they would. The only articulate cry he had been able to distinguish had come from the remote west corner, away from the mouth of the Temple: 'Real tennis this afternoon, Jamie?'; to which another voice, presumably Jamie's, had called back no and sorry and something about Henrietta.

David felt the sun hot upon his eyelids and relaxed absolutely still. From the direction of his right ear he heard a voice whisper, 'He's dead!' Another voice, as if in explanation, said, 'He's probably got exams. They have them in the summer.'

'Stop,' David said aloud, without consulting himself or opening his eyes. There was a moment's silence, broken only by the sound of feet slipping on the gravel, and then a voice he recognised as the second speaker's asked:

'Do you mean *us*, sir?'

Suddenly David smiled. He opened his eyes as much as the unaccustomed sunlight would allow. 'I'm not a sir. And I'm not dead.' He was looking up at a grey sock with a wine and navy blue band around its top. Above this his painful eyes could make out a bare brown knee and the hem of a pair of flannel shorts. The choirboy twisted slightly and the copious skirt of his black opera cloak shaded David's eyes from the sun.

'What *are* you doing down there?' the boy asked.

Before replying David withdrew a fountain pen which was tucked into the boy's sock and had leaked, staining the wine and merging with the blue. He handed it up towards the sky. '*Ich habe genug – gehabt!*' he said: all his German derived through Bach. To his delight the boy laughed, seeming to sense a conspirator.

'So've we!' he said; then added, 'Hamley felt sick at Communion.' David sensed rather than saw Hamley nod.

As his shaded eyes accustomed themselves to the light he realised he was looking straight up the gold beam of the boy's thigh into the shadows of his widely belled shorts. Before David could look away the boy seemed to sense his unease. He flexed his knee slightly forward and sideways like a fashion

model so that the hem of his shorts closed around his limb. He
made no attempt to move his footing. Instead he distractedly
screwed the toe-cap of his shoe into the gravel. David noticed
the initials *A.S.* crudely worked in brass tacks on the sole.
Alessandro Scarlatti? He still hadn't seen the boy's face.

'D'you know anything about Frogs?' the boy asked, ceasing
for a moment to ruin his shoes.

It was then that David, squinting over his chest, became
aware of an elderly don about fifty yards away who was staring
at him in amazement. For no reason he laid his hand on the
boy's ankle.

'About what?'

'Frogs. Model 'plane engines. Mine won't go.'

'Do you buy your fuel made up?'

'Yes.'

'Well, try screwing the compression right down, and adding
one part of ether to five parts of the fuel you get from the shop.'

'All right. I'll try that.'

'Why aren't you with the rest of the crocodile?'

The boy gestured with his shoulder. 'I had to hold the basin
for Hamley. He felt sick again in the eleven o'clock.'

'What was it this morning?'

'The fried bread, I think,' said Hamley, speaking for the first
time from somewhere out of David's sight.

'No; I mean the service.'

The boy standing over David twisted his body round so that
the opera cloak billowed out behind him. David's eyes travelled
up the neat creases of his grey shorts. Scarlatti was a sartori-
ally conscious child, excepting the ink-stain on his sock. 'Oh,
"Sing joyfully unto God our Strength", Mundy, and sermon
by the Lord Bishop of Dorchester or someone.'

Hamley had begun to shift his feet. Perhaps he was thinking
of lunch. The boy standing over David seemed more reluctant
to move.

'D'you use a glove to start your engines. Or did you when
you had them, I mean?'

David grinned up at the sky. He still couldn't see much of
the boy above his blue elastic belt.

'No. You don't want to be afraid of it though. Just get used
to flicking the propeller sharply down against the compression.
Your finger comes away naturally.'

'That's what I'm afraid of! My *finger* coming away! I'll try the way you suggest, though; and with the special fuel.'

The boy made flicking motions in the air with his hand, and blew a rapid succession of popping sounds from his lips. As he did so he bent forward and David saw his face. The smooth curve of his hair line was broken at one temple by the absurd, conical hat. David hardly noticed it.

'We ought to go now,' the boy said. 'Perhaps I'll see you again.' He turned on the ball of his foot and ordered Hamley into line abreast. A moment later a clear voice rang out across the Great Quad. 'Don't forget! *Ich habe genug gehabt,* too!'

David raised the hand with which he was exploring the extent of the indentation where his hair receded. Involuntarily, he felt more liquid than when he had been playing the metaphysical game. He got up, looking at his watch. Twelve forty-five. He had a number of acquaintances living in college who might give him a drink if he looked in at their rooms, and his friend, Lang, whom he'd continued to know since they'd both left the same school two years ago. He decided against the acquaintances, and then against Lang as he remembered he was currently receiving instruction from Rome, and that at this hour there was bound to be a row of Jesuits perched on his bed like carrion crows on a gate. Last time he'd looked in on Lang there had been a Spanish Jesuit in attendance who was smoking Turkish cigarettes. David had had to talk himself rapidly off-stage, feeling for the doorknob with his hands behind his back.

Instead, he decided to get a sandwich in a pub, and wandered out through the west gate. On the pavement three American ladies were stating in triplicate their reasons for not entering St Cecilia's. The thesis that 'all the *insides* were the same' might have pleased Swift. David negotiated a don who was inexplicably manoeuvring a battered Ford on to the pavement, and crossed the road to the Wasp's Nest where he had beer and a polythene-protected and apparently reinforced sandwich.

After lunch David strolled aimlessly in the Great Park. The summer had appeared early. The air carried the scarcely perceptible hum of extreme heat. It was one of those peculiar Thames Valley afternoons when the sunshine may bring body and soul together on the brink of Elysium, but where bliss is held at bay by some invisible and enigmatical presence. Throughout his first year David had watched the same sunlight creeping along the stone balustrade outside the dormer window of his room in St Cecilia's until it licked the pencilled mark that defined tea-time. Now he sat in its full warmth, listening to the rhythmic thud of rowlocks coming up from the river and looking at the great crescents of blossom scattered from the St Cecilia's trees. He felt relaxed; securely lulled, as if new life had entered him. Nevertheless the sense of an un-staged drama remained. Perhaps it was like a consumptive's fear that the coughing might begin again.

## 3

O N an impulse David decided to put in an appearance at his language tutor's open-house tea. He might even leave him his paper on the absurdity of Anglo-Saxon at Oxford called *Try Cantab*. There was a lot to be said for the enraged followers of the school who claimed the language to have been invented by a bunch of mad German philologists in the nineteenth century, and quoted the names of editors such as Quirk and Grimm to support their claim. Confirmation was badly needed, though. He might suggest to the company that if while wandering in Mercia or Northumbria any of them should detect a small scholar with a Germanic face inflicting runes upon honest English tombstones with a coal chisel they should apprehend him and ask his business.

David shook himself free from a line of thought that was apt to produce unwelcome pressure cycles, and took a number two bus out to North Oxford.

A black claw seized his neck from behind, pinning his shoulders to the back of the seat. For a second he thought a West Indian conductor had gone berserk, and he was to be the first martyr in a caste war; then he saw it was the handle of an Italian umbrella that was throttling him.

'For God's sake!' a voice said. 'Wait for me!' A moment later a person David hardly knew collapsed on to the seat beside him and buried his face in his hands. Meanwhile David freed himself from the umbrella.

'You're Rogers, aren't you?' Crawley said, sinking his teeth into the upholstery of the seat in front. 'No, don't answer!'

There was a pause in which David lit a cigarette and became uncomfortably aware of passengers turning their heads.

'Rogers . . .' Crawley said, and stopped, as if unable to admit the diagnosis was cancer. 'Rogers, if you only knew the moral responsibility of writing *anything* for these ten thousand bewildered youths!'

'You do okay,' David hazarded.

'Shut up, will you. I must talk to you because I suspect you can *read*. Don't you play – a banjo, is it?' Crawley had hold of his umbrella again. It was martial law. 'Ninety per cent of this university can't, you know. They haven't got ears, eyes or minds. Just sex-organs, beer stomachs . . . nicotine-lined lungs.' Crawley's key had sunk tragically into the minor. It leapt suddenly into the major. 'Rogers, that's not a cigarette in your mouth, is it?'

'Yes.'

'Please put it out of the window.'

David threw the cigarette away. Perhaps the man's mind had snapped.

'Now can people really *read*? It's a question that tortures me, Rogers. Do they derive anything at all? From *anything* any more? Look at what Christ inspired once! Look at Him now! Dead even to the corrugated Edwardian widows who crawl out to His service on second Sundays. Look at Raphael, Rogers! Angelo even, poor sod. Dante! A beautiful story inspired great men and peasants alike. What have we now? Consumer goods shovelling us into the sea. Telly and hideously bent tin – Christ, man, look at that *car*!

'They call Oxford a melting pot,' Crawley went on. The upper deck was now empty save for the two of them. He could afford to lower his voice. 'But it's not. Our ten thousand courses are parallel. There is no communication.'

'Where there is it's not very democratic,' David said. Crawley hadn't heard him.

'God!' he whispered. 'Communicate, Rogers! You may not play that flute of yours very well. Keep trying though. That was my stop. I must leave you now.'

'That's okay by me,' David said. Crawley rose in a trance and felt his way towards the stairs.

David knew North Oxford well from the walks with which he had occupied the afternoons of his first year while he waited for the sun to reach the pencil mark on the balustrade, and allow him to put the kettle on. The danger here was not from traffic but from the rabid teeth of the perverse little terriers that always seemed to go with history dons. This was a square mile of silence, ruffled only by the stolen Scout on a bicycle, the obstetrician's basset hound, and the lawn-mowers of opposed half-acre squirearchies. Two small boys ambled past David in the gutter talking about rockets. He turned his head, and the silence seemed visibly to be restoring its equilibrium in the wake of the pigeon-toed figures.

A practically pubescent girl wearing nothing but knickers opened the Furlows' door. She stared up at David through spectacles with only one lens. 'Yes?'

'Is your father at home?' David asked. The girl said nothing. 'I'm David Rogers. One of your father's pupils,' David said desperately. He was hypnotised by the grossly exaggerated eye behind the single lens. The child still made no move to admit him.

'I-mutation?' said David evenly. 'Ash? Thorn? Yok, then? No?

> *May your eyes mutate and decline,*
> *Italicised in paradigm!'*

The child showed no sign of softening before the compliment.

'Umlaut!' David cried, slapping a hand to his stomach to clinch the matter.

The little girl smiled faintly, sceptically perhaps, pushing the door open with her big toe. 'You panic easily, don't you?' she said. 'Tea's in the garden if you really want some. Harold's here,' she added possessively, indicating the garden through the depths of the house with the same bare foot. 'I'm meant to have made a cake but I've been reading *Jane Eyre*. What do you think of the female novelists?'

'Mansfield's okay.' David was cautious. 'Woolf and Murdoch rather more so.'

'*The Waves* puzzled me rather,' the girl said. She took a brassière off a hat stand and began putting it on.

'Me too,' David confessed.

'You're rather an ineffectual person, aren't you?'

David looked hard at the magnified eye. 'Supposing you come out to the garden in ten minutes and tell me why there are no female composers,' he said.

He walked through a succession of book-lined orangeries as he had been directed. He had reached the glass door leading into the garden when the identity of Harold was revealed to him with an uncomfortable jolt. Harold Ricks was the demented St Cecilia's don who had been staring at him so incredulously that morning in the Great Quad. David became aware that the palm of his hand had stuck to the door-knob. He pushed open the door and shook himself free.

'Why, Rogers!' Furlow cried. A heavy armchair had evidently been lugged out from the house, and his tutor was reclining in it in his habitual position on his shoulder blades. David advanced, as he supposed beaming, over the lawn.

Apart from Ricks, and a second-year contemporary of his own, Brougham, the only other people present were a rather bohemian-looking woman, whom David imagined must be Mrs Furlow, and, sitting some yards away in evident gloom, what could only be a French *an pair* girl. North Oxford imported these to heave coal.

When he had introduced David to the bohemian woman as his wife, and gestured towards the French girl, who was called Susanne, Furlow pointed to a treacherous little folding chair and said, 'When do you think people stopped sleeping in the nude?'

'Have they?' David asked blankly. He was aware of Ricks staring at him like a bird through eyebrows like briar bushes.

'I take it you mean, sir,' said Brougham, nestling his chin into the pale-blue cravat thing that served him for a tie, 'when did people begin to indulge the habit of wearing night clothing at all, as opposed to possessing them and abandoning them only . . . um . . . periodically . . . in the proper pursuance of . . . eh . . . matrimonial rights?'

'It,' said David.

'I beg your pardon?'

'Night clothing's a singular noun.'

Brougham ignored him and turned back to Furlow. 'I think that's fair, sir?' He had coloured slightly and twisted his head towards Mrs Furlow and the silent *au pair* girl. The cravat thing was rather like a blanket cushioning an Easter egg that had been dipped in cochineal.

'Yes, quite,' said Furlow. 'You see, there's plenty of evidence to suggest that medievals, for instance, slept in nothing at all: prints for example always show people naked in bed. Before you arrived, Mr Ricks and I were wondering roughly when the practice continued to. I don't think the Elizabethans even had night-shirts. Ricks?'

The old man had nothing to add. He still looked at David as if he were some sort of isotope with the lead casing off.

'There are "sweaty night-*caps*" in Shakespeare,' David hazarded, biting into a conical macaroon. 'And the author of the *Ancrene Riwle* directed that his anchoresses might wear woollen socks in bed if they were cold. That was Middle English times . . .'

'I know. It's very interesting.' Furlow was sitting forward in his chair now musing. He probably really did think it was interesting, David realised with horror. Furlow slowly raised the cigarette which was dangling from his big sheep dog's paw. He drew in a mouthful of smoke with studied leisure, and then gasped it back into his lungs with a rapid convulsion of his whole body. David thought of the breakfast cereal shot from guns which had mystified his childhood. Furlow had begun pummelling his face. He raised his glasses beneath his right hand and violently massaged his cheek-bones. The little finger of his left hand corkscrewed into his left ear and, seeming to discover something embarrassing, the whole process froze.

Silence had descended on the North Oxford garden. Mrs Furlow had disappeared into the house, and Brougham was sipping tea with well-bred affectation. Even Ricks had taken his eyes off David, and instead was contemplating a row of gold tooth-picks in the waistcoat pocket of his hairy suit.

Unkindly ignoring Brougham, who was about to offer him one of his cigarettes with the college crest on it, and which were in fact Senior Service disguised, David turned to the French girl.

'Have you been on our river?' He instantly realised this might be like snapping a lead at a dog one has no intention of walking.

'Please?'

'*River*,' David grinned; making balancing motions with his

feet in the air, he directed a phantom punt pole into Ricks' stomach. But the girl only looked at him more eagerly. 'No, please?' She put her chin out and looked supercilious.

Heaving a huge breath as if he were taking on smoke like Furlow, David made an expansive gesture, and intoned with idiot punctuation, 'Lovely English summer!'

'Please!' the girl echoed, apparently satisfied, and David became aware of Ricks watching him with a little frown that might have been photographed on a grandmother.

'It has something to do with the belated emancipation of women; but only a little,' Furlow's daughter said. She had materialised beside David's chair. Her brassière must have been hung up on the hat stand again. 'The main reason is that male energy is creative and exploratory. They're go-getters, if you like. Female energy is more introspective. I think it's mostly devoted to having children, and then holding the family together.'

The little girl looked up at David almost as to a fellow intellectual. He was oddly touched. 'So you see,' she went on, 'that's why there are no female composers and very few female painters. There are writers. But that's an introspective energy. I think of painters as cave men fighting for their lives : against real enemies, but also against imaginary ones, whose terror Freud modified a bit for us.' She laughed; kneeling naked beside him. 'Do you like my Vesuvian protuberances?'

On the verge of panic, David remembered she was the reluctant cook. He bit gratefully into another macaroon – 'I like them.'

'Good,' the owl-child said. 'Do you like being thought well of by dons' wives?'

'I'd not thought about it.'

The girl nodded slowly. 'If you do I should keep your hair cut shorter.'

Furlow's daughter had gone. David got to his feet, killing an impulse to look at his watch. Furlow was evidently still unable to withdraw the finger from his ear, and Brougham was caressing the beard of a Pekinese, motivated no doubt by the same prompting that had once caused David to jab at an electric fire with a poker at the Master's sherry party.

'We've seen the real thing, haven't we, Salamon?' David said kindly. 'An embryo intellectual,' he explained, not letting Brougham escape. 'Oh, rather!' Brougham said.

David turned to Furlow. 'Goodbye, sir: thank you.' Furlow raised the hand that wasn't engaged with his ear.

At the gate David was congratulating himself on having escaped without another bout with the Cyclops child, when there was a shuffling behind him, and a hand was placed on his shoulder. The hand felt like the leathery skin of a rice pudding, which might rupture at any moment, revealing formless pulp. It was Ricks.

'There you are, Rogers,' he said unnecessarily. 'It *is* Rogers, isn't it? Yes, I have got a note on you. I wanted you to know, though, that in all my years at Cecilia's I've never seen such an extraordinary sight as I saw in the quad this morning. Quite astonishing!' The old man was panting after his effort to catch David. 'You know, I suppose, those young boys pass through the Great Quad to or from the choir school about six times a day. Quite pretty some of them, probably, though I don't notice children myself. But I've never before seen an under-graduate *talk* to one. Are you a homosexual?'

Ricks had once asked a freshman, 'Young man, are you a virgin?', to which the man was alleged to have replied, 'In front, or behind, sir?' David merely shook his head; foregoing any pretence at wit. He recalled the picture of Ricks coming into the Schools to lecture and stripping off his trousers in an attempt to clear the hall of women.

David lit a cigarette for Ricks, and said goodbye; turning a moment later to watch him shuffling away down the strict perspective of Charlbury Road. He turned himself to the way he had come, and walked through the scarcely opened blossoms of Belbroughton which a light wind scattered at his feet.

Half an hour later David stepped out of the back gate of St Cecilia's where he had returned to collect accumulated post. It was only half past five and the sun was still hot, washing the buildings a deep gold. He sat on the terrace, looking out over the Great Park where it stretched towards the river. The grass was already browned in patches beneath the trees, and it was covered with a hum of insects.

His post was the usual assortment of religious society cards which had continued to follow his soul since a rash resolution of togetherness had caused him to sign it away to all sects in the freshman's panic of his first term.

He struck out wildly with a rather ostentatious card, but

missed the hornet that seemed to be circling his head. Stiffening,
he looked up to where, a long way away, a .75 cc Frog engine
must be making angry orbits between earth and sky.

David smiled faintly at the thought of having made some sort
of contribution to the gigantic foundation of which he was a
member, and turned his face towards his digs in Walton Street.

## 4

D AVID had taken his digs for a year with the option of
a second; a settlement which no doubt reflected his
bourgeois predisposition for artificial security. He had been
able to decorate it himself, borrowing a steel-grey carpet
from his home, washing the walls with a pink emulsion, and
painting the woodwork in a grey that matched the cerebral
cortex, and so might be expected to delude it into anaes-
thesis. A small upright piano he had been able to import by
the simple expedient of sawing off its legs on the pavement
below and then sticking them on again with Bostik reinforced with six-inch nails. Otherwise the room was simply
furnished, and ordered meticulously with further regard for
the cerebral cortex. David had all the bourgeois' obsessional
urge to hide unseemliness in drawers, and so apart from
some boxes on top of the wardrobe which contained photographic equipment, the only other visible object was a large
photo of the Greek horses on St Mark's in Venice, which he
had stuck directly to the wall after consultation of a neigh-
bouring scientist's slide rule.

David had entered the house with half-closed eyes as was
his habit. The tenement was not a slum but its neighbours
were. The pale yellow brick was as much like a public lavatory
as the rest of the row, but the frontage had been painted with
undergraduate rents, and stood out a glaring canary among
the grimed blacks and greens like Virgil's mysterious fruit
in the primeval forest. Its tenant hierarchy, reading towards
the sky, though without implying divine allotment, consisted
of a barber in the basement, who could sometimes be seen

abusing his wife, Mrs Kanter, who owned the building, a
Balliol scientist who had breakfast, and David himself who
did not. The Balliol man's rooms carried a clause which
made him responsible for sweeping the stairs.

David collapsed into his desk-chair, opened the typewriter,
and wound in a sheet of foolscap. He was too tired to reach
any of the relevant books off the shelf above him. Gloss, then.
He flicked the ribbon indicator to red to brighten the overall
effect, and like Crawley biting the bus seat, sank his teeth
meditatively into the key casing where the word *Remington*
had long since been licked away. He hit the paragraph release
to jar his teeth, and then hit it again. The mechanism crossed
the page in bold jumps, but no inspiration came even when the
bell pinged. He got up to look at the St Mark's horses, circled
the room, running his finger over the rack of L.P. records, and
then hurled himself into his chair again from a yard's distance.
He began to hit the keys; pummelling at each meaningless
symbol. Then he reduced the keyboard pattern of his first line
to a single horizontal plane, opened the piano, and struck the
series of chords it represented. Appalled, he stumbled back
to the desk for the third time, and began to peel off a sallow,
summer night essay for his Lit. tutor.

Perhaps an hour later David played a passage of Mozart on
the typewriter. The keys flew into the sacred circle; inextri-
cably jammed cheek to cheek. It was rather like the Oxford
girl race. Improving on the new game, he half depressed the
letter *G*, suspending the slender finger in space. With his other
hand he beat down three letters simultaneously. *T* got there
first, bruising the wretched *G* intolerably so that she let out
a metallic whine. Probably a black man called Tosca and a St
Hilda's girl with a head full of adolescent socialism and racial
tears.

David beat out a line of Xs to represent a gap he might
fill later. Why didn't he have his paper produced in rolls and
perforated like bumf? He'd once produced essays for a whole
term at a single sitting, and might tonight stray through Swift,
Pope and Johnson without pause. On.

After a further hour David reached into his pocket for a
cigarette, panicked, thumbed through the stubs of his cheque
book, and hit the keys with renewed fury, without making so
much as an inter-space.

*Dear Sir,*

*I have just received your invoice for work carried out on my Series 4 in March, and should like to raise two points.*

*My initial letter with regard to the paint-work sounded your responsibility with considerable restraint. I did however enquire whether any, and what, cost might be incurred by myself. As no reference was made either in your reply, or when I saw the Managing Director at the Works. I assumed that this matter would be attended to under the obtaining warranty. I was, too, prepared to accept an unexplained fault in good faith.*

*The second point relates to the labour charge for what amounted to a routine adjustment and lubrication service. I have read the handbook clause explaining Works' charges as 'consistent with expert workmanship', expected, and I hope got just this. However, your labour quotation of £7-10-0 represents some 15 man/hours, or 2 astonishingly intensive man/days. Could there have been some clerical error?*

*It is not my habit to query bills. As I hope to be able to avail myself of your Works' facilities in future I should be grateful for some explanation of this.*

*Yours Faithfully, D. Rogers.*

David rose from his desk and, opening the wardrobe for a fresh packet of cigarettes, his eye fell on the level of the whisky. Aloud he said, 'My total capital is three hundred pounds. I'm damned if I'm going to spend it.' He returned to the desk.

*To the Insurance Company*

*Dear Sir,*

*With regard to the delay of payment for the receipted bills now in your possession I have only one thing to say. As you already know, my car was stationary at traffic lights, and had been stationary for some minutes, when the car of Mrs Shepherd collided with its rear. Only my concern for Mrs Shepherd's obviously hysterical state prevented my summoning the police in order to prefer a charge of*

*dangerous driving. As I see it, therefore, your liability is*
*established beyond all doubt.*

*If, however, Mrs Shepherd is prepared to sustain the costs*
*of an action at law simply for the privilege of presenting*
*your company with a mistaken account of the accident*
*well and good. Meanwhile I suggest you impress upon your*
*client the advisability of supplying you with factual infor-*
*mation, such as may enable you to honour my receipts with*
*cash payment within the next forty-eight hours.*

*I remain, Sir,*

*Yours Faithfully, D. Rogers.*

Suddenly weary, David opened his wardrobe and drank the
last of the whisky. It was 2 a.m. He tore off his clothes, folded
them, stood back contemplating them for a minute, and then
crept down the un-dusted stairs to see if the Balliol atom
man had left any milk outside his door. He hadn't. Two cats
broke off their copulation on the landing. They stared at him
shocked, their faces masks of terror, then scampered away.
The house was quite still.

## 5

D AVID woke at eleven o'clock. Without bothering to brew
himself a cup of Nescafé, he cut out the paragraphs of the
essay he had written the night before and glued them, together
with any other relevant scraps of typescript he could find, to a
roll of paper he kept for the purpose. His Lit. tutorial was at
three.

Around midday he wandered down to Joe Lyons at Carfax
with his scroll under his arm, pausing to deliver a reprimand
to a small girl playing in the gutters of Walton Street, who had
poked her tongue out at him.

There was already a crowd in the shop, David trundled his
tray along the formica shelf, giving plenty of room to a blind
man in front of him. There were metal studs on the surface

of the shelf, and the blind man's tray bumped over them slop-
ping soup. David watched him ask for the beef. The second
girl behind the counter poured a ladle of gravy over the meat;
then, seeing that the man was blind, checked his tray with a
wet finger and gave him another ladle. The meat nearly floated
off the plate.

David took his sandwich and glass of Russian tea to a
corner table. He apologised to a woman for treading on her
red toe-nail, and glowered at her child which was brushing ice
cream on to the underside of its chin like shaving lather. There
was a man on a step-ladder attending to the fans which had
broken down. The eaters had glazed eyes and the room was full
of smoke: sharply defined steel-blue coils of virgin smoke that
rose from forgotten butt-ends; and formless masses of yellow
smoke etiolated by lungs. David broke through the sticky glass
doors into the sunshine.

He walked down to St Cecilia's, determined to be by himself
in the Great Park until it was time for his tutorial. At a quarter
to three he was looking at his watch when he heard the sound
of the Frog again. This time it didn't startle him, and he realised he had half expected it. He went into the back lodge of
the college, scribbled a note about stomach upset, childish and
inexplicable vomiting, and thrust it together with his essay into
the messenger box. Then he walked towards the river and the
direction of the high-pitched sound.

He reached the low iron railings of the choir school playing
field and paused for a moment. The boy hadn't seen him. He
was quite alone in the middle of the field, holding the control
handle of the 'plane, and leaning backwards against the centrif-
ugal force as it circled above his head. Then he must suddenly
have caught sight of David, because he raised his free hand,
brought the 'plane into a bumpy landing, and came towards
him over the grass. David noticed that he was no longer
wearing the grey flannel suit, but light grey cotton shorts and
a blue blazer with a device derived from the college arms on
the breast. He had a silver wire across his front teeth, though
David couldn't conceive why. As he came up the boy removed
the plate and dropped it in the pocket of his blazer.

'Well, it works!'

'I know,' David said. 'I heard it last night.'

'What's your name, by the way?' The boy had raised one

foot on to the bottom rail of the fence. He was still wearing the black shoes.

'David. David Rogers.'

'Shall I call you David, or Mr Rogers?'

David laughed. 'David, I should think. I thought you must be Alessandro Scarlatti, because I saw the *A.S.* on the bottom of your shoes yesterday. Are you?'

The boy smiled quickly, and his upper teeth showed to the gum. 'No; I'm Antony Sandel. Actually, I was christened Antony, but I'm called Tony. My aunt calls me *Ant*, though – because "you're just like one, boy!"' he added in evident parody. For an instant his gum showed again. 'Do you want to come and see the 'plane?'

David climbed over the fence, and they walked out into the field. The 'plane was a scale model of a Tempest, and beautifully made.

'The tyres blow up,' said Tony.

'Did you build it yourself?'

'Yes. I usually make one every term. My aunt, that's my *good* aunt, gets me kits.'

'Do you live with your aunt?' David asked; then regretted the impertinence.

'Yes. My parents are dead. We haven't got much money, and that's why I'm here really. You see, we get paid. That is, a sort of scholarship. For singing, I mean.'

'I'm very sorry,' David said. 'About your parents, I mean.' The boy's diction seemed to be infectious. 'What about the bad aunt?'

'Oh, that's my uncle and aunt. They're all right really. I think they've got too much money though. But they take me skiing sometimes; and on their yacht in summer – as you've probably noticed,' he added philosophically, if inexplicably.

'Noticed?'

'Yes. My legs.' The boy pushed his sock down and pulled the leg of his shorts up to his groin. The contour of his muscle was very faint; like the ridge of a sand bar under the golden skin. He had clearly forgotten about the 'plane.

'How old are you, Tony?' David tried to make the question sound like a *non-sequitur*. He was alarmed.

'Thirteen. I should be going on to Glenelgin next term, but they want me to stay on here.' He moved his head towards the

distant spire of St Cecilia's Temple, though without taking his
eyes off David. 'I wouldn't mind so much if conditions weren't
so *incredibly bad.*'

'How do you mean?'

'The food. Lloyd, he's a boy in my form, was sick five times
last term.'

David smiled. 'That's probably just your age. I had hundreds
of tummy upsets at my prep school.' The thought crossed his
mind that his tutor was probably reading his note at that very
moment.

'I don't think so,' the boy said seriously. 'Take Hamley
yesterday and the fried bread. It was the fried bread, I'm sure.
No, the food *is* bad,' he repeated, moving the rudder of the
'plane back and forth for emphasis with his toe. 'Sanders was
going to organise a strike last term and refuse to sing. But his
voice began to break, then he got hair, so it wouldn't have made
any difference if he had come out on strike.' The boy gave the
'plane another poke with his toe. 'I hope I don't get hair.'

Wildly, David wondered whether the child was contemplating some traumatic connection between this 'hair' and his
voice, or whether he was thinking about the beauty of his body
again. He didn't need to wonder for long.

'I mean it spoils it, doesn't it – your tummy. Look. The line
should be smooth like this.' He had turned his body away from
David so that it showed a profile, and impatiently restraining
the jutting creases of his shorts with one hand, he inscribed
a slow curve in the air with the other close to the front of his
stomach, making a cup-like indentation at the bottom of the
stroke. 'You see?' He looked up smiling, and gestured towards
the Temple again with his head. 'There's a statue in the chapel
which is smooth like that. It's much nicer than Sanders.'

'Tell me about Sanders, and about the choir school,' David
said. He was beginning to feel responsibility for this extraordinary child.

'Well, Sanders has left actually. The school's not too bad.
We've got one decent master called Mr Simon, who's got a lot
of art books, but he's got to leave at the end of this term. He
seduced someone, I'm afraid.'

'I see. You'll miss the statues in the art books?'

'Yes. I like statues. And paintings, too, really. But statues
more. The matrons are decent but I don't like the Ghoul. In

fact, I rather hate the Ghoul. He used to call me *his choirboy*. It's rather wearisome *being* a joke.'

'I don't understand.'

'Oh, you know . . .'

David was surprised that the boy seemed to have few inhibitions about mysteries; though probably it was only because they still were mysteries. He found he had dug his heel deeply into the hard ground. 'I don't think you're a joke, Tony.'

The boy was lost in some world of his own; moving his feet idly in the grass, which was very brown in the middle of the field. He nodded towards the Temple for the third time that afternoon. 'I'll have to be clocking in over there soon. Back to school, change into best suit, left-right crocodile, and then all those vestments! At least we don't have to wear lipstick like I did in Vienna.'

'Have you been to Vienna?'

'Mmm,' the boy nodded. 'Last summer I did an exchange with a boy from the Vienna Boys' Choir – a boy from Kings and one from the Chapel Royal went too. But they wear lipstick for concerts.'

'That's why you were so quick with my German yesterday then!'

'Yes. I only know some libretto, though. Oh, and how to point out particular cream cakes.'

David smiled up at the sky. 'So do I! I've been to Vienna too.'

'Have you really!'

'Yep! Look, Tony, can you come out to tea with me?'

'We're not allowed to,' the boy said automatically; then, after a pause, 'How?'

David looked round at the empty field, and the buildings of St Cecilia's far away. But his thought was interrupted by the boy's excited voice.

'I know! Verrucas.'

'*What?*'

'Verrucas! A boy in my dormitory's got them. If I touch his bare feet with mine I'll catch them and be off games!' The child was quite radiant; like one of his statues floodlit for photography.

'Well, they don't take root as quickly as that, you know . . .'

'You'll see! I'll be over there by the fence at half past two tomorrow – we play games on the upper field, so no one'll know.'

'But –'

'Isn't tomorrow any good?' The boy's voice had dropped a semi-tone, becoming hesitant for the first time.

'All right,' David said, 'I'll be there. But I'll want to see a note saying, "Sandel is off games and allowed to fly 'planes".'

'Do you want me to put on my best suit?'

'Do you usually put on your best suit to fly your 'plane?'

'No, I s'pose not.' Tony looked at his shoes, then archly up at David. 'Why do you look at my eyes like that? Do you think they're *wild*?'

'They're big,' David said, and felt foolish.

The boy nodded without smiling, and began to wind up the control wires. 'My great-grandmother was a gipsy – one of the real Romany queens – and my great-grandfather was a Swedish prince. All our family are passionately conceived; or that's how my aunt puts it. Grandfather was a commoner of course, and since then we've been very English. He and my father really ran the Foreign Office. I'm the last of the Sandels.' He wiped some oil off his finger on to the grass and tucked the 'plane under his arm. 'I've got to go now. Goodbye.'

For a second David thought he was going to shake hands. Instead, he adjusted the turn-over of one of his socks and began to walk away. A moment later he called back. 'David, what'll I do with the 'plane?'

'Bring it,' David said. As the boy turned again he became aware for the first time of a man and a girl leaning on the railings some way behind him. They were looking into the field without interest. David watched the receding figure in light grey and blue until it was out of sight. Then he sat down on the grass.

# 6

DAVID hadn't been to the Maypole Cellar since his first wild weeks as a freshman. He stood on the stone steps looking down into the mass that was seething to the music of a single trombone. The weird, pastel colours were like a sand-storm in a Turkish bath. Henry Moore's tube stations didn't touch it. David felt sick.

Beneath his feet the steps were wet with bottled beer, still containing tiny bubbles that stared glassily and then popped, closing their million eyes on him. Here and there was a darker pool, or slowly expanding promontory of draught Guinness. He saw Gloria lolling on the rostrum near the trombone player. No one knew who Gloria was, or what. David didn't now know what he wanted Gloria for. He had tangled with her his first year. It had seemed mature and contemporary.

He fought his way through the pulsating body on the floor. A girl shouted a protest. David held course for Gloria. He could make her out more clearly now through the steam rising from the dancers. Her hair was the same badly hung blackout curtain he remembered; her mouth a candid gash. She must be about forty. David looked down at her as he approached and thought, her limbs are like joints of meat ineptly dispatched by the butcher. Gloria swung the blackout curtain aside as he came up.

'Henry!'

'No.'

'Well, Samuel then, or something! Anyway, I know you.'

'Dance with me, Gloria,' David said.

Gloria seemed to rise with the heavy wing-beat of a harpy. They moved on to the floor.

'Come here often?' David asked.

'Let me ask you a question, darling.' Gloria was pressed so tightly against him that he was almost winded. 'Where have you been? I always knew you weren't like the other boys. Have you been sitting over books? Or playing that square instrument of yours? Or *sleeping* with it . . .'

'You can't sleep comfortably with a piano,' David interposed practically.

'What then? Undergradu*ettes*?'

David didn't reply. He'd had three double whiskies at the Wasp's Nest and the room was filling with wool. He dropped his chin on Gloria's shoulder. 'Shut up, Gloria. I hate your guts.'

'Now, darling! That's not very kind, is it?' The rumbling passed over David like a mill-race. He was an exhausted swimmer trapped for ever in the pit of the mill-race. Nothing could stop the waters.

They'd been jostling steadily towards the entrance. He must have said some more offensive things.

'You've had a long day, darling,' Gloria said. 'It's past tuck-up time.' They'd arrived at the doorway, and she catapulted him off her stomach as if she was a horse ridding itself of a tiresome fly.

David closed his eyes as he lurched over the bridge above the barber's basement. He shut the front door with exaggerated caution, and climbed the flights of stairs like a drugged octopus. When he had folded his clothes, he scoured the atomist's hairs out of the bath and turned the taps on. He went back to his room and smoked a cigarette, sprawling naked in the armchair. Then he emptied half a bottle of Mrs Ranter's Dettol into the bath.


# 7

T HERE were two letters waiting for David in college. One was from his Literature tutor, and read:

*My Dear Rogers,*

*I am very sorry to hear you have been ill. Thank you for your essay. I am afraid I was really able to make very little of this, though, despite the evident care you had taken to edit it for me. Perhaps you would be good enough to come and see me at 6 tomorrow (Wednesday).*

*Sincerely, J. Thompson.*

The other letter was addressed to *Mr D. Rogers,* and had also come through the college messenger service. The boy must have dropped it off at the lodge on his way to Communion as it was dated *6 a.m. Tuesday!* David read the rather angular hand.

*Dear David,*

*I touched Lloyd's feet and I think I've got verrucas now.
I told matron I had verrucas and it's all right because she
put me off games.*

*Lots of Love, Alessandro Scarlatti (Security!)*

David left his car by the Botanical Gardens. Just before half
past two he walked up to St Cecilia's Great Park, skirting the
nearer corner that was Christ Church Meadow.

The boy was leaning with his back against the fence, with
his elbows spread on the top railing, staring at the sky. The
'plane was at his feet. As David came up he took a cap out of
his blazer pocket, un-crumpled it, and set it with some concentration on his head. It had the same badge in miniature as
the blazer. 'Come on,' David said. The boy picked up the big
model, and they walked back towards the car.

David opened the driver's door and the boy scrambled in on
the other side, putting the 'plane into the boot behind them.
He was still wearing the cotton summer shorts, but David
noticed from the way they hung that they were a different pair.
Following his eyes, Tony wriggled over on his side and pulled
up the skirt of his blazer.

'Look!' he said, and added with pathos, 'The Ghoul.' There
was a heel-mark on his seat, faintly outlined in black. 'They
were clean this morning and it doesn't rub off. It's coal,
because he has to stoke the boilers.'

David couldn't help smiling. 'What were you up to?'

'Well, he was reading us a story to do with history and it
was about a wagon full of silver coins called *dollars* in Spain
which fell over a cliff – and they all spilt. The story was called
a *Rain of Dollars,* you see, r.a.i.n. Well, I drew a picture of an
*American* dollar with a crown on top, and passed it to Hamley.
D'you see? R.E.I.G.N. But the Ghoul caught me. He made
me bend over in front of the whole class and spoiled my clean
shorts. I think he likes to,' he added, 'to beat me, I mean. He
does it sort of slowly.'

David had stopped laughing.

'Would you beat a boy for doing that?' Tony asked. It was
one of his philosophical moments, which David was coming to
recognise.

'I would say he was probably one of the brighter boys in the class,' he said. 'But not aloud. Or to him.'

The boy nodded as if they were talking about someone else. 'I agree, really.'

'Right. Now, put your plate back in. I like it.'

Tony took the plate with the silver wire out of his pocket and picked some bits of fluff off it. He clipped it over his teeth, pushing it up with his thumbs, and then grinned at David. 'Where are we going?'

'Burford, I think. I know a good place for tea there.' David let the clutch in. Oddly perhaps, the boy had hardly noticed the car. Now he accepted their destination uncritically. He was staring out of the window, and said in a tone at once formal and far off:

'Can you have me back in time for Evensong, please?'

David flicked the boy's cap off and tangled his fingers in his hair. Tony slid down the seat, and cupped his body in an attitude of languor, grinning up. David disengaged his fingers with a downward brush over the boy's brow. The traffic was thinning. They negotiated a roundabout, and the by-pass stretched before them.

The Bowdenex cable drew open the twin throttles with a long, smooth pull beneath David's foot. The needles of the rev counter and the speedometer rose together. Irresistibly the rev counter pushed the speed needle before it in a steadily increasing arc. The boy had put down the fire extinguisher he had detached from the dash clip and was gazing ecstatically through the windscreen. With horror David recalled the boy. He didn't even know whose boy. He let the cable recoil sharply into its sheath. The twin needles before his eyes faltered, and then fell back together, still linked in diminuendo. David realised he was shaking.

Slowing to thirty he manoeuvred through the blanket town of Witney and out on to the road running over the Cotswolds to Burford. The afternoon was very still. Away on the right the watercolour greens of the Windrush valley lay under haze. Above a line of slender poplars on the horizon the sky was contorted with white coils of rope where the U.S. Air Force had laid its vapour trails. David knew that in a few hours a wind would spring up in the valley. The lowered sun would transform the poplars to fine traceries of burnished copper gauze, and the wind would pull the vapour trails apart like a skein of silk in the hands of an idle god.

Tony was looking down towards the valley. 'What's the stream called?'

'The Windrush.'

The boy thought for a moment. 'I think that's a beautiful name,' he said presently.

David stirred at the return of the odd sophistication. 'Higher up another stream joins it which is called the Evenlode.'

'I expect there'll be dragon-flies down there,' the boy said. 'Can we go and see?'

David stopped the car. When they were half-way across the sloping fields the boy asked, 'What are you studying at the university?'

'English.'

'*Just* English?'

'Yes.'

'How do you know the name of the stream?'

'I used to walk here my first year.'

'Didn't you have any friends?'

David smiled and pointed out a dragon-fly on a stone; but it wasn't a dragon-fly. 'No, Tony. It wasn't that, I don't think. I just like being by myself most of the time.'

'That's funny. No other boy at school makes 'planes, and I like being alone too . . . There's Hamley . . .' Tony was drawing the toe-cap of his shoe slowly through the water.

David laughed. 'Come on!'

Back at the car David took a clean piece of rag and soaked it in petrol. 'Now then, your shorts!'

Obediently the boy bent over. 'Don't be an ass, Tony. I meant you do it.'

The boy took the rag and dabbed at the coal stain, twisting his head over his shoulder.

'And just ask this Ghoul to wipe his feet before beating you up,' David added.

'All right. I will!' Tony was apparently satisfied with his sartorial repair.

David had chosen the Bay Tree because he imagined their habit of encouraging customers to cut their own slices from the selection of home-made cakes was likely to appeal to the boy. Also, the hotel was run as a training establishment for

young ladies, and one was spared the lingering of un-tipped
waitresses. There were few people on the terrace. The air was
filled with the gently spiralling seed cases from the giant elms
which flanked the garden. While their tea was being prepared
Tony ran about on a lower lawn, trying to catch them as they
fell.

Tony certainly did justice to the tea, though David had twice
to deflect the cake knife to a more obtuse angle to counteract
the boy's modesty. He ate almost too properly, and seemed to
have made easy adjustment from whatever lore might obtain
in the school dining hall. The winged elm seeds covered the
terrace and table and settled lightly in the boy's hair, while the
young ladies were equally fond in their attentions to David's
brother . . . Or was it son? Or . . .

'Can I ask how old you are?' Tony seemed to have read a
part of his thoughts.

'Nineteen.'

The boy addressed himself again to the gateau. He glanced
towards the house and the girl standing by the cakes. She came
out looking alarmed. Tony cocked his head on one side like a
sparrow and smiled enquiry at her. David conceded to himself
with a twinge of discomfort, that he importuned superbly.
Perhaps it was outrageous. But the doubt passed as a sudden
gust of wind blew another show of elm seeds down on their
heads. Tony shut his eyes and gripped the arms of his chair as
if at the dentist's.

'She looks like a matron,' he whispered when the girl had
gone, and another slice of cake lay capsized by its icing on his
plate.

'If you want some more chocolate when you've finished that
you'll find some due south of your nose,' David said.

The boy put out his tongue and searched his chin for the
chocolate. Chocolate had built up in a drift on the wire of his
plate too. Uncannily, he removed the plate, and after a glance
at David, rinsed it in his tea-cup and clipped it back into his
mouth. The wire gleamed hypnotically.

Tony was fumbling in his pocket. He produced a crumpled
letter. 'Can you help with this?'

'What is it?'

'It's a letter from a French boy. Last term our French master
went to a French school and he fixed it up that some of the

boys there write to us and we write to them. Only they write in English and we write in French. It's the sort of thing peda-gogues do.'

David took the letter and read:

*Dear Antony,*

*I've received your letter yesterday and I answered so quickly I can. I'm very glad to hear from you. I've not received letters from Oxford and I ask you, if it doesn't bother you, to write with me. I hope you're glad to read this words.*

*I've look at your photograph and I've to write you're very pretty, I don't think find more nice boy than you.*

*Since we write one another, I go speaking about french pubs and Sunday. Here the pubs are open from The morning from 6 o'clock to 4 in The morning. All the people can go into its; The boys like The men. The women like The boys and The girls. In my town there is 8 pubs for 6,000 inhabitants. For French man The Sunday is the amusement day. Here it remembers us, Morning – Go up at 9 o'clock – pub then Mass. At 12 o'clock – dinner With chicken (often). Afternoon: – from 2 to 3 pub. At 3 picture till 6. At 6 Ball till 8. From 8 to 9 Supper, From 9 to 9½ pub. From 9½ to midnight or 4 Ball. At 2 or 4 'Midnight' supper.*

*In your next letter speak me about english pubs and Saturday please.*

*Hoping to hear from you very soon,*

*Your Friend, Gaston de Yonghe.*

'What is one to do?' Tony asked desperately when David looked up.

'I think it's *cafés,* not pubs, he's curious about,' David said. 'We'd better try and explain the difference. Who is this Gaston?'

'A choirboy in Rheims.'

David nodded. 'Do we have to be honest? Or shall we wander back and forth between the High Altar and the pub?'

'I think we'd better be honest.'

David took a sheet of paper from his wallet. 'Okay – dictate.'

Five minutes later he passed the completed letter to the boy.
Tony looked at it critically. 'Shouldn't a gateau have a hat?'

'*Accent circonflexe? Mais oui!*'

'*Alors!*' Tony said loyally, tucking the paper in his breast
pocket behind the Tudor rose. He stretched his legs under the
table and adjusted his blue elastic belt. 'Sometimes it's trying
being a schoolboy.'

David smiled. 'Tell me about Sanders' proposed strike.'

'Oh, I think he was going to put a notice on the altar saying,
"Feed My boys better, or I'll leave this place: J. Christ".'

David frowned momentarily; but the boy went on.

'It wouldn't have worked. We're not allowed up to the altar.
It's sacrosant.'

'"Sacro*sanct*."'

'Oh yes; thank you.' Tony had begun to brush the cake
crumbs into the palm of his hand; then stopped. 'Can I take
these back with me?'

'Crikey!' David was astonished. 'Is it as bad as that?'

The boy laughed. 'I've started to keep tropical fish. The book
I've got says they can have things like cake crumbs sometimes.
They like sugar. But you have to be very careful with them.
Especially about buying them. Sometimes you get a bad one –
I mean a weak one – and it dies. Sometimes they're not even
proper tropical fish. But we get mine from Harrods.'

'Are they proper, strong ones?'

'Yes,' Tony said, 'but there's an awful lot of deceit in the
tropical fish world.'

The boy's legs were stretched out under the table. He flexed
them suddenly, pressing his ankles against the sides of the
chair like a jockey with short stirrup-leathers, and his knees
were quite square.

'Something's bothering me,' David said. 'You worry about
the slightest mark on your shorts, yet you let ink leak on to
your sock, and grind your shoes into the gravel and trail them
in streams. Why?' To his embarrassment a deep flush spread
over the boy's cheeks, as if the reflection of a fire had been
caught in a copper screen.

'Socks and shoes don't matter much,' he said, '– or not
these old ones.' He plucked distastefully at his clothes. 'These
are pretty awful too.'

'You look very . . . fine,' David said. Then he was angry with himself for substituting the last word, and because even then he'd fallen back on a facetious tone.

'Thank you,' Tony said. He met David's eyes so seriously that he jerked forward impulsively and began dusting the elm seeds out of his hair.

'Brush one hundred times forwards and one hundred times backwards,' Tony said happily beneath the buffeting.

They had reached the Botanical Garden, and the boy had retrieved his cap and 'plane from the boot. 'When can I see you again?' he asked blankly.

David span one of the 'plane's wheels on its hub. It was true that the tyres were inflatable. 'I don't know, Tony. How long do verrucas last?'

'All term,' the boy said without hesitation.

'What about Saturday?'

'Shall I be in the same place?'

David nodded. He straightened the boy's cap. 'Better bring the 'plane, Tony. Go straight back now.'

David crossed the barber's bridge, and climbed the stairs with his eyes open. He corrected the angles of chairs misplaced by Mrs Kanter's domestic industry, and then sat down at his typewriter. Ten minutes later he wound out a sheet of quarto and looked it over.

## TROPICAL FISH

Tropical fish
Are a delectable dish
Much favoured in the Orient.

But to Ant
They simply can't
Be anything but orn(i)ament.

These rare marine fauna
Then, normally orna-
Ment the tables of Chinamen.

But to Ony Tony
(When proved *Bona
Fide*) they're stock for his aquarium.

To you or me a fish
Is a fish
Whether gold, or tropical, or merely cod.

But to Ant
They're sacro*sant*
And certainly not food.

David sealed the rhyme in an envelope and posted it.


## 8

THERE was no row of Jesuits perched on Bruce Lang's
bed. Having established this with a peep David opened
the door fully, nearly upsetting a table on which the works of
Thomas Mann were disposed in the unmistakable confusion of
crib books. Though he was now eight months on the road to
Rome, Lang still had his digs in the attics of the retired canon
of Bath, who was St Cecilia's Dean of Divinity, and high func-
tionary in the Temple. The situation, Lang would tell you, was
comfortable since the canon was never loaded.

David entered the room, taking care not to look at the
colour photo of the Pope above the mantelpiece. His Holiness
held a small bird. Facing him, on the opposite wall, was a more
modest representation of Lang as the Christ in the Chester
Mystery Cycle they had once performed at school. The east
wall was bare save for a two-foot crucifix, complete with
contorted Saviour. David touched his forelock.

'*Grüss Gott, Gott!*'

'David, that man died for you!' Lang roared.

'Yes, Bruce; I know.'

'You don't consider there's a certain impertinence in
commending God's attendance upon God?'

David looked at the effigy again. It reminded him of the
family guest house at St Jacut in Brittany which was run by
nuns. They all carried two-foot models, and when they waited
at table the feet of the Redeemer clanked against soup tureens.

'I was thinking of *L'Abbaye*.'

'Oh,' said Lang flatly. He got up and poured David a glass of port, although it was only five o'clock. He had put down the porcelain bowl he had been turning in his fingers, and David picked it up. It was a finely wrought vessel of egg-shell thinness with narrow, fluted channels which spiralled up from its base to the crenellated lip. It had once been a cup, whose cleanly broken handle had been disguised by a cleverly faked continuation of the pattern, so that it was now a bowl. But the colour did not quite match, and the brilliant jay's-wing blue of the original glaze had proved inimitable.

'When do you think it was restored?'

Lang had sat down in the brown corduroy chair again. 'Probably quite soon after it was made, though as you can see it was too late. It must have been properly glazed and baked again. It's early Crown Derby; sometime in the last quarter of the eighteenth century I should think.'

'Was it so highly valued in those days that someone should have taken the trouble to restore it even then? After all, it's only a tea-cup.'

'Probably. That blue under-glaze was a trade secret of the pottery at Derby, and withheld even from the London branch. The gilding's perfect, but whoever did it couldn't manage the blue. It's possible that the thing was restored at the London pottery at Bow.'

David replaced the hybrid on the table and sighed. 'I expect I'll come over in the end, Bruce!'

'Where?'

'To the Scarlet Lady – under the incense – you know.'

Lang laughed.

'It must be wonderful to have your way carved out for you,' David went on, running his finger up one of the grooves on the bowl. 'To have a pathway ready hewed through the mountains, and follow it happily masticating in your nosebag – blinkers on the trail. And all the awesome pomp. The sweet-smelly smoke, and those nose-picking plebeian acolytes toddling round with watering-cans tinkling little bells. Then the doctrine of happy accommodation – flexible as any bulrush when the emotional gales of March are blowing. Ah, blessed idiosyncratic interpretation!' David felt rubber bands behind his ears involuntarily spring the corners of his mouth apart. He restrained the childish triumph badly.

Lang was looking down the several yards of his legs, and had one eye closed. 'You remember then?'

'Father!' David mimicked with confessional solemnity. 'In March last year, after seeing an Italian film at the Scala, which was on the Index too, I swore tearfully to my heathen friend Rogers that Resurrection of the Body must take place at four-teen years of age exactly, for otherwise it were pointless. These were my very words, Father. What must I do now?' David dropped his voice an octave, and answered himself, 'Repeat four hundred Hail Marys, my son.'

Lang had raised the heavy cushion behind his head to the full extension of his arms. Now he hurled it with a grunt. The cushion missed David, upsetting the table, and completing the disorientation of Mann. David got up and tossed it back. 'Isn't this stuff on the Index, anyway?' He was restacking *Joseph and his Brothers, Felix Krull,* and *Death in Venice.*

Lang had settled back, and was looking tiredly at David. 'Mann was deeply religious, and probably one of the greatest thinkers of the century.' He seemed to be putting little wings on his words.

'Whole shelf's a bit unorthodox I would have thought. For a good Roman. What about this lot?' David ran his hand over the spines of Gide, Sartre and Proust. He stopped before twin volumes of Peyrefitte in French, *Les Amitiés Particulières* and *Les Clefs de St Pierre.* 'Omigod!' he murmured, pulling out the last, and looking at Lang in horror. 'Oh, Bruce! There must be a Papal Bull already in the post. You must hide, man!'

Lang was making motions with the cushion again, but changed his mind. Instead, he said, 'If you had only read the elementary *bases* of your own school, Milton's *Aereopagitica* for instance, you'd know that ever since good and evil came into the world "as two twins cleaving together" man's sole preoccupation has been with their distinction. He must learn, if I remember rightly, to "apprehend and consider vice with all her baits and seeming pleasures, and yet abstain, and yet distinguish". That way he becomes the "true war-faring Christian" . . .'

'Sure, sure,' David murmured. 'Milton was worried about something else, you know. Rome, my boy! The "wolf with privy paw". The implemented of the Inquisition – who'd gaoled Galileo, and broken Da Vinci's toy helicopter.' David pointed at the bed where the Jesuits were accustomed to sit. 'Who knew that you mightn't pervert geography next, or suppress the humanity of Greece – to whose "polite wisdom" we owe it, after all, that "we are not yet Goths and Jutlanders"! Mind you,' David added, 'Milton wrote before the invention of Anglo-Saxon in the nineteenth century. We *are* now Goths and Jutlanders, though through no fault of yours this time.'

'Thank you,' said Lang. 'Incidentally, Milton studied Anglo-Saxon, though he probably knew even less than you.'

David was incredulous. 'Really?'

There was a fixed smile on Lang's face. David thought he was growing to resemble the Spanish Jesuit.

'I stick to my point,' Lang said. 'We must read all; and be responsible.'

'Rome's umbrella!' David muttered. 'The aura of mystery and entertainment that draws Europe's masses more surely than telly. Of course, most of them don't have telly – or coats when it rains. When you've no money for the cafés, there's always the incense house on the corner!'

'You're being very silly, David!' Lang was suddenly angry.

'Probably. But I don't like this fascist stuff. "We the elect have a duty to the masses: we know."'

'Intellectual superiority need not contradict humbleness,' Lang said gently. 'You know I'm arrogant, David, but that's beside the point here.' It was like Lang to use any weapon, and he knew David was too weak to attack sentiment.

David took on port. 'You bamboozle me with doctrinal manoeuvre. Would you rather we talk in Italian; or perhaps Spanish?'

'I speak neither, as you well know.' Lang had slipped down into the chair, and his long body jutted out of it like a breakwater.

'By the way,' David went on, 'talking of raincoats and responsibility, do you still maintain that it's equally worthy to drop half a crown down a well in dedication to God as to spend it on clothing for refugees? It's another of the convert's dictums I've got a note of.'

Lang didn't answer. He hoisted himself from the chair and sloped over to the bookcase. He took down a volume and turned back to David. 'I've modified my diagnosis of your mind,' he said. 'May I read to you?'

'Please!'

'Very well then. Leslie Stephen on that remarkable man Sir Thomas Browne – probably not the least of the studies you've neglected.'

'Good God! Don't tell me the Medical School still reads the *Religio Medici*?'

'We don't, I do, and shut up,' said Lang carefully. He began to read.

'"Sir Thomas's witticisms" – or read David Rogers's – "are like the grotesque carvings in a gothic cathedral. It is plain that in his mind they have not the slightest tinge of conscious irreverence. They are simply his natural mode of expression; forbid him to be humorous, and you might as well forbid him to speak at all . . . He is a mystic with a sense of humour, or rather, his habitual mood is determined by an attraction towards the two opposite poles of humour and mysticism . . . He seems to be held back from abandoning himself to the ecstasies of abstract meditation chiefly by his peculiar sense of humour . . . His is the sentiment of reverence blended with scepticism. It is a contradictory sentiment. But then the essence of humour is to be contradictory."'

Lang looked up. 'End of quote. Nutshell,' he said. 'Incidentally, Stephen wrote before the Freudian analysis of the function of wit and humour as being that of reconciling opposing impulses in the mind by verbal dexterities and ambiguities. His perception's pretty shrewd.'

David was astonished. 'But, Bruce, you wouldn't want me any other way, would you?'

'It would take seven years on a couch, and cost rather a lot,' Lang said practically: 'And afterwards you'd be hard put to write the lyric for so much as a nursery rhyme.'

'I'll think about it.'

'So will I. Remember I'll be qualified and able to certify you in three years.'

David nodded dubiously. 'Pack up the piccolo, eh?'

'You'd have to hand in the lot, I'm afraid. But it might just free you of the boy business.'

There was silence for some moments. David gulped down smoke like Furlow.

'Would you like a fourth glass of my port?' Lang asked a little dryly.

'No, Bruce; absolutely no, thank you.' David let his eyes

stray about the room. Lang was a better St Cecilia's man than he. The tobacco jar on the mantelpiece all but had the college arms on it. 'Why don't we take a trip down to school next Sunday?'

'No, David. I've said never again, and meant it. Not after the way you behaved last time.'

'Oh, yes. But it was those sinister omens, remember? Electrical storms, and those *owls* hovering over the Plain.'

'You know it was nothing of the kind!'

'Oh, all right.' David was struggling. The rubber bands were fastened to his collar and eyelids. 'Look, I really came to ask you to peel off layers of memory and produce a man of the past.'

'We're drinking port, not wood alcohol!'

'I know – wood port, actually. I mean recall an earlier stage on your journey to beatification. Not as far back as Confirmation, which is always understandable given that one's been born British, or even as far back as low Anglicanism, but to *high* Anglicanism – to your St Cecilia's Temple days . . .'

'Why?' Lang asked warily.

'I want to use the organ.'

'Very understandable, but these things are best done within the sacrament of matrimony.'

David opened his eyes with a jerk. 'Why, that was superb! The double First Jesuit couldn't have put it across so suavely! I *meant* the Temple organ.'

Lang looked sheepish. 'What do you want to know about it?'

'Simply whether that mad organist is likely to play it around midnight, and whether any of that lot are liable to nip in for a pray at that hour?'

'I can't guarantee an answer to either, and anyway, if you want to play the thing why don't you ask? Why *do* you want to use it?'

'I'm composing a cantata.'

'Aren't they usually orchestrated?'

'Yes – so'll mine be. But I can convert for organ as I go along. Adds extra spontaneity.'

Lang considered his port. 'I don't think old Bull's likely to play in the middle of the night; but obviously people go into the Chapel to pray at all hours. I don't see why that should disturb you?'

'I'm shy, you know.'

Somewhere above the attic the St Cecilia's clock began
to strike. The sound seemed to crash down on them. David
thought he could hear Lang's collection of porcelain tinkling.

'Lord – tutorial!'

'Lang. or Lit.?'

'Lit. But what's the difference except that Thompson never
turns up until ten past the hour? Goes to the lavatory between
each tutorial. I've got to fly, boy!' David was up with a grunt.
'Thank you, Bruce. Good port. I really must give you one of
those wall-shields with the college arms on it.'

He closed the door and picked up his gown, which he'd
thrown down outside. To work, Rogers. Public School and the
Old-Stone B.A. is the pathway to success. They start angling
you that way when you're seven. How can they be wrong? He
clattered down the back staircase that served the attic rooms.

## 9

D AVID paused outside the canon's door. The Great Quad
was deserted, and the evening sun was washing the buildings with gold. There must have been some wind in the world
outside for high overhead rooks were drifting along vacant
diagonal planes with their wings quite still. Probably they were
being blown from the great beeches in the park. The echoes of
the clock had died away and David thought of the carp coming
to the surface again in the pond, and then of the goldfish,
whose splendour was being eaten away by a skin virus.

There was a movement in the mouth of the Temple on the
far side of the quad. A small boy emerged, pulling an opera
cloak over his shoulders; another appeared, and then Tony.
Tony walked towards the Hall and stood looking down at a
new gargoyle the masons had left lying on the terrace. He
raised one foot and put it down on the tenon at the base of the
creature's head. He fumbled in the jacket pocket of his suit,
and then raised his thumbs to his teeth. The boy continued to
stand alone like a pocket Napoleon. He seemed far away; an
ant, almost, inside the battlemented castle of St Cecilia. He

stared up at the scaffold-covered front of the Hall, and David could tell by the way he held his head that he must be screwing up his eyes against the sun. The boy's cloak stirred slightly; it caressed the back of his bare knees, and then floated out behind him. David let his eyes travel up from the boy to the rooks wheeling high above the college. A moment later the sixteen boys had gathered together and the column of black cloaks began to move out across the Great Quad. It wound round the pond and passed between the gigantic doors beneath the Bell Tower.

The canon was on top of him. David turned to go, but it was too late. He was still in his vestments and must have come straight from the service. His approach was like the progression of one of those mechanical bears that amble along sniffing the ground when you pull them behind you on a string. The old man peered up at David. He had sausage skin instead of eyelids. 'What can I do for you, young man?'

'Nothing, sir. Thank you. I've been calling on your attic lodger.'

'Good heavens! Is there someone living up there?' The canon put both hands on the stick beneath his chest. His eyes clouded as if a bit of the sausage membrane had strayed. 'Why yes, of course! Young Kitchener. A fine Greek scholar, and a military sort of fellow too. God bless my soul!'

'No, sir,' David stammered. 'Lang. Bruce Lang. And he's a Roman.'

The canon appeared to be recollecting himself. 'One of the Paraveccini twins? Claudio, perhaps – or Hippolyt. I must ask him to breakfast.'

David felt a bit like Tony with the Ghoul around. 'I meant a Catholic,'

'Ah! Would we were all as tolerant as Paraveccini! His cousin, Karl of Saxe-Coburg, is such a very nice fellow too – why!' he teetered around like a weather cock, 'I do believe that's his man over there!'

David followed his gaze. The only person in the quad was the Master, making his way briskly to his Lodging.

'Such fine fellows these Prussians,' the canon mused.

'Do you know the Sandels?' David asked. 'The last of the Sandels?' He realised he'd spoken the name purely for the kick of doing so.

'We've never had a Sandel up,' the canon said. 'Never heard of them.' He put his head and one hand to his door. David opened it for him. 'I do hope you'll come to breakfast,' the canon said, and disappeared.

'Nut case!' David muttered. 'The whole place is one multiple nut case. It's criminal to send little boys in here even in crocodiles.' He crossed the quad to the J.C.R., passing only Brougham, whose head was cushioned in a new scarf.

There was a letter from Mrs Shepherd's insurance company promising their 'advices' in the matter of the car accident. What was the mysterious lore that reversed singulars and plurals in the business world? David wondered. On the rare occasions when he had a suit made his tailor referred to 'the trouser'.

There was a letter from Tony too. David opened it second like a child keeping the tinned peaches for last. He took a knife out of his pocket to slit the envelope cleanly.

*Dear David,*

> *Thank you very much for the poem. I think it is jolly good. Saturday will be all right because my verrucas are worse and I poked them with Armstrong's sheath-knife to help. I had a parcel from my aunt with jelly babies and some Brighton rock. I gave the jelly babies to the Ghoul's dog. Would you like the rock because I don't like rock?*
>
> *Lots of Love, Tony.*

*P.S. I will bring the rock in case.*

David took a card and an envelope, and shoving aside a runic review called *Medium Aevum,* sat down at one of the J.C.R. desks.

'Good!

### 'BRIGHTON ROCK

> Alas! Eternal Brighton Rock!
> Aunt has sent yet another stock.
> You can go on biting,
> But can't eat the writing,
> As far as you bite on
> It still says, *Brighton.'*

David sighed. Lang was probably right about him. After a moment he added:

> 'Jelly babies
> Give dogs rabies.
> Give the Ghoul's hound
> One pound
> Regularly!'

Stamping the envelope, as he wasn't sure whether the messenger system delivered to choir schools, he put it in the J.C.R. box.

Thompson's staircase was at the back of St Cecilia's Small Quad. The landing was covered with mud from last term's rugger fields. David looked out of the window. Below him was a wing of domestic Tudor done on the cheap, but the roof tiles were old stone ones; thick, and chipped at their lips like oyster shells.

There was a movement behind him. Turning, he found Thompson's door open, and the back of his earlier pupil going down the stairs, David waited respectfully. Sure enough Thompson emerged and descended, looking neither to right nor left. When he returned he looked straight through David and entered his room again. David could now decently knock on the half-open door.

Thompson was an intense, bird-like man who made quick, meaningless movements which were apt to be alarming. When David entered he was standing in front of the fireplace. He dropped his chin on his chest like a marionette expressing embarrassment, looked up sharply, and as promptly dropped his head again. David thought he could hear his chin hitting his thorax.

'Ah, Rogers!' he said, the last syllable getting lost in his tie. 'Sit down.'

David sat, first moving a set chessboard. Thompson never actually played chess, but when a world champion in Moscow seemed frozen in stalemate Thompson quietly thawed him out in the privacy of his room.

'I'm going to talk to you, Rogers.' Thompson looked up. The puppeteer had yanked the head string violently. 'I hope you won't mind. No? Very well then.' He grabbed the sheets of

cardboard that were David's essay. 'Swift. Awful! But Johnson
– Samuel! Where are we?' He shuffled David's boards like
giant cards, then began to read in a nervous monotone.

'Zzz. "The many and obvious fallacies in Johnson's literary
criticism have caused some critics to deny him any power of
imagination. This is at once true – and absurdly false. Johnson
had in fact a terrible imagination, as Mrs Thrale's custody of
Johnson's padlock, and much else besides, suggests. But in the
pre-Kraft-Ebbing darkness Johnson had no choice but to deny
himself its licence with all his might. Simply, Johnson equated
imagination, or the pre-valence of imagination at least, with
madness. Johnson says as much himself in several places . . ."
Zzzz. Paragraphs. "For Johnson, then, imagination meant two
things: it was responsible for what he called his *vile melancholy*, but it was responsible as well for the sexual fetishism
which he had no hope of understanding, and so could only
conclude to be madness. That is why, in his criticism, we
find Johnson denying creative power to the imagination of
poets, and insisting, as Hagstrom phrases it, that 'mental
actions be relegated to primary perceptions'." This is rubbish,
Rogers. Absolute rubbish. But then you go on. Zzz. "There
are, however, curiosities in Johnson's criticism which are not
so smugly explained by a flip through a textbook . . ." Now,
Rogers, we may be smug. Yes, we are smug, I think. You are
smug. But we never *flip* through a textbook. Ever! Are you in
love?' Thompson was looking straight at David with his head
collapsed on one shoulder.

'No,' David said: he'd spoken more violently than he'd
intended.

'Have you a nice girl?'

'I had one once, sir . . .'

'Yes, yes! I don't mean you should go that far. Just walks.
Literary teas. With a volume of Donne. Know what I mean?
Better work!' For some reason Thompson was jangling his
hands like an athlete limbering up. 'Won't do, Rogers. It's
smug, smart, pretty, slick, *facile*. Understand what I mean?'

David gazed at a cornered pawn on the chessboard.

'Are you what the New Science calls neurotic?'

'Well, yes. Rather,' David said lamely. In a minute they'd
both be weeping. He liked Thompson. If it ever came to

Calvary Thompson would be there with vinegar. He wouldn't know what to do with it; but he'd make the gesture.

'We'll say no more about Johnson.' Thompson was decisive.

For some time David had felt pressure building up in his pre-frontal lobes. Now there was the faint prompting of a soprano line.

'Have you got anything on Thompson? *Thompson,* Rogers? The poet!'

'Oh, yes.'

'That's better. Not one of your sillier glosses, I hope. Thompson's an ancestor of mine,' he added inconsequentially.

'I think I left Thompson in my room.'

'Come!' Thompson's descendant was advancing on him like a Thurber creature. David surrendered the file.

Thompson began to buzz quietly. Then the buzzing became articulate. '"For Thompson, surely, is less a poet than a curious indicator to which the literary historian may point to demonstrate innumerable things. It is perhaps unfair to pick out single lines of Thompson like, 'The foodless wilds / Pour forth their brown inhabitants'. But the sad and the prosaic may be found equally readily in whole passages:

> 'The bleating kind
> Eye the bleak heaven, and next the glistening earth
> With looks of dumb despair; then sad-dispersed,
> Dig for the withered herb through heaps of snow.'

This is a nicely observed picture of offended sheep; but it is also abominably funny, which of course it was never meant to be."'

David swallowed. An ancestor, the man had said. But Thompson's buzzing had dropped an eighth, and the harmony become almost whimsical.

'"Thompson is said by Dobree to have been most successful in his sentimental cameos. Perhaps wrongly, I found these hard to take.

> 'In vain for him the officious wife prepares
> The fire fair-blazing and the vestments warm;
> In vain his little children, peeping out
> Into the mighty storm, demand their sire
> With tears of artless innocence.'

When one has read *Winter* one is prepared to believe anything
of Thompson, and so it is without surprise that one discovers
him to have been the author of *Rule Britannia*."'

The new Thompson accomplished a roll into the Minor. 'Zzz
– ZZZ. "Before discovering the places where Thompson was a
poet – and there are some discoverable by him who wades long
enough . . ." ZZZ.'

David's chair began to vibrate. It was astounding. A piccolo
man with the tonal depth of a bassoon. The rumbling became
articulate again.

'"Despite his two faults of excruciating diction and diffuse-
ness, Thompson sometimes hits the ball when it soars red and
unmistakable into the sky. My examples come from Dobree,
because I got sleepy long before Thompson got his eye in."
Zzz. "In passing one might note that Thompson's diction is
not all hackneyed. He was a pioneer too, and seems to have
invented a new verb, to *thick-urge,* as in the phrase:

'. . . a blackening train
Of clamorous rooks *thick-urge* their weary flight'."'

The contemporary Thompson threw out his chin and tossed
the file into David's lap. 'I suppose you know you could get a
First if you weren't just damn silly?'

David mumbled and moved his shoulders around like
Fernandel. He found now that if he tacked 'Sir' on to a
sentence it sounded wrong. It was a secret of voice inflection
one lost after school. He said nothing.

David bundled towards the door. Thompson seemed to be
snapping at invisible mosquitoes. He looked over his shoulder
at the bottom of the stairs. Sure enough Thompson was
going to the lavatory, and pretending to anyone who might be
watching that he wasn't.

'Stay just where you are, Rogers!' Crawley ordered.

The outside door of Thompson's staircase had closed
behind David. Crawley backed steadily away from him like
someone about to deliver fair play with a six-gun. From ten
yards Crawley called loudly:

'What news, you old bugger, still on probation then?'

The gaggle of tourists that passed between them at that

moment did nothing to muffle the cheerful shout. When David opened his eyes the tourists had gone and Crawley was coming back towards him with a furious scowl. 'Won't do,' he said, shaking his head.

David was nettled. 'I should ruddy well think not!'

'Testing the inane greetings of this place,' Crawley said absently. 'Look, Rogers, I can walk with you just as far as the Great Quad. I'm doing another charity job for the blind.'

'Your dependent ten thousand?'

'Yes.' Crawley looked up sharply. 'And work doesn't come easily with a girl – I'm getting married.'

'Funny,' David interrupted relentlessly, 'Thompson's just been advocating one for *better* work.'

Crawley stopped in his tracks. 'Our work is not the same, Rogers. You're an academic; but I'm alone. I'm an artist.'

'No! That's a big word, you know.'

'Please let me speak,' Crawley said. 'I must leave you in ten yard's time and I know what it is that's going to destroy the world. Lack of communication – *reciprocal* communication: cultural, political, intellectual – whatever you like. But more, it's snobbery and self-deceit, which are artificial, protective barriers that prevent communication. You see Cowley workers streaming out of the dogs. What do you feel? Rogers! I'm asking you a question, for God's sake!'

'Oh! Superior. That I'm a better bloke – an entity with a brain something more than brute. That I should meet them on some level. But one never will.'

Crawley had sat down suddenly in the Small Quad. He stared at David wildly. 'I've communicated!'

'Or I have,' David said. 'You have to leave me here, remember?'

'You're the first person I've reached! The first of my people!'

'I thought we were all your bloody people,' David called over his shoulder.

He walked through into the Great Quad. The sun had sunk below the battlements leaving a slab of sleepy warmth trapped between the walls. He stepped out under the Bell Tower and there it was; a hot orange inexplicably glued to the spire of St Aldate's.

David made his way to the number three bus stop, and then had to stand. Port and sherry with Thompson sandwiched between them. No, two Thompsons. A shadowy poet, and a convulsive bird-man in Glengarry tweeds. It was too much. A baby was staring at him like a cameo of Thompson's. It brought up wind, lolling over its mother's shoulder. 'Me too,' said David. 'But it'll go with a bang when K. looses the I.C.B.M.s aligned on Brize Norton. No time for decisions, let alone revisions. No time to finish a song.'

Mrs Kanter was on the first landing.

'Oh, Mrs Kanter. My little brother will be coming to tea with me here on Saturday. I hope you don't mind?'

The woman beamed. 'Why, Mr Rogers, of course not! I didn't know you had a brother though!'

'Yes. He's at St Cecilia's choir school.'

'How lovely! And how old is he?'

'Thirteen.'

Mrs Kanter slapped her girth. 'I'll make you a cake then! Does he like chocolate?'

'Very much,' David said without hesitation. 'But, please, you really mustn't bother . . .'

'Bother! Don't you be silly, Mr Rogers. Whose house is this now?'

'Why, yours.' David was puzzled.

'Well, just don't you be silly in it, then!' Mrs Kanter announced triumphantly. David smiled. The dramatic way the working class delivered their rhetoric seldom wanted ingenuity. 'And it's no bother,' Mrs Kanter went on, 'just don't you worry about it. I'll have it in your room dinner-time Saturday. You go on now!'

David knew a command when he heard one. 'You're very kind. Really.' He closed the door and hurled himself on to the bed. 'Lousy liar, Rogers,' he said aloud. He felt in the cupboard beside him. 'You deserve MacVitie's digestives instead of dinner.'

## 10

'THANK you for those other poems,' Tony said when David met him at the bottom of the field. There was a flush along the high line of his cheek-bones, and he was wearing his flannel suit. He hadn't brought the 'plane.

'Well, they're not poems really. Just rhymes.'

The boy had pulled himself up on to the fence, and now he perched there looking at David oddly. 'I like them very much.'

David smiled. 'Come on. I hope you don't mind being my brother this afternoon. We'll have tea at my digs. My landlady's made a cake for you.'

'We won't have to have tea with her, will we?'

'No, of course not!' The boy seemed relieved. He smiled happily as he got into the car. 'Before I forget – the rock!' He pulled a huge stick out of his pocket. 'Think of it as a symbolic gift if you like.'

David stowed it away ceremoniously. A disquieting thought occurred to him. 'Tony, you're not an alto, are you?'

'No, soprano. Well, that is, actually I'm rather unique . . .'

'I know.' David was looking at the line of the boy's nose. Unexpectedly, Tony twisted round giggling. He seized the lapels of David's jacket and tugged them.

'I meant my *voice*.'

'All right. Tell me about your voice.'

'It's almost mezzo,' the boy said, releasing David. 'I'm first soprano, but I can sing most of the alto range as well.'

David started the car. Excitement had tightened his stomach. He began mentally to revise his soprano line; dropping it into cool grooves like the fluting on Lang's porcelain bowl. 'You do like singing, don't you?'

'For specially favoured patrons, yes,' said Tony. David glanced at him. His tone had held an odd mixture of emotions. But now his attention was distracted by the shops they were passing. 'There are frog-flippers in that window,' he said.

David felt breathless on the stairs. He didn't want Mrs Kanter to pop out; yet a part of him wished that she would. She didn't appear, however. Sure enough, in the middle of his table was a chocolate cake covered by a paper hat. Tony's grey eyes widened.

'Who's the hat for?'

'The cake, of course. To keep the flies off.'

'There aren't any flies.'

'No.'

The boy was standing by one of the high dormer windows. He had hung his cap on the back of the door as they'd come in. Now he said apologetically, 'I'm sorry my suit is rather worn.'

David looked up from arranging cups. 'It's very nice, but I'd wondered why you'd put it on?' Tony, he realised, matched the cerebral-grey paintwork of his room.

The boy looked confused. 'It's all-wool,' he said at a tangent. 'New College have ten per cent of nylon in theirs – but I like their red, white and black socks better than ours.' He looked down depreciatingly at his wine-and-blue-topped stockings. 'Our suits are better, though.' He moved his knee forward. 'Feel.'

David felt the hem of his jacket. 'You're a funny boy, Tony,' he said lamely: he had cut out 'little' just in time.

The boy wandered away, petulantly almost, and struck a chord on the piano. Then he swung round, suddenly animated. 'The Ghoul's always on at us about looking scruffy and about New College,' he said. He thrust his hands into the pockets of his shorts, then splayed them out, drew them up over his stomach, and rocked back on his heels. Then, catching sight of David's gown on the back of the door, he unwound himself, draped it over his shoulders, and took up the same stance again. Leaning right back on his heels, and struggling to control an inane grin, he mimicked: '"The boys of New College School, which on an old map you will see is situated, not inappropriately, at the apex of Lovers' Lane and Saville Road, *never* look scruffy! What's more, their manners . . ."' But it was no good. Intoxicated by his own performance, Tony folded up in mezzo-soprano giggles, and fell back on the bed.

After a moment he scrambled off again, straightening the bedspread. 'They have to take their caps off to cars on zebra crossings, too,' he said in his own voice, when he had recovered.

'"Manners Maketh Man" – belated Wykeham foundation.'

Tony had discovered David's tripod. 'Do you take photos too, then?' He seemed to have forgotten both his scorn for the nylon in New College's suits, and his covert admiration of their socks. 'So do I! Isn't it funny.' He had perched on the edge of a chair and was looking intently at David with the grey eyes under brows which a god must have pencilled as the final expression of his own wonderment. 'About you and me, I mean. You know about model 'planes, and about music and about photographs as I do. I think we're sort of bound . . .' Tony looked down; he'd lost his composure.

David stared across at him. He was a ravishingly beautiful boy. The word 'ridiculously' rose in his mind, because it alone could express the enormity of the boy's beauty without conceding its terror. And this, of course, was just the nervous brinkmanship Lang had accused him of. 'I think so too, Tony.' He got up impulsively. 'Tea! I'll show you the camera afterwards.'

The boy looked up again with a brilliant smile. David went out of the room to fill the kettle. When he returned Tony was kneeling on the hearth-rug, turning over the pile of records he had tipped out of their rack. He had inverted his right hand; the third and index fingers were in his mouth, and his nose was nuzzled into the palm. As David entered the room, he quickly withdrew the fingers. David pretended not to have noticed, and lit the gas ring.

'Do you know any more poems – I mean rhymes?' Tony asked.

David spun the dead match into the waste-paper basket. 'There's one about the rug you're sprawling on.'

'What, this *mat*!'

'Exactly. It's mohair. I think the rhyme should particularly appeal to you.'

'Go on, then!' Tony grinned.

'All right. It's called *The Mohair Sheep*.

> The mohair sheep
> Is two feet deep.
> He may be worn,
> Shorn;
> Or tinned,
> Skinned.
> Spread flat,
> As a mat,
> He will dispose
> Of cold toes;
> For he has a pile on
> *Superior to nylon.*'

David spoke the last line with deliberation. Tony laughed and ran his fingers through the long hair of the rug.

'Did you make that up?'

David had to admit that he had.

'Just *now*?'

''Fraid so.'

'Good Lord!' said the boy slowly. He turned his head into the shaft of sunlight coming through the window, and then back into the shadow. It was like the effect you get when low cloud chases a band of gold across the face of a cornfield. Tony began to laugh. 'I'm sorry! I really am! But I think it's a goat, not a sheep!'

'Blast!' David said. The kettle was boiling.

Feeding Tony was an unpredictable business. Happily, Mrs Kanter's cake assumed precedence over the meringues and eclairs David had imported. The boy began almost too properly with bread; modified the regime with strawberry jam, making careful equation between the pulp and the whole fruit, and then started in on Mrs Kanter's cake. Eventually he sat back and nodded towards the pile of records on the floor.

'In that Vienna Boys' recording did you notice a bad German accent in Mendelssohn's *Elienchor*?'

'No, I don't think so.'

'Well, there is one; and it's me.'

'Really? I hope they paid you a suitable fee. They must make thousands out of those recordings. My God! And I had to pay special duty on that to import the native genius of Sandel!'

'Yes, we're often exploited.'

'Like Tropical Fish? How are they, by the way?'

'Oh, very well, thank you.' Tony seemed to have drifted off somewhere.

'Shall we play the record?' David suggested.

Tony was back in his body with a bound. 'What! When you've got the real me? We don't want anything canned like the mohair sheep-goat!'

David looked into the sun. For a second he had to compress his lips tightly.

'Can I see your camera first, though?'

David fetched the camera and handed it to the boy. Tony had got up too, and was bouncing gently on the edge of the bed.

'What sort is it?'

'A Rolleiflex 2.8.E2,' David said, and felt rather foolish.

Tony turned the reflex over curiously. 'Does it take very big pictures?'

'Well, you can enlarge them pretty big if they're black and white ones.'

'How big?'

'Oh, about the size of that wall.'

Tony looked at the wall. 'I don't believe you! You're joking!' David heard him swallow. Perhaps it was a nervous gesture that made him suddenly straighten his tie. 'Do they really make paper that big?'

'You wouldn't use paper. You would black out the room, paint chemicals on the wall, and project the negative on to it from the other side of the road. Then, still in the dark, you'd swab down the wall with more chemicals, using one of those brooms on a long handle they have for washing trains. Finally, you'd sit in the middle of the room squirting it with a hose for about three hours. After that you could turn the lights on, and there'd be a huge Tony permanently printed on the wall.'

David glanced at the boy. The tie-straightening hadn't been nervous at all.

'Can we?' Tony asked.

'Definitely not! It would be rather complicated, and might annoy my landlady.'

'The water, I suppose.'

'Exactly.'

Tony looked into the viewfinder. 'Show me how it works. It seems to have a lot of knobs.'

'What's an aperture?'

'An opening,' Tony said without hesitation. 'It needs to be very wide for colour. But why *does* the film need more light for colour?'

'For the same reason that you don't go out to paint roses in your garden at midnight – or even at dusk. Your eyes, and the film, need more light to see colours accurately.'

'Can you take colour inside?'

'Well, you can.'

'Can *you*, I mean?' Tony was looking at the gold bars of his thighs, where they protruded from his soft shorts; then he looked down distastefully at the wine and blue band of his socks.

'It's better in sunlight.' Tony nodded sagely. 'Do you like taking photographs?'

For a moment David hesitated. 'Yes – and no. It's an impure art; yet one with the demands of art proper, I suppose – like writing music. It's fascinating; but it can become an obsession – a technological, and a visionary obsession.'

'How do you mean – an "obsession"?'

David came back to him with a jerk. He looked at the boy sitting beside him on the bed. 'It's rather like combing your hair ten times a day; like knotting your tie in just the right place and – and worrying about your suit.'

Tony got slowly to his feet. With sudden violence he dragged crooked fingers through his hair; he pulled his tie viciously aside, and then, for good measure, seized the front of his shorts and drew them round over one hip, so that they hung absurdly twisted. He stared back at David with a look that mingled defiance with a conspiracy altogether alien to his years.

David got up, and pressed him briefly against his side. 'We sing! What's it going to be?'

Tony grinned wildly, and then looked at his toe-caps. 'Well, my speciality – my showpiece that is – is Mozart's *Benedictus* from the Requiem. But we need an alto, a tenor and a bass,' he added doubtfully.

David looked at him incredulously. He thought of the soprano melody reaching high up beneath the fan vaulting of Rheims, where he had once heard the Requiem performed live. 'Can you really do that?'

'Oh, yes.' Tony was almost off-hand, but was looking at his toe-caps again.

'You won't want whisky, or something?'

The boy giggled; but David hadn't meant it as a joke. He doubted whether he would be able to control his fingers.

'Tell you what,' Tony said. 'Let's keep that until we can rake in Hamley or someone for the alto. I'll just do the *Laudate Dominum* from the hundred and sixteenth psalm-setting now. Do you know it?'

David sat down heavily on the piano stool, and pummelled his face like Furlow. The truth was the anti-climax must hurt him more than the boy knew. The serenity of the soprano *cantilena* demanded a discipline no boy would tackle casually, and even then it was something an English boy was unlikely to have been trained for. He looked up.

'All right. I'll keep the violin line going to support you, and just throw a hand at the orchestra when I get the chance. I'll play the introduction twice, so you'll know where you are. Okay?'

Tony nodded. He had become very attentive. The plate with its silver wire was resting in a little pool on the top of the cheap upright.

David began to play; feeling the notes, not seeing them. 'That's your violin now,' he said quietly.

The next few minutes David was never to be able to recall with any reality. His fingers explored the depth and resonance of the boy's voice, and then the voice was informing his fingers directly, so that the accompaniment rose to support it in perfect harmony. Tony's voice was uncanny in its control and projection. It opened before the senses like the living petals of a flower whose evolution has been miraculously speeded in a Disney film. It was smooth and firm like the play of a fountain: a stream of silver when it aspired to the sky, its source was mellow as pewter. Over the lower soprano range his tone was superb: almost mezzo, as he had said; almost alto, and yet not quite either.

Tony was reaching for his plate. He clipped the wire over his teeth.

David said, 'You're the greatest advance in music since they curled up the French horn, Tony!' He had put his arm round the boy. Feigning exhaustion, Tony sank down on to his knee. The patches of heat were on his cheeks again, and David sensed the exhaustion only masked embarrassment. He said nothing. Tony shifted his weight and snuggled his hip into David's stomach. David closed his eyes. His mouth and nose were filled with the boy's fine hair. 'Off!' he ordered.

Deliberately the boy twisted round. He pressed his hot, frightened face against David's mouth. David felt the silver wire cutting his lip. He compressed his eyes more tightly. The purple patches deep inside them exploded into pendants of fire. Gently he pushed the boy off his knee.

'I've written you a cantata,' David said blankly. Tony was still flushed, but with a triumphant radiance. David took a manuscript from the top of the piano. 'Here. Look it over while I clear the things.'

He stacked the tea things on a tray, and carried the uncertainly tinkling crockery to the bathroom on the other side of the landing. He sat down on the cold linoleum, and was overcome by uncontrollable shaking. He bowed his head and extended his useless hands before his eyes.

When David returned to his room Tony was lying curled up on the mohair rug. With one hand he was idly turning over David's manuscript score: the other was inverted, with the third and index fingers contentedly buried in his mouth. The boy's jacket was undone exposing a pullover, with the wine and blue bands at its neck and waist, which tightly sheathed his torso. Doubtless all-wool, too, David thought inconsequently. Then he realised that although Tony had seen him he hadn't taken the fingers out of his mouth. Instead, he indicated a page of the score with his unoccupied hand, and looked up.

'This bit's Bach,' he said through the wet fingers.

'Very probably! It's difficult not to crib a bit sometimes – usually it's unconscious.'

Tony withdrew the fingers from his mouth, wiping them on the rug and not his suit. 'I like it,' he said clearly.

David said nothing. The boy had regained his composure, and his colour had returned to the dulled richness that was like antique gold; but he didn't want to risk saying anything which might bring the passion back. 'I thought we might perform it together if you can come again next Saturday.' Tony gave the mohair a heavy blow. 'Damn! I can't. It's the last night of the Eights, and the Ghoul wants me to go down and sort of support the college boat. He's a bit funny about boats, and rowing and things.'

David refrained from suggesting that the Ghoul was a bit funny about more than just boats and rowing and things. Instead he reversed the upright chair at his desk, straddled it, and looked over its back at the boy. 'Tell me more.'

Tony drew up his knees beneath him on the rug. He shrugged his neat shoulders casually. 'Well, the idea is that I have to wear white shorts, and my own blazer and boater . . .'

'And look pretty on the St Cecilia's barge!' David finished for him.

'Well, yes.' Tony seemed to be looking for small animals in the fleece of the mohair.

David controlled himself with difficulty. 'Tony, this Ghoul has no business to suggest such a thing. I – I think it's absurd. I mean – do you really want to do it?'

Unwittingly, he seemed to have released an appalling dilemma in the boy. For a minute Tony shook his head desperately, still searching the fleece of the rug. Then he cried out, 'No! Well, no! I think it's silly too. And I hate the Ghoul, and I – I like being with you but . . .' He seemed unable to finish the argument.

'What is it then, Tony?'

The boy's reply was almost sulky. 'You see, well . . . I thought I might be able to keep the white shorts afterwards.'

'I see.' David got up and walked round the room. It wasn't the moment to face his own jealousy, or weigh the morality of pandering to the boy's odd vanity. 'Who am I?'

'David.'

'Exactly. And this afternoon I'm your . . .?'

'Brother?'

'Even so.' David stopped. 'Now supposing I were to buy you your blinking white shorts – always supposing the things come in all-wool . . .'

Tony had taken up a corner of the mohair and buried his nose in it.

'I'll *remain* your brother – I don't see why the hell I shouldn't. On Saturday next I'll take you out. Official. Filial concern for your wardrobe. Aunt's orders. Overhaul. Family celebration or whatever. However . . . you'd better know nothing of this until your headmaster announces the impending visit of your brother. Is that clear?'

'Think so.'

'Right. Now stop behaving indecently with that woolly rug.'

'Yes.' Tony dropped the corner of the mat at once.

'I was going to suggest that you break out tonight, and that we have a shot at the cantata with the Chapel organ. But it would have to be at about eleven o'clock, and I think you'll be too tired . . .'

'No, really, I won't be!' Tony said urgently. He held out his watch, and David had the impression that his objections were being anticipated methodically. 'My watch is luminous, and I

never go to sleep early. Then, tomorrow I'll have a bad cold
and spend the day in bed because I've got the matrons taped.
Really it will be all right!'

'When does the master on duty do his last round, or
whatever?'

'It's Chambers tonight. He doesn't.'

The boy explained the layout of the back of the building, and
at last David said, 'All right. Then one, you mustn't leave the
passage until I meet you; and two, you must take the day off
tomorrow.'

Tony said, 'I promise.' He was calm now.

David laid a finger on his nose. 'Tell me – what's it for?'

Tony moved his nose up and down beneath the finger. He
grinned widely. 'What?'

'The wire.'

'Oh, the side ones!'

'I thought it might be calculated decoration. Or perhaps an
artificial sounding board for *coloratura*.'

Tony brought his right foot up and placed it against the calf
of his left leg. Perilously balanced, his hips swayed. '*Ho! Hum!*'
he said darkly.

Tony picked up the manuscript score. 'I'd better take this
and look it over this evening, hadn't I?'

'Yes.' They synchronised their watches; David more
self-consciously than the boy.

On the stairs Tony said, 'Should I say thank you to your
landlady for the cake?'

'Put your head in there,' David replied. He went on down
the stairs.


## 11

D AVID crouched in the shrubbery. In front of him, in the
darkness, was a totally strange house. There was no
question of *déjà-vu*: somewhere he had done this before. Then
he had it. Of course! Lang would remember well enough. He
had been drunk then, and had had a crazy uncertainty that
if he was apprehended he had only to say, 'Don't shoot; I'm

drunk!', and that everything, mysteriously, would be all right. David smiled as he thought now of Lang, tucked up in bed and befuddled by port. He began to move forward again.

An ill-tethered bull suddenly loomed up at him; but proved to be a rose bush. He was under the walls of the house and had found the back door. With infinite caution he turned the handle and it gave before him. He was standing in a narrow passage. At least he'd made the right house. In the gloom he became aware of a row of caps and raincoats hung on pegs, and a line of Wellington boots with numbers painted on them was ranged along the wall beneath them.

As his eyes became accustomed to the light, David realised that the passage in which he was standing gave at right angles on to what must be the front hall. He moved cautiously forward. It was in fact the hall, and in the middle of it a night-light was burning.

Suddenly David froze. A lavatory had been flushed inches from his ear. A door banged, and a small boy in a dressing-gown was bundling sleepily towards him along the passage. He glanced up at David: 'Good night, sir.'

'Good night,' David said gruffly; but the boy had already gone into a downstairs dormitory. David retreated to the back passage. It was five to eleven.

From above him he heard a board creak; then the descent of slippers on uncarpeted stairs. The next moment Tony was beside him. The boy had put on his flannel shorts and a pullover on top of pyjamas. Now he took a coat from one of the pegs.

'Will you be warm enough?' David whispered. Tony nodded and grinned. He was wide awake.

The climb into St Cecilia's was accomplished with only minor abrasions to David's forearms as he lowered the boy over the six-foot wall into the Master's garden. Someone must recently have oiled the Temple doors, for they swung open without a creak. The great Chapel was dark and silent, but David could sense the proud expanses of Gothic space soaring above them. It was deliciously cool after the black-treacle night. 'Have you got the score?'

'Yes,' the boy whispered back.

'Right; lead me to the organ loft!'

Tony led him surely through the darkness up the aisle. Then

they were climbing wooden stairs. There was a click, and a deep humming filled the darkness. 'It's all set,' Tony said more loudly.

David felt about him, and a faint light sprang up over the two-manual instrument. It was a beautiful thing: probably the finest early English organ in the country, it had been built by Thomas Dallam between 1605 and 1606. He looked at the boy. 'Think you know it well enough?'

'Well enough,' Tony echoed confidently. He took the score out of his pocket and laid it on the music rest. Then he took off his coat and folded it up on the floor. Standing again, he contemplated his strange array of clothes. 'Feel how thick my behind is.'

David felt. 'Like an apricot. Only the fur's grey,' he said. 'Now, let's get on with it.'

The boy drew nearer, looking over David's shoulder. David's hands began to move over the manuals. Now his feet joined them unthinkingly, with an integral continuum of the rhythm. The sound of the organ came up from the darkness below, and filled the darkness above them. David adjusted stops, and drew out the *vox humana*. The chorus whispered, then fell deferentially away, leaving only the melody of a single reed. He nodded his head.

Tony was in his element now. The sensuous animal had entirely disappeared, and his whole being had become an instrument of sound. His voice flashed. It became fluid and irrepressible; seeping into the black crannies of the rood screen, and aching its soft cadences against the invisible petals of the fan vaulting. Now it floated down as reluctantly as an autumn leaf, or plunged purposeful as a cormorant from a height. As surely it rose again until the walls and ceiling of the great Chapel must be left mysteriously gilded. There was no doubt at all about the alto depths. Tony could negotiate anything sung by the late Kathleen Ferrier.

The Chapel lights had come on. Abruptly the boy's voice broke off. David dropped a phrase, caught it as it slipped, and continued to play. He put out his hand to reassure the boy, and then stopped playing altogether. Footsteps were echoing on the stone floor below them; then their note changed unmistakably to a wooden thud on the organ-loft stairs. Lang appeared at their head.

'Christ!' David exclaimed.

'No, not this time. Just me.' Lang looked curiously at Tony, and then back at David. 'Traditional scene,' he murmured.

'Vertical drop,' David countered pleasantly, motioning towards the parapet.

Lang sat down at the head of the stairs, drawing a packet of cigarettes from his pocket. Then he apparently thought better of it. David meanwhile had recovered.

'The road to Rome doesn't lie this way.'

'But perhaps for you the road to Ithaca does,' Lang replied unequivocally.

'This is Tony,' David said.

Lang looked disinterested. 'Hallo, Tony.'

Tony said nothing.

'David,' Lang began heavily, still toying with the cigarettes, 'infringement of copyright . . .'

'Don't you think we'd better talk French in front of *the child?*' David enquired ironically.

Lang looked sour. 'I rather doubt if it would be any use anyway.' He heaved his gangling form to its feet, and tentatively pressed a note. When the sound had died away, he looked deliberately from the instrument to the boy. 'What's the tune tonight? Manual; or oral?'

David got up. His fists were clenched with rage and his jaw quivered, 'If you want to be martyred in an Anglican conventicle, Bruce, just stay where you are for five seconds longer!'

Lang raised an appeasing hand. 'That might be a little awkward – so good night, David.' He gestured towards Tony. 'And don't forget to take that home where it belongs.' He turned and clumped heavily down the stairs. A moment later the Chapel was plunged into darkness again.

'Do you know him?' the boy asked.

'Yes; it'll be all right. But I think we'd better stop now. I'm sorry, Tony – and thank you!' Suddenly David smiled in the bluish light that illuminated the organ. 'I suppose you know that yours is no ordinary voice?'

'Oh, yes.' Tony was dispassionate. 'The next few months should see me at the peak of my career, I think.'

'Can I stick with you?'

'You can be my manager.'

✧

'What did he mean – about *Ithaca?*' Tony asked, when they had successfully negotiated the Master's wall, and were advancing through the shrubbery.

'I don't quite know,' David replied after a moment. 'Ithaca was the home of Odysseus, where he returned after his wanderings. Things weren't altogether happy when he got back. But you don't often need to take Bruce seriously.'

'I see. I will be able to come out with you on Saturday, though, won't I?'

'Don't worry! Just wait till the headmaster tells you I'm coming.'

They had reached the door. David lowered his voice. 'Now don't forget to take the day off tomorrow. If I see you about, there'll be trouble!'

'I promise.'

'All right. Good night, Tony.' He watched the boy tip-toe down the passage. At the corner he turned and waved. David waited until he heard the door closing safely above him, and silence settle once more over the house.


David swallowed four grains of Seconal with a mouthful of the Balliol man's milk. He took a bite of the Brighton rock, and lay back on his bed thinking about the boy. The Seconal dropped doughnuts on his eyes. He could hear the boy now, and see him too. But he was beginning to see something else: Tony reflected in the ground-glass screen of the Rollei. A thousand facets of Tony revealed by the multiple eye of a fly. A thousand faces in some surrealist film trapped in the bubbles of a glass of champagne. He closed his eyes more tightly. He was being catapulted down at one of the bubbles. For a second it ballooned up to meet him: a shimmering convex surface with Tony encased inside it. The bubble broke, wetly tickling his ears. His face was pressed against the warmth of Tony's pullover. Then he was through that too, and plunging into darkness.

## 12

T HE week seemed interminable; and the heat was scarcely endurable. It was a clammy, sick-room heat, that swabbed the body with sweat, and peeled the paint from outside window-sills. David tried to play the piano, but his fingers slipped off the keys as if someone had anointed them with glycerine. He wiped his fingers on the mohair, and tried again, but with the same result. He wondered whether he should pick a fight with the barber or the Balliol atomist. He decided the barber might prove too tough, and the atomist, with Finals approaching, lived leaded in his room, or some Parks Road laboratory, like an isotope. Apparently he still ate breakfast; but he had acquired a stock of pre-1945 U.S. war surplus dried milk in tins, which he mixed with Nescafé. He had forgotten to cancel the third of a pint of strontium delivered daily at his door, and David drank it regularly.

On Sunday Mrs Kanter trapped him on the landing. He learnt that his little brother was 'sweet', 'a cherub', and that he was 'such a good-looking boy'. David shuddered. Somehow he slid a smile on to the sweat of his face like a water transfer. He liked Mrs Kanter.

During the mornings he spent long hours working on the Series 4, and cursed the convention that prevented race meetings being held mid-week. At lunch-time he bought vaguely green bits and pieces from a delicatessen in the closed market. In the evenings he had sandwiches and beer at the Bird and Baby. He suddenly felt the need for a splash of colour, a summer freshness in his room. He bought a selection of oranges and lemons, and then searched the cattle market for a bowl to put them in.

The card in the bank said Tuesday, and banks weren't often wrong about things like that. David stepped into a telephone kiosk, still bundling the dirty notes they always seemed to give him nowadays into his wallet. He ran his finger down a column

of the directory. He would never have believed the place had
so many affiliated offices and telephones, but there it was –
Headmaster, Choir School: the Rev. R. H. Jones.

David read the name in dismay, then looked quickly in the
G.P.O. mirror. 'Jones,' he muttered, 'the *Reverend* Jones.'
He dialled the number and inserted four pennies. One came
straight through. Why did people always give him notes like
tramps' underclothes and pennies too thin for lavatories? He
dropped in a square-jawed George VIth and spun the dial
again furiously.

'Jones?' a voice said.

David pressed button A. Counterpoint, he thought. 'Hallo?
Headmaster? This is Tony Sandel's brother. Look,' David
could feel the comma in the air; a beautiful, Wagnerian pause,
'I'm going to be in Oxford on Saturday, and I wondered
whether you'd let me take Tony out for the day?'

'Why, certainly, Mr Sandel! I'm so glad.'

'My name is Rogers, actually. A half brother.'

'Why, of course! How silly of me. Mr *Rogers*.'

David prayed that Tony's aunts never went near the place.
With luck even the bills went straight to executors. 'Well, that's
very good of you. Actually, I'd rather like to have him out to
dinner too. It's something of a family anniversary,' David lied,
ignoring the G.P.O. mirror now.

'Certainly,    certainly!'    Jones'    voice    became    almost
reproachful. 'But won't you come and have lunch with us
first?'

'Why, yes. Thank you.' It was one of those decisions one
could worry about afterwards. 'That's settled, then. I'll tell
Peter straight away.'

'Tony,' said David. 'Tony Sandel.' He didn't see himself
picking choirboys out of bran tubs.

'Merciful Heavens! What can have come over me!' Jones
said, like a splash falling from an alcoholic's glass. 'Saturday
lunch, then; you'll take *Tony* out for the afternoon, and for
dinner!' The Reverend had recovered triumphantly. David
looked curiously into the earpiece of the receiver to see if the
man's smile was visible there.

'Thank you, Mr Jones. I'll look forward to seeing you on
Saturday then. Goodbye.'

David put the receiver down, and leaned heavily against the

glass wall of the kiosk. It was like being in a battery incubator that had short-circuited. 'Checkmate, Ghoul,' he said aloud.

There was an insistent thumping on the side of the kiosk. David brought his nose to the glass like a goldfish. Daylight didn't become Gloria. She opened the door and squeezed into the kiosk, parting the curtain of hair before her eyes. The sprung door pressed her against David.

'Driven to the call-box system?' she purred. 'Thoughtless Wolfenden.'

'You seem to have got off the streets yourself,' David said, struggling for air.

'That's rather horrid, darling.' Gloria was fingering the knot of his tie. She pushed his Adam's apple up out of the way like a tiresome door latch. The latch fell back into place involuntarily.

'You know the Proctors' regulation about undergraduates not loitering where they might make "undesirable acquaintances". Blow, Gloria. Or at least let me.' He realised that she was undoing his tie. 'What are telephone boxes made of, Gloria?'

'Why, glass mostly, I suppose.'

'We're in one,' David said, delivering the words singly like eardrops.

There was a sharp rap on the door. David caught a glimpse of a ferociously wielded plastic umbrella, and of a queue forming outside. He heaved Gloria out and stood on the pavement. She'd gone, he realised, drawing a hand across his body like an octopus taking leave of a favourite rock.

'Young man, were you molesting that woman in there?'

It was the woman with the plastic parasol; an ugly looking, sawed-off job. Dook, David thought. Deep South. Brize Norton.

'I must ask you to tell me your name and college,' the woman squeaked, looking round at the queue for support. David looked at the sawed-off and decided to forget Dook.

'Cymbeline Smith,' he said pleasantly. 'Magdalen. I'm a Fellow.' He limped away.

There was no mail in college. David looked up at the square of sky above the Great Quad. What must be God's Wednesday sun blazed motionlessly above the clock tower. Perhaps He just wasn't reckoning on withdrawing it tonight. Then what?

The academic year would be upset, and there would be embarrassed consultations at Greenwich, he supposed.

He wandered across the Great Quad, which Nero himself
wouldn't have scorned for chariot races, and went out into St
Cecilia's park. A long way away a figure was sitting by itself
on the fence at the bottom of the school field. Even as David
watched another came up to it and pulled it off the railings.
Tony followed the other boy reluctantly, kicking listlessly at
the baked earth. He flexed his ankles like a finely bred trotting
horse; then he began an exaggerated goose-step, putting his
hands on his hips, and throwing back his head. Suddenly he
turned a somersault.

David bit his lip and set course for Walton Street. It was
nearly half past five and some of the shops were beginning to
close. Suddenly he veered off the Cornmarket and through the
doors of Messrs. Elliston and Cavell. Hunches, he reflected,
finding himself in *Prams,* were best played out instantly.
Possibly this lore was becoming a conditioned reflex with him.
He threaded his way through *Perfume,* and found a depart-
ments directory.

David took the stairs. A girl lolled behind a broad counter.
She had orange lipstick laid on with a palette-knife; a reaction
probably to the uniform black dress she was wearing. David
consulted an imaginary piece of paper in his wallet.

'It is you that does New College School, isn't it?' His voice
held a shade of calculated distraction.

The girl nodded. She was investigating her hair with a
pencil which had a road safety Belisha beacon on the end.
David consulted his piece of paper and hummed a few bars of
Buxtehude. He looked up again.

'I want a pair of socks.'

'Size?' The girl seemed to have found whatever she wanted
with the blinking beacon.

'I've no idea.' David was vague again.

'Age, then?'

'Thirteen.'

'Has he got big feet?'

'Certainly not!' It occurred to David that she couldn't yet
have been broken in on *Nylons,* calling brown *oatmeal,* and
yellow *honey.*

'Six-and-a-half, I should think,' the girl said. Some of the lipstick had rubbed off on to her teeth. She opened a drawer behind her, and flapped a pair of socks down on the counter. It was true. The grey socks had a brilliant red band, a pure, baby-wear white one, and a black one. Poor Tony.

'They look flat,' David said, 'two-dimensional.'

The girl thrust her arm into one, and looked at him pityingly.

'Oh, I see. I suppose they've got nylon in them?'

'These *are* the socks, you know,' the girl said.

A small woman like a well-drilled Guinness bottle was advancing from behind another counter. 'All right, Peel.' David thought she was going to blow a whistle. Peel moved away. 'Can I help you, sir?' asked the guide mistress in mufti.

David put preoccupation carefully back on to his face, and indicated the socks. 'I've just bought these,' he said slowly. 'I wonder though if you could tell me whether you do an all-wool flannel suit?'

The half-pint woman came to attention. 'We only stock an all-wool nylon reinforced one. It's very warm, and it's the uniform. Achilles.'

'I beg your pardon?'

'*Achilles* brand.'

'Oh, I see.'

The woman appeared to be engaged in some mathematical equation with the socks on the counter. She reached behind her without looking, unhooked a grey suit from a row of them, laid it on the counter, and began to fold it up. 'This is his size,' she said with the certainty of Confucius. 'That will be just seven pounds all told.'

'You misunderstand.' David was alarmed. 'The suit must be all-wool. It mustn't have long trousers as this one seems to have. And, anyway, I don't want it just at the moment.'

The woman abruptly ceased patting and folding, and looked him sharply up and down as if he was a delinquent Brownie. Then she must have remembered Lady Baden-Powell, for she suddenly softened. David prepared to clasp her left hand. 'You'll have to go to Harrods or Neal Frazers for an all-wool flannel now, sir, I'm afraid.'

'I see. Harrods or Neal Frazers. Thank you very much. I'll just take the socks.'

'Very well, sir. I expect you'd like our current Boys' Wear catalogue though, wouldn't you?'

'Yes, please,' said David humbly.

The woman trotted off, and David's gaze strayed over the display cards of elfin-eyed little boys strutting around in Chilprufe underwear, and an assortment of brilliantly coloured prep school caps. Perhaps they were afraid of losing pupils in the snow. He picked up a pair of pants that was lying on the counter and looked at them curiously.

'Good afternoon,' an unsteady voice said behind him. David swung round. It was Ricks. The old man tested the point of a toothpick protruding from his waistcoat pocket, and exclaimed, 'Extraordinary!'

David dropped the pants uncomfortably. 'Men's Department, ground floor, sir,' he said.

Ricks smiled like one of the poet Thompson's deprived sheep and pottered on his way. The woman proudly placed the catalogue before David on the counter. Politely he turned the pages. More elfin-eyed boys waving seaside buckets and starfish. 'Sun-splashed Colours for Smaller Boys'; 'Ladybird Underwear with Latex waists'; 'Tough Sailcloth Shorts (chunky style in dove or Breton-red)'; 'Tomboy Play-clothes both Rugged and Gay'; 'Crew Neck Sweater (white and Caribbean blue)'; 'School Shorts (mid-grey and slate)'.

'Thank you,' said David. He'd come to 'another superlative welted shoe for the junior boy', and a 'cool lightweight sandal'.

The woman seemed disposed to regard him indulgently. 'Have you tried the Cathedral School stockist in Queen Street for the suit? I believe they have the Beau Brummell make, but I'm not sure whether they're a pure wool. All the school suits are a standard shade nowadays.'

David smiled to himself as he imagined Tony debating whether the obvious attraction of Beau Brummell brand outweighed its being associated with Christ Church. 'No, but I think I'll stick to Harrods and Neal Frazers.'

'Very good.' The woman began feeding the socks into a paper bag. 'Between you and me I think they may still stock a finer cloth than we often see in the provinces.' To David's horror she suddenly winked deprecatingly.

'Oh, grand! Jolly good, then!' he said hollowly. He picked up the parcel and descended in the lift.

David hadn't forgotten the frog-flippers. He stepped out into the Cornmarket again. The sun was trained down it like an ultra-violet searchlight. The tar-macadam was melted wet like Negroes' lips at the edge of the road. Cowley jostled on the pavement and overflowed amongst the traffic. Here and there was a gaggle of gown: suede-booted, sun-glassed and loud-voiced; many with girls folded over their arms like plastic raincoats. They owned the place; they said so, and that was it. David paused for breath. Cowley or the gown must go. There just wasn't physical space for both. He didn't mind which went.

He fought his way through the crowd. Outside the Co-op he pressed himself flat against the window and looked in his wallet. It was disgraceful that St Cecilia's didn't supply her choirboys with frog-flippers gratuitously.

'A very good model this,' the man said. 'They've just been tested in the South Seas. And you can wear them as snowshoes too, see?' He bellowed with laughter; then became confidential, and lurched towards David across the counter. 'What size, son?'

David opened Elliston's paper bag and consulted the socks. 'Six and a half.'

'They'll be for a nipper then?'

'For a boy.'

'Ah!' The man's jaw was late Neanderthal. 'Nippers love flippers!' He guffawed helplessly, beating a hairy paw on the counter. 'What colour, now?' gasped the ape at last, clutching his stomach. 'Grey or black?'

'Grey.'

Australiopithicus bundled the flippers into a bag and twisted its neck. 'Anything else, son? Mask, snorkel – anything like that?'

'The boy doesn't need a mask or a snorkel,' David said. The innuendo was wasted.

'Fair's fair, then. Fifty-nine and eleven. We don't charge for the bag!' The man began to bellow again, David waited to see if he would clap the money into his mouth.

'I'm glad I've found you, Rogers,' Crawley said. David had the impression that the words were intended to express some profundity, rather than his physical seizure by the elbow. 'I have to buy some Oxford marmalade for Jean. Please accompany me.'

Crawley steered him through the doors of a grocer and

stood looking blankly at a row of hams. 'Have you any ideas at all about the state of culture among the working class – do you think we've come to the right place . . . miss?' he said experimentally to a shop girl, 'I want the marmalade counter.'

'I've only one pair of hands now, haven't I?' the girl said. 'You'll have to wait your turn, won't you?'

'Oh, very well,' said Crawley. 'When it is my turn, it's a large tin of Oxford marmalade I want.' He turned back to David, who by now was suffering the familiar sensation of being stared at that seemed inevitable when one was with Crawley. 'They'll never become creative again, Rogers, but something must be done to raise the threshold of their receptivity.'

'Who is this exactly?'

Crawley looked at him curiously. 'The working class, Rogers. What have they in their lives? The Music Hall's dead, the church is dead, even pub singing is dead. What have they?'

'Telly?' David suggested dutifully.

'Exactly! Every bloody thing in their lives except sex is canned, man!' Crawley made a gesture that embraced grocery shelves and last-minute shoppers. 'And it's not only the working class. I could name you a dozen professional men with families who slump down in their chairs at five-thirty and switch on the box with the hand that isn't feeling for the slippers. Often they don't even look at the thing. It's just necessary environment, together with drawn curtains and lounging children.'

'What are you objecting to: telly as an institution; or the fact that it's present and yet ignored? You haven't sold a play to the B.B.C. by any chance?'

'I'm objecting to the fact that they have no goals except physical prosperity and bored survival. Sometimes, just sometimes, mark you, they'll make facetious pretensions to other values – unprompted apologies, simply perhaps because you or I are around. We believe in education, chaps, what ho? "Must send the boy to a public school, Crawley, old man; only thing, really, wouldn't you say? Teaches a lad *values,* I always think. The wife's with me in this, Crawley. But then we've always tried to give him a good start. Bought him some books, you know, the other day. Has he shown you his books? He's a good lad. I can say that for him honestly, though he's my own. He's good about the television too; *selects* his programmes, which is more than you can say about our neighbours' children. Oh, he'll do. Have another drop of whisky, then we'll feed."'

Crawley broke off the charade and looked pathetically at David. 'And what's behind this? Partly it's an acknowledgement of guilt. Reluctant, of course, because they've still the saving suspicion that they're incomplete human beings. For the rest,' he shrugged, 'it's fear. Fear that they or their sons may somehow fail to measure up to the accepted image of the caste. But what happens if you try to define that image? You can't. It exists only as a vague projection of their own self-esteem, and since that, like everything else in their lives, is unintelligible, how can its aspirations have coherence?'

Crawley was staring gloomily at the hams again. For some time the shop girl had been lolling on the counter looking at them dryly. David became aware that a man was standing at the door, and that they were the last customers.

'Yes?' the girl said.

'A tin of Cooper's marmalade was what I asked for,' said Crawley. 'We must do everything in our power for these people,' he said to David. 'The medium for their self-discovery sits in every drawing room. It's up to us to provide an attractive primer, and then to lead them towards some sort of fulfilment – what does this mean, *threepence off?*'

'It means it's just two shillings and nine pennies. These brown ones are the pennies,' the girl said, helping herself from Crawley's hand.

'Our society is sick, Rogers; and the sick are responsible to no man. Take none of its dictums for granted. Test its every premise.'

'Yes,' David said humbly.

'Good night,' said the man at the door.

David wandered up Walton Street resolving to spend the next day fitting new valve springs to the Series 4. If only there were a race now! For an hour his purpose would become simply defined. More importantly, perhaps, he would be away from Oxford.

Sweeney's wife, Glad, was waiting for him at their basement window. 'If you're going to have women singing in your room like that Saturdays we'll make a complaint to Mrs Kanter,' she said. 'It's not right.'

David put the socks and flippers away. He peeled an inch

of greaseproof paper from Tony's rock and took a bite. He
wondered whether he should listen to Tony's bad German
accent on the Vienna Boys' record, but decided against it.
He wondered whether he could play the *Benedictus* from the
Requiem without convincing Glad that he'd spirited in a whole
harem, but decided against that too. He ran his finger blind
along the bookshelf, but it stopped at Donne.

David threw open a window and looked at the sky. It was like
blood and water in a Japanese sunset. And there were the silver
darts, high up, their wings swept through a clean forty-five
degrees: machines of matchless beauty, and of madness.

He adjusted the lamp on his desk to give the room a
comforting glow; then climbed into bed and pulled the sheet
up so that it lay across his lip beneath his nose. He stared at
the ceiling. After a moment he felt in the bedside cupboard and
drew out one of McVitie's wholemeal digestives and a copy
of *Cherwell*. He looked sleepily over the news headings, and
masticated the biscuit under the sheet, while the fold of linen
grew warmer on his lip. He opened the paper and allowed his
eye to bounce like a punctured football down the column of
personal notices. About three-quarters of the way down the
page the football came to an uneasy halt. Violently, David sat
up. He read the notice again.

'Dissident Protestant requires immediately to meet beautiful little-boyish *girl,* preferably Catholic, with a view to holy
matrimony. Applicants should measure 32–30–32 o.n.o. (the
flatter the better): remedial orthodontic appliance and skinny
brown legs an advantage. Apply in first instance: Bruce Lang:
St Cecilia's. Advertiser purposes deflect friend hyacinthine
heresy.'

For some time David wandered round his room muttering
incoherently. Then, overcome by sudden weariness, he
collapsed into the chair at his desk. Prudently, he wound only a
small card into the typewriter.

*Dear Bruce,*

   Cherwell *is really not very funny – however well-meaning
your intentions. Lay off.*

*Yrs. D.*

He thrust the card, together with an insulting ten-shilling note, into an envelope and addressed it to Lang. With a kinder second thought he removed the money. He took another bite of Tony's rock, and climbed into bed again.

## 13

A CCORDING to the English weathermen the anti-cyclone, which had blanketed the country with muggy air for the past few days, had now begun to 'collapse'. David, however, had once been told that the only way to determine Oxford's weather accurately was to ring the U.S. Air Force at Brize Norton and talk humbly about garden fetes, giant marquees and insurance. This he now did, and was immediately put through to the 'meteorological hut', which he imagined most probably looked something like Munich station. There he was informed in Dakotan tones that clear sunshine all day would not exceed 70 degrees centigrade, but that between five and twenty minutes after midnight rain would begin to fall, and continue to fall for roughly eleven hours. The speaker apologised for the approximations, and after switching in a tape-recorded invitation to a baseball match next Thursday, rang off.

David decided he might safely leave the Series 4's hardtop in the garage. He settled down with a cigarette, and looked at Lang's letter again.

*My Dear David,*

*Notoriously, society has always forced the role of jester upon its oddities. This I think is what is happening to you. Medically speaking, the situation will become dangerous when the persons about you cease to exist in their own right, and become subjective distortions of your mind. Watch carefully for that time, and try to pray.*

*There have been a couple of responses to my advertisement so far. A pair of St Mary's girls, who insist, however,*

*that anything they might do for you they must do together.*
*Does this attract you? The other applicant is a town girl.*
*She says she would 'dress up' and that she's 'done that sort*
*of thing' for other people before. Thinking about this, it*
*occurs to me that you could say 'shorts off!', or whatever*
*it is you do say.*

*None of these has quite the lascivious, wriggly look of*
*the choirboy, but something better may turn up.*

*Please get in touch with me at once. Let's talk about*
*this.*

*Ever, Bruce*

David leant back and exhaled smoke. What a long way people
would go in the maintenance of a lie. Lang lived a lie, and
Crawley's professional families were intent on following
another that was only less explicitly defined. He, David,
professed a series of lies with each new relationship he made,
and this was because his guiding lie had as yet no definition at
all.

There was the weekly lie with his tutors, the uneasy explo-
sive lie with Gloria, and a whole host of lesser lies that were
like sextant readings designed to establish position, and
provide corroborative assurance of identity. Only the more
frequently recourse was made to such soundings, the obscurer
identification became, and the paradox must eventually panic
the traveller.

The boy alone demanded no lie. The gaining of his company
might call for subterfuge, but this was irrelevant, and a mere
technicality. Where Lang's guiding lie was a priest-smothered
God, and the professional families' a muddled expediency, his,
David's, might prove to be the boy. If it was so, the deception
had yet to be revealed to him.

He got up. The maintenance of the personal lie might well
explain the conflicts of men. Tony, he was sure, could happily
liquidate China because their choirboys' shorts were all wrong,
while he had no illusions about himself. Glad, Brougham, and
God knew how many Fellows of the Academy of Music were
already as good as annihilated by his own pride. The thesis,
though, might safely be left to Crawley. He would clearly
martyr himself in the emancipation of his people. In the end he
too would have lived out his lie.

Almost timidly David struck a series of chords on the piano; testing the only constant truth he knew.

At a quarter to one David drew the car up in the school drive. He observed with alarm that the front garden was filled with concrete gnomes. Undeterred, he rang the bell, and wondered whether this would be a proper occasion for that authoritative form of words, 'My name's Rogers.' He decided it would, and waited for an answer more easily. After two further rings, irreproachably spaced, the door was opened.

There stood before him a young man wearing a disillusioned smile that was both fixed and faded like some tragic recording of natural photography left on a surviving wall at Hiroshima. Without moving the monument the man said:

'Yes?'

'My name's Rogers. I believe you're expecting me.'

'Oh, yes?' The man made no move to admit him. After a moment he said, 'But why did you ring?'

David wondered how the Friends of St Cecilia who organised the annual choristers' party would react to this man, whose mind the little boys had clearly murdered. 'I had supposed it usual,' he said gently.

'Oh, I see. Here we just come and go.'

David noticed a gnome that was heading for the gate with a concrete brief-case, and another that was making straight for the porch with a garden roller. 'Yes; I suppose so,' he said.

The young man now ushered him into the hall. 'School's finished,' he said.

David affected dismay. 'No! What about government assistance?'

'Morning school,' said the man, without any change of expression.

David could now hear the hubbub of disbanding classes. The man pointed to a door and directed him to wait. 'The Reverend Jones should be down in a minute,' he said, and disappeared.

This was indeed the hall David had glimpsed on his night excursion. There was the nightlight, now extinguished. The walls were panelled with oak. From one a rather mangy bear's head gazed down at him. The others were given over to colour prints depicting the life of Little Jesus. Little Jesus, possessed of downy Pre-Raphaelite beauty, in the Temple; Little Jesus leading a woolly string of lambs, which were surely without authoritative precedent; and Little Jesus hitting a nail with a hammer in the carpentry shop. 'He's just like us, you know,' David murmured, looking curiously at this last.

The room to which the martyr had directed him was very differently furnished. The panelling was an identical continuation of that in the hall, but was covered with a variety of cinema programmes, duty rotas, and blessed country bus schedules. Elsewhere the confusion was scarcely credible. There were half-consumed bottles of port and handle-less coffee cups full of sugar; a litter of little transparent triangles from Woolworth's geometrical sets; stone jars of ink; old gym shoes; spineless books; a squash racquet in three pieces, and the front wheel of a bicycle. Barely concealed behind a sofa in one corner was a modest barrel of bitter, with a ream of new pink blotting-paper under the tap to catch the drips.

David leant against the mantelpiece and closed his eyes. Opening them again, he realised the shelf must be a repository of confiscations. There was a stone knotted into an expensive lawn handkerchief with a Cash's name tape that said 'Lavington'; a mechanical mouse with silk whiskers; a long-barrelled Colt with a bronco in relief on the plastic butt; a bazooka-like device designed to deliver a rapid succession of Ping-Pong balls; and a wide selection of plastic missiles from cornflakes packets.

There was a hiss from the door. David turned to find Tony's head poking round it. The boy grinned with a mixture of excitement and confusion. The colour had seeped over his cheek-bones.

'It's all right,' he said quickly. 'The Ghoul's got Hunter to do the river. He's a drip – but another of his friends. By the way, the Ghoul's not called the Ghoul really. He's Mr Gould, so you'll know if you meet him.' Tony took a look over his shoulder. 'I've got to go now, so I'll see you after lunch. I didn't think you'd have the nerve to come to lunch!'

'Thank you,' David said gravely. 'You'd better hop it.'

The boy seemed reluctant to go. He was looking at him oddly. But he nodded and disappeared.

'Ah, Rogers! I'm so sorry to keep you waiting.' David swung round and clasped the Reverend Jones' outstretched hand.

'I expect you'd like to wash?'

'Thank you.'

Jones began moving towards the door with a crab-like

motion. David kept step with him. Suddenly Jones stopped and looked at him searchingly. There could be no doubt about the sweetness of the smile David had caught lingering in the telephone receiver. Probably the reverend could drink lemon juice without sugar.

'Do you know anything about cubbing?'

David was relieved to be able to speak honestly. 'Well, I was blooded and all that when I was about Tony's age, but it's a long time since I actually rode to hounds.'

Jones was looking at him curiously. 'Dear me no, Rogers! Not blood sports. *Wolf* Cubbing.'

David was beginning to feel he wasn't on the same plane as the people in this place. Perhaps he shouldn't have become Tony's brother after all.

'Well, let me know what you think in your own time.' Jones resumed his motion towards the door.

'About what?' David hazarded wildly.

Jones stopped again. 'Merciful heavens, Rogers. I'm so sorry! I meant of course about your taking them on for us. It would only be two hours a week on Friday evenings – I think it's Friday evenings.'

David frowned. He had the impression that wolf cubs divided their time between tying knots and sitting in a circle round Big Wolf (D. Rogers) yapping: Big Wolf (D. Rogers) had graciously to howl in return. But he was sure he had told Jones that he was simply visiting Oxford, and not resident in the place. 'It's kind of you to ask me,' he managed to say. 'As you suggest, I should like a little time to think it over.'

'Dear me, yes! Quite, quite.' Jones had clearly forgotten the subject, as too he'd evidently forgotten that David might like to wash. They had moved out into the hall, and through a pair of swing doors. Jones said:

'Sit there, will you, Rogers, there's a good fellow.' David sat as bidden. He saw with horror that the room was full of choirboys. Jones had passed on through a further doorway and abandoned him.

In fact he was sitting at the head of a long table looking down at a staring double row of some thirty curious faces. On his left was a similar table, with fewer boys and, hopelessly out of reach, a master, who anyway didn't seem to be wholly present. Still further away was a girl at a serving table with a long spoon

poised over some sort of cauldron; while at the other end of his
own table was a man of evidently artisan class with large hands
and a leather apron.

David had observed just so much, and concluded that this
must be a junior annexe to the dining hall into which Jones
had passed, when he became aware of a small boy with a towel
about his waist standing beside him and respectfully shifting
his feet. Meanwhile the thirty pairs of eyes at the long table
remained fixed on him. He raised his eyebrows to the small
boy in the makeshift apron, who was evidently some sort of
child-labour menial. The boy wiped his hands professionally
on the towel.

'Do you want a staff ordinary, or a staff small?'

'You tell me?'

'Well,' the boy appeared to consider, 'a staff ordinary is
bigger than an ordinary ordinary, and a staff small is bigger
than an ordinary small. Or you can have an ordinary with a
small of potatoes or something.'

David's head reeled.

'Mr Robinson has a staff large,' the boy added helpfully.

'I think an ordinary ordinary, please.'

The waiter boy departed, and David turned to the boy on
his left. Unobtrusively, he indicated the big-handed man at
the other end of the table, who if anything was looking more
bewildered than himself. 'Who's that?'

The other boys had now begun to talk and clink glasses.

The boy David had addressed took a look at the man and
said, 'I think he's the man that delivered the ice cream, sir. The
headmaster told him to sit down there and have lunch.'

David was unsurprised. Still, the man didn't look genuine.
Perhaps he was a Pot Hall man pursuing some practical joke.
At that moment the bewildered fellow caught his eye. David
nodded to him, and turned to the boy on his right.

'And what's your name?'

'Hunter, sir.' If the child rubbed his knees together as he
spoke David couldn't see because they were under the table.
He tried to picture the said Hunter in boater and the rest of
it. He had a china-like sort of prettiness, and raven hair cut
rather too lovingly in a fringe. David didn't think he would like
Hunter very much. His question, however, seemed to have
loosed thirty inhibitions, and he was suddenly besieged.

'What are you going to teach, sir?'

'Sir, were you in the war, sir?'

'Sir, is it true that Stukas *scream?*'

'Sir, Cason's got a Dinky Toy Javelin with drop-tanks on, but Javelins don't have drop-tanks, do they, sir?'

'Oh, shut up, all of you,' said the boy on David's left. 'Let the wretched man eat.' Clearly he was the born shop steward every school discovers.

The waiter boy had put a plate down in front of him. David looked up from it and caught the ice-cream man's eye again. He called down the table:

'I recommend the ordinary ordinary!'

The man grinned uncertainly. 'Good afternoon to you too, sir!' he called back bravely.

David was convinced now that he was really a Pot Hall Calvinist sneaked in to pour plant hormones into the choir-boys' porridge, which was what the stuff before him most nearly resembled. The honour of St Cecilia's stirred within him. The man must be watched. He turned again to the boy on his left who seemed disposed to regard his welfare as his personal responsibility. But the boy, who evidently considered that the wretched man had now had grace enough in which to eat, got in first.

'Who are you?' he asked simply.

'Tony Sandel's brother.'

'You don't *look* like him.' A small boy with spectacles said this suspiciously.

'Are you coming to teach, sir?' asked Hunter.

'No. Just to take Tony out.'

'Why are you *here* though?' The boy with spectacles had a spoonful of stew poised in front of his mouth with the tip of the spoon resting against his closed teeth. No doubt it was waiting for some river lock or portcullis to open.

David sensed vaguely that Froebel had forbidden the use of irony when dealing with small boys, and so said nothing. Instead he turned to the neighbour on his left again. 'Who are you then?'

'Crockett.'

'He's related to Davy, sir!' called someone from lower down the table. 'Really? Born in Tennessee?'

'No, Anglesey actually. Or rather just off it.' Crockett seemed possessed of a superior social accomplishment.

'On a mountain top?'

'No, a motor yacht!'

'But reared in the backwoods?'

'Knightsbridge, I'm afraid!' Crockett acknowledged the breakdown of the game apologetically. 'All our names end in y,' he went on, evidently anxious to establish his descent from the hero of the Alamo beyond doubt. 'I'm Henry, and my father is Harley, but it's difficult to bias John Crockett – that's my little brother. He won't be called *Johnny,* and he thinks Davy was silly anyway, because he says no one could really kill a bear when he was only three.'

'Oh, I don't know.' David was looking at the mess of steam pudding and custard that had been put down in front of him. Evidently the waiter boy had decided he was an ordinary ordinary customer whatever the fare.

The noise in the room had risen considerably. David looked towards the man at the table on his left. He had the appearance of a Dickensian usher. Once or twice he said, 'Quiet!'; but it was more like the commendation of a Romantic poet than an effective injunction. Meanwhile he eyed space and tucked into his stodge. Then he got up and left the room.

Hunter interrupted his reverie reproachfully. 'Sir, Miss Poole has been making signs at you for seconds.'

David looked up in alarm. The girl with the ladle was ogling at him, and silently mouthing vowels as if running up a *do-re-me* scale behind plate glass. He wondered for just how many seconds she had been making such signs, and for how many more they might be expected to continue. Crockett came to his rescue.

'Oh, it's second helpings. She signals, you announce them, and then the second-servers rush. It's quite easy,' he added sympathetically, 'you just say "seconds".'

'Seconds,' said David.

'No *custard!*' yelled Hunter after the flying heels of the second-server. There was no doubt that the Ghoul's mascot's voice would reach the St Cecilia's eight. Conceivably it might shatter the hull.

'*L.e.s.s. n.o.i.s.e.,*' the girl mouthed at David, quite silently, but with a labial definition that must have won the lip dictation prize at any school for deaf mutes,

'Less noise!' said David. At that moment a heavily built man of about forty came through from the further room. Out of the corner of his eye David became aware of Hunter behaving like a budgerigar in expectation of another. He shifted his small behind on its perch, and puffed out his chest.

'Who's that?' David asked, though he had little need to.

'Sir, that's Mr Gould, sir.' Hunter had clasped his knees under the table, and sucked his lower lip into his mouth.

'Sir, we're making less noise, sir, and can I ask you a question?' a boy half-way down the table said.

David nodded gravely.

'Well, sir, you still haven't told us whether you were in the war, sir, were you?'

'Break-in a bronco, little boy,' David said slowly. 'Or take a canoe across the Atlantic. If that's not enough, try sticking pins in a cat, and letting it scratch you.'

The boy began to giggle delightedly. Whichever of Crawley's families he came from could already be proud of him.

'No, honestly, sir, *were* you?'

'Fetch me a carving-knife. I'll stick it in your stomach; and perhaps you'll forget war.'

The rhetoric was fatal. David couldn't have indulged little-boy blood lust more successfully if he'd tried. Half the table clutched their stomachs and began to groan in ecstasies of expectation, rolling their eyes at him.

Some sort of fight seemed to have broken out.

'Sir, Cason's going to blub!' a boy called.

A boy opposite the one who must be Cason let out a kick under the table. Cason did begin to blub, silently into his custard.

'He wets his bed!' the boy who had delivered the kick called out to David.

'He has to have pills too, sir!' another yelled triumphantly, elbowing Cason contemptuously in the ribs.

'And he has to see the doctor every week – drip!' The, speaker addressed the last word bitterly to Cason himself.

David eyed the principal protagonists warily. 'Really? *I* wet my bed, *I* have pills, and *I* see my doctor every Thursday.'

He was aware of a stunned silence in the room, and of eighty eyes staring at him. Cason seemed to have discovered a guinea in his progress through the stodge, but was unable to believe his fortune.

'Gentlemen!' David said, seizing on the silence. 'There will be no more talking in this room until the end of the meal.' He got to his feet and became aware of Jones standing in the doorway. Jones caught up with him in die hall. He said:

'There'll be coffee in the Staff Room – your brother should be changed in a minute. Rogers?' he added, evidently troubled, 'about the question of that resident post. You will let me know, won't you?' He clapped David on the shoulder, and wandered off shaking his head.

Tony appeared in the hall. He was carefully attired in his suit and what looked like brand new black shoes. As soon as they were in the car he asked, 'Did you talk to him?'

'Who?'

'The Ghoul?'

'No.'

'He beat me again.'

'Why?'

'Well, he was telling us that Pitt reformed London and introduced a new system of taxes. I said I didn't think there were taxis in London in those days.'

'Then you deserved it.' David was uncompromising. 'Anyway, I thought the Ghoul taught maths.'

'History too,'

'Tony, let's forget about the Ghoul. You haven't said Hallo yet.'

The boy slid down in the seat and grinned up. 'Hallo!'

David stopped the car at the school gates to let a pedestrian pass. His stomach suddenly contracted.

'That's that man, isn't it?' Tony cried.

David accelerated out into St Aldate's. Lang stood staring after them.

## 14

'I've been doing research,' David said. They were waiting for traffic lights. 'All the best wool comes from Neal Frazers. There's a branch in Cheltenham apparently. That's where we're going.'

'Are you really going to buy me – new clothes then?'

'Sure.' David took a quick look at the boy, and let in the clutch as the lights turned amber.

'What about the white ones?'

'The white whats?'

'Oh, it doesn't matter,' Tony said quickly. 'I meant the shorts for cricket,' he added after a moment. 'You see, we've got a match against Kings in Cambridge on Wednesday, and I think my verrucas will be better again.'

David threw him a suspicious glance. 'I thought you didn't like cricket much,'

'I don't. I want to see the statues in the Fitzwilliam Museum. I usually manage to escape for an hour.'

'Doesn't the school provide the eleven with whites anyway?'

'Oh, yes.' Tony was vague. 'But they lend them out to anyone who's playing, and they're not very nice.'

'I see. Who else do you play matches against?'

'New College, of course; and Christ Church. They're pretty useless though, and we always beat them. Once I hit a six right into Merton,' Tony added modestly.

David smiled. 'Which reminds me. I've got a present for you – two, in fact. I'm beginning to suspect I shouldn't have got the first, though.' The car was coasting steadily along the Witney road. David reached into the back and produced the socks, still in their bag. Tony unwrapped them, gave a gasp, and then folded up with laughter. David found the flippers. Tony became grave.

'You're very kind to me,' he said. 'How did you know I wanted some?'

David inclined his head non-committally. Clearly the boy had forgotten. Tony now stripped off his shoes and socks and put the flippers on his feet. He pulled up the hems of his shorts the better to admire the length of his brown legs. The neon-topped socks were happily forgotten.

Tony seemed to sink into a dream, alternating his attention between the countryside through which they were passing, and his own legs which terminated in the absurd rubber feet. The U.S. Air Force was being proved right. It was warm, and a light breeze shifted the boy's hair in the open car. They were running again along the valley of the Windrush; only today the air was clear, and they could see the silver ribbon of the stream as it meandered through the fields. In the distance still, was the spire of Burford church. I must find cherries and hang them on the boy's ears, David thought irrationally.

'We didn't see any dragon-flies, did we?' Tony said.

'No.'

'Or where the Evenlode joins the Windrush.'

David was strangely moved by the boy's remembering the names of the two streams.

'There was something I wanted to ask you.' Tony still clutched the hems of his shorts. Holding his legs rigid, he moved them up and down while he looked at his feet. 'It seemed easy last night . . .'

'Go on.'

'Well, it's . . . You don't think I'm like a girl, do you?' David let the cats' eyes kick rhythmically at his offside wheels. 'Crazy question. No, Tony. I think you're like a boy.'

'Good,' Tony said with finality. 'I think a boy can be better than a girl.' He seemed content to let David work out whatever he might mean. It was obvious that he didn't know himself. After a moment he added, 'Did you like me with those elm seeds or whatever they were at that place where we had tea?'

David smiled. 'I know that if I say yes you'll produce a handful and sprinkle them in your hair now!'

Tony became suddenly animated. He began to beat his rubber feet up and down on the floor of the car. 'I thought we'd buy a cold chicken or something for tonight, and have it in my room,' David said after a while. 'I've laid in some stocks of film too.'

Tony looked at him. 'Colour as well?'

'Colour as well. But you get better effects with black and white. And you can't be as big as the wall in colour.'

Tony compressed his lips. David glanced at him quizzically. 'Don't worry! We'll use them both. I'd really like you in your dashing opera cloak – as you were when you first broke in on my peace.'

'As a matter of fact it was you who said "stop!",' Tony amended, truly enough. 'But the cloaks have been put away, and I probably couldn't get one. We have gowns in summer.'

David was puzzled. 'But it was definitely a cloak you were wearing that Sunday.'

'Yes. That was because our gowns had been to the cleaners,

but they sent them back to your dons' Senior Common Room, I think it is, and they got lost. You see, they're long gowns — much longer than yours,' he added in explanation.

'Oh!' David said, visualising the mean proportions of his Commoner's gown. 'I certainly wouldn't put it past our dons to steal your gowns. Their own are shabby enough.'

For some minutes the car ran on through the open-faced fields, and neither of them said anything. There were clouds like yellow satin cushions in the sky.

'I know today isn't *ended* yet, but when am I going to see you again *after* today?' Tony asked this suddenly.

'I don't know.' David flexed the sprung steering wheel, thinking. Out of the corner of his eye he could see that the boy had produced a diary. 'When are you next free? You've got Cambridge on Wednesday. What about Monday?'

'Funeral,' said Tony. 'One of your dons. Then on Tuesday I've got a wedding,'

'You certainly see life.'

'Yes, we do,' Tony was thoughtful. 'We usually get five shillings for weddings, because it's overtime. We don't get anything for funerals though. Not that we'd want it,' he added, as if sensing some impropriety.

'That brings us to Thursday then.'

Tony turned another page of his diary. 'Blast! I've got a concert at Christ Church. Their first soprano was run over crossing St Aldate's and they've asked for me.'

'Of course,' David echoed hollowly; but he was appalled. 'Was he badly hurt?'

'I don't think so. Just bruises. It was only an undergraduate on a bicycle.' Tony considered his rubber feet for a moment. 'He must have felt rather a fool.'

'Who?'

'The man.'

'Yes, I suppose he must. So it looks like the week-end again?'

'I'm afraid so.' Tony was apologetic. 'It's an awful nuisance when one's professional life interferes with one's personal engagements. Shall we say Saturday then?'

David nodded. 'Two-thirty on the fence.'

Tony had turned to the back of his diary and appeared to be studying something intensely.

'David?'

'Yes?'

'What's a *homosexual*?'

David glanced at the boy, but he was concentrated over the diary. 'It's a person who's attracted to someone of the same sex.'

'Same sex?' Tony had looked up.

'Yes.'

'It's a Greek word then?'

'You're a bright boy! The *homo* part is: the rest comes from Latin.'

'Am I one because I'm *attracted* to you?'

'Well, no. It means a more mature attraction.'

'Like grown-ups' love?' The boy's tone was one of aggressive inquiry.

'It can be.'

'I see.' Tony turned another page of his diary studiously. 'The other word is *pederast*. What's that?'

'Tony, where on earth did you get these words from?'

'Sermon,' Tony said simply. 'I asked one of the matrons what "pederast" was, and she said she thought it was what you stood statues on. When I asked her about the other word - she said she was busy, so I assumed it must be one of those words we aren't supposed to know, and that I'd better ask you. Our dictionary is someone called Chambers' and it doesn't have either.' He'd become quite heated by the idea that knowledge was being withheld from him.

David smiled. 'I see. Well, your Greek should help you with that one too. What's ερaστής?'

'*Love* – no, *lover*.'

'And παιδ?'

'*A boy*.'

'Exactly. So you put them together.'

'*Love-boy*?' Tony hazarded. 'Or *lover-boy*! But that sounds like one of those modern songs with impossible harmonic groupings.'

'Your diction can be priggish, to say the least.' David laughed. 'No – it means someone who loves boys.'

'Not "Jesus loves us" and all that stuff?' Tony said suspiciously.

'Not really. It's difficult to distinguish between the different meanings of love. Words don't always help because people put different interpretation upon them. That's one reason why I write music.'

'But wait a minute.' Tony was confused. 'There is only one sort of love, surely?'

'Probably; at least I think so. A second ago, though, you were a bit reluctant to admit God's love at all.'

'Well, we get religion about three times a day,' Tony said, 'yet our masters are atheists or hypocrites. It's muddling. If all loving's the same what's the connection between praying which I don't want to do *thoroughly,* and kissing, which I do? I mean, Sanders, I think I told you about him, the boy who had hair, used to have this photo of Bardot, you know, and take his shorts off in front of it and say he *loved* her. Then . . .' Tony broke off; gathering his concentration furiously. 'Then, Mrs Jones says Saint Francis loves the birds – she means the feathered sort. So – so think of Mrs Jones saying that, and of Sanders taking his shorts off and going stiff in her drawing room at the same time. Do you see?'

'I didn't meet Mrs Jones this morning,' David said. The outburst had startled him and he needed time. 'I think you must think of all forms of love as aspects of a single force, which none of us can completely understand. It's because love can take so many forms that it can be used for good, or it can be used selfishly.'

'Like sex?'

David gave the boy another look. 'Like sex, or like anything else. You see, Sanders, when he wasn't simply showing off to you all, wanted to find some sort of happiness – and sense of security, maybe – with the film actress; Mrs Jones, though of course I don't know her, may be looking for her happiness by caring about birds and other wild life. When people pray thoroughly, as you put it, it's because they're looking for just the same security, and happiness, and sense of belonging with God. At your age you can't possibly know where you'll most happily belong in the end. Some people spend their whole lives without discovering what they can really love, or where they'll best belong. Certainly I don't know yet.'

'One's *age!*' Tony said with astonishing irony. He was running his finger back and forth along the dashboard. 'I understand a bit better, though. But what's the difference between those two words. I mean homosexual and pederast?'

'Well, the first is a very general term; and the second is a specific or particular term.'

'For a man who loves a boy?'

'Yes.'

'What's the *specific* term for a boy who loves a man?' Tony had been addressing David directly; now he seemed to have discovered some new interest in the dashboard, and was tracing the grain of the walnut with his finger-nail.

'I don't know that there is one. Perhaps people don't take you seriously enough to invent a special word.'

'They take us seriously enough if we miss practice,' Tony said with some heat.

David was perplexed by his own clumsiness. 'Do you often take words down from sermons?'

'Yes – interesting ones. I wasn't sure whether I'd got these right though because Hamley was making such a noise unwrapping fruit drops.'

'What! Quite openly?'

'Oh no. He pulls his hands out of his sleeves and just sits there without any arms. Then he unwraps sweets. Or plays with himself, I think. Only he doesn't eat sweets so much now because once the prayers finished too soon, and when we stood up for the anthem, and Sir Vernon Bull raised his baton and everyone was quiet, Hamley suddenly choked. A sweet came whizzing out of his mouth and we could hear it bouncing down the nave like a marble. We didn't giggle, because we never do,' Tony went on, 'but you know how the Master sits in that box thing quite near us and his eyes are always open as if he's stuffed? Well, he shut them, and sort of *sank* into the box. There was an awful row. So Hamley doesn't eat sweets quite so often. He still does something with his hands though, because often when we stand up Hamley hasn't any arms and has to share my book. It makes the choir look pretty sloppy if you ask me, but no one's been able to cure him.'

The car ran on across the Gloucestershire Cotswolds through a changing pattern of sheep, forests and sunshine. David threaded his way into the centre of Cheltenham, and found a place to park in the Esplanade.

Tony stripped off the frog-flippers and pulled on his own

socks. He carefully knotted the Cherry Blossom shoes and combed his hair in the driving mirror. Then he cocked his head on one side and grinned deplorably. 'Oh!' He collected himself. 'The elm seeds!' He made to feel in his pocket with a frown.

'Come on, ass!' said David. 'And just see you behave, because I'm feeling nervous.'

They paused beside the car, and David laid his hand on the boy's shoulder. 'It's a new suit you really want, isn't it?' Tony's face filled with pleasure and confusion. They crossed the road and walked past a jaded row of Regency houses. David pushed open the shop door, hoping this wasn't going to be like taking a normal child to a sweetmeat emporium. Until the end of the month he had only thirty pounds in the world. All of it was in his wallet. His grandmother's capital of three hundred pounds was melting now without pain.

They found themselves in a hall given over to fluffy baby-wear, and cots with suck-proof knobs, and bunnies painted on their hygienic Formica. There were eiderdowns for similarly miniature persons, which a placard claimed to be *Tubable*.

They passed through *Junior Miss* and plain *Girls*, while Tony looked at his toes. At last they arrived unmolested at what appeared to be the appropriate place. Tony started fingering a wax boy who sat dejectedly on a tuck-box in the middle of the room. The initials of the new boy were apparently B. H-B. The tuck-box said so. Benjamin Hawker-Brash or whatever looked very unhappy.

A round man advanced on them.

'Good afternoon,' David said. 'I want a couple of flannel suits for this boy.'

'All-wool,' Tony interposed. He had looked at David in amazement for a moment.

'Certainly, sir!' The man rubbed his hands together. He rocked back on his heels considering, and looked Tony up and down. 'Now, sir!' He swung on David again. 'Will it be with knickers? Or the long-trouser suit?'

'*Shorts*,' Tony interrupted dully. He seemed to have taken a dislike to the man, who now advanced on him with a tape measure. He got down on one knee, but Tony inelegantly took a step backwards. 'I'm size eight,' he said quickly. David was startled and a little embarrassed by the boy's coquettish

behaviour. He had an uneasy feeling that this was Mr Neal
Frazer himself. The man now conducted them to a cubicle and
discreetly withdrew. 'I hope you've got clean underpants on?'
David asked when they were alone.

Tony looked up surprised. 'I don't wear pants in summer.'

'I see.' David wondered whether he should call loudly
for pants, but decided against it. Mr Neal Frazer might feel
disposed to throw them out.

Tony changed into the first suit. David had to confess that
the effect was resplendent. The boy put his belt round the
shorts without threading it through the loops.

'Why not wear it now?' David suggested.

'Have to anyway,' Tony said, peering down at his stomach.
'The buttons are too stiff.'

David smiled. 'Well, I hope the legs are liftable.'

Tony pulled experimentally at one of the legs of the shorts.

'All right!' David said quickly, 'We'd better see if they've got
an identical blue belt to complete the mint tuck-box boy effect.'

Mr Neal Frazer produced the belt. 'Stockings? Anything like
that?'

'We have our own socks, thank you,' said Tony.

'Oh, yes.' David remembered. 'One pair of white cricket
shorts; same size, the woollier the better.'

Tony had begun threading the new belt into his shorts, and
acknowledged this with an extravagant movement of his hips.
Mr Neal Frazer bundled up the parcel and David paid up
fifteen pounds odd.

As they stepped into the afternoon sunshine David lagged
behind. The boy undoubtedly had an uncanny sense for the
sartorial complement to his own beauty. Tony perched on the
pavement's edge. His head was cocked on one side, and he
looked down the street into Brize Norton's freshening wind – a
golden calf arrayed in soft silver. They began walking together
along the Esplanade beneath the lime trees, and David had the
sense of a transparent bubble that enclosed only themselves
wherever they went. There was no relevant world outside.

Suddenly he thought of the French surrealist film where
a boy loves and eventually masters a wild stallion in the
Camargue: how he mounts it beneath the thunder, and it
carries him out, galloping faster and faster, irresistibly into the

sea. David stepped hastily back into the sunlit bubble beneath the sober Cheltenham limes.

'Thank you for the clothes,' Tony said. 'They're really too big just to say thank you for, though.'

'The spectacle's its own reward.'

'How *do* I look?' Tony stopped suddenly.

'To me? The way Van Gogh's yellow chair looked to Van Gogh, I suppose. I wish I was a painter, not a photographer.'

'You're a composer,' Tony said.

Cheltenham being synonymous with cash. County, colonels and horsy kids, the Cavendish House menu:

> Teddy Bear Tea for Children:
> Honey sandwiches
> Chocolate biscuit
> Teddy Bear Ice-Cream
> Orange Squash
> Or,
> Glass of Milk

Tony didn't think much of this. Instead he opted to eat tea *à la carte,* with the proviso that a Teddy Bear Ice-Cream be transferred from the *table d'hôte.* David settled for the same.

Some sort of fashion parade was conducting itself informally amongst the tables. Models churned slowly about the room like restless autumn leaves. Tony, with one paper napkin tucked under his chin and another in his belt, had reached the Teddy Bear Ice stage, and fed steadily on. David leant back and lit a cigarette. The school lunch had not altogether agreed with him. Meanwhile his own Teddy Bear Ice was long since sunk drunkenly on its stomach, and now, with its forepaws melted, was breasting the pool of its own substance.

Tony looked up. 'Don't you want that?'

'Don't think so.'

Tony reached across, exchanged plates, and got his head down again.

The waitress had been disposed to regard Tony indulgently. David decided that if she called him 'dear' he would scream once, shrilly, and then break something. It's odd, he reflected; all the women I come across are intrusive and motherly, Mrs

Kanter, Gloria, Ricks, and now this. 'By the way,' he said aloud, 'what happened to the letter we wrote that French boy?'

Tony tugged home some stray dribbles of Bear with his tongue. 'Oh, it went off. He wrote back and said please would I send him a "tin-can of the English beer".'

'Incorrigible.'

'Shall we?'

'No. I won't voluntarily direct a Frenchman on the road to alcoholism. Besides, your respective English and French masters might begin to suspect Rogers. No, hell, why not? Let's see. I suggest Bartram's Black Export. It's horrible.'

The fashion parade continued to eddy about them. A woman moved her bottom around for David's inspection.

'Have you got Bartram's Black Export?' he asked the waitress.

'I don't know, I'm sure. There's Christian Nithsdale's Paris Sack Line soon. This is very nice too.' She indicated the bottom.

'It's horrible,' said Tony, who wasn't to be put off from ordering the beer.

'My bill,' David said quickly.

Tony sat down in the car, after carefully dusting the seat. The frog-flippers were forgotten in the contemplation of his new splendour. David had contrived to buy a barbecued chicken, tomatoes, tinned mangoes, a bottle of Moselle, fresh cherries grown suspiciously large beneath the shadow of Harwell, and even a can of Bartram's Black Export. Now, as they sat in the car, David found two double cherries and hung them over the boy's ears. Tony turned to face him and lowered his eyelids. David produced the slim bottle of Moselle.

'I make you Sir Tony Cherry of Sandelwood with this sweet white wine.'

With elaborately feigned delicacy, Tony removed the cherries and ate them.

The car climbed up out of Cheltenham on to the high, exposed ridge of the Cotswolds between Andoversford and Northleach. At perhaps a thousand feet above the deserted road an American B.47 was circling. It banked languidly through the nearer segment of its arc, while the late afternoon sun glinted along its slim, silverfish belly.

'It's waiting to land,' Tony said.

David pulled up the car in a lay-by.

'What are you going to do?'

'Signal.' David un-dipped the spotlight and clamped it to its bracket on the windscreen. 'D'you know Morse?'

'A bit.' Tony was doubtful.

'Never mind. Just shade this thing with your flippers.'

Tony got the grotesque rubber feet, and held them as a mask to the lamp which David directed towards the sky.

'Now!' He began flashing the spot; spelling out the coded letters for the boy: 'G.o. H.o.m.e.' He paused; then repeated the message.

The bomber continued to circle for some time. Then it banked away, and was lost over the western horizon.

'It *has* gone home!' Tony exclaimed delightedly.

'Somehow I don't think so, Tony.'

Suddenly the giant bomber appeared from behind a hill, lined up with the long road. It drew steadily nearer, coming straight at them now at scarcely fifty feet. The limp anhedral of the wings with their six engines under-slung in pods gave the plane a droop-shouldered look. Only at their tips did the slender wings curve upwards again; flexed like fencing foils they quivered, supporting the weight of the great machine as if on springs.

'They've opened the bomb doors!' Tony yelled above the scream of the jets. He stood up on the seat and gripped the windscreen for a better view. His voice turned to horror. 'They've dropped *a bomb!*'

It was true. Hurtling down from the 'plane was a small black object. It landed in the road not ten yards from the car, which shuddered as the shadow of the bomber crashed over it like a tidal wave. Gradually the bellowing died away.

Tony stood staring fixedly at the object in the road. Very slowly he un-damped his hands from the windscreen and pressed them over his ears.

'Tony!' David put his arm round the boy and shook him again. 'Tony!' The boy still stared at the package in terror. He didn't seem to hear. David reached up his other hand. Gently he turned the boy's head. Now he was looking into David's eyes; but without seeing them. David lifted him down into his arms. 'Tony, I'm sorry . . .' He couldn't find words.

It was some seconds before Tony stirred; then he smiled. 'A dud.'

David nodded; he was too shaken to speak.

'Shall I fetch it? You don't think it will be radioactive?'

'It won't be radioactive.'

Tony left the car and ran across the road. He came back with the package. It was a heavy oilskin bundle about eighteen inches square. Stamped on it in white stencil were the words *Desert Survival Pack*. Pinned beneath the legend was a note written with a ball-pen: 'Suit yourself, Mac.'

Tony unrolled the bundle, which had pouches like a tool kit. There was one empty, angled pouch that had evidently contained an automatic. Otherwise the kit was apparently complete. There was a remarkable folding fishing rod and an assortment of dry flies; a rubber torch and an ugly knife; morphine, a variety of labelled pills, and some matches in a tin; some condensed bars like squares of plywood; half a pound of chewing gum; and a sheaf of notes on the dietetic values of certain fish and herbs to be found in the Siberian Steppes.

David unwrapped a stick of gum and closed Tony's jaw on it. He pocketed the morphine and pills, and gave the pack back to the boy.

'You might try offering one of those condensed bars to the school cook, raw,' he said. 'But I expect if you boil them gently over a low fire of yak dung they'll turn into Chicken Maryland and Angel Cake.' He picked up a minute, brown nugget. 'That one's certainly Cranberry Sauce. I imagine this bigger one's Waffles with Honey.'

Tony smiled his own full smile; moving what he imagined was an American jaw on the gum. He began to extend the telescopic fishing rod.

## 15

'Y ou haven't finished the rock!' Tony had his elbows on the mantelpiece, and was looking indignantly at the thick rod, whose pinkness the opaque paper only modified.

David smiled. 'No. I take a mouthful after cleaning my teeth, and then suck it all night. Usually there's some left in the morning.'

'I see.' Tony didn't seem to see. He was looking thoughtfully at the third and index fingers of his right hand.

David arranged the provisions on the desk. Tony had found the Rolleiflex and was following him about the room with the lens like a news-reel man. He turned the camera round, pointing it at himself. David cast a tablecloth into the air a primitive fishing net. It settled over the table. 'Cedarwood, Sandel, and sweet white wine,' he incanted.

Tony grinned. 'Are you going to make me drunk?'

'No. Strictly rationed.'

Tony turned back to the camera. He pressed one of the creases of his shorts with his finger and watched, fascinated, as it sprang into place again.

'Food first,' David said. Tony tilted his head on one side. It was as if someone had ingeniously grafted tomato skin beneath the golden olive along his cheek-bones. 'I'd like a camera like that,' he said, sitting down. 'They've got a photographic club at Glenelgin – I'd make prints as big as your wall. I know how to make small ones with contact paper and just sunlight.'

David was surprised. 'We must do some together. What made you choose Glenelgin? Or was it your aunt's idea?'

'They wear shorts.' Tony considered for a moment. 'But of course they're blue ones.'

'All-wool?'

Tony was evidently troubled. 'I don't know. I only really like grey ones though.'

'And white ones,' David said, trying to humour him. 'Just for the occasional sporting exhibition in Cambridge.'

Tony produced a rather wan version of his smile.

'You'll get used to them.' David tried to sound reassuring.

Tony stood up. 'Maybe. The grey goes best with my skin, don't you think?' He folded back one of the legs, where it lay over his thigh. It appeared to have a three-inch hem that could be let down as he grew. David couldn't envisage Tony's growing. He searched his mind for some counter to an exhibition of self love whose morbidity must have appalled him were he not himself involved with the boy, and so an accomplice to every aspect of a libido to which pathetic solicitation such as this evidently contributed a large part. But then perhaps the morbidity did appal him, and the indecision he felt when confronted by it only added to his sense of helplessness.

'You're a bit of a crook, Tony,' he said lamely. He squeezed the boy's leg with dutiful brevity. Tony's mouth assumed an ambiguous attitude, which might have been either the suppression of scorn or a consciousness of modesty.

Tony turned away with one of his slow, gyroscopic movements. He sat down and let his chin sink on to the tablecloth. 'I annoy you, don't I?' he said, staring steadily at David's eyes.

David carved the chicken with a strength and surgical verve that surprised him. 'A bit. But then that's probably inevitable.'

'Hell!' Tony said, springing up again, and looking round the room. 'Protection. Last time I had a new suit like this I spilt coffee all over it. I felt sort of *raped* because it was spoilt.' He shuddered luxuriously; and suddenly David was angry. He pointed to his chewed silk dressing gown on the back of the door.

'Put that on. Pooh Bear. Then come and eat.' He deposited half the chicken on Tony's plate with a thud.


David drained his wine and got up from the table. 'Right! Photos.'

Tony lifted the dressing gown off his shoulders, then held his arms rigid at his sides so that it slipped dramatically to the floor. He stood in the emerald pool like a silver Venus. 'How many are you going to take?'

'Fifty or sixty I should think. See how we go.'

'*Sixty!*'

'Yep.'

'Is it good colour?' David smiled and busied himself with the photo-floods. If he fused the whole house it would bring Sweeney up. 'Now, grab that Oxford Companion from the shelf, curl up on the mohair, and really read it.'

Tony settled himself on the rug and began to read the *Oxford Companion to Music*. He looked up suddenly. 'Hey, David! It says here in a heading, "Choir Boys and Press Gang". And lower down it's got, "Choir Boys: ill treatment of", and, "Nineteenth Century neglect of"!'

'Better read it up. See what it says about midday meals. Does it mention St Cecilia's particularly?'

Tony looked up again; his lip hovering above his gum. Deliberately David pressed the cable release.

David watched the image of the boy, brightly reflected on the ground-glass screen of the Rollei. Constantly he altered the angle of the camera and the lighting. Occasionally he attracted Tony's attention away from the book, sometimes altering the position of his head with his hand, similarly perhaps, though more gently, than Sweeney moving those of his clients in the chair.

He clipped a supplementary lens on the camera and took just the boy's eyes from six inches. Curiously, with the magnifying screen down, he looked at his nose in profile. Its contours were of the kind plastic surgeons manufacture for fashion models. It occurred to David that by taking some careful elevations he might be able to sell blueprints and keep Tony in frog-flippers for life. There'd be pseudo-Sandel noses in *Vogue* for years.

David felt the uneasy obsession of the art beginning to take hold of him. It was hot in the vicinity of the floodlights. He tore off his tie and rolled up his shirt-sleeves. He knew that he would come covertly to love each finally evolved picture. But they would be unreal. Tony couldn't be represented in black chemical stains on white paper, and it wouldn't be him he was loving at all. The photos could only be an empty security, not unlike that which he suspected the boy of deriving from his clothes. The morbidity of his attempts to retain Tony's image suddenly oppressed him. Yet the effort must be made.

Tony hadn't noticed the several changes of film, but now he looked up.

'Hallo!' David smiled his exhaustion.

Peering out from the bright cage of light Tony seemed alarmed. 'You look like the Ghoul after he's rolled the cricket pitch!'

'It's hot work. But I think you'll get a couple of sixes, anyway. Now, forget about the book. I want more full faces.'

'I'm hot too,' Tony announced a few minutes later. 'I'm going to undress so you can take me nude like a statue. Is it all right?'

'If you want to. I'm about ready for a smoke-break.'

'Find me a coat-hanger first, can you?' David obeyed,

and then settled himself rather self-consciously in the semi-darkness which surrounded the floodlit area like an auditorium.

Tony took off his jacket and arranged it carefully on the hanger. Removing his tie, he dragged pullover, shirt and vest over his ears together, folding them as a complex on the chair. Beneath the chair he moored the Cherry Blossom shoes like twin Argosies, and after stripping off his socks, he smoothed them out with his hand until they were flat and two-dimensional like the curiosities David had suspected in Messrs. Ellistons' shop. Finally, despairing of the new shorts, he undid only the belt before wriggling out of them with extravagant movements of his hips and behind.

'The butterfly emerges from its silken cocoon,' David said, as the boy folded his shorts over the hanger. It had been a small epic in its way. 'I sense a problem, though.'

Tony pushed the clothes-laden chair away, 'What?'

'I've no idea how to take nude photographs.'

Tony sucked his lower lip into his mouth, and searched for pockets he hadn't got. Motivated by a similar perplexity David scratched his head. He moved the camera back.

'I think you'd better just stand. Now, face me with your arms relaxed at your sides. Okay. Move your right foot forward a bit, and take your weight on your left leg. Look at the floor . . . disinterestedly.'

'I think this is right.' Tony was doubtful. 'Show me – the way you showed my head.'

David moved the boy's right knee slightly.

'Do you want to see the bruise on my behind the Ghoul made?'

'For pity's sake, not now! Anyway, I thought we'd made a pact not to talk about the Ghoul.'

'I know!' Tony cried. I'll hold a wine glass!'

'You will not!' David said coldly. 'Stay balanced as you are, and relax.'

As David returned to the camera the boy wilfully shrugged his shoulders. Then, in the moment when he released them, his whole body resolved itself into unconscious harmony. His eyes continued to brood on the floor. David made a second exposure without breathing.

Steadily he concentrated on the Rollei; working with it in

what had become a precise and accustomed rhythm. But it wasn't a happy or complete union, and never would be. For all that, he worked jealously with the camera's eye, becoming so absorbed with its narrow satisfaction that he had the sense of not having used his own. Tony seemed unconsciously to adapt himself to the camera's needs; changing his pose at will, or at a sign from David, though always maintaining within it an equilibrium that seemed founded on an almost blasé exhibition of unknowing.

The myopic monster must be sufficiently fed. David looked at the boy with his own eyes. He was anything but the skinny child Lang had chosen to envisage. The carriage of his head, and the careless stance, gave a profound harmony to his naked body whose beautifully modelled chest, smooth belly, and firm, flat pubis, were perfectly proportioned. The beauty was more compelling, perhaps more unreal as well, because of its obvious transience. His body had achieved strength and definition that was almost a linear severity after the formlessness of childhood. Its neatness hadn't yet suffered the imbalance and dislocation of adolescence.

'Look a bit more malign,' David said. The camera might not be sufficiently fed after all.

Tony scowled, thrusting his chin out. He became conscious of his pose, and its rhythm was spoiled.

'I've a final idea.' David reached behind the wardrobe for a bamboo cane he kept for closing his upper windows, and tested its spring.

'Oh Lord!' Tony sighed. This time there was no cause to admonish him. He said it with a resignation that was almost reverence.

'Don't be an idiot, Tony!' For all his exhaustion David couldn't help laughing. 'I want you to bend it almost to breaking in your hands, and then across your shoulders.'

The actions, as he had hoped, influenced the boy's entire stance, giving it harmony again.

David pointed at the rug. 'We'll finish with Boy on a Bearskin. A tummy-sprawling Sandel kicking its legs.'

When it was done David sank back exhausted in his armchair. Concentration, and the heat of the photo floods, had made the heaviness of the night more oppressive. His head swam. 'Get dressed, Tony Bear. Private beaches are the proper

place for bare Sandels. How do you spell the footwear sort?
There should be another pun somewhere.'

'With an *a*,' Tony said. He slithered into his shorts, fastening
the snake-clasp belt, but leaving the flap of the waistband loose
so that it hung down exposing its dark silk underside. Tony
noticed it, and raised an admonitory finger to nose. 'Never
leave that undone when the Ghoul's around! He grabbed a boy
by it once and his shorts ripped open. The Ghoul was fright-
fully embarrassed. Mine won't, though,' he added, tugging
thoughtfully at the flap.

'Just shut up about the Ghoul!' David buried his chin in his
hand in an effort to control his anger.

Tony slid the flap back on to its fastener. He walked slowly
across the room, kicking out his bare feet before him as he had
done on the day David observed him in the field. He trailed his
hand along the shelf of books like a child drawing a stick over
park railings.

'I can annoy you, can't I?' he said, when he had drifted back
to where David was sitting. He eased himself over the arm of
the chair on to David's knee. He showed no trace of his former
embarrassment. David didn't attempt to push him away.

Tony stretched out his bare arm and took a lemon from the
bowl of fruit on the table. He held it above their heads and
appeared to consider it. He's a butterscotch boy in silver foil,
David thought. Tony dropped the lemon deliberately into his
own lap. David picked it up, then let it fall again. Tony waited
for him to repeat the game. When he wouldn't, he twisted his
body and pressed against David, burying his face in his neck.
David found the lemon and held it under the boy's nose. Tony
bit into it deeply and the saliva, flowing over his teeth like
Niagara, ran along his silver wire, and fell in bright drops on
his naked shoulder. David could taste the sharp juice on his
lips.

Tony suddenly drew away; bracing himself with his arms
against David's shoulders.

'You know what I said this afternoon? About boys being
better than girls?'

David nodded. He sensed that kind of rhetorical preparation
that seeks permission to proceed.

'Well . . . there's something I don't understand . . .' Tony
seemed momentarily at a loss; the challenge in his voice

replaced by petulance. 'You know how people hug girls − in films, for instance. Well, I don't see how they can hug them *properly.*' Tony brought the word out fiercely, as if, stumbling through puzzlement, aggression had presented itself as the only possibility of progress. 'I mean, don't their *breasts* get in the way?'

David said nothing. There didn't appear to be anything he could say. But for Tony, the question itself seemed to have proved of sufficient release, and he no longer looked for an answer. He had begun to hug David properly.

To David, the moment of happiness was precariously poised, as the beauty of Tony's nakedness seemed to have been, when he had stood before him on the floor. A sense of impending loss, of a possession that could have no perpetuity, threatened to obscure its fulfilment, stealing reality even from present awareness. His arms were locked about the boy, their every nerve exposed. Tony was polished walnut and soft wool. But he was a displaced part of David himself, that had mysteriously returned. He was whole. A dug-out canoe become a living tree again.

'I've got to take you back to school.'

Tony made a contemptuous noise. David said nothing more. He was the wind's breast, and the boy's body a guttering candle flame. He was a moth, pressing against the ceaselessly shifting planes. His hands were cold. He held them against the flame. His palms were vibrant as drum skins. He squared his hands constantly to the hard facets of the wandering flame. But he could find nowhere to rest them.

'Fainted tiger-meat,' Tony said. 'Bite somewhere. My nose just fits your eye.'

Tony went wild. He beat furiously against David like a stranded fish determined to crush its life before the last air dies in its blood. Then he fell still. David's hand moved restlessly back and forth over the boy's ribs with the motion of a captive leopard. He pressed the butt of his palm against the tensely sprung cage.

'Tony, I'm taking you back *now*,' David said. 'Home . . . to school.' He lifted him on to his feet.

They stared at each other, bewildered by the cruelty of interruption, because neither of them had willed it.

## 16

'T HE trouble with you,' Lang said, 'is that you evolve a comfortable epigram and then expect the world to live by it. It won't, you know.' He sat in his armchair and sipped port. 'What you're gaily saying in effect is that that choirboy is your mistress.'

'Not yet,' said David. 'And anyway I think Tony would call it hugging.'

'Nevertheless, you do, it seems, hop into bed with the child.'

'Not yet! I'm telling you! Can't you understand? We did nothing of the kind. What may happen tomorrow . . . I don't know.'

'Then you don't propose to set him up in a flat? Or perhaps stare into oases like Alfred Douglas with some painted Arab boy?'

'Douglas was a bastard and a hypocrite, and Tony doesn't like paint.' David was confused. He wondered why he had come. The room was hot and there was a rumble of thunder outside. He looked at his watch. It was seven minutes past midnight. Even as he noted the time, a heavy drop of rain fell on the window. Brize Norton had said something about rain a long time ago. Lang was still saying something.

'Of course, I don't propose to turn you over. But if you must corrupt . . .'

'Oh, don't be so bloody silly!' Some of the thunder was in David's head. 'I came here for friendship,' he said awkwardly. 'What do I get? Wisecracks and platitudes. Have you no stones? Perhaps you'd feel better if you lit that censer.'

He turned away and leant his forehead against the raised sash of the window. Lang always opened it when he arrived to let the smoke out. The rain was pouring down now. It flooded over the pane, ran along the lip of the sash, and dripped on to the sill. David thought of the saliva running along Tony's silver wire when he bit into the lemon. He turned back into the room.

'Can't I love without volunteering for Calvary? I will, if you'd like to knock up a cross and a charge.'

'Masochism,' said Lang. 'And morbid self-pity as well.'

'I agree. But then there's something inherently pathetic about having to justify loving.'

'A cat purrs if you stroke it,' Lang said slowly. 'All young animals solicit cuddling. A boy, being a higher one, simply goes about that – to say nothing of inviting touching in exciting places – more subtly. He would just as much have enjoyed some mechanical device, or even this Ghoul creature's, dropping that lemon.'

'And being embraced by a ten-ton grab perhaps?'

'No. My point is that, technically, the sexual act – and in whatever combination – is indulged for its lone pleasure's sake.'

David clapped his hand to his brow, 'Oh, my God! All right! So what a miracle that he found *sex with love* first time!'

Lang considered his crucifix. 'The argument so far seems to be that because there's a possibility of the child's indulging casual practices in the future you're justified in giving him what you fondly imagine to be a more complete relationship now? It's really very noble of you. Like making a clean haul of a bank to forestall anyone else's bungling it later on.'

'Maybe.' David was uneasy.

'Then why don't you admit that lust determined the incident earlier this evening, and jealousy the illogical rationalisation of it you're making now?'

'You're asking me to justify an act of love, but without any reference to the mutual attraction of the lovers. I can't do it . . . As to lust and bank robbery, they're the wrong words. Their connotations are seizure of advantage. The event wasn't like that at all.'

'The boy seduced *you*, I suppose?'

David smiled to himself, remembering. 'Nothing happened. And if it had . . . it's neither here nor there. Besides, I can't admit seduction. Once again the term presupposes censure. What one does happens.'

'And you're making a smug defence of the accident.'

'No,' David shook his head slowly. 'A bit vain, perhaps. But then some vanity is probably inevitable when one loves . . . and finds oneself loved.'

Lang stretched, and the gesture seemed to fill the room.

'I'll concede that the boy has some sort of crush on you; even that you were justified in embracing him. Bed, though, would be a different matter. I've no doubt that psychologically your argument about the happy merger of love and sex is sound. However, in this instance, the psychology and morality are irreconcilable.'

'With respect to your first point,' David mocked Lang's idiom gently, 'if you really see love in terms of bio-chemistry on the one hand, and the terminology of schoolgirl stories on the other, then I'm sorry for you. Nothing is more sickening than attempts to plant hedges between love and sexual passion. I don't blame you for that here. It isn't your fault. Something in the human mind takes care that other people's sex shall always be inconceivable. We nervously acknowledge our fear of it whenever we make a dirty joke.'

Lang had put his hand up. 'Can I just slip in that your irreverence before God has a similarly nervous origin?'

David bowed. Lang at once ceased to be a suppliant.

'Which leaves the question of morality.'

'I'll have port after all,' David said, getting up. 'I'm racing in the morning.'

Lang waved a benign hand, but, surprisingly, the decanter didn't multiply. David helped himself liberally. Perhaps Lang would be able to replenish the draught with more concentrated prayer later on.

'You're mad,' he said.

'You should be in bed – alone.'

'You're impotent, Bruce.'

'I beg your pardon?'

'I said you're impotent . . . and an old man. You and I are sitting in our cave in bearskins. There's Tony there too; and a neighbour-tribe concubine you've clobbered on the head and dragged in by the hair. All around there are fierce beasts and men out to get you . . . Nasty things. I take Tony to my corner and ignore your presentation concubine. Not so good. No children. Very rightly you equate no children with death. There'll be no one to protect you in your old age from the things outside. What do you do? You impress upon anyone you can – it's not difficult – that such deviationist behaviour is deuced awkward; wrong; very evil – in that order. They hand the dark secret down the generations and we have conventional morality. You've initiated what's virtually become a conditioned reflex.'

'So murder is harmless too? It just weakens the efficiency of the tribe a bit?'

'No. There are two distinct kinds of morality.'

Lang groaned. 'Of which one is Rogers' morality of personal convenience, I don't doubt.'

'No. Yours.' David said. 'Your morality of convenience and convention. Plenty of illegitimacy in the cave in one age; bigamy in another, and so on. Then there is the other – and only real morality – whose definition depends upon harm done to somebody else. Obviously murder is censurable. Both the victim and anyone near to him suffer. Making love to Tony on the other hand is not censurable, if only because I know it is not hurtful. As I say, it'd almost certainly be beneficial.'

'To whom?' Lang asked distinctly. 'What about me being assaulted in my cave for lack of your precious progeny? Aren't you responsible to my infirmity?'

'Ideally, yes. But then, ideally, you would be to mine.'

In the hiatus Lang refilled both their glasses.

'How can you be sure the boy isn't hurt?'

David watched the level of the decanter curiously. The reduction of a moment of happiness and human communion to an academic discussion of its advisability seemed to him to be without meaning, so that he could only reply wearily.

'One can be sure of nothing. But if you're driving at the idea of deviation's being somehow *instilled* during youth, it's a fallacy – as you'd discover if you read your textbooks. Where a condition isn't innate, then the sort of imaginative sensibility where it may take root obviously is. Germination is as arbitrary as anywhere in nature. Remember the sower whose seed fell on differing soils? It's more arbitrary than that, because man has a mind, and *its* susceptibilities – *its* responses are limitless . . .'

'So good minds, and stony – evil minds.'

'Or yielding and *unyielding* minds? No, the pun's out of place. Say simply, normal minds and abnormal minds. And normality of mind isn't necessarily a virtue.'

'You should be on a committee,' Lang said dully. 'I still don't follow this tenuous suggestion of yours that because bigamy is accepted in one age David Rogers can take choirboys to bed in his.'

'You've got it all wrong.' David was patient. 'I implied no such connection. I instanced another deviation from the norm merely to demonstrate the arbitrary nature of conventional morality. Incidentally, I wish you'd drop this choirboy angle – it isn't nice.'

'No,' said Lang. He drained his port. 'Nevertheless – to pursue other ages – no doubt you'll be reminding me next of paederasty in Lacedaemon?'

'On your insistence. What was the result?'

'I don't know. Wretched small boys wandering round clutching sore behinds, I imagine.' Lang was at his smoothest.

'On the contrary, there was no adultery or neurosis.'

'You astound!' Lang affected incredulity.

'What was Plutarch's Latin for "neurosis"? But this is all rather a stale line, you know,' he went on, dubiously consulting the dregs of his port. 'Greeks and Gide; free-love; scraps of D. H. Lawrence . . .'

'I'm not suggesting Christ co-habited with anyone.'

Lang's response, sensibly enough, was to ignore him.

'Incidentally, what about the aborigines of Kimberley who are temporally presented with boy wives when the tribe happens to be a bit short of girls?' Lang spoke with increasing irony. 'Then, let's see, we've the Dorian boy-marriage-by-capture, the Crusaders' little pages, the Chinese professionals, modern Turks and Albanians, the American hobo's *prushun* – though I believe they've recently been replaced by pumpkins . . . Goodness, what a lot of precedents you've overlooked !'

'I don't do quite so much vicarious reading,' said David. 'The sooner you're put away in a monastery full of other solitary monks the better.'

Lang stretched his long legs. He was unmoved by the childish jibe.

'But what about your reclamation, David? My offer of marriage still holds good.'

'Sorry,' David said, deliberately misunderstanding him. 'Try Ricks. I only like boys.' He felt suddenly tired of the bickering game. It could serve no purpose. Yet they both went on playing it mechanically.

'That plural betrays you,' Lang said.

'It was figurative; adapted to jest.'

'I know. But who else would? It demonstrates what I said earlier. One day you'll slap out an epigram like that and it'll bounce back disastrously. Few people's intelligences are going to admit the sort of intellectual latitude you demand.'

'Maybe,' David said. 'But I can't deny Tony for all that. Call it perverse pride if you like. Whose side in this argument are you on now, anyway?'

'That of rationality and the angels – as ever,' Lang said piously.

'I see. Bruce sticks to the big battalions, but can lend a Samaritan hand to heresy where he chooses! Talking of parables and my marriage, did I ever tell you about the hippopotamus?' Lang was now looking at him wearily: he shook his head.

'Well. There was a rather restless hippopotamus, see? And its friends and relations, other hippopotami, observing its distress, all came and stood around it in a big circle one day – the way hippopotami do. They said, "August!" – that was his name – "August! We strongly advise marriage." August nodded his head safely; then he said, "Yes. But I don't know a camel."'

Lang looked quite blank.

'A *parable,* Bruce! Surely you understand such things?'

David looked at his watch. It was three in the morning. That left him only seven hours to change the Series 4's rear axle and get over to Silverstone. Outside it was still raining. He got up.

'So you're maintaining your stand then?' Lang asked. His enquiry was oddly tentative, as if he supposed the silence might have produced conversion.

'Presumably. Isn't it as inevitable as your sticking to yours? Intolerance arises from two things – contradictory ones: a man's guilt, which only finds absolution in the solidarity of the herd; and the necessity of maintaining whatever is most precious to himself as an individual. He feels that his salvation depends upon it. Who can say it doesn't?'

'Then we're each of us condemned to isolationism?'

'Surely!' David was excited. 'And no doubt your God cunningly devised it like that to make us ultimately dependent upon Him. I don't know. What I do know is that you'll never stop people coming together in love. You'll never know what makes them sympathetic to one another, and it's probably as impertinent to enquire as it is to cast judgement. Perhaps even discussion is meaningless, if only because one can have no valid part in other people's reality.'

Throughout this speech Lang had been shaking his head. Now he said:

'This isn't a defence of your behaviour, but an hysterical admission of your being alone. The damnable thing is that you like it. One could almost believe that you'd involved the boy to achieve it.'

'No,' David said; and when he reached the door, 'No.'

'Wait! I haven't finished yet.' Lang got up with an agitation that was unusual in him. 'You're trying to resurrect Peter. This Tony is a projection of him. But the folly of it is that through a combination of the child's precocity, and your own need for some sort of orientation, you've entered into a relationship that you would have found unthinkable with Peter. Peter's death might have given you a lot of valuable things. Instead, you let it make you an outsider. The realisation you're looking for can't be found with this bloody boy. Not only is it wrong, but by seeking to transpose fantasy into actual behaviour you're not finding yourself but getting more hopelessly lost.'

'Maturity *is* the modification of the fantastic by the real.'

'Of course!' Lang was nervously picking up various society cards on his mantelpiece. 'But you're proceeding from the wrong fantasy. You must *know* it can't work. Yet some bloody-minded conception – preconception I should say – drives you on . . .' He faltered, and looked away. 'It's something you didn't use to have . . . this cussedness.'

David watched him steadily; still holding the door-knob. Now that the inanity between them had evaporated he felt relieved. Yet the uncertainty, from which they both acknowledged the inanity as springing, wasn't diminished.

'You're right, anyway, about the loneliness,' he said. 'I found Tony in a vacuum. Beyond that . . . what? I love him. Of course it may be that everything we know is an illusion. What have we that's absolute?'

David lay sprawled for a moment on top of the Master's wall. He was soaked to the skin. The thunder still rumbled overhead like tanks marshalling in the uneasy dawn. Sheet lightning flickered like giant flash-bulbs, weirdly protracted in slow motion. It lit the sleeping edifice of St Cecilia's and the soaring buttresses of Tony's Temple.

'Good morning, sir,' a voice said.

David looked down into the night porter's torch.

'Now don't fall, sir. Just let me have your name.'

'Tony Sandel,' said David. 'No . . . wait a minute. It's David Rogers. I'm not sure. I don't think it makes much difference . . .'

'Soon know,' the porter said soothingly. He seemed to consult a list of some sort. 'Mr Rogers, sir. We don't appear to have a Mr Sandel.'


The shape on the pavement wasn't a dustbin. It was Crawley. He sat hunched under the rain with his feet in the gutter. They stared at one another.

'I'm waiting to see the sunrise,' Crawley said. 'It's something I've never done before.' He trailed his finger in the torrent flowing beneath his knees. 'Rogers . . . Jean's left me. It was yesterday afternoon. We went to Abingdon on the top of a bus. I think we looked at the river . . . there were ducks and things. She stamped her foot in a teashop and said, "Take me home!" Everyone turned to look . . .'

'Did that worry you?' David was cautious.

Crawley seemed unable to find words.

'You see, Rogers, with her I was . . . real. Myself. She gave me . . . validity. Something I couldn't find here. She doesn't belong to the university. We could be real together. We were going to be married . . . No, don't sit down in the rain, man.'

'I'm soaked, anyway,' David said.

'Funny,' Crawley began to muse again. 'Love's an elaborate thing. One reveals so much. Builds so much. So many inter-dependencies. And then . . . Do you have a sheet of paper?'

David produced a page of blank score. 'I've nothing to write with.'

'No! No!' Crawley said, almost in agony. He crouched over the gutter, sheltering the sheet of score from the rain, and began to make a paper boat. A lamp standard near the Taylorian splashed a pale light on the road. Crawley launched his boat with its pin-stripe sails. It carried only a few yards along the gutter and became stranded.

'I'd sensed it coming. I can see that now. But somehow one doesn't believe it. Because one doesn't want to, I suppose. Have you another bit of paper?'

'What will you do?' David asked.

'I don't know. I won't find another Jean. One re-adapts, doesn't one? Life would be unbearable if one didn't. I suppose I'll grow another mask.'

Crawley made to launch the second boat, then crumpled it in his hand. 'We used to play Pooh-sticks at Godstow,' he said. 'You know the game?'

'Yes.'

Crawley rallied suddenly. 'Blast the emotions of women! The trouble about them is that one never knows what's real, and what the artifice of the moment. But Jean wasn't like that. Or rather, we'd gone beyond it. Beyond the initial manoeuvres of courtship. Those can be more trying than fun for a man.

'I'll do other things I've never done before,' he went on, becoming gloomy again. 'I'm going to smoke and drink. Really I'm not here to see the sunrise. I didn't want to dream. I have a recurrent one. I'm clinging to a rope . . . it's vertical, suspended from nothing, going nowhere. My hands begin to slip and they burn. But it doesn't matter because I'm too tired to hold on any more . . .'

'You can hold on to a spanner, I bloody hope?' David said after a minute.

'A what?'

'Tools. I could use help on a car that's got to be ready for a race track by morning.'

'Racing?' Crawley looked helpless. 'It's against University Regulations, isn't it?' Nevertheless he stood up. Near the Radcliffe he startled the night with his first cigarette. When the coughing died away, he said, 'Look, Rogers, I don't think I know your name.'

David smiled faintly. Less than half an hour ago he'd forgotten it himself.

## 17

T HE track was murderous: that was immediately apparent. The rain had stopped, but the damage was irreparable. The converted perimeter of the old airfield glistened damp yellow under a morning mist. Here and there were streaks of burnt rubber beneath the transparent film of moisture. Patches of oil spread slow rings of colour that twisted in agony like fallen rainbows.

David buckled his helmet, and squared his shoulders against the squab of the Series 4 as it vibrated beneath him on the starting grid. He looked over towards the straggling line of spectators by the pits. Girls in sheepskin jackets and headscarves. A few limp mums with papier mâché national emergency coffins. All that was usual for a club event. Immediately on David's left a slim-nosed Lotus Seven was sniffing the ground like a dachshund. David let his own revs dwindle and listened to the snuffling. Over-square Ford 105E probably. He could leave it standing on the grid. On his right was a Zagarto-bodied Fiat-Abarth, its engine buzzing like a bee in a tin. Rich man's car. Not a hope in hell. Behind him were scattered an assortment of Sprites and Berkeleys, a Morgan, a Fairthorpe, and a Turner. Thoroughly business-like all of them. The Series 4 was the nearest approximation to a road car, if only because he'd forgotten to knock off his hub caps. Gentleman Rogers.

The starter had raised his flag. David ran his revs up to 3,500 and held them steady. It would mean a new clutch. So be it. Inevitably, he began muttering into the scarf around his mouth. 'Boys' Bumper Annual,' he said. 'Big Red Racer. Picture covers, and pages like blotting-paper. Daring Dick. Watch it . . .'

The car's back wheels lashed the grid. Instinctively he checked the slide and was away. 'Rogers in the lead,' he said smugly into the scarf. The Abarth whined past him, and they were both glancing treacherously into the sharp right-hander

of Copse. 'Rogers gives way saving the life of a rival driver,'
David muttered.

The cars roared down Hanger Straight like the charge
from a shot gun. Stowe Corner. Tears streamed from David's
eyes, tickling his ears. Insane alignment. He might never have
been to school at Brands Hatch. The Series 4 slashed broad-
side across the track into Stowe. Too fast. 'Discs,' David said;
calmly now. He clamped the pedal: dragged the wheel down
for twelve inches; relinquished it for six. He hauled it round
another eighteen, and let it spring back nine. His strength had
concentrated like anger in his fingers and wrists: otherwise all
his body, save his calf muscles, was relaxed. The car squirmed
dangerously in his hands like a live weasel. But he was through
now; aligned and accelerating on Club Corner, an arrow still
quivering from the shock of the bow. 'Rogers' estate to pass to
Tony Sandel. Codicil. Port for Lang.' He was through Club.
The gentle sweep of Abbey Curve received him like a greased
blowpipe. The hay bales fused together, A Cresta Run of
butter-pats. He was rocketing away down the home straight.

'Rogers, as he lay dying, stretched out his arms towards
the lovely ladies with flowers in their hair, and said, "Give me
lilies with full hand. Make my coffin of sandalwood, and I'll
sleep happy with the ants. Pour a libation of white wine into the
Temple, and then let Sandel sing . . ."' The car took Woodcote
like a trolley-bus with an upper deck load of mercury. David
didn't care. 'Afterwards do not neglect to feed Sandel sufficiently . . .'

The words left his lips but not his ears. He wondered whether
his taking part in the race was anything more than the gesture
of an enfeebled mind. A form of non-genital exhibitionism;
and one where he was his own audience and commentator. He
threw the car accurately into line for a corner. What did the
exercise of power conceal? Was Daring Dick a confrontation
of emptiness? Driving racing cars was patently a pursuit of the
insane.

Sobered, David sat on the tail of the Turner. Someone
had cruelly dented her backside, peeling the paint to the bare
aluminium. He moved his wheel to the right and the Turner's
rear slid left across his windscreen. He brought his left hand
down, but couldn't get past on the other side either. For some
moments he moved his wheel in slow arcs to and fro, whilst the

tail of the Turner oscillated back and forth like a shuttlecock between his windscreen pillars. He bounced the image off the pillars at the exact moment of contact every time. Dick had found a new game.

But the Turner was pulling away. David scowled. The car must be powered by a Climax engine. He thrust out his jaw and relaxed his forearms. Steadily he drew out the Bowdenex cable that opened the throttles; a long, satisfying pull. The engine whined up to a diabolic crescendo.

Still the Turner drew away. They'd been nose to tail through the long curve of Becketts, and were now flat out on Hanger Straight. Suddenly David stiffened. The shock, cramping his forearm, exploded the fingers of his left hand like a bomb casing. The Turner was shitting on the track. At least one con rod had gone clean through the sump, flooding the ground with oil. David snatched his gear lever through the gate. The box howled in protest. He stood on the brake; at the same time dragging the car from its trajectory as sharply as he dared. Too late. His off-side wheels ran, locked, into the spread of oil. The car slithered wildly, span, struck a hay bale, and keeled over with a rending of naked metal on the road. In seconds it was a ball of flame.

David's back was broken. Somehow he'd become detached from the car. Searing pain in his legs grew fainter as warmth spread through his head.

Dark forms stood over him. They were wrapping a sheet about his body, and he fought against it because he couldn't die yet. He was watching another sheeted figure, standing upright on a hillside. Small creatures milled about its base. They had four-cornered hats and black wings like eagles. He knew now that they were going to unveil a statue. The black figures were prancing around it. He had to know what it was. The form beneath the shroud was hard, angular. Tony's body must be carved from box wood; his lips tinted with the blood of a cherry tree. It might be transparent as water. When he realised this panic seized him. He was afraid for the crystal figure because its chest was ice cubes and might melt in the sun. It couldn't be destructible.

David saw the boy once more. He alone was standing before him. He felt that he had created the boy; sculpted him in clay that is nearly dry; its graphite texture tolerant of fine etching.

In the moment of consolidation he was exhausted, unable to move except to throw away his tools. He would never need them again. He was afraid of their strangeness.

But now something was wrong. Perspective had contracted as swiftly as a jazz trombone. He was hurled against his creation when he should stand back from it; cast into the terror of its inception. Then he knew that he had not created the boy, and would never begin to comprehend him: that like a fly struck to the floor during the performance of a symphony he might only lie helplessly beneath the alien music.

## 18

'APPARENTLY you nearly died.' Lang was peering unemotionally down at the bed.

David was laid upon his back. One of his legs was encased in plaster and raised above him as if determined to take a gigantic step up the wall. Over his head was a series of blocks and tackle more appropriate to the Pool of London than the hospital ward in which he supposed he must be lying.

'After deliberation,' Lang went on, 'I've come to the conclusion that it's a pity you didn't.' He had sat down on the edge of the bed and was subjecting the dock equipment to a professional scrutiny. David's head appeared to have achieved a state of weightlessness and a tendency to float off the pillow.

'How's that?'

Lang met his eyes and smiled. 'David, you're now a member of the Roman Catholic Church.'

'I'm *what!*'

'You came over. In delirium, of course. But the faith and the will were there and, well, in such extreme circumstances that is enough.'

David made to speak, but Lang raised an imperious hand.

'Had you died, I'm confident that all would have been well, but *now,*' he indicated David, 'we have to deal with a new resistance – to say nothing of the accumulation of sin since what we had supposed the final absolution. It's going to be tricky,' Lang added thoughtfully. 'The restoration of a salvaged wreck.' He curiously adjusted the salvage equipment above David's bed, and the plaster leg rose helplessly as he manipulated the wires.

David found his voice. 'D'you honestly mean to tell me that while I lay here unconscious you had Jesuits perched on my bed with their ears clapped to my lips?'

'More or less,' Lang confessed modestly. 'It was rather like the conversion of Wilde.'

'Oh, Bruce!' David brought a hand up to ballast his head.

'The Fathers would be distressed if they could hear you now. Their vigil was no short one, you know.'

'I'll bet it wasn't!'

Lang laughed suddenly. 'The Jays *were* here – but of course you're not a convert really – not yet. Incidentally, you're not popular with the Society of St John.'

'Oh? Jays pipped them at the post for the *near* credit of my soul – with Benedictines running a close third? Something like that?'

'The ambulance brigade,' Lang explained dryly. 'Apparently you rose as from the dead and laid one of them out.'

Some memory was returning to David now. 'They tried to roll me up in a shroud. A winding-sheet – you know . . .'

'Blanket. Elementary treatment for shock.'

'Oh,' David tried to move his body, but his waist seemed to be restrained by more plaster. 'Now, supposing you tell me the whole story, beginning with where I am. But first of all, it isn't Saturday yet, is it?'

Lang was looking at him oddly. 'It's Thursday.'

David looked down at his incarcerated form, and dwelt clearly upon his predicament for the first time.

'Okay. So where am I?'

'Acland Nursing Home.'

'And what does that little notice say?'

Lang crossed the room and peered at the discreetly framed notice on the wall. '"The foundation of the Acland . . ."'

'Guts, man, for God's sake!'

Lang returned to the bedside chair, where the length of his legs reduced his posture of professional attention to absurdity. 'Twenty-four guineas a week, excluding surgery,' he announced. Despairing of dignity, he reversed the chair, straddled it, and gazed at David intently, while resting his elbows on the chair's back.

'Where on earth am I supposed to get twenty-four guineas from?'

'Nearer two hundred, actually.' Lang was looking puzzled again.

David's alarm was growing. 'Now wait a minute. On whose authority was I cleaned up as a private patient? And surely a place like this doesn't take people still covered with blood . . . casualties? Why wasn't I taken to the Radcliffe or somewhere?'

'You were; initially. As to the authority which moved you here, that was the college. The Senior Dean discovered on battels that you subscribed to a health insurance scheme. So, when the Radcliffe intimated that they were tired of you, the college had you moved here on battels though less I imagine from any sense that it was indecent for St Cecilia's men, or even ex-St Cecilia's men, to die in public, than because it was the obvious thing to do.'

David now clutched his head with both hands. It had become ludicrously articulated like Thompson's. 'Singly, Bruce! Come slowly! The Radcliffe were *tired* of me?'

'Yes.'

'Now ex-St Cecilia's men?'

Lang's perplexity had become a frown. 'You mean you don't *know* that they sent you down?'

'You're the first visitor I've *consciously* received, man, damn it!' The day of awakening was proving something of a trial.

Lang had risen in confusion. 'David! I had no idea . . . they told me you'd been conscious for several days . . .'

'On and off. I remember now. A doctor and a nurse, I think. All internals, though.'

Lang began to mumble something, but David cut him short.

'You couldn't have known. Of course, I knew all along that racing cars is against Proctorial Regulations. But we're not quite through.'

'How?' Lang looked up.

'Since when has your intended profession taken to moving patients around whilst in a coma, and within days of a major accident? And what about that two hundred quid? Did the ambulance man claim damages – or have I undergone a little surgery on the local private table?' As he spoke, David gestured towards the notice on the wall.

Lang, who seemed to have regained his customary composure, promptly lost it again. A frown furrowed his brow like the work of a drunken ploughman. He started to take a copy of *The Times* out of the pocket of his hairy sports jacket, then apparently thought better of it.

'David, I told you a moment ago that it was Thursday, and it is. But it is Thursday the first of September. You've been unconscious for just over ten weeks.' Lang, who had been looking at him steadily while he made this announcement, now handed him the paper.

David took it, but laid it down without looking at it. His body had gone strangely cold. Gooseflesh had colonised his neck, and was making inroads behind his ears and along his cheek-bones. When he moistened his lips they felt like Ozymandias' stones in the desert.

'I promised to meet Tony. On the fence where we often met. He must have sat there waiting . . . and I didn't come . . .'

'You *look* well enough,' Lang pronounced: he had taken a turn about the room. 'But if I don't go soon they'll as like as not throw me out and prefer manslaughter. I only got in anyway because the house surgeon is one of our part-time instructors. You're supposed to be resting.'

David didn't smile. 'Your visit has proved bloody salubrious so far. Just supposing you go off and persuade someone to produce one of those wandering telephones. A place like this must have sockets in every room.'

Lang was holding up his hand. It was that empirical gesture of his that commanded mute attention. One day it must be enlisted to help open graves. Now he merely said, 'News! As regards that wretched small boy, I collected a number of letters from your pigeon-hole in the J.C.R. which I imagine are his. At least, the handwriting has a spidery quality and a tendency to protract itself diagonally across the face of the envelope in a manner that suggests it could only be that of a choirboy. The characters appear microscopic or ballooned, and the script, in a word, might be said to mince over the paper. Further,' Lang continued reminiscently, 'I couldn't help remarking that the postcard – there is one – carries a superfluous capital X and a zero, while the illustration strikes me as being a strange choice for a child.'

While Lang unwound himself, David had stretched a hand out of the bed. 'You seem to have scrutinised my post with the eye of a lover yourself.'

'My devotion to it didn't end there, I assure you!' Lang produced a large envelope from his breast pocket. 'I sealed them in here, so that they might be preserved from thoughtless abuses such as bending, atmospheric pollution and so on. Also,' Lang fished in another pocket and produced a card of ribbon, 'I bought this after some consultation with a young woman in Woolworths who assured me that pink would be "nicest" for the purpose.'

David's outstretched hand had become inanimate during this pantomime. Now it was allowed to close on Tony's letters. He drew the fathom of pins and needles back to the bed.

'Tongue, please,' Lang said curtly.

'What?'

'Put out your tongue!' David put out his tongue.

'Mmmm!' Lang shook his head. 'You know, you haven't smoked for ten weeks yet your tongue still looks like a doormat. Makes you think, doesn't it? All right, I'll see what can be done about a telephone, though probably my name will be struck off the medical register before it's even on it as a result.'

'It will be anyway if you insult your patients' tongues . . . Always stop at the "Mmmm!", and don't hazard matey remarks.'

Lang looked at the envelope, which David had made no move to open. 'I'm going to wander round the lawn. Only don't take wing like a Tinkerbell. I don't want to have to come hunting for you in Kensington Gardens or wherever that fragile correspondence comes from.'

## 19

WHEN Lang had gone David considered the envelope, and then looked about him in the small room. He had no previous memory of it, and so presumably he had become fully conscious for the first time that day. It was strange there had been no medical interruption while Lang had been with him – no beating of tambourines, or even ritual admonitions to rest and save his strength. But then perhaps he had been coming half-heartedly to the surface for some days, and his recovery had been predictable.

David looked again at the large envelope in his hands. His eyes strayed away from it across the cream-walled room which was quite bare save for a single, pale lily in a pewter vase, the chair on which Lang had sat, and an ill-disguised Victorian commode, whose achievement would doubtless become his sole physical ambition in the weeks that must follow. In fact the commode did literally stand in the pathway to the light, for it was placed in front of what he now saw to be a french window giving on to a series of terraced lawns. At the bottom of the garden was an oak whose bearing only mocked the subservience of his own absurdly trapped mortality. It was four o'clock, but already late afternoon. The sunshine was thinned like a painter's sunshine: diluted with turpentine so that it flows irresistibly cold to the corners of the canvas. The same chill had suffused the entire scene which the window framed. The softened, melon-flesh green of the oak leaves, and curling grey petals from the collapsed rose heads, were already allied in their gradual submission to the tonal equality of winter. For the first time the freak result of his accident was fully comprehensible to him. He had slept into the autumn.

David turned once more to Lang's reinforced envelope, realising that he had only sought to delay the moment when Tony must leap out alive from the pages of his letters. The postcard bore the earliest date, and had been sent from Cambridge on June the 8th; the day Tony was to have played in the match against Kings. The message said simply: *Nought not out! See you on Saturday. Love T.* It carried in addition the symbols to which Lang had referred, while the picture was a photograph of a statue, which suggested that Tony had made the Fitzwilliam Museum after all. Like Hamley standing up for the anthem, the statue had no arms.

Of the further letters the first was dated June 12th, or the day after the proposed meeting by the fence. David opened it without allowing himself time for thought. Tony's voice came to him quite as clearly as he'd feared:

*Dear David,*

*Did you forget on Saturday? I was there at half past two.
I hope you are not ill or anything, or that you were tired
of me. Anyway, I thought you must have forgotten. Then I
looked all along the fence in case you had left a message. I
missed Evensong. There was an awful row. Mrs Jones was
wild. I said I thought I'd lost my memory like in a film I saw
once. Then Mrs Jones said, 'The child is upset, Harold',
and squashed me into her bosom. Will you write soon?*

*Lots of Love, Tony?*

*P.S. One of my fish died. I think it was the thunder.*

David passed the sleeve of his pyjamas over his face and
opened the next letter mechanically. He wished to God that
Lang had opened them months ago, and that the discretion
that was at this moment withholding the telephone had yielded
to common sense when Lang first saw the postcard. Still,
he'd spun the Series 4 into that Turner's oil through his own
stupidity. A careless betrayal of his academic career was one
thing: a betrayal of Tony another. Desperately David looked
through the french window, but there was no sign of Lang.
There wasn't even a bell connected in the room, and he had
nothing more substantial to throw at the window than his
wrist-watch. He might as well have been in a straitjacket.

The second letter was post-marked ten days later:

*Dear David,*

*I haven't had a letter from you yet. I know you are ill. I
hope you get better soon. But don't worry if you can't write.
Can you ask someone to tell me where you are?*

*I've got it in my diary that your term ends tomorrow
so after practice this morning I went along the quad and
rang the bell of the Master's Lodging to see if he knew
where you are. I think it was a butler who came because
he had a tailcoat like a conductor. It was the same man
who took our caps at our party there at Christmas. He
called me 'Master Sandel', and said that Sir Eustace and
Lady Janet were in America. Then I said that I wanted
to know where you were but that it was all rather private,*

*and he said there was a don called Mr Ricks, I think, who knew most about 'the young gentlemen', and would I 'be pleased to follow' him. There was a maid dusting things in the hall and the butler said, 'Smith, receive any callers whilst I escort Master Sandel across the quadrangle.' Then he led me right across the quad holding his arms stiff at his sides. I thought I was supposed to keep step with him like in gymn but it was difficult as there was a gale blowing and my gown kept blowing up almost over my head. When we got to the don's rooms the butler said, 'Excuse me, sir, but one of the choristers, Master Antony Sandel, is anxious to determine the whereabouts of Mr Rogers, and has called at the Master's Lodging, I thought it proper to refer Master Sandel to yourself, sir.' The don said, 'Thank you, Mekin,' and the butler went away. When he had gone the don looked at me and said, 'Extraordinary!' He was a tiny little man with white hair and looked quite nice. He son of shuffled right round me in a circle while I stood still and tried to follow him with my head. When he got round to my front again he said, 'Extraordinary!' just like before. Then he took his gown out of a cupboard and put it on. I suppose because I was wearing mine. When he came back he said, 'So you're a friend of Rogers?' I said, 'Yes,' and he walked right round me again. Then he gave me a glass of lime juice.*

*After that he was very nice – rather like my grandmother who's dead. He said you were in hospital but he thought you would get better soon and would write to me. He said that there were 'some difficulties with the college too' but that I mustn't worry and that he had been thinking about you 'very hard' in the last few days. He had a file, like the ones we have for geography but bigger, which he said were notes about you. He wrote some more notes in and said, 'Extraordinary!' when he looked at them.*

*When I was going he said he hoped I would come up to St Cecilia's when I was 'grown up' but that he would be dead. Then he called his scout to show me back into the quad and said I mustn't worry again. So now I know you are ill but I don't know where you are. I hope you get better soon. I hope you don't mind my asking the don about you.*

*Lots of Love, Tony*

David drew a long breath. It would take Tony to call on the
Master when he felt it to be advisable. Heaven knew there
were enough fourth-year men, and even incorrigible ex-G.I.
Fullbrights, whom the very sight of the door-bell in the Great
Quad would cripple. The thought of Tony's erupting upon
Ricks, who of course had never seen a boy, was equally superb.
Still, the idea of Ricks inspecting Tony as an alien species
was disquieting. In what context, too, might Ricks have been
'thinking hard' about himself? Anyway, it was something that
Tony had learned within a fortnight that he was ill and had not
abandoned him, though the knowledge would have done little
to explain his continuing silence. Presumably, too, Ricks had
been unable or unwilling to reveal his whereabouts when Tony
saw him.

There was still no sign of Lang. Though he had only been
gone some twenty minutes, the sun had already dropped down
behind the garden wall, and it was both colder and darker in
the room.

David opened the final letter, which had been posted about
three weeks after the last in Budleigh Salterton. He had read
only a few lines when he became aware that this letter differed
distinctly from either of the previous ones. It was not that
the interim weeks appeared to have worked a greater despair
in the boy, nor was there any sign of an outraged patience.
The letter involved only a present, but it was a present whose
composition was an unconscious sum of its past. Tony wrote
as someone newly possessed of a finer awareness. Of maturity
even; though maturity was too gross a word.

David returned again to the beginning of the letter and, as
he read on, the ill-defined sense of some new dimension in
Tony grew, and with it there was splashed on to his mind's
eye a vision so absolute in its power to command him that for
the moment while it lasted he seemed to be struggling for the
survival of his senses. The image had been simply of the boy,
as he was, writing a grubby letter with a ball-point on a hillside.

With all his force David swung his suspended leg at the adjacent wall. What might have been a whine of protest came from
the other side. The plaster spattered down on the bed and he
grinned inanely at the dent, denuded of its glossy paint. It was
like the backside of the Turner. David lashed the wall again for

good measure and this time the human origin of the protest
was unmistakable. He turned again to the smudged letter:

*Dear David,*

*I still haven't got your letter yet and I think it must have
got lost in the post. Our postman has only one leg, so could
you send another letter?*

*I had to tell my aunt about you – a bit, because you're
my friend and I don't know where you are. She said you
were probably all right, but I don't know how she can know
if I don't. I asked her anyway though.*

*We had a concert here. I had quite a big part and wore
your other suit. They want me to sing, in something of
Vittoria's I think, at a hall in London. It may be on tele-
vision. After the concert here a little girl came up on the
platform and gave a bunch of flowers to a lady who gave
a talk about how good the concert was. Then she stood on
her toes and kissed me. Everyone clapped. I think it was
all sort of arranged. I wiped my face and they all shouted
'Shame!' and laughed. Afterwards I washed my face. I've
written a letter to London and said I'll only sing if I'm
not kissed like that. There's a more professional concert
in Exeter soon. The one here was local, you know. There
probably won't be talks and drippy flowers in Exeter. I am
in demand! Ho-hum!*

*David, I'm writing this on top of a cliff here. There is a
liner I think going past, but it's too far away to see its name
or how many funnels it's got. I don't know why I did something funny. I hope you won't be offended or anything, but
I don't think you will. I rolled the other new suit into a ball
with stones in and dropped it into the sea. I think I did it
because of what you said about worrying. I've got some old
cotton shorts on which are dirty but I don't mind. I've got
very brown so I think you would like me! I can't be bare
because we aren't allowed to be here. I've got my sandals
off though. I've still got the other best suit, only just for
concerts.*

*Near here there's a stream that runs into the sea. It's
called the Otter. I thought I'd tell you because I know you
like the names of streams. You can drink the water high up.*

*If you follow it down through the bracken to the sea and taste it every hundred steps you can feel it getting saltier on your tongue. Then it is the sea.*

*David — I don't know why I go on saying 'David' like that: I hope you don't think I'm a drip. David, I haven't any friends here and sometimes I'm horribly bored. There's only a boy of my age. He keeps on wanting to play silly games and follows me round. I don't like that so I just walk away. I said he was filthy and I'd tell his mother. (Of course I wouldn't have though.) That settled him! He bought me a choc-ice. I put it down his neck. He has very ugly clothes — Terylene. Sorry!*

*I'm quite looking forward to next term and also I'm not. It's hard to explain. I feel I've grown out of it. The place irritates me. Mrs Jones specially is fussy in a stupid way. Anyhow I'll be able to see you often and I have to go back for the extra term because old Bull wants me. Most of the work will be in the early part of the term. We've got some recordings to make for the Argo company then too. Kings are all right in that flowery way, you know, but we've got more 'guts there'. That's confidential! The man who was at our concert here told me. Oh, the man wants to buy just me for one record and have a picture on the sleeve. I said I must ask my aunt and you first.*

*I've got to go now. The grass is boiling hot and there are midges and the liner has gone. I'm going to put two fourpenny stamps on this so they'll feel it's important and you'll get it.*

*Lots of Love, Tony. XO.*

*P.S. Have you done your photos yet? Perhaps we could have one of the ones of me as a statue on the record sleeve. No, I suppose we couldn't!*

*Love, T.*

David folded the letter back into its envelope and stared at the deserted flying trapeze above his head. It was dark outside and there was nothing else to look at. His eyes caught the scar his plaster heel had made when he'd kicked the wall and he wanted suddenly to apologise to the occupant of the room next door.

Lang carried in the phone as Mekin might have done if asked to handle such a device. Evidently though, Lang's distrust had a less dignified cause.

'This,' he announced, untangling himself from yards of flex, 'could prove my undoing, with your death making for the actual indictment. You'll make a maximum of two unemotional calls of such duration only as is strictly needful, and I myself must have left the sanatorium within fifteen minutes. Meanwhile the entire British Medical Council is strategically disposed throughout the garden and each of its members armed with a copy of the Hippocratic Oath.'

Lang paused, and David looked at him dryly.

'You know, Bruce, I've been listening to a child . . . a boy . . . who derives more unselfconscious sense from monosyllables than you could hope to convey after a five-year course at a school of Subversive Oratory. What's more, his effects aren't obtained like clotted cream – that's to say he doesn't wander round a garden with a verbal simmering-pan coagulating rhetorical fats. Even if he did, he wouldn't at a time when someone was waiting for a telephone which only he could bring. Now give!'

Lang raised his eyebrows, and still withheld the telephone. When he opened his mouth David could see that something big was coming.

'Believe me, David, I should be the first to uphold the superior accomplishment of innocence. But I fail to see how you may be said to have upheld the innocent state of the said choirboy Hildebrand Kirtle, or whatever his name is. Your pose is hypocritical.'

Lang shot out the last word with unprecedented simplicity. Somewhere a temple screen had probably split in two.

'The name's Tony Sandel, as you well know,' David said. He was feeling more than a little weary. 'As to innocence, we have different conceptions of it. To me innocence is right standing in relation to truth. I hate whatever offends against it. I hate illusions. Life is like one of those fields in Normandy which the Germans were afraid the allies might land paratroops and gliders in. So what did they do? They painted obstructions on canvas where really there was nothing but an open field. The allies lacked the nerve to make a landfall. If they had they might have brought liberation where it was unthinkable before.'

'And who in this colourful panegyric are the Germans?'

'Not just convention. Convention's often right. But blind adherence to a convention that mayn't be questioned if only because the act of questioning would itself offend the convention. Incidentally, by "convention" I don't specifically mean conventional morality – as you might be tempted to suppose.'

'Oh?' Lang had raised his eyebrows, which were rather like suburban doormats. The telephone was still out of reach.

'No. A whole colony of self-delusions – amongst which I'd number some of the gambits of Rome. Though not the basic idea, maybe,' David added.

'Basic *idea!*' Lang threw up the suburban doormats to heaven for spring-cleaning.

David exploited the confusion by grabbing the telephone. It wasn't plugged in.

'As with all your emotional philosophies, David, you fail to deduce a convincing conclusion.' Lang had carefully realigned his eyebrows in their customary place. 'You implied a moment ago that you hadn't betrayed *your* innocence because you hadn't offended *your* truth. What causes you to suppose that the boy's innocence isn't spoiled?'

David abandoned the attempt to hold his head on the pillow. 'Neither Sandel nor I were aware of any ugliness . . . far from it. We were drawn together without thought. We landed in one of those fields that had been dishonestly disguised. So far neither of us has been disappointed with what we found there.'

Lang had given a shrug. The shrug, perhaps, of a minor fisher of Galilee who had caught another net-full of empty water. Neither of them spoke. David lay back exhausted. Cold spread over his body like a tide. Once – perhaps many times before – his own words had failed to leave his ears. He looked steadily at the scaffolding. For an instant terror hung over him quite as menacingly as ever it had done in the form of the music-room ceiling at home. When he spoke again it was uncertainly.

'Underneath the words . . . what's real? *Am* I living a lie? So many odd things can become precious to a man . . . and he fanatical about them. You know – a dry-fly fisherman, say – who thinks the world's insane. Could I be on a hobbyhorse too? If I am, what about Tony . . .'

Lang had got up. 'You're one of Nature's trapped poets, David. A mad one, I think.'

Startled by the directness, David looked at him quickly. Then he saw that the telephone was plugged in. 'Now, wait a minute!' he said. 'There's no doubt *you've* a façade. What's the mystery beneath *it?*'

'You're impossible,' Lang said.

## 20

T HE Medical Council were showing considerable restraint. So far they had failed to erupt through the french window, nor indeed had there been any other disturbance, though Lang had already outstayed his fifteen minutes' grace.

David asked the hospital switchboard for the Budleigh Salterton number. His stomach was taut. Lang, he noticed, was frowning, and he raised his eyebrows to learn more. Lang took the cue.

'I'm just wondering what this aunt or whatever is going to think when a *strange man* rings up asking for her pretty ward.'

David said nothing. The line had gone dead. Suddenly a female voice reached into his ear. It was like a tremolo heartily sustained on an oboe.

'Prudence Laying. Yes?'

'Miss Laying, my name's . . .'

'Yes, David; I know.'

'Yes. I'm ringing . . .'

'From the hospital; they told me.'

'Why, yes . . .' David cast a helpless glance at Lang, who had drawn nearer. 'Miss Laying, I wonder whether I might. . .'

'Ant is in London for the day.'

'Ant?' Someone had dried up David's mouth with a flamethrower.

'Antony. My nephew!'

'Oh, of course! Forgive me . . .'

'Now, just a moment, young man.' The oboe had gone into a firm andante. 'The operator told me the call was coming from the hospital. Is that right?'

'Yes. I'm . . .'

'Very well then. In that case I must first speak to your doctor, as I have quite a lot to say to you.'

Throughout the conversation Lang had been listening in with his neck strained towards the receiver. Now he suddenly slapped his hand over the mouthpiece. David looked at him in bewilderment.

'Lie! For God's sake lie, man!' Lang hissed.

David stared at him stupidly. Then the reason for Lang's alarm dawned on him. At the same time the shock of witnessing so complete a *volte-face* in Lang seemed to have lubricated his mouth. He looked quickly at the receiver, which Lang still held muffled.

'To meet melodrama with kind, boyo, I may lie to find Tony; but to deny him, never. You've got the wrong station for triple cock-crows – so desist – for Pete's sake!'

The exchange had lasted only seconds. With a shrug Lang deferred the situation to higher authority, and abandoned the receiver to David.

'I'm sorry,' David spoke again into the black bowl. 'I was interrupted. No, I'm quite well enough to talk. All I wanted was to let Tony know I'm all right. I haven't been able to answer his letters because I was involved in an accident. In fact I've been unconscious for ten weeks.'

'That's extraordinary, and most unfortunate! I do hope you'll be better very soon. But I think you've already answered the challenge I had to put to you.'

'Challenge?' David glanced at Lang, who was struggling like Deiphobe endeavouring to rid herself of the possession of Phoebus.

'Yes. About the nature of your relationship with Antony.'

Phoebus had got the better of Lang. He was visibly breaking up.

'Now tell me,' Miss Laying's voice continued, 'do you intend to go on seeing my nephew?'

'Why, yes!'

'Good. That's settled then. You had better keep up this half-brother pretence.'

David swallowed.

'There's no need to prevaricate, David.' Miss Laying must have ears like a bat. Possibly her eyes could track sputniks in daylight. 'I was most intrigued when Mrs Jones rang up to say that Antony wouldn't be needing a new suit because his brother had turned up unexpectedly and bought him two! I had the impression that Mrs Jones was not only going out of her way, but that she doubted Antony *had* a brother.'

'Then you . . .'

'I concluded that anyone whom Ant had persuaded to indulge his vanity must have discovered a mutually happy relationship with him.'

'Then what did you tell her?'

'Tell her? I told her that I should not expect to find the cost of the telephone call on my bill!'

David let his head roll on the pillow. His mouth gaped at the ceiling. The only infringement of the morality he had outlined to Lang had been his involving Tony in one lie – the brother pose. Since no one could deny the right of this Laying to summarily elect brothers, or to ordain anything else for that matter, he was absolved from his only sin. Lang was sunk in meditation on the tail of his bed. David was startled from his own vacancy by another injunction from Budleigh.

'Don't trust her! That woman's stupid, as you'll discover if you meet her.'

'I only caught a glimpse of her when I was at the school . . .'

'What did you think of her?' Miss Laying shot the question. 'I don't know, she didn't speak to me. She *looked* like a brief stack of doughnuts. Sort of dumpy.' David had been steadily warming to Miss Laying. Now he was finding words. The conditions of human communication were odd. 'Tony, I know, regards her as something of a dark presence. I don't think he's quite clear why he does though.'

'No children for one thing.' Miss Laying was positive. 'What do you think of the Ghoul?'

'The . . .?'

'The Ghoul, David. *Gould!*'

'Oh! A sad man, I think.'

There was a snort in David's ear, like a rogue elephant wondering in which direction to charge. It didn't ponder long.

'He's perverse! Ties boys up.'

'Ties . . .?'

'Ropes the Wolf Cubs to trees to demonstrate reef-knots.'

David tried to envisage Hunter bound to a tree. It didn't
seem quite right somehow.

'Anyway, he's left.'

'Retired?'

'Yes. Great Scott, though! I'm talking backwards. I've told
Jones to offer you the post if you want it. He seems to have
been most impressed by you.'

'There was some crazy suggestion the moment I stepped
into the building,' David said slowly. 'As a matter of fact I'm
now free . . .'

'Then accept it. You might make Ant's last term at that
dreadful little school human. Anyway, I'll tell him you're safe
as soon as he gets back, and explain why you were unable to
write. Whatever you decide, take care of him.'

'I'll do my best,' David said, and put the receiver down.
Then it occurred to him that neither the astonishing Prudence
nor himself had said goodbye. Well, sometimes people didn't.
Lang was only partially restored. The spiritual dilemma looked
like being a long one. At any rate it engrossed him entirely, for
when David phoned Jones, and promised to confirm his intention of filling the post vacated by the Ghoul in writing, Lang
made no protest beyond a symbolic tearing of his hair.

Now David was able to relax. Conceivably his comfort lay
in once more becoming officially, if remotely, connected with
the body corporate of St Cecilia. But then, conceivably again,
perhaps it did not. Either way, the job would be more honest
than others open to disgraced St Cecilia's men. He might well,
for instance, become rent collector for her many scattered
slum lands; or even the incumbent of one of the cosier livings
she owned.

Lang had risen from the foot of the bed. 'You know, David,
your condition is still what the bulletins would call critical. My
own diagnosis is that your brain's suffered more damage than
was at first supposed. It always flirted with the lunatic fringe,
but now it would appear to have completely succumbed. The
last half-hour hasn't been a happy time for a friend to have to
have witnessed. I'm going, but I'll have a few words with your
nurse on my way out.'

David waved his arms. 'No, stop! There're a lot of things I
still want to know.'

'Like what?' Lang was expansive. For all the new pose,

which was clearly a temporary defence flung up to prepare the party line, he was visibly cheered. Perhaps by the knowledge that Miss Laying wasn't searching the attic for a horse-whip.

'Like what the hell you're doing in Oxford in the vacation, for one thing?'

Lang inclined his head.

'I thought as much. Your brother's keeper. Well, what about the car?'

'I eventually sold it to a motor fiend with black fingernails and pebble-lenses who was apparently on the spot with spanners within seconds of your crash. Your engine, it seems, was a "sweetly-blown 100E with a genius valve job" – did you know that?'

David laughed.

'The proceeds,' Lang went on, 'I burned. Fifty candles, distributed for modesty's sake between The Chaplaincy, Campion Hall, Greyfriars and St Bennet's, and dedicated in equal division to the salvation of your own soul and that of that wretched small boy. There was exactly two shillings and sixpence remaining from the total balance of two pounds ten, which I expended on this Penguin edition of Thomas A Kempis.'

Lang produced a Penguin Classic bordered with sacramental purple. David bowed as best he might as he accepted the gift. There was something touching about the thought of twenty-five candles burning for Tony with bright daggers of flame.

'So the Series 4 was written off. What about me?'

Lang made the transformation to a temporal physician whose attentions were conscientious, if reluctant, because necessarily mundane. He pulled what is called a long face. 'Initially, I understand, there was subdural haemorrhage, which meant boring a hole in your skull and draining it discreetly like a coconut. That's where I'm afraid they may have evacuated too much – or, again perhaps, too little.'

David began tentatively exploring his skull.

'Oh, you won't find it there now.' Lang was reassuring. 'It will have healed; despite the remarkable thickness of your skull. So odd that, by the way, that they took photographs and measurements.'

'Oh.'

'After that,' Lang spread his hands, 'severe concussion continued until a few days ago. Previously, though, you seemed nearer consciousness on several occasions.'

'And that's when you called in the Jesuits.'

'Yes.'

'Tell me no more.'

'All right.' Lang was surprised. 'As regards bones, though, you only had a cracked left hip, and a fairly nasty complex fracture of your right leg.' He indicated David's humiliated member. 'Bone protruded indecently from your trousers.'

David regarded the plaster sourly. At least the Jesuits didn't appear to have written their initials on it. 'And what date do you calculate for the Resurrection?'

Lang looked wary.

'Come along, Bruce! When comes the promised time? When do I stand erect again?'

'You can't,' said Lang. 'Not in that abdominal plaster. That's why I was going to suggest you practise flirting with your nurse. You have the perfect alibi.'

'Full marks,' David conceded a little wearily. 'You know bloody well I meant when will I be on my feet again.'

'Can't really say.' Lang assumed professional ethics again. 'Fractures should be healed by now, so I imagine the plaster could come off any day. Then if your head is all right, your body will still be very weak. I'd say three weeks. Only don't quote that at the Establishment or they'll keep you another six.'

David frowned. 'Just tell them that Rogers *purposes* to be up in three weeks.'

'No.' Lang turned at the door. 'I'll look in again in a few days. There's an accumulation of less personal letters, for one thing. By the way, your landlady apparently called, and also sent your, *brother* a chocolate cake. That tutor of yours, Thompson, was here too. Broke in because he wanted to see for himself whether your concussed state looked any different from your normal tutorial one. That was before they'd sent you down. He came again afterwards. If you hear a shot in the corridor it'll only be the Medical Council executing summary justice.'

David smiled and raised his hand in farewell.

✧

David lay back on straightened pillows. A nurse had provided paper, a meal like soft soap, and a half-hour's delay before the pills. He had tried Donne to no effect:

> For every hour that thou wilt spare me now,
> I will allow,
> Usurious God of Love, twenty to thee.

It hadn't worked. The pills would come.

The letter to Thompson must wait. It wouldn't be easy. He'd not been wrong about Thompson; but he'd wronged him. Mrs Kanter and Jones must wait too; as must the telegram to Harrods to replace the tropical fish the thunder had killed.

David was exhausted. The nurse had left the curtains undrawn. He could see the oak tree standing out against a deep sky, that had the clarity of Christmas. There were no clouds, but a wind had sprung up. David had an almost Wordsworthian apprehension of the magic that lay hidden in the winds. Thompson, he reflected, would probably be astonished at the idea. But then he had a no more explicable, or less deeply rooted, love for the autumn as well. It wasn't a death wish, because no season held such exhilaration for him. Yet the sense of quietus was there: a sense of journeying down the emptying corridor of the contracted days, resignedly, but with a keener expectation that bared the senses until, everywhere, they could watch, and hear the shallower breathing of the world. Now this expectation was heightened in him, because he had been reborn with a new body on the threshold of autumn; and because of the sense of a new dimension in Tony, whose mystery he had only glimpsed in the heavy summer.

David wrote a few words with the pencil he'd been given. He filled half a page. Tomorrow he could write again. Then he began to use symbols which he better understood; which Tony would better understand as well. He struggled to contain the ocean which the manuals of the organ might release beneath his fingers. Instead, he drew out a simple line of melody that flowed swiftly glinting like the Windrush or the Evenlode in the sun. But the new stream, running like dimpled glass over the cheeks of the boulders, was the Otter; and David allowed it to

get saltier as it tumbled towards the sea. He released the organ
to meet it with a smiling, tidal embrace. Then, of course, the
Otter was the sea.

David swallowed the red pills. He held out the letter to the
nurse. 'Would you put two fourpenny stamps on it? You see,
the postman at the other end only has one leg.'

The nurse poked a thermometer under his tongue. She lifted
his limp wrist with three firm fingers and nodded indulgently.

## 21

DISPOSED on her bed Gloria looked like something
toppled over in the cast rooms of the Victoria and Albert
Museum. As the facetious image passed through David's mind
he hated himself for the nervous insulation he knew it represented. He was discovering Gloria's real kindness, but custom
died hard. Now he tangled his fingers in her hair. It was something to hold.

'Go on,' Gloria said. 'Tell me about Peter.'

Instead, David smiled at her slowly. 'Gloria, I think you're
the only adult I know. We pretend to be grown-up here. Really
we're all of us self-involved children.'

'Aren't you saying *we* when you mean *I*?'

'Maybe!' David laughed. He moved his leg, which was still
stiff.

'I've listened to a lot of you,' Gloria said. 'You're more
self-pitying than most.'

David looked at her quickly; then grinned. 'Probably. The
world's a pretty pitiful place. Just sometimes one finds something, or someone who's not.'

'My, aren't we glum! *Peter!*' Gloria said firmly.

'Oh!' David was off-hand. 'Peter was just a kid.' He could
hear his words continuing into the room: not a boy, or a child,
but 'a kid'. It was the nervous, distancing device again. Aloud
he went on, 'My landlady's basement lodger makes some bitter
remarks about public schools — though God knows he's no

cause to – except that I annoy him. Or rather used to, when I'd nothing better to do. Poor old Sweeney . . .'

David lit a cigarette and let his head fall back on the floor. His hospital hair cushioned the shock. 'I'll give you an example of public school mores. Sex Talks. Outside doctor . . . a specialist . . . steams in. Pretty giggles in the second and third forms. Blushes and feet-shifting in the fifth and sixth. First: colour slides about flowers. Graduation: birds and bees. Then astonishing photos of the female body. As a throwaway, the chap mentions he's the father of fourteen daughters. One begins to see why. Okay. So far it's been honest. But the lies are coming. You can sense the chap relaxing even his cock in his attempt to be casual. The audience beginning to quiver like a heat haze. "About these homosexuals," he says. "Don't get involved, boys. Ill tell you why. I knew a homosexual once, and his mother died. He shot himself. There wasn't much else he could do."'

Gloria leant over the bed suddenly and kissed David's ear.

'Hang on. You haven't had the scientific proof yet. One of the boys did . . . A few days later. Only he hadn't got a gun, and the pathologist said the rope must have broken first time. Apparently the police can tell when a tree's been climbed twice too . . .'

'Was it Peter? Someone you knew?'

'It was Peter,' David said slowly. 'But do you ever *know* someone you love?' He looked out through the un-curtained window; down towards the canal at the bottom of the narrow garden.

'That's your axe then?'

David looked up.

'No. I've none to grind . . . or not consciously. It's all blacked out . . . Unreal. Perhaps I didn't believe it at the time. You can't think of a child of fourteen hanging himself . . . or not when you're only seventeen yourself. Sometimes, though, I get a nightmare glimpse of the state of his mind. This, maybe slight, but tender, wonderful thing he'd found, made monstrous by irresponsible lies. Of his struggle to maintain its Tightness, for him, and at that time . . . Then of the struggle's breaking him . . .'

Gloria was sitting on the bed; her legs over the side against which David leant his back.

'Why d'you think he did it, David?'

'I don't really know. Virtually over nothing at all. I think he got silly the way little boys can and kissed a prefect . . . in front of a notice board. His housemaster had been talking to him about it. It all added up. That wasn't the tiny column the Headmaster gave *The Times,* though. Funny that!' David laughed suddenly. 'Until then one had thought the Headmaster, *The Times,* and Test cricketers were God's truth.'

Gloria began swinging her legs idly. 'He must have been unstable and neurotic in the first place anyway.'

David said nothing.

'Then you ran away?'

'Just as fast as I could. Europe. Then North Africa. I was sick of white faces . . . but more ashamed of my own. I wanted raw elements . . . beauty and ugliness mixed. You can't imagine the squalor of Tunis . . . Or the beauty of the Arabs. They have the most regular teeth in the world . . . Hair as black as the windows of their houses . . .'

David drew away, and sprawled his half-naked body out on the carpet. He could hear owls calling near the canal in the darkness, and the sound of a radio came through the wall of the semi-detached house. 'I'm sorry, Gloria. To have made such a nuisance . . . and fool of myself.'

Gloria had something on at last. She was moving about the room, doing ordinary, human things. Now she was lighting a gas-ring.

## 22

T HERE could be no doubt that Mrs Jones was large. In fact she was built like an ice-breaker, and gave the impression of being a woman who would be perpetually on manoeuvres in home waters. David found himself hoping that home waters might be limited to the flat in which he was standing. Now Mrs Jones threw up her hands impatiently, and with a quick smile at David, which was strangely tight in the flabby, chow-like surround of her face, hustled out of the room in search of some missing item of tea equipment.

David had spent the morning incarcerated with Jones in an under-stair cupboard effect with a Yale lock, which evidently served the school as operational headquarters, and where he had received some sketchy improvisation as to the nature of his duties. Since, until his arrival that morning, Jones had forgotten all about his engagement, these would themselves be improvisation. Nevertheless, it was at some sort of timetable that Jones was now scratching away in the corner.

The early afternoon David had spent alternatively unpacking armfuls of clothing and possessions in the large first-floor room until recently inhabited by the Ghoul, and collapsing into an armchair before the leaded window with its distorting diamond panes for a cigarette. He had been on his feet now for ten days, but still felt weak. The window gave on to a prospect of St Cecilia's Great Park, where it lay flanked on the south by the river. The northernmost horizon of David's vision was marked by the back of Corpus and the squat tower of Merton, standing like a castle of gold ingots in the sun; while away on the right was The Plain obscured by trees, whose winter starkness would eventually reveal the colder, greyer stone of Magdalen Tower. The prospect was one ideally calculated to render Magdalen Tower Fever chronic in any sufferer. David told himself he was not one. And yet the view before him, allied to the feeling of standing beneath the first, crystalline archway of the autumn, which never failed to rediscover in him those emotions that were as old and mysterious as memory itself, had plunged him into an uncertainly luxuriant sadness. If it were true that he was no sufferer from the fever, and that the abortive termination of his career had left him with no regrets, then at least his present mood convinced him yet again that happiness was a fantasy of retrospect. Now, as he sat in front of the window with the university distanced from him both in time and space, and yet still visible before his eyes, it would be surprising if he hadn't reviewed the past without some indulgence and remorse. But then, he told himself, there had been no life before Tony. And while it might be as an alien, as a townsman even, that he was now considering Oxford across the Great Park, it was, after all, only nearer to Tony that circumstances had brought him. The strangeness of his environment, and of course the imminence

of Tony, must be contributory causes to this feeling of barely
sub-hysterical sadness, which might at any moment be startled
into an irrepressible and idiot joy.

Tony, David had learned from Jones, would not be coming
on the school train that arrived at five, but for reasons of his
own had elected for a later one that would deliver him about
eight. David had been unsurprised at the news, and interpreted
the delay in the light of recent letters from the boy whose tone
made it clear that he proposed to regard himself as the guest
rather than pupil of the school in what he considered to be a
charity term. Presumably he had broken his journey to do the
statuary at the Tate or somewhere in more leisurely fashion.
David was unconcerned, and even relieved at the news. It
would give him more time to settle in. He felt he needed the
time badly, and should like to be able to spend an hour flat
on his bed before meeting again with the physical presence of
Tony. Already his apprehension of that moment was acute. For
as Tony stood in his mind it was as a series of memories, each
seemingly contained in its own diaphanous bubble of sunshine,
which had mysteriously survived fresh and intact throughout
ten weeks' unconsciousness. To these there had been added in
the weeks of his convalescence both such myriad projections as
were loosed in his mind by the suggestions of Tony's letters, as
well as those countless, poignant, and often terrifying images,
that came from he knew not where. He had in effect no real
picture of the boy. In the absence of the photographs, all of
which still lay unprocessed, the loved face remained characteristically veiled. When the veil did part it was fractionally, and
through the working of a diabolical inconsequence whom no
agency of human will might command, or even petition. When,
fortuitously, the living image of Tony's face did appear like
this, the consequence was such a stunning rupture of David's
faculties that he was becoming convinced that if the Virgin
really had once appeared to Lang on the towpath at Wimborne
it had perhaps been neither so funny, nor so comfortable an
occurrence as David had chosen to suppose.

With his unpacking completed, he had just determined
neither to look back into the past, nor further into the future
than the end of the coming term, and Tony's departure for his
remote Scottish school, when he was summoned to the Joneses
by a small boy, who had presumably been delivered early by

car. Retrospection was the function of the morrow, while thoughts for the morrow itself inevitably proved to be a useless expenditure of psychic energy. Or was this, he wondered as he followed in the footsteps of the small boy, who was disconsolately and inexpertly playing with a yoyo, only as much as to say that his being had become so involved about Tony as to admit of neither a past, nor a future dimension; or indeed of any sphere of influence other than that which, like the filings clustered around the magnet was directly responsible to Tony's gravitational field.

David laid his hand upon the shoulder of the boy in front of him, and took the yoyo. He coiled the string about the axis of the bright yellow spool, and relinquished it confidently into the void, while the child watched him intently. Sure enough, when he gently tugged the string at the nadir of its fall, the bright spool sped upwards again, ferociously devouring its lifeline as it came, until it bounced off the tips of his fingers. The rhythm established, the yellow disc danced hypnotically up and down in the dark corridor, while both their eyes followed its motions in silence.

'I think I can do it now,' the child said.

David released the string, and caught the spool in the air. 'The secret's in the rhythm; the timing of when you pull the string. You must get the *feel* of it.'

The small boy looked at the dead object in his hand as if afraid to make the experiment.

'There's nothing to be frightened of!' David laughed. 'Just so long as it is you who are holding the string, and aren't sitting on the yoyo.'

A thought seemed to occur to the child. 'If you had a big one, I mean a very big one so that you *could* sit on it, and you hung it from the ceiling, could you ride up and down?' He looked enquiringly at David.

'No! The string must be held by a person, who knows just when and how to *pull* it.'

'A person who can feel it then, like you said, but big enough to hold a big one?' The child looked up at the ceiling.

'Yes,' David assured him, 'then it would work.'

'God!' said the child devoutly. 'God would be big enough, and He can feel.'

David wondered whether he might legitimately parcel this

infant into one of those ventilated boxes the railways employ
for transporting guinea-pigs and send him to Lang. Meanwhile
the metaphysics were becoming too much for him. Still, he
owed a duty to the establishment. 'Yes,' he admitted, 'God
would do very well. If you are quite sure that it is God who is
holding the string, then by all means sit on the yoyo. But until
then, be sure that you hold the string yourself.' David turned
to keep his appointment.

'Thank you very much, sir,' said the child, who must have
decided that David was a sir.

David had left him, still in some perplexity, and made his
way to the flat where he now stood while Jones, oblivious of his
presence, scratched away at the time-table.

Mrs Jones padded into the room clutching a sugar basin.
'Sorry to keep you waiting, Mr Rogers,' she said in tones such
as one might address to a tradesman. It was true David was
still standing.

'Not at all.'

Somewhere in the building a bell was ringing, presumably
summoning such boys as had arrived, and members of the
staff less privileged than himself to similar refreshment. Mrs
Jones was now bent over a table pouring tea.

'One lump, two, Mr Rogers?' She sang this like a descant.

'I don't take sugar, thank you.'

Mrs Jones straightened her gargantuan form and advanced
upon David with a cup of tea and a plateful of highly-coloured
commercial pastries. 'Are you a Protestant or a Catholic, Mr
Rogers?'

This question, like the last, carried a certain assumption
about it. For a second David was tempted to give it the same
reply.

'I was brought up as a Protestant.'

Mrs Jones nodded. 'I only asked, really, because we shall
have two Catholic boys with us this term and we've been
wondering who's going to take them to their church.'

'I see.' David was doing some wondering himself. He was
in fact weighing the sound of that unnecessary 'really' in his
mind, and speculating as to what clue it offered to the character of Mrs Jones.

An awkward situation had now developed. Mrs Jones stood
before David holding the plate of cakes in one hand and the

cup of tea in the other, while David, in the absence of an invitation to be seated, still stood supporting himself on the walking-stick he had taken to carrying. The position might have been resolved were he to have taken only the cup and left Mrs Jones holding the saucer. But unfortunately he was also hungry. As Mrs Jones showed no signs of solving the deadlock, David smiled apologetically.

'I think I'd better sit down if I may.'

Suiting the action to the words he sank into a chair and tucked the cane between his legs. He relieved Mrs Jones of the tea and one of the cakes, and noticed that she was regarding the cane with distaste. It was made of black ebony which terminated in the carved head of a negro, and David had discovered it in the cattle market on his first morning of freedom from the nursing home. It was perhaps an unfortunate support to have chosen at a time when colonial emancipation had become a universal demand, and some pleasantry to this effect was forming in his mind when Mrs Jones' next remark confirmed him in the opinion that she would probably not have been able to grasp it. In fact she said:

'We've had a lot of trouble with foreign boys in the past. You know, they're really so *different* in their ways.'

'Yes,' said David, who saw no other possible rejoinder to this profundity.

Mrs Jones had collected a cup of tea and one of the larger cakes, and now stood planted in the middle of the hearthrug. Her eyes were extraordinary. They were light blue and large, yet wanting in any attractiveness due to an excessive protrusion. These, together with the heaviness of the surrounding face, one of whose chins Mrs Jones was in the process of scratching, suggested that her temperament was selfish and unstable. Probably she took pills for a heart, and was conceivably a member of the Cardiac Fellowship. Following this uncharitable line of thought, as with his eyes he followed the abortive figure of Mrs Jones down to the carpet, David couldn't help observing that her massive legs were reminiscent of some species of tropical pot-plant in the foyer of a Brighton hotel.

'Headmaster, do drink your tea up before it gets cold,' Mrs Jones said irritably.

David glanced over his shoulder, half expecting to see a row of boys, or perhaps servants, before whom Jones' prestige must be upheld. But there was no one. He passed his eye round the room. The centre-piece appeared to be a large tele-vision set, before which was drawn up the settee where Jones was crouched. Apart from these items of furniture there were two further armchairs and a bureau whose extended leaf bore a stack of notepaper whose letter-head announced it as coming from The Headmaster, St Cecilia's Choir School. A book-case ranged beside this contained a copy of the *Public and Preparatory Schools Yearbook* for 1957, an *A.A. Road Maps*, a very large Bible, quite the smallest *Pocket Oxford Dictionary* David had ever laid eyes upon, and an assortment of volumes in shiny dust jackets whose subject matter he guessed would be confined to various aspects of the English rural scene. The pictures on the wall had been chosen with the same wholesome and conservative eye as those in the hall which had horrified David on his first visit. Here, in fact, they were Gainsborough's *The Blue* Boy; and another scriptural scene with emphasis on the suffrage of little children. Above the mantelpiece, and between two Stafford dogs whose hideousness placed their authenticity beyond doubt, two further little children, poeti-cally ragged urchins this time, and perhaps the good poor, were depicted launching a toy boat on what might have been the Serpentine.

David's eye recoiled sharply from the china spaniels, and took refuge in Mrs Jones. 'These foreign boys are on some sort of exchange with a couple of yours?' he hazarded. He had rejected 'ours' as sounding rather presumptuous at this stage of his employment.

Mrs Jones transferred the attention of her scratching finger to another chin. David saw now that it was a nervous gesture.

'Well, yes, that's it really. Two of our boys have gone to these foreign boys' schools.' Mrs Jones paused, as if doubting whether she'd given the first chin sufficient attention. 'The Headmaster and I think it's so nice if boys can get away like that for a term, you see.'

David said he saw. 'Tony, I know, was very grateful for his term in Vienna,' he added, partly to sustain the pleasantry, but more for the sake of pronouncing Tony's name aloud.

'One of our this term's boys comes from Vienna. Oh, I do hope he won't be as naughty as the last one, Headmaster!' She turned to Jones, who merely grunted. 'He was the only boy in our time at the school whom the Headmaster had to send home. He stole apples,' she explained.

'How dreadful!' Too late David realised his acting couldn't match the boldness of the words, and hurried on. 'Where does the other one come from?'

'From Paris.'

'I think I'll put Hans Gunther von Manz, and the other boy, Rassignac, in your special charge, Rogers,' Jones interrupted. 'You can give them English tuition, or anything you like when you're free.'

'Right,' David said heavily, in a tone which he hoped suggested that he was already giving consideration to a carefully devised course for these two unknowns.

Mrs Jones cleared the tea things. She looked with even greater distaste at the Negro's head on David's cane. David noticed that Jones hadn't called him 'my dear boy'. Jones seemed a more timid, and certainly less natural, man in the presence of his wife. He sorted out some papers that had become stuck to the hot-water jug.

'We still don't know whether Hamley's supposed to be going to Vienna or not, dear. Can you get on to Colonel Hamley and find out?'

Mrs Jones groped more resolutely at her neck, and her eyelids drooped momentarily in assent. David, for his part, couldn't contain a smile. He thought of Hamley, whose stomach couldn't support a slice of fried bread, faced with a plate of Viennese pastries veritably inflated *mit schlagrahm;* and of the armless Hamley, to whom a long hour in the Stephansdom might have been extended as a courtesy. And suddenly, no doubt through some unconscious train of association, the veil parted in David's mind to reveal an image of Tony as true to the life as if it were before him at that moment in the ground-glass screen of his Rolleiflex. Tony's face was contorted with horror as he regarded a lipstick in the outstretched hand of a wardrobe mistress, over whose forearm were draped a number of sailor-suits. But David hardly noticed her. His mind was reeling back before the magical interplay of line and colour that made up the composition of Tony's face. The high, almost disdainfully pencilled arches of the brows above his grey eyes; the strangely fragile structure of the cheek-bones sweeping back to his impish ears; the too perfectly moulded fashion model's nose; the incongruous suggestion of a tried compassion that lurked about the jaw and lips of a face whose texture and colouring was otherwise that of innocence, and which played, perhaps, the larger part in dividing Tony's beauty from any pretty boy of a similar age. All this, and particularly the superbly-cut lips, which were parted in horror at the proffered cosmetic, David endeavoured to transfer into memory as soon as the first shock of recognition was past. But then the image was gone; lost, if not irretrievably, then at least beyond summoning in the crystal reality of its original form. Memory might reproduce the scene, but only as a blurred photograph.

David got to his feet and discovered he had cramp in the toes. Seizing his stick, he hobbled to the door and opened it for Mrs Jones who was trundling forward with the trolley. He smiled at her almost indulgently as she departed.

He recalled his remarking to Tony that he wished he were a painter, and Tony's indignant assertion that he was a composer. The Symphony in G was still only a collection of disjointed themes with an inspirational key change, which alone would require a weight of time and mathematics to orchestrate. The unorthodox vocal sonata, on the other hand, which when completed and recorded in the manner he proposed would represent an entirely new employment of the boy soprano, was barely begun. The blight here was time. Tony was thirteen and eleven months. His voice might lose control tomorrow and be dead within ten days. Alternatively, it might enter a period of gradual decline drawn out over a period of months, when it would be criminal to put it through the arduous tests the sonata would demand at a single run through, let alone the rehearsing that a satisfactory professional recording would involve. Though David had had no formal training in the choral field, he knew Tony's was a voice that might happen once in a generation. Furthermore, the boy seemed to have achieved a peak of training that was no mean credit to St Cecilia's, and to be possessed as well of an innate musical intelligence, the lack of which left many technically accomplished boys' voices helplessly wanting in any imaginative interpretation. Tony, in a word, was a genius. But his genius, like his physical beauty, must soon decline.

David, oblivious to the huddled form of Jones as Jones was oblivious to him, stared out through the window to find his melancholy echoed in the garden where the sun had left what must be Mrs Jones' personally-tended rose beds. He scowled at a further group of concrete gnomes. A white cat, perhaps the one the boys called Palestrina, uncurled itself from beneath the feet of one of them and slunk round to the western side of the building to enjoy the last of the sunshine. The problem was not new. One trained a boy hard, perhaps from when he was eight. At twelve he might be fit to sing, and sing with increasing usefulness for eighteen months or two years. But just when his lungs were beginning to be able to support, and his throat to control something other than thin squeaks, and more, when he was beginning to have some intimation as to what music was about, he was finished. Who enjoyed the brief season of his achievement anyway? At St Cecilia's, a few old ladies who tottered in from Headington and North Oxford, and a clutch of those smooth Anglicans who didn't know a soprano from a piccolo. Not for the first time David asked himself why he had never been to hear Tony sing in the Temple. He was still unsure of the answer.

Where it concerned Tony, the problem of the brief season was particularly acute, being obviously complicated by personal feelings. As with the photographs, David felt compelled to record a permanence; but a permanence that would be of more universal appeal, and also more living to themselves. He could hope for none greater than that Tony should perform a work of his own. For the time being at least the boy had the voice; and he had both the musical intelligence, and the lungs in his scaled-down Donatello chest.

'I'd better make myself more familiar with the school,' David said.

Jones passed a hand through his thinning hair. 'Yes, you do that, Rogers. Excellent idea. Good heavens, that train'll be here any minute and Samuel's not arrived. Hayden will have to take first duty. Watch him, Rogers. Watch him and learn, there's a good fellow.' Jones looked down triumphantly at the paper on the table. 'Your first job will be to escort the school to prayers in the Chapel tomorrow at nine.'

'The *college* Chapel?'

Jones looked surprised. 'But of course, my dear boy!'

'Right,' David concluded uneasily. As he turned to the door

he had hastily to flatten himself against the wall. Mrs Jones was agitated and her colour dangerously heightened.

'Emergency, Headmaster!' she announced. 'Emergency!'

David had the impression that the words were a recognised signal at which the whole household must spring into some carefully rehearsed sequence of action. He stiffened instinctively.

'That *ball-cock* in the boys' *bathrooms* again,' said Mrs Jones.

David's puzzlement cleared as he recalled Mrs Jones' showing him what she termed the *geography* of the house on his arrival. 'I'm quite an experienced hand with lavatory cisterns,' he volunteered to Jones.

But the Headmaster was already following his wife meekly into the hall. David turned less hurriedly into the wake of the odd couple. It occurred to him to wonder now whether the Viennese who had 'stolen apples' with such unprecedented consequences had not perhaps urinated thoughtlessly in the Great Quad or on to Mrs Jones' rose beds.

There was nothing methodical about David's exploration. Instead he strayed more or less aimlessly about the still largely deserted building. The train had evidently not yet arrived, but the occasional swish of tyres on gravel announced the delivery of boys being returned by car.

From the doorway of one of the dormitories David was able, unobserved, to witness the odd spectacle presented by the reunion of three of these. At first the boys, plucked from their holiday environment of familiar homes and informal clothes, then dressed up and driven through the September afternoon to be deposited at this focal point, barely recognised each other's existence, or else were prepared to do so only with a formality that was both touching and comic. Gradually, as a new toy was dragged from a night-case and reluctantly shown, a name, or a common memory recalled, or an argument begun, the adjustment quickened visibly. Then, with the impatient hand on a sleeve demanding the return of a Dinky-toy, or the now uninhibited laugh at the recollection of what somebody had done with his milk, the pattern of readjustment was complete, and the home environment of parents, sisters and brothers had become as remote and unthinkable as the school one must have seemed only hours before. As the secure sense of familiarity grew with the greater frequency of physical and mental contacts, so the noise grew also.

The scene was one David was to discover in different forms, and among different groups, in all parts of the building. Here and there, too, sitting on the one righted chair in a form-room whose furniture was otherwise stacked in an untidy heap, or else wandering listlessly down a corridor, and feeding himself periodically from a paper-bag in his pocket, he came across the born outsider. One of these was brushing-up a geometry theorem, another was talking soulfully to some offspring of Palestrina in a dark corner, and a third had discovered a box of coloured blackboard chalks, and with tensed face was expressing himself luridly whilst he still might.

Wherever David went he was constantly struck by the beauty of such boys as he met. 'Yes, *sic*' he owned to himself aloud. Of course, there was nothing like Tony's, and probably nothing, he told himself dryly, that wouldn't have suffered disillusionment after a few weeks of the familiarity that a classroom must impose. But now, and recently released as he was from the long period in hospital, he found himself at moments overwhelmed by the wealth of so many young forms, while the confinement of these supple bodies in their uniform clothes disturbed him not a little. He became acutely apprehensive of the impact Tony must have upon him that night. Meanwhile, he reflected, the pleasure he took in some of the boys he saw about him now was not very far removed from the sudden upsurge of joy he had experienced among the wildly blown trees and scattered rooks when he had taken his first faltering walk in the Great Park. And if this were so, there should be no matter.

David discovered the art-room in what, when the building had still been a private house, must have been a conservatory. He stood for a moment before the one wall that was not made of glass, and where there were pinned a number of exhibits on bluish-grey sugar-paper. The paintings were no different from those that might have adorned the similar room at his own private school. There were in fact exactly the same aeroplanes, decorated with exactly the same swastika, for which inheritance Captain W. E. Johns, rather than parental experience, was most probably responsible. David surveyed the collection for a common denominator, and saw at once that this was a direct reflection of the energy and restless movement with which the arrival of the school train had now filled the building. Yet there was something more, that he could only define as joy. Or perhaps it was more nearly expressed by what the Christians called Witness. An aeroplane might not fly, but that it must have fire spurting from its guns and bombs falling simultaneously from its belly. If a ship was not creaming along over an expanse of ocean but was for some reason confined to harbour with heavy black anchor-chains at each end, then a man, if not two, must at that moment be falling from the mast. Again, that old faithful, the two-dimensional cottage in rural setting, positively belched smoke into the summer sky from an altogether unjustifiable number of chimneys.

Tony, David reflected, looking at this last, could sit still and talk. He could write letters or settle down on his hilltop to read music. He had become consciously cerebral, where the authors of these paintings had not. But he had lost none of their innocence.

'That's mine,' said Hunter, who had somehow appeared beside David. 'The house . . . Sir?' Hunter looked up, and David noticed that the rather precious raven fringe of the Ghoul's boating mascot had evaded the scissors for too long. His piercing blue eyes were not unattractive. 'Sir – is it true that you're teaching Mr Gould's classes?'

'Some.' David nodded abstractedly. 'Why?'

The boy looked abashed. 'Sir, well, it's just that Mr Gould let me be form monitor, sir, and – '

David cut him short. The little boy's expression made it apparent that he was putting forward his prior claim to mother-love, and was looking automatically to the Ghoul's successor to fulfil his need. 'We'll see.'

'Thank you, sir. Thank you very much, sir!' Hunter ran off as someone called his name, and David turned away in some perplexity. It came to him uncomfortably that the job he'd landed was primarily that of a nursemaid. And tomorrow he must escort the crocodile.

Although the uncarpeted building was now a chaos of slamming doors, shrill cries, and racing grey forms, some of which checked themselves dramatically to stare at him with a feigned horror or alarm, and even with an unfeigned delight: who seemed to be under some compulsion to screech to a halt before him on the polished floors, mutter 'Sorry, sir,' before walking respectfully past him, and then breaking into an even noisier run again, he found his way to a large, empty assembly hall that occupied most of a western wing.

He paused for a moment listening to an authoritative voice which was shouting, 'House-shoes! No supper until you've changed into your *house-shoes*, I said, idiot . . .' before closing himself into the comparative silence.

Before him in the empty hall was a Blüthner concert grand. David gave a low whistle and opened the keyboard almost fearfully. He struck a chord, and concluded that someone must have held St Cecilia's Choir School in pretty high regard: Somehow he couldn't see the Governing Body of the college voting away the money for a piano such as this. He struck a further series of chords. Shafts of late sunlight came through the western window to melt in dazzling pools on the polished mahogany. Without further ado David flexed his fingers and went straight into Rachmaninov's Third Concerto, albeit that the orchestration might only be heard in his head. The move was a bold one after his incarceration. Still, he was in uncritical mood – so much so that a moment later he broke off to raise the giant's top before commencing again.

David's exuberance swelled irresistibly. He flew off the crest of Rachmaninov's most shamelessly conceited wave at a tangent, spontaneously endowing the Third with a gratuitous orgasm. Then he continued the improvisation in an ecstasy. The Blüthner was superb: so sensitive that it thundered, rippled, and mewed as if actuated directly by the electrical impulses that coursed through his brain.

The child whose head was just visible, and who was staring at him through the angle formed by the piano's lid and its support, was weeping profusely. Hallo! David thought. The born audience of Tchaikovsky: a romantic heart. He stopped playing abruptly.

'Can you play the piano?'

The child said nothing. He stared at David with red eyes, but came round to the front of the instrument. He was so brand-new that David half expected to see labels attached to his uniform.

'What's your name?' he tried again.

'David.' The boy got the word out, but the acknowledgement of his own identity was too much for him. A fresh supply of tears welled up in his eyes and ran an erratic course down his cheeks.

David nodded. 'I'm David too. But I can't tie my tie as neatly as you can.' Too late he saw his mistake. The child's face was now awash with tears.

'Mummy did it.' The sobs became convulsions. 'I forgot my lamb.'

After a moment David pulled out his pen and found a piece of paper. He drew a short down-stroke and barbed one end obtusely, like an anchor. He held the paper against the music rest; then looked at the boy intensely. 'Its nose . . . Is it like that?'

The boy nodded in bewilderment.

David's eyes narrowed. 'And *black cotton?*'

'It's black.'

David bit his lower lip in deeper perplexity. 'Now eyes . . . Glass or felt? Quick!'

'Brown glass ones.' The child sniffed, and left a silver smear across the cuff of his flannel jacket like the path of a snail over a stone. Tony, David reflected, would have been horrified. But he was busy calculating relative angles with an unreservedly furious frown. At length he drew in the eyes and looked searchingly at the boy.

'In about that position?'

'Yes!' The boy's interest was visibly marked.

David looked at the boy with an amazement that was still troubled with suspicion. After a long moment he pulled himself together and shook his head. He drew a long narrow U, and then blocked it in the middle like a half-filled test-tube, shading over the lower portion. 'Think carefully before answering, David,' he said. 'The lamb is white. This is one leg. What *colour is* the lower part of the leg?'

'Brown,' said the boy without hesitation.

David was far away. 'I thought so! As if it had been dipped in chocolate.' He returned briskly to the present, and found a postcard in his wallet. 'Mine got lost years ago.'

Understanding spread over the child's face. 'You can still get new ones, I think,' he said anxiously.

'No matter,' David said. 'We'll send for yours.'

He addressed the card as directed.

'Do we have reading and writing here?' the boy asked.

'I hope so!' David abandoned deception with relief. 'I'm not personally writing home for everything you've forgotten.'

The boy stood the test bravely.

'At my other school we had finger-painting. I'm going to have trombone lessons because Daddy plays the trombone for the London Philharmonic. Are you really called David too?'

David decided his work was done. The child was fully loquacious again. He got up from the piano. 'Do you know how long a trombone is when fully extended?'

The boy shook his head, suddenly suspecting a difficulty.

'At least once times my size of David and two and a half times yours.' He made towards the door, leaving the child to puzzle this out.

How long Miss Poole of the second-helpings had been standing there he blushed to think. She was more attractive than he remembered her, and she was looking at him as if he were some particular sign of the zodiac.

'Jean,' she said.

'I'm David,' said David. 'And this is a namesake's summons for a soft-toy.'

## 23

David lay on his bed. It was ten to eight. The staff supper had passed off easily enough. It had been a ragged affair with people coming and going so that he didn't know whether he had now met all his colleagues or not. Apart from Jean Poole, there had been another matron, the sallow-faced man whom he thought of as a curate, who had greeted him so distractedly on his first visit to the school, a round, middle-aged man, Samuel, and a younger, mousy man, Wallace, whose natty dress suggested emotional compensation. The Joneses had not been present, nor had the duty-master, Hayden, whose voice, nevertheless, had reached them clearly from several parts of the building. When this happened the curate trembled as if submitted to a charge of electricity.

Now David closed his mind to them all, and wondered whether heart-beats really might in fact be audible as cornered secret agents invariably fear. He tried to see himself suddenly confronted with the strangeness of Tony, and wondered what he would do. There must be considerable shock in the blazing colour and live warmth denied him so long. Beyond that he could make no prediction as to what would follow. He suspected he would need compulsively to make some physical contact with the boy, but that this would be impossible for him to initiate because they would meet as strangers. Perhaps they might shake hands.

This time there was someone coming down the passage, and the step was the uneven footfall of someone carrying a heavy case. To beguile a sudden self-consciousness, David fixed a parody of boredom on his face and gazed over his chest at the door. The mask twitched about his lips. He couldn't keep his face still and was trembling all over.

Tony knocked thunderously, and then was standing within the threshold. He dropped a case on the floor, pushed it further into the room with his foot, and then closed the door with his hands behind his back. Instantly David recognised small changes. An attempt had been made to part the thick fringe of his hair, and Tony was wearing a long-trouser flannel suit which reflected the light in silver facets like some incomparably rich elfin armour, setting off the grace of his slight form. Tony smiled with the peculiar liquid dimension which dazzled, and David saw that the wire was gone.

'Portrait of one bad prep school master!' he announced.

'Bad?' David echoed wildly. 'Lazy, then,' Tony emended easily. He stood in the middle of the room before the spluttering gas-fire. 'Stand up!'

David obeyed; swinging his legs off the bed. Tony had placed one hand fiat on the top of his head and was standing stiffly to attention. 'Nearer!'

David didn't understand. Tony closed the gap which separated them so that his body was almost touching David's. He strained his eyes upwards at his hand, and then slid this horizontally off his head so that his hair fell willingly back into its old fringe. The blade of his hand bumped against the bridge of David's nose. 'Thought so. Up to your nose.'

The explanation, now that it had come, didn't sound wholly

valid. Tony's eyes were laughing three inches beneath David's own. Then the boy's smile became self-conscious.

'What do you think of them? I bet they're the last thing you expected to see . . . Don't think they're *symbolic*, or anything.'

David smiled. 'I like them.'

Tony undid his jacket; holding it open like wings so that David might better admire the long trousers. He looked down almost morbidly at his own waist, pinched by the elastic belt, then flicked his eyes up at David again. Even the distaste in his voice could barely ruffle the moulding of his nose, 'You don't think I'm getting *fat*?'

Even had the absurdity of the question not betrayed the boy, his eyes now did. David was trembling at the carefully engineered proximity.

'Crook!' he said meaninglessly. Slipping his arms round the boy's waist, he let his forehead sink on to the cushioning fringe.

David felt a muscle in his jaw twitch. It was like embracing a symphony; something ultimate. Tony's body didn't yield. He stood there formally; triumphantly playing some private game of his own. Then suddenly he squeezed David with a tight, childish passion, and, uncoiling himself with an equally violent reaction, flopped back into the armchair with an ecstatic grin. David also sat down; at ease now himself.

Tony spoke first; jerking upright in the deep chair, and feeling in the pocket of his jacket. 'I've got a present for you. I had to stop off in London and get a proper box for it, so that's why I'm late. Close your eyes!'

David did so, and then opened them again to find Tony slumped back in his chair, studying his tie with a bashful expression. The small box that had been placed in his hand was plastic and had a transparent lid. David read the name of a London dentist, and then raised the lid for a better look at the pink plate and gleaming platinum wire. Tony's chin was still lowered, but he was looking up through his lashes, and his lips were poised uncertainly between embarrassment and laughter. David smiled.

'I couldn't have thought of a nicer present. I'll keep it always like the Cheshire Cat's grin!'

Tony was instantly alive again. 'You won't find any food or anything on it. I cleaned it up specially.'

David produced the compendium of statuary which he had
bought with the credit Blackwells had allowed him on a sackful
of Anglo-Saxon textbooks. Tony opened the heavy volume
across his knees in amazement. A moment later he exclaimed,
'Ten *guineas*? That's more than a suit with shorts!'

'But I trust less worthy of being dropped into the sea!'

Tony looked up sharply. 'Who told you that?'

'Why, you did.'

Tony frowned. 'Oh, so I did. I wish I hadn't thrown it away
now.'

'So it was an impulsive sacrifice rather than a standing
resolution?'

Tony's eyes narrowed as he thought this out. He nodded;
then smiled wickedly. ' 'Fraid so!'

David shook his head. 'And why the long suit?'

'For dignity at concerts and recordings,' said Tony
awkwardly. 'But I still prefer shorts . . .'

'For vanity,' David finished helpfully.

Tony closed the book and laid it on the floor beside him.
He tried vainly to draw his brows down from their high arches
into a frown, at the same time compressing his lips ferociously.
The effect was merely comic. 'Do you know something, Mr
Rogers? You are talking to the *head-boy,* T. Sandel, and even
privileged members of the staff are advised to keep on the right
side of him.'

David burst out laughing. 'I don't believe it! And even if you
were I should still take the greatest pleasure in spanking your
bottom as a public example in the dormitory.'

'*Dormitory*?' There was no mistaking the provocation in
Tony's scorn. 'The head-boy, let me tell you, has a private
bedroom.' Tony spaced the words emphatically, and added,
'It's just along your corridor. Don't knock.' He sprawled back,
reviewing David's discomfort at leisure with his most outrageous expression.

David ignored the suggestion; and Tony's thoughts seemed
to become more properly disposed again.

'What happened about the car? How long have you been up
for now?'

David told him.

Tony was feeling in his pocket again. 'That don, Mr Ricks,
sent me a letter in the holidays *telling* me where you were, but

that old bag of a Jones woman didn't send it on. Now I suppose I'll have to write him a letter saying I'm sorry I couldn't thank him for his letter because I hadn't got. . .'

'It (his letter) before today,' David volunteered.

'Thank you!' Tony sighed wearily. He passed a hand through his hair; and then did it again with a sudden, gentler curiosity. 'Have you got any shampoo?'

David shook his head with a smile.

'Blast!' the boy said abstractedly. He curled his legs beneath him in the chair.

'One plucks them up.' David made the irony light. 'Stops them becoming baggy at the knees.'

Tony was indignant. 'I *know*. Anyway I don't care about this suit because I've got your other one still new.' Nevertheless he tugged at the trousers, revealing, and obviously approving, of the gold shins and grey ankle-socks that became displayed.

'All right!' David was patient. 'Supposing you just tell me about the B.B.C. concert and the recordings.'

Tony looked up quickly. 'Didn't you see the Vittoria?'

David shook his head. 'Alas. No telly for weak patients. . . . It was on the first night of my awakening.'

Tony nodded, remembering. 'They had a small screen in front of us so we could see *ourselves*.'

'It's called a monitor screen.'

'Oh. Anyway, I could see *us,* but not *me.*'

'How very odd.'

'I mean they didn't show me close, I don't think, though I couldn't watch all the time.'

David smiled. 'Tones, didn't it occur to you that if people tune in to a concert it's not for the purpose of inspecting one-hundredth part of the cast – T. Sandel, head-boy?'

Tony looked numb. 'I suppose not.'

'Aural and visual works of art aren't compatible – which is why opera is absurd,' David hurried on, offering this muddled consolation as something Tony might dig for if he chose. 'What about the record, though?'

Tony's enthusiasm returned in a flood of animation. He took a deep breath. 'Well! It's all done. It took three days and I stayed with my other aunt and uncle who take me skiing some-times, you know. Wow, was it exhausting! A full twelve-inch

L.P., do you realise that, boy!' Tony was bouncing on the chair, and thumping his fists on the flat leather arms.

'And who supported Sandel, head-boy?'

'Oh, yes.' Tony simmered down a little. 'Six sopranos and two altos from Westminster Abbey. But they were only, well, chorus, you know,' he added, finding what he considered the right amount of modesty with difficulty. 'Seven of the songs are just me. Oh, and one of the sopranos was a weedy kid who hadn't a clue and had to be dropped after rehearsals. That makes it only five.'

'I've no doubt you extended your professional sympathy to him very nicely.' Even as David spoke, a little dryly, he sensed the futility of bringing restraint to the boy. He must accept that, or else involve them in all manner of destructive antagonisms. Or was he seeking to absolve himself from responsibility?

'Well, yes, I did!' Tony said hotly.

'Okay!' David laughed. 'What did you sing?'

'The other boys were all very good,' Tony said in slow, almost sulky, parentheses. He became earnest again. 'There are some bits and pieces of Schubert and Bach that we all did . . . Oh, and Bruckner's *Um Mitternacht,* which they let me do in the end . . .'

They let you loose as an *alto?*' David sat up in astonishment.

Tony spread his hands. They said it was a freak effect, and that's why I had such a time persuading them.'

'It is.' David was thoughtful. 'When this recording comes out we'll have professors of music from all over nosing about the place.'

Tony smiled with unfeigned delight now.

'Who is "they", anyway?'

'Argo.'

'And?'

'Oh, some London orchestra, with their own conductor, I think. Someone I'd never heard of at any rate.'

'So, we're going to have Sandel, alto, and Sandel, soprano, on the same record.'

'*Master!*' Tony emended.

David inclined his head. 'As is only proper. But that's not the point. I only hope people will think you're twin brothers, or we'll have the likes of Percy Scholes peering down your throat and making notes. Yes, "open wide!"' David picked up the plate in its presentation box. 'Still, what about the soprano twin?'

Tony smiled. The name on the little plastic box could have been world famous with a little unethical advertising.

'Well, Bach: *Sheep may safely graze,* first.'

'With the full Flagstad resonance?'

Tony heaved a chestful of air, 'Certainly! Then, Schubert's *Ständchen* – the opus 135 one; his Ave *Maria,* for the innocent choirboy touch; and Handel, *I know that my Redeemer* . . . Now, where are we? Ah, yes! Schubert once again. *Salve Regina;* and, finally, Mozart's *Laudate Dominum,* from *Vesperae solemnes de* something or other . . . '

'*De confessore.*' David got up to turn the gas-fire lower. His smile had a helpless breadth about it. 'That's certainly going to town in a popular way! You know, people are bound to compare the Handel with the Lough recording?'

Tony closed his eyes and slid a few inches lower in his chair. Airily he waved his hand. 'Just wait. Have no fear. Master Antony Sandel, first competent soprano of the stereophonic age, will not let you down.' He opened his eyes again. 'Anyway that recording was practically before Caruso, and they'd only just learned to make records at all, the man said.'

Tones, whatever the man said in the interests of encouraging stereophonic Sandel, the H.M.V. recording will take some equalling. Just bear modestly in mind that the repertoire you've described is quite a bold one.'

'I know.' Tony was confident. Morosely, he added: 'Do you think you're going to be a schoolmaster for life?'

'I sincerely hope not!'

'Good. I'll save you yet.'

'Explain!'

'About the man again.' Tony was firmly set on a tangent. 'He said he *would* like a photo . . .'

'To enhance the innocent choirboy touch?' David interrupted. 'Your own qualification about the *Ave Maria,* remember? I don't think we've got one that looks suitably holy.'

Tony leapt up and seized him by the lapels: his face was a comic mask of ferocity and excitement. 'Look, Mr Rogers, sir, weed, if you think you're going to bully me this term you wait!' He thrust his blazing eyes to within an inch of David's.

David passed his finger over the boy's nose. Tony dived head first back into his chair. He checked the somersault half-way, and regarded David through his legs. In a different voice he said, 'Can't we send one of the photos anyway? The man said it didn't have to be in vestments, and only had to be a face.'

David couldn't prevent himself from smiling. Tony poked his tongue out; then, finding he couldn't sustain the contortion, slithered his body into an upright position again.

'All right.' David relented. 'But I still have to process the photos.'

Tony seemed satisfied. 'When will you do them?'

'Soon.'

The boy looked up quickly. 'Pedagogue already!' he sighed. More seriously he asked, 'David, when are you going to have finished that music you want us to record? Can I look at it yet?'

David thought for a moment. 'I'd rather you didn't. It's still a mess, and I'd like to finish it first. But I'm working on it as fast as I can.'

'All right. Only don't forget I'm fourteen next month.'

'I'm already searching publishers' lists for further works on statuary.'

Tony said nothing.

'Don't worry,' David went on, 'there's lots of time.' As he spoke, with more confidence than he felt, he looked at Tony's face to become aware that there were facets of the boy's personality still quite unknown to him.

'I don't know,' Tony said slowly. Abruptly he came out of his dream. 'What really annoyed me about the recording was that I wanted to do a piece of the Vittoria, but they said I couldn't. . . That bit in the *Recessit Pastor* part with the terrific soprano phrases, you know.'

David shook his head.

'What!' For perhaps three seconds Tony listened, intensely poised and with his eyes shut; then loosed the astonishing crescendo phrase flawlessly into the still room. With his hand, he followed the rising wave of sound as if he were launching a paper dart. David recognised the line, but was stunned by the musical feat. To pause in the middle of a conversation, and confidently pluck such a phrase from its choral context without so much as a hum, let alone a tuning-fork, was a musical

exercise comparable, perhaps, to the linguistic one of spontaneously rendering Anglo-Saxon riddles in modern Chinese.
Tony had simply closed his eyes, heard his choral support and
its tempo, and launched himself with split-second timing.

'Whatever's the matter?' The boy was alarmed. 'Did I miss
it?'

'No,' David said dully. 'You hit it all right.'

Tony beamed. 'You recognised it then after all?'

David nodded. He got up to draw the curtains on the
autumn night. 'Tones?'

'Yes?'

'If I were you I shouldn't worry much even when your voice
does begin to go. For one thing you'll almost certainly have
a decent tenor or bass when you're eighteen or so . . . And
even if you haven't, or don't want to sing, then you'll still have
got a musical sense that's more immediately accessible than
anyone's I've known.' David turned round; then couldn't
help laughing at the boy's expression. 'You'll soon sober-up!
I envisage stiff lessons in composition and harmony. You may
have got your scholarship and be reclining on your laurels, but
it's not going to be a slack term, Sandel head-boy, or no.'

Tony was putting on his pet hedge-sparrow act.

'Incidentally, if you behaved like that when Argo were calling
you stereophonic Sandel, and promising you loud billing on
record sleeves, I'm surprised they didn't turf you out of the
studio . . . And now it's your bed-time.'

Tony had bounced out of his chair again, and taken the
same excited grip on David's lapels as before. He shook him
violently. 'Only if you come and talk to me in my bath. I haven't
warned you about any of the things in this crazy place I must;
or given you the love my aunt sent . . . and the advice. About
old Hayden too . . . all sorts of things . . .'

Not for the first time, David found himself acknowledging
that Tony was a highly nervous creature, on top of whatever
else he might be. Or rather, whatever he was originated in a
highly nervous basis, that was not unlike his own. 'You don't
happen to sing in your bath?' he asked suspiciously.

'No, never!' Tony was tugging him about all but hysterically.

'All right then. I'll join you in five minutes . . . But cool off a
bit.'

Tony paused to pick up his case; then looked round.

'You know, even the words you use are getting like the establishment.'

'Out, quick!' David commanded.


Tony dropped a large emerald towel on the floor and a similarly coloured flannel into the bath. He lowered himself gingerly into the water, grinning inanely at David as he did so. 'The one good thing about the first night of term in this place is that all the juniors cut their baths so there's some hot water left for me,' he said. 'This is the last decent bath I'll get unless I work an off-games racket and have them then.'

David looked about him. The room was bare except for a towel-rail which was cold, a nibbled cork bathmat, and a rickety chair, parts of the surface of which were still covered with a thick yellow paint, whose white lead base had become sticky through long exposure to steam. David perched himself instead on the rim of the bath, and wondered whether Tony proposed to put on some sort of aquatic show. The wretched boy had already drawn his attention to the area where his shorts had prohibited the even tan that covered the rest of his body. Now David watched the dissolving pattern of tiny indentations made about his waist by the band of the pants, which presumably he did wear in winter. Tony lowered his head for a moment beneath the water, blew three bubbles, then raising his head and legs simultaneously with a powerful contraction of his stomach muscles, balanced his heels on the hot and cold taps. He reviewed his legs with satisfaction.

'Shorts again tomorrow,' he announced thoughtfully.

'Less silver more gold.' David's indulgence carried a hint of irony. 'Only don't forget to hang up the long all-wools carefully so as to preserve the creases.'

For a moment he thought Tony was going to throw the face flannel; but he only muttered :

'Right, Rogers!' He fished around for the soap, and then blew his nose on his flannel to see if it would annoy David. It didn't. Disappointed, Tony asked:

'What do you think of the staff?'

'They seem a nice enough bunch to me.' David was guarded.

'Has Samuel shown you his collection of moths yet?' David remembered the round man. 'No.'

'What about that old fraud Hayden?'

'I haven't met him yet.'

'Oh boy! Just you wait!'

Tony's face split into an almost hysterical discomposure and he sent a shower of water flying into the room. 'He teaches C.E. geography straight from the army manuals because he doesn't know anything else. Then every few weeks he has a general knowledge test – I ask you!' Tony slithered round on his side in the bath and threw this excitedly up at David. Then, clearly imitating the absent man, he went on. '"Question one: On what famous ground is the Eton-Harrow match played, eh? Question two: When does the Flat Season start? – *Flat* season, boy, you know what *that* means – no more questions. Hurry, boy, number three now: Who was Master of The Grafton before the Kaiser's little balls-up? – no, you cannot be excused, Hamley, old boy. Shut *up*, Ferris!"'

Tony gave a low whistle as he lobbed the soap into a comer of the bathroom. 'Blackboard duster,' he explained. '5A has a proper ministry model with felt and a wooden back. The classrooms that only have an old school sock from the sewing-room are the lucky ones, I can tell you!' Tony sank back on his shoulders. 'Then there's his coughing. He smokes sixty a day. "Two hundred Seniors for me, Jakes, old boy, if you're going up into Oxford. My account at Grimbly's, you know. Just say Major Hayden, what? Oh, and look in on the cigar maturing room, that's if you don't mind, old boy. Tell 'em the Major'll be along soon about that home-grown stuff of his they're curing. They'll know all about it."' Tony pointed with a dripping hand towards the door. 'Exit Jakes humble and humiliated,' he said with satisfaction.

As Tony finished speaking heavy foot-falls sounded in the corridor outside. The boy wrung out his flannel, and then carefully laid the emerald rectangle over his lower abdomen. There was a rap at the door, and the voice David had heard about the building throughout the evening bellowed:

'Sandel!'

Tony blew a stream of bubbles over his chest and moulded the flannel more delicately in position with his hand. 'Here we go! You'll get it now! All about his horse Wellington who had to be shot in the South Bucks '33, although she had "good bone, old boy"; and his dear old spaniel bitch that got distemper . . .'

The door was thrown open and David found himself facing an emaciated, though still rugged-looking man of about sixty. His first impression was of a moustache that was less stained than sticky with nicotine, and of a nose like Bonaparte's, but bigger. When the man spoke his nose swung through several points of the compass.

'Deuced sorry, old boy . . . This one's broken barracks, what?' He indicated Tony with an orange finger.

David waited while the newcomer fought off a paroxysm of coughing. 'Must be . . . new feller Rogers, eh?' The old campaigner was struggling manfully with his diaphragm. Now he had it under some sort of control. 'I'm Hayden,' he spluttered.

'Major, Gunners,' Tony put in formally. He submerged again. The Major ignored the boy, and David held out his hand. 'Yes. I'm David Rogers. How do you do.'

It was inconceivable of course, but the soldier's hand seemed to have imparted something like liquid nicotine to his own.

'You two are related somehow, aren't you?' the Major asked without curiosity.

'Intimately,' said Tony, who'd raised his head. He submerged it once more, and the spluttering of bubbles suggested he'd been overcome with giggles.

David stilled the anger that flicked through him. It would be wiser for the moment to ignore the boy as the Major was doing. The Major spoke again in sharp bursts as if afraid that a long sentence might bring a return of the coughing.

'By the way . . . Are you a mild . . . or a bitter man?'

David stared at him. 'Mild, I think. Usually, that is.'

The Major stared back in turn. 'No, no, old boy. That won't do at all, I'm afraid. Must know one way or the other for the barrel.'

'Barrel?' David echoed stupidly.

'Yes, old boy. Common Room beer barrel. Aren't you with me? Didn't Wallace tell you, eh? We vote in either mild or bitter each term. Strict ballot. Majority wins . . . All that.'

David remembered the barrel he'd seen tucked away in the staff room with a wad of blotting-paper under the tap to catch the drips. 'I see. Then I'm still mild.'

The Major was confused. 'Awkward that, old boy,' he said

slowly. 'Complete deadlock . . . Fifty-fifty.' He frowned. 'I'm bitter myself. Gould was a bitter man too.'

'You're telling me!' said Tony. Either the remark was beyond the Major, or else he hadn't heard. He continued to frown at the bathmat.

'Perhaps,' David hazarded, 'the problem might be settled in one of two ways. Either we could persuade a brewery to supply us mild and bitter ready mixed, or else you yourself in the capacity of O.C. might be allowed an additional, casting vote.'

The Major looked up at David with new respect. There was considerable emotion in his bloodshot eyes. 'I say, old boy, that's dashed handsome of you, you know!' The trouble returned to his brow. 'Have to put it to the others though. Jean, now . . . Don't think she likes bitter much.'

'Does Jean subscribe to the beer?'

'Rather, old boy. Universal Suffrage here, you know . . . Gotta do the democratic thing. That's the problem. Can't throw away cricketing principles over a thing like this, eh? . . . Not after a life like mine.' He shook his head sadly and was lost in contemplation of the cork mat.

'Sir!' said Tony heavily. 'How long till lights-out now?'

'Eh, what?' The Major looked up from his dream. ' 'Bout two minutes, Sandel. Move, boy! On the command.'

'I haven't washed my face yet,' Tony said dryly.

'Well? What about it then, eh?' The Major's nose swung through several compass points.

'I don't know! I really *don't*!' Tony contrived to distil the essence of pity in his voice. He heaved a sigh as though he had become suddenly weary of life, then, patiently, he indicated the position of the face-flannel, the Major, and the door, with three uncompromising gestures of his head.

The Major retired with a grunt.

'That was just childish and rude,' David said, when he'd gone.

He saw the colour beginning to rise on the boy's cheeks, suffusing them from below with a rich stain. Tony was about to say something, but David checked him, clasping his head firmly in one hand as he leaned over the bath. Instead, the boy plucked the flannel from his groin, and folding it laterally, laid it across his eyes.

'Tony, listen,' he went on. 'I don't care how you behave

towards your masters – that's their problem. But don't talk
to them like that across myself. All right?' David peeled the
flannel from the boy's eyes to find them closed underneath.
'Tony? You'll only make my position impossible here if you do
. . . And yours, come to that.'

A few moments later Tony opened his eyes. Then, as David
had got up and was standing beside the bath, he called:

'Catch!'

Before David realised what was happening, and with a single
movement that combined incredible agility with an almost
lunatic degree of confidence, Tony had leapt wet and naked
from the bath and was sitting with his arms about his neck and
his legs locked around his hips.

'You know, I haven't got quite as many suits as you,' David
said mildly. He lowered the slippery, dizzy-eyed creature to
the floor, and rolled it up without ceremony in its emerald
towel. Tony lay inert except for his quivering eyes and lips. His
sprawled, mocking candour was effortlessly contrived. David
closed his eyes, and opened them again determined to see only
Tony's innocent beauty . . . what presumably other people saw.

Tony got up with a single harmony of movement that was
as consistent as the phrase of music he had so unexpectedly
uttered less than half an hour before. He wound the towel into
a turban about his head, and walked slowly, stark naked down
the corridor, placing one foot carefully before the other as if he
were balancing on a single crack between the bare boards.


David sensed that something was wrong as soon as Tony came
in. He had returned to his bedroom and was smoking a cigarette before the fire. Tony knocked, and then entered the room
without waiting for a reply. He was dressed in cornflower-blue
pyjamas, and over his shoulder on coat-hangers were slung
the suit he had been wearing, and what was evidently another,
though enclosed this time in a polythene wardrobe-bag. He
avoided David's eyes, and spoke jerkily.

'Can I hang these in your cupboard? This cellophane thing's
got the other suit you bought me in.'

'Never bought you anyhow,' David said; but when Tony
didn't smile, he waved towards the wardrobe. 'Yes, of course.'

Tony didn't open it immediately. Instead, he laid the clothes on David's bed and then went over to the window where he poked his head between the drawn curtains, holding them together about his neck so that only his back was visible to anyone in the room. 'David?' Muffled though the voice was, its tone was that peculiar one that demands an answer, or makes a formal request to proceed.

David struck a match. 'Yes?'

Tony spun round into the room again with a movement that was at once restless and slow. His eyes still wouldn't meet David's. 'David, d'you remember those fashion models we saw in Cheltenham?'

'Yes.'

'Do they have boys like that for boys' clothes anywhere?'

'I don't think so.' David began to suspect what was coming.

Tony came back towards the fire. 'I should like to show clothes like that . . . I mean all different ones. I could have cricket shorts and a white pullover and carry a bat like they carried umbrellas, or gym things, or our summer shorts, you know, or those sort of puffed bathers with blue and turquoise squares that boys wear at Cannes . . . And of course best suits like these . . .' Tony shook off one of his slippers and turned the gas-fire up fully with his toes so that it roared loudly in the silence. 'Then I'd just wander round between the tables! I'd take my cap off and people would inspect it and ask how much it was . . . People would feel my clothes . . .'

'I don't like the *people* . . . or any of it much.' David found he'd been startled to the protest involuntarily. He was angry and confused. As the boy had been talking there had grown in him the awareness that the whole thing was some sort of intensely nervous preamble, though to what end he had little idea. He suspected the fantasy wasn't wholly serious.

'Well, not just *any* people,' Tony went on, There was a flavour of truculence in his voice now, and he seemed to be doing elaborate exercises with his bare foot. 'I'd always come to you first.'

David was silent. The half-inch of ash fell off his cigarette before he could jerk his hand over the saucer he was using as an ash-tray. 'I won't always be there. Tones.'

'No.'

The boy's voice was perfectly matter-of-fact, and David instantly felt self-conscious. Tony was standing facing squarely

away from him, with the back of his legs resting against the
arm of the chair, and was idly reversing the winder of his
watch with his finger so that the ratchet mechanism purred in
the stillness. Then suddenly he turned round and his face was
contorted with a violent flow of tears. As suddenly again, and
as if the sensuous and beautiful boy were somehow left behind
him in his haste, he scrambled blindly over the arm of the chair
and butted his trembling face into David's chest. As David's
shock subsided, the boy began covering his face with kisses.

Gradually Tony's sobbing ceased. He began to find articulate
expression for his grief. Often the words were so simple that
they must have appeared naive had not his earnestness defined
their importance. Sometimes they were oddly conjoined as he
floundered for expression. They came as fast as the tears that
had preceded them.

'In the holidays . . . when you weren't with me . . . I thought
you might be dead . . . or killed.' The tears started to flow
again, but now Tony wiped them away impatiently with his
hand. Violently he shook his head. 'And I was rude . . . In the
bathroom to the Major. But it was because of seeing you again.
I was all excited and silly.'

Tony went on, speaking faster; his thoughts following illogical sequences, pouncing haphazardly into the present and
the past in his determination to exorcise all pockets of doubt
remaining in his mind.

'In your room . . . when I came to tea and you were on the
piano-stool and I kissed you . . . It wasn't because I was a
drip like Hunter. And before that . . . when I first saw you . . .'
Tony sniffed, and was crying again. But he talked on carefully,
feeling for words. His tears had become incidental to his voice;
something remote from himself that was to be ignored. 'You
think it's because my father's dead . . . And you know, and you
think I want you instead of him . . . But it's not . . . Because it's
different . . . how I love you.'

'Tony, you don't have to explain. You see – how to put it.
When I was an undergraduate we used to have a fashionable
catch-phrase – the way you'll have crazes for particular expres-
sions here. People would say, "don't rationalise". It makes
more sense than many of the people who used it realised, and
means "don't try to explain" . . . And especially not what is
most deeply inside you. You see . . . human beings are very

near to one another. Nearly every feeling they have is common to all of them. Even if it weren't so, then I understand how you feel . . .'

Tony had nodded with an acceptance that was only partial and conditional when David had spoken. Now, in a voice that was nearly his normal one, he said:

'It's not like that . . . You're not like anyone else either. Sometimes, when I have dreams, you're there . . . And you do all sorts of things to me . . . things you wouldn't know. And you undress my clothes. Well, I wouldn't let just anyone do that, would I?' Tony looked up suddenly; his eyes blazed as he flung the question.

David shook his head. He met the boy's eyes without betraying surprise. In fact he was marvelling at the uninhibited confidence, or else the dangerous dynamic of mental turmoil, that had proved powerful enough to force this confession to the surface.

'But it was like that as soon as I met you in the Great Quad . . . And before that too. I'd always wanted someone . . . But I couldn't let anyone unless I loved them . . . Then I loved you because you were so kind and what I'd always wanted and so good looking . . .

'You know when you asked me to tea in your room the first time?' The boy's tone was now straightforwardly conversational. 'And I twisted my clothes around? Well, that was because I wanted you . . . to straighten them again. Then in Cheltenham, when I tried on the new shorts, of course I could undo them really. But I wanted you to . . . like I spend hours thinking about sometimes.' Tony lowered his eyelids; though only momentarily. 'I was excited – you know – underneath. And I'd left my pants behind half on purpose. I really do wear them in summer . . . It would be pretty disgusting not to.'

Tony had retreated on to the arm of the chair and drawn his knees up to his chin. He had kicked off his other slipper so that his feet didn't slide off the leather, and with his right hand was idly exploring the contents of the waste-basket David had filled in the course of his unpacking.

'Tony, why did you really throw away the other suit?' David gestured towards the wardrobe, still lying on the bed. 'I don't mind two hoots. It's just that I'd like the picture straight while we are at it.'

Tony turned his lip down. 'I only *sort* of know.'

'Do you often throw clothes away?'

'Once I put a pair of my shorts in the boiler here . . . But that was different because a man touched them.' David frowned.

'How?'

'Hamley and I were buying sweets – at that wholesale shop in St Ebbes – and an old man patted my behind – no, *rubbed*; it was sheer sex. I was wild because I thought he'd made them dirty so I burnt them in the stoke-hole.'

'And the suit?'

'Well,' Tony tugged his hair with a violent gesture of concentration, 'after the night you hugged me properly I thought it was *wrong* to keep the suit because when I've got clothes I like on I feel *I'm* loving *me*, not you. D'you see?'

'I think so. But why keep the other suit then?'

Now Tony was baffled. Slowly, he said, 'I thought I might change my mind. You see, I'm very particular about clothes.'

'No!' David smiled broadly. 'I'd never have guessed it!'

Tony drove his fist into his ribs. 'Right, Rogers!' The threat, as usual, failed to materialise. But then Tony was serious again. 'I suppose I really like the grey suits because I think they make me look my best . . . Sort of sweet and sexy . . . For you,' he added quickly: he'd dropped his eyes over the 'sweet' only to raise them shamelessly again with the 'sexy'. 'Then, well, I just wanted *one* brand new to keep . . . For a bit, anyway,' he finished lamely.

'Because one of a thing is more valuable than two,' David suggested. 'And you keep it newly wrapped so that if I should somehow fail you will still have its emotional security. You will still have *something* to love that's really a projection, or part, of your own self. Or perhaps it's of another boy.'

Tony thought for what must have been a full minute. Then he said, 'You do understand.'

David smiled. 'Perhaps. But remember, to me at least, you're equally "sweet and sexy", as you horribly put it, in anything. Don't *you* worry what you look like. Now put the thing in the wardrobe.'

Tony slid off the chair to do so, then checked himself. 'David, why did you say just now that the suit was a *projection* or part of *another boy?*'

When David didn't answer, Tony said:

'It's funny you should. When I was about ten there was a boy next door with a suit like ours. He was terribly beautiful and I wanted to hug him . . . but I was afraid. I think it was after that that I started liking the suits more.'

Tony paused again when he'd opened the cupboard. '*You* won't put it in the boiler in the middle of the night, will you?'

David laughed. 'I promise! Only try to stop thinking of yourself as your own silver wool teddy bear.'

Tony came back to the fire. He was smiling happily again. He hoisted himself on to the arm of the chair and picked something out of the waste-basket. It was a tube of lipstick David had discovered tidying out the room. Tony now studied it with distaste, and David was reminded of the strange vision he had had earlier in the day.

'Where did this come from?'

'I turned it out of a drawer.'

'It must have been part of the acting make-up the Ghoul looked after.' Tony twisted the milled base of the tube thoughtfully. 'It's rather obscene, isn't it . . . like a dog. David? Are you going to sleep with me tonight?'

'No.' David looked quickly at the boy, but if the naivety was studied there was no admission of it in his face.

Tony simply nodded without emotion and retracted the lipstick. Then, as an afterthought, he extended it once more and slashed it carefully across David's brow, and then vertically down his nose. '*In Nomine Domini,*' he said, getting off the arm of the chair. He lobbed the tube back into the waste-basket from the door. 'You don't have sugar in your tea, do you?'

David shook his painted head.

'I'll bring you some as soon as the bell goes in the morning. It'll be in a glass, I'm afraid, but you soon get used to the *barbarities* of this place. I'll pinch it from the Jones' early-morning lot – I've got the kitchen pretty well organised. Oh! I nearly forgot! I've got something else for you.'

He disappeared, and was back a moment later with a bundle under his arm. 'My gown!' he announced triumphantly. 'I've got a spare one so you can keep this instead of the B.A. one you would have got if they hadn't sent you down. It's just the same.' He held the gown up and inspected it critically. 'It may be a little small. They're specially tailored for all the choir.' He bundled it up and lobbed it to David with a grin.

'Tones,' David said, in a rather vain attempt to cover what he really felt, 'the Vice-chancellor never bestowed a more coveted degree, nor ever indeed with such engaging informality.'

Tony bowed low in his cornflower pyjamas and said good night.

When the boy had gone David worked for two hours on his vocal sonata – more accurately it should perhaps have been called a concerto. The school was silent, and he began to move bars into the inevitable pattern that would eventually represent some small imposition of order upon chaos: perhaps his own sole emotional security, and not so very unlike Tony's magical suit hanging in its moth-proof polythene in his wardrobe. He knew every pitch and resonance of the boy's voice as well as he knew the range of a piano, and was able to summon and test its finest detail in his mind as he composed. It was its fulfilment at which he aimed.

As he worked, drawing out the tangled ribbons of melody and plaiting them into coherence across the living face of the page, he thought of the significance of Tony. The road he himself had followed to their meeting had lost definition. Past time had no more relevance. There was only a present; and perhaps a future.

Exhausted, David put the manuscript in a drawer, and got into bed. He resolved to put Tony and the boy's problems out of his mind for the night, and was surprised to discover he could do so. Tony was safe; within a few yards of him.

David turned out the light and slid his head beneath the newly-starched pillow-slip belonging to some boy called Lavington and closed his eyes. A single penguin was wandering around on an ice-flow, quite aimlessly, and in a world that was cool, barren and absolute like bars of Bach. For a long time David watched the penguin, conscious only of its slow, awkward movements, and of the pressure of Lavington's pillow on his cheek. Then the slide changed in his mind, and the world was warmer, but still muted; eminently respectable like Harris tweed. There were hills like mulberry eiderdown, and a sun dissolving into a beaten-copper loch. Then, as the slide changed again, he was looking at another aspect of the same Western Isles, where the fractured limb of a headland, out flung, was thankfully being licked, soothed by the Atlantic.

## 24

'WHERE are your garters?' Tony frowned belligerently. The lamb boy was too petrified to speak.

'Oh, all right! Just pull your socks up, and *straighten them.*' Tony turned impatiently on his heel. 'School!' he yelled. 'Hurry up into line!'

'Sir, are you *in love* with Miss Poole?' asked a little boy, after being meaningfully nudged by his companion in the crocodile

'Silence!' yelled Tony. There was an unpleasant edge to his voice

'Davies says you were talking to her,' the boy muttered by way of explanation.

'I'll see you after prayers in the prefects' room,' Tony said coolly: he had sneaked up on the other side of the double column. He took up station beside David, and made a wide gesture with his arm which is usually associated in westerns with the cry of 'Wagons roll!'. The school moved down the drive past the gaping concrete gnomes and through the wrought-iron gates into St Aldate's.

The early morning sun had washed the pavements gold, and rendered the silver-suited crocodile an alarmingly conspicuous affair. Fortunately there were still few people about. David turned his head and reviewed the column. The conclusion he came to was that he had never exactly envisaged Rogers in this capacity. He shrugged himself deeper into his duffle-coat. At least the university term hadn't started yet.

'You cold?' Tony asked.

'Bit.'

Tony looked over his shoulder at the crocodile. '*They'd* better not be,' he said awkwardly. 'I told them "no coats" because we look better in our suits. Coats in summer, yes, if you like,' he added thoughtfully, 'because our blazers and cotton shorts

don't add up to much. But in the winter terms when we wear
best suits all the time, no.'

David opened his mouth with a view to challenging this
logic, but changed his mind. They passed through the college
gates. Tony nodded graciously to the porter in the lodge who,
to David's confusion, touched the rim of his bowler and said,
'Master Sandel.'

David looked up to become aware of a crisis. Cutting diagonally across the quad, down one of the paths whose radii
branched out from the pond, was his scout Haggert. Even
Haggert, he knew, would look straight through one unless his
existence were first acknowledged; but he couldn't decently
ignore him. He looked at his watch and decided the risk was
justifiable.

David smiled good morning, and the column came to a halt
some twenty yards from the pond. Haggert had been walking
with his eyes dead ahead and a broom at the trail, but instantly
came alive when David spoke.

'You'll be back with us then, sir?'

David smiled and shook his head. 'Not exactly, I'm afraid.
I'm through with Academe . . . Or at least its rarefied levels.'

'A bad business, sir, and I know it.' Haggert inverted his
broom and prepared to lean on it, which was a bad sign.
Inexplicably, he winked at one of the boys behind David. 'I
heard all about it from James in the Buttery, sir, and I told him
just how disgusted I was, sir, them sending you down when
you were lying unconscious in the hospital too. And I said why
pick on Mr Rogers the only real gentleman I've had on my
staircase in years, sir? Cars and high spirits I said is natural,
and even if he shouldn't of been racing, that's no reason to
send him down unconscious and *in absurdum* in that Lord
Petrey's on fours phrase, sir . . .'

'"*Absentia*", I think.' David smiled.

'Oh, right, sir.' Haggert had begun the fatal process of
rolling a cigarette. His eyes had lost focus. 'There's them of
the gentlemen as between you and me, sir, that's no good,' he
said sadly. 'But though you've been living out of college this
year, sir, I've always remembered you as the best. I used to say
to Mrs H. sometimes before cycling down from Headington,
it's worth it. May, just for that Mr Rogers. He's what the
gentlemen was once. Then when I was doing your rooms, sir,

and dusting that photograph of your little brother as was killed in the earthquake, the tears would come to my eyes, sir, and I'd think Mr Rogers is the best we've got. He's *human*, sir, if you take my meaning. He'll give himself to something worthwhile like a government that's fair for once, or education like I see you've done, sir . . .'

Haggert broke off to lick the edge of the cigarette-paper, and David seized the advantage quickly.

'You were always too good to me,' he said. 'Now I've gone and done you out of a Degree Day tip!' Turning his back as best he could on the school, he gave Haggert two pounds, which he tucked into his apron.

Haggert grinned. 'Thank you, sir, though I don't know why I let one as good as you do it. I hope you'll see to it as a favour to me and Mrs H. that you beat some sense into young Haggert here, sir!'

David stared at him.

'That's him with the sly look, sir.' Haggert pointed with the broom. 'You just watch him.'

David followed his glance to a boy a couple of yards away in the waiting crocodile. Earth gape, he thought dully, Rogers has done it again. But Haggert, completely un-offended, was wishing him good luck. He picked up his broom and was gone.

'School, stay just where you are!' Tony said loudly.

David came out of his daze to find Tony had gone forward to the pond alone. He looked at the school, some of whom were becoming restless, and went up to the boy with mounting exasperation. Tony turned his face unsmilingly and stared into his eyes.

'Was it consummated?'

David looked at him uncomprehendingly.

Tony's jaw was quivering with rage. 'You haven't got a brother,' he said. 'Only me.'

'Tony . . .'

'Why did you lie to that man?'

David sat down suddenly on the coping of the pond and pressed his knuckles against his forehead. He looked up again. 'I didn't. Haggert is highly imaginative.'

'But there was a photo?'

'Yes.'

'Whose?'

David looked unseeingly at the school twenty yards away.
He became aware of the otherwise empty quad sleeping quietly
in the morning sun, and of the slight figure with its uncanny
beauty and poise standing beside him. He looked at Tony, and
while a part of him acknowledged the absurdity of the scene,
he was overcome by a tenderness that made him inarticulate.
After a moment he regained control of himself.

'He was a boy at school. I loved him the way one only can
at seventeen.' He turned desperately to Tony. 'Why – far from
knowing him as you suggest I hadn't the guts so much as to
*speak* to him in two terms. That photo was taken by a friend of
mine somewhere in the grounds while I wrapped my head in a
towel in my study for embarrassment.'

The inflexion of Tony's voice hadn't altered when he spoke
again. 'You told that man he was killed in an earthquake. *Why?*'

David buried his head in his hands again. 'No. That was
Haggert's fantasy again. I once told him the boy was dead.'

'Boys don't just die nowadays,' Tony said with devastating
logic.

David got to his feet and looked carefully into his angry face.
'No. He killed himself. He was just fourteen.'

A fallen leaf came drifting across the gravel with a crablike
motion, supported on its crisp, curled edges, and stopped at
Tony's feet. He raised his shoe and crushed it into the ground.

'Why?'

'No one really knows. There was a love affair with an older
boy . . . And a row with his housemaster . . . Then they found
him. I think the master said something the boy couldn't believe
. . . and that somehow it destroyed his mind.'

David watched Tony's face, and could see him searching
desperately for an explanation.

'Was he . . . like Hamley?' His voice was indignant.

David shook his head. 'The whole thing involved only a kiss.'

Tony stared into the pond. 'So he killed himself,' he said
slowly. Then his whole face became charged with fury. He
swung savagely on David with parted lips. 'The drip!' he cried.
The miserable stinking little wet weed!'

'I'm sorry.' David picked up the crushed leaf; crumbling it
completely before scattering its fragments on the water. 'But
we must hurry up into the Chapel, so call the school.'

'No,' Tony said petulantly, 'the head-boy is thinking.' He

raised one foot on to the low coping of the pond, and put his cap on his knee as if to conceal its nudity.

David felt desperate. 'Tones, we can talk about the whole thing later if you want to; but you can't hold the other boys to ransom like this now.'

'Can't I, hell!' Tony said unpleasantly. 'They'll do what I tell them.'

David shrugged his shoulders with more confidence than he felt. 'Okay . . . I'm going to count five and then chuck first soprano Sandel into the pond . . . And if you go on staring at your own reflection like that I won't need to as you'll probably leap in . . . One!'

'Very funny!' Tony said sourly. 'The Ghoul made those sort of jokes and you haven't been here twenty-four hours yet.'

'Two and three,' David said steadily. Suddenly he wanted to embrace the boy. If he might only do so for the purpose of throwing him in the pond, that was the way it must be. Tony looked at the creases of his shorts, and at what were clearly a new pair of wine-topped socks. He tugged unnecessarily at the hem of his jacket before staring at David for a second. Then slowly he turned his head.

'Hurry up, school!' he yelled. 'You're *late!*'

The waiting boys re-formed the crocodile. Tony put his cap on again. It was one of those gestures no medium will ever record; which, perhaps by the very transience of their nature, leave the world richer.


The school filed into the Chapel and took their places automatically. The lamb boy, David noticed, was looking alarmed. He found a place for himself in the choir stalls nearest the altar, and sat down. Tony had disappeared. David looked about him. The silence was absolute, and he wished someone would at least drop a hymn book. No one did. He realised that the majority of eyes were turned towards him; waiting. Tony had still not appeared. He racked his brain for the privileges of the laity within the Anglican Establishment. It was as void of remembrance as the silence.

With sudden resolution David went to the lectern. He gripped the eagle's pinions, surveyed the school apologetically, and dropped his head. 'Let us pray,' he said.

There was a stirring in the Chapel. The school, he supposed, though his eyes were tightly shut, must be getting on to its knees. So far so good. David reflected uncomfortably that this was one of the most revered places in the country, in comparison with which King's, Cambridge, was upstart, even a little vulgar.

'Our Father,' he said loudly into the great vault.

The response was instant and unanimous.

'*We chart 'n Heaven . . .*'

'And we're off,' David thought with relief.

The school was rhythmically pleading for the coming of the Kingdom when he felt the tap on his shoulder. Jones must have materialised from the vestry: at least he was in full regalia. David gave way. Jones took over neatly. Tony, David saw as he turned, had also reappeared, and had occupied the stall he had abandoned. He sank down beside him while the school forgave unspecified trespasses. Tony raised pleading eyes to heaven; then rolled them at David. His rigid form was convulsed with giggles, whose impulses transmitted themselves to David. 'We didn't giggle, because we never do,' he could hear the boy saying primly in his memory. Tony put his right hand in David's jacket pocket, and David removed it. Tony put it back again, and there apparently it had to remain until the conclusion of the service.

Eventually Jones stopped praying. A hymn was sung without music. It might have been better had David been able to conduct it; but then the entity was distorted for him by the proximity of Tony who contrived to lend it the arbitrarily selected effects of Carmen, Madam Butterfly, and the dying Mimi. David realised that he was being treated to an assertion of Sandel on something like the scale of a Moscow May Day. Tony, in a word, was demonstrating. The performance ended on an 'amen' which Tony embellished with the passion of a first-night Melba. In the few seconds of silence before Jones pronounced the blessing, David turned to look at him and was met by a mockery that was made the more unnerving by two patches of red and green light that were thrown on the boy's face from the rose-window above the altar. Tony moved his head; the lights played with his eyes, and David felt he must cry out aloud. A spasm of vacuity replaced his abdomen, as if a cold horseshoe had been laid against the skin beneath his sternum. Tony still had his hand buried in his pocket. As Jones pronounced his last recommendation, and what must surely be the ultimate 'amen', he withdrew it. He smiled so that the lozenge of red light touched his lips. Then he turned his face into the shadow.

## 25

THE morning passed quickly. Jones proved amiably disposed towards the misunderstanding in the Chapel, and was, as David had suspected, a different man when away from his wife. The morning's teaching resolved itself into little more than the discovery of names. With the morning break David postponed Tony's first music lesson in order to get to know his colleagues better. The occasion in the staff room was marked by thick tea and paste sandwiches. David eulogised as best he could on the value of raffia-work to one of the two ladies who came in by the day, and he also supplied the Major with three cigarettes. Rain and mist had descended on the Thames Valley, quickly choking the promise of the crystal morning, and the Major stumped out in a trench-coat with two subservient batboys to inspect the rugger pitches, and returned with a frown to borrow a fourth cigarette. As the bell was going his morning was made by the arrival of a ready-mixed barrel of mild and bitter. He took the next period off to install it, and the form he was supposed to be taking, left to their own devices, apparently knew better either than to make any noise, or register a complaint.

After lunch Jones peered into the gloom and said: 'French and English with the middle school in the Hall, I think, Rogers.'

Finding Tony, David was told that in the days when he had deigned to join the game, he had almost been murdered as a result of being the only boy to change into gym things; and that he had better plug his ears with something.

David soon discovered why. The game bore no resemblance to anything he remembered from his own prep school days, and in fact there seemed to be some dispute as to whether

it was called *French and English,* or *British Bulldogs.* As far
as David was concerned each title equally well expressed the
spirit of militancy he refereed. The carnage was devastating.
A minor Arnhem rendered the more horrific by the surrepti-
tious expression of personal animosities as the civilised veneer
melted in the heat of battle.

One boy was chosen and stood in the middle of the floor.
The others, gathered at one end of the room, had to rush past
him and reach the opposite wall. The boy in the middle had
to seize one of the mass and lift him clear of the floor, when
there became two Bulldogs, or Englishmen; and so it went on.
The obvious thing would seem to be to get lifted up with the
greatest possible speed and the least pain, but few appeared
to see it like that, and those who did were carefully ignored
in favour of more violent and co-operative assault later on.
Meanwhile teeth, nails and shoes were freely employed as the
occasion required, and the floor was rapidly littered with the
bloody and tearful forms of those left for dead.

David watched with a fascination that at times he suspected
as unhealthy while Crockett succumbed to his own personal
Alamo, and until Hunter's struggling body had been dislocated
by the simultaneous assault of four avengers, with the aid of a
fifth who carefully strangled him with his tie, and then blew the
whistle with which Jones had thoughtfully provided him.

He turned desperately to the Blüthner as to Orpheus.
Gradually, with muttered threats and sly, retributive kicks, the
beasts were stilled. After some minutes of Tchaikovsky, which
David would have found unthinkable except in such an emergency, they began to dress themselves and gather round the
piano.

David stopped playing and looked curiously at the company,
seeing many of their faces for the first time. Without warning
he exploded a fist over a chord that would have jarred Winifred
Atwell. The jam session was on.

When David subsequently looked back over the wild hour
which followed it was to review a small miracle. Something
called the 'junior percussion cupboard' was broken into, and
there appeared a collection of tambourines, cymbals, drums
and triangles. Pictures came off the wall for timpani, a washboard was mysteriously discovered, and as a crowning effect
some wild-eyed genius brought a dozen steel foot-rules which

he proceeded to scatter over the wires of the Blüthner. The makeshift orchestra went to work with a spontaneity and cohesion that was astounding. The spring of the boys' musical abilities was called forth by the insistent rhythms as the animal had been revealed by the Bulldog game, and, likewise, proved itself to be very far from square.

In the middle of a dynamic interpretation of the *St Louis Blues* David became aware of Tony standing in the doorway with the corners of his mouth turned down. He returned a moment later with what seemed to be a glass of tea, but which proved in fact to be whisky which David subsequently discovered him to have liberated from a bottle of the Major's in the staff room. Still without speaking, the boy returned a second time with a mirror, which he placed on the music-rest and adjusted to reflect David's hands.

Perhaps it was half an hour later, when St Cecilia's middle school was savagely embroidering the hottest boogie David knew, that Mrs Jones opened the door and switched the lights on and off twice in quick succession. She didn't actually say 'Time, gentlemen, please'; but the intimation was there. David stopped playing. 'Tea, sir,' one boy said. Another looked at his watch. 'It's not,' he retorted; then hazarded: 'Mrs Jones can't bear jazz, sir.' David nodded. The boys began to pack up their instruments and return the pictures, washboard and steel rulers to their more usual, if mundane, places.

At about six o'clock, when the lower school was rowdily enjoying its early supper in the tutelage of Jean Poole, David allowed himself to be persuaded out into the cold to buy the Major cigarettes. He was just leaving the tobacconist-confectioner's opposite the main gate of St Cecilia's, having discovered the Major was mistaken in supposing himself to hold an account there, and subsequently having had to part with a pound which he never saw again, when he witnessed a sight that must have embarrassed any member of the currently sitting Roads Committee who happened at that moment to glance out of the Town Hall windows a hundred yards away. In the gathering gloom and rush-hour traffic Tony emerged suddenly from the college gates at the head of his choir in their opera cloaks. Barely looking at the triple stream of cars, and without breaking step, Tony led the choir straight out into the roaring thoroughfare of

St Aldate's. David held his breath in fear while on all sides the
astonished traffic came to a standstill. Looking neither to right
nor left Tony raised his four-cornered hat on behalf of himself
and the other fifteen boys, and then they were safely across.
David found his teeth were so tightly locked together that he
relaxed his jaw only with difficulty before he could speak.

'What on earth did you have to do that for?'

'Hallo!' Tony was surprised.

'Do what?'

'Cross the road?'

'Oh, I see.' Tony indicated the confectionery shop into
which the choir were now milling, having broken ranks. 'We
sometimes come over to buy sweets after Evensong . . . Only
it's strictly unofficial, and you aren't here . . . Understand?'

The boy had taken hold of David's lapels and was pulling
him backwards and forwards on his feet. He followed the
direction of David's eyes, while the crowds making last minute
dashes to newstands and the general post office jostled around
them.

'I should make the best of it!' Tony smiled, pulling him
forward particularly violently so that for a moment he was
almost engulfed in the black cloak. 'I'm retiring soon.'

'The hat is ridiculous,' David countered weakly. 'It makes
you look like a diminutive Venetian nobleman . . . a baby
Doge, perhaps. As to the whole effect, well . . . A Dark Angel.
The sort of thing that might have sent Milton or Bunyan diving
under the bed.'

Tony gripped the wings of the cloak, and with a rapid movement locked them about David's waist. Just as unexpectedly
he released him. 'If I wasn't here in my professional capacity
I should have to attack you for that, David,' he said slowly.
There was only dream-logic in his tone.

The choir were beginning to assemble on the pavement;
stuffing bars and paper-bags into their pockets. Hunter had a
slash of brown blackboard chalk running from his collarbone
to his knees. Tony had been following David's glance. Now
their eyes met.

'He was cheeky,' Tony blurted, and turned scarlet.

'Don't you want to buy anything yourself?' David asked.
The question made time. He was revolted.

Tony shook his head, silently counting his raven-like flock.

Some of it was still in the shop. 'I'm cold,' he said, shivering suddenly. 'Have you had the fire on in your room all day?'

'Since lunch.'

'Will you play me some of the B Minor Mass after supper? . . . Oh, and I've got something I want you to help me with.'

'As long as you don't appear in that hat.'

'"Somebody's Academic and Ecclesiastical Robe Makers",' Tony read, having taken off the hat, and peering inside it in the fading light.

'You're the ecclesiastical part, absurdly enough.'

'"Episcopal" would be more dignified,' said Tony. 'I should really be made a Boy Bishop to terminate my career . . . Hunter could wash my feet.'

'There are times when you're quite as revolting as anyone at that place,' David said, nodding towards St Cecilia's. 'Probably I'll never know why I tolerate you the way you are . . . God save Sandel at least from an Eton and Cecilia's varnish.'

The choir were now collected on the pavement.

'Right away in your pocket, Lattimer,' Tony said to a child who couldn't have been four foot high. He grinned at David. 'Now we return.'

David looked at the seemingly impenetrable streams of traffic. 'I think I'll throw in my fortune with yours.'

## 26

TONY sat on the bed with the cricket bat clasped between his thighs. He was making no progress in his attempt to roll on a new rubber grip. The gramophone scraped for a second, and there was a metallic click as it switched itself off. It was the curate, whom David had discovered had read maths at Jesus, and held a diploma to teach the violin, who was on duty. In the silence it was his voice that could now be heard, together with the dragging of slippered feet, and the running of taps and banging doors, which were the sounds of the school going to bed. Tony had apparently intimated to all the staff that he had made Mr Rogers responsible for seeing that his light was out, so that they needn't trouble to make the trip to the east wing.

David put the B Minor away while Tony watched him.

'When do you think my record will come out?'

'I don't know. What did they say?'

Tony stopped struggling with the bat handle. 'They didn't. It was recorded five weeks ago though.'

'Probably should be quite soon now.'

Tony looked doubtfully at the gramophone. 'If we're still here.'

'What do you mean?'

The boy moved the bat handle about between his legs as if it were a joy-stick and he was fighting to control the plane in a storm. 'Doesn't this place *bore* you? I mean, you must be able to get a better job . . . not teaching little boys with immature minds? What was that miserable drip Hunter doing dancing round you this afternoon with a piccolo?'

David sensed Tony had reached his point. He wasn't altogether sure what it might be. 'It wouldn't be quite proper to be bored on my second day, you know. I've got the teaching to do . . . and meanwhile we're together. I don't think you could have it better than that.'

The boy said nothing for a moment. David frowned at the floor.

'You know we all have to learn an instrument here?' Tony went on.

David looked up.

'Well, somehow you'd just expect a drip like Hunter to learn the piccolo, wouldn't you?'

'You're making an ass of yourself, Tones . . . No, you're quite mad,' David added more resolutely. 'And I don't believe you're specifically jealous at all . . . What is it then?'

'There are tramps behind the station,' Tony said, tapping the bat against his shoe. 'Did you know that? I might go and visit them. Or I could walk out of here. You'd feel pretty silly then, wouldn't you?'

'Probably,' David said, watching him steadily.

Tony took out a pen-knife. 'See this? Which bit would you cut off Hunter? Because I'm going to do it . . . And torture him . . . Why are you looking at me like that?'

'I'm thinking you're upset, and that it's making you very unpleasant. Just why I'm waiting to find out.'

'*Upset!*' Tony snorted. 'First you're the Ghoul only twice as dirty and now you're Mrs Jones! You think I wouldn't let the tramps touch me, don't you? You don't think I'd dig this in Hunter's balls!'

'Tony, I don't suppose for a moment that the tramps exist; and if you wave that knife in front of another boy I shall have to take it away from you.'

The boy reversed the knife in his hand; holding it like a dagger. At the same time his body tensed on the edge of the bed. 'Go on! Just try! Now!' The words ran into each other with the fluidity of hysteria.

David went towards him holding out his hand; and the next moments developed the characteristics of a dream sequence, or something filmed in slow motion. The knife curved savagely down. He saw the skin of his wrist gathered like a worm-cast or the paring of an apple; then the blood rising sluggishly as if startled in its nakedness. The fury faded in the boy's eyes to be replaced by something duller, but equally dangerous. His body didn't relax at all. David stepped back to find some part of his mind dispassionately acknowledging that the boy's gipsy blood had bequeathed him something more than his beauty.

'I want us to be away from here and just together,' Tony said. There was no apology, or any other concession in his voice. He tossed the knife to David, careless of the fact that the blade was still unclasped. 'You can't kiss me and next minute think you're my schoolmaster. It's ridiculous. And I'm not just anyone's boy, you know.'

'Then you might abandon revolting fantasies about tramps behind stations,' David suggested.

'That Hunter needs his new suit dragging round the garden,' Tony said, not listening.

'You've already made a pretty vicious symbolic job of it,' David said, remembering the chalk mark.

'I'll do it again.'

'It was a thoroughly ugly gesture.'

'What do you think of his suit?'

'*I* don't notice these things!' David protested. 'As far as I'm concerned there are a crowd of children here and one lunatic Amazon.'

'Like hell you don't notice them! You're going to be a typical soft, sticky queer like the Ghoul in no time. Probably you'll brush Hunter's hair fifty times on duty nights. And that's *all* you'll do.'

'I'm sticky all right,' David said grimly. There was blood on the carpet now. 'And the jerkier moments of your adolescence seem likely to leave me mashed, never mind soft. Since when, incidentally, have you been calling people *queer*, like any jealous girl who's failed to make a conquest?'

'Don't change the argument,' Tony said irrationally. 'You're not getting cissy and ineffectual and giving orders and I'm getting you *out*.'

'Thank you,' David said dryly. 'Meanwhile you might refrain from either *torturing* my pupils or wrecking their clothes because neither are your rivals.'

'"*My pupils*", you see!' Tony shouted triumphantly.

'I'm going to get this wrist bound up,' David said.


'Can't you take over my regular piano lessons from old Mrs Culham?' Tony asked when he returned.

David studied Jean's bandage. 'I don't think I've met any old Mrs Culham yet, and anyway I'm not qualified to teach the thing, I just play it.'

'Balls!' Tony retorted. 'I'll tell Jones you're a Fellow of the Royal Academy.'

'You'll do nothing of the sort . . . Besides, I don't think Mrs Jones would believe it.'

'The jazz, you mean?' Tony guessed. 'It takes my aunt to deal with that woman. I think she's probably the only person who can.'

David smiled faintly. 'What about this bat?' he said, as Tony began toying with the roll of rubber again. 'What do you want a new grip for anyway? The bat itself looks practically brand new.'

Tony was indignant. 'It's two seasons old! I want to put it away for the winter.'

David couldn't help a smile spreading across his face. 'There's hardly a single ball-mark on the blade.'

'Well, I hardly ever hit them!' Tony was now smiling happily back.

'Swordsmanship might prove to be your natural sport,' David suggested.

The boy looked away. With a terrific effort he got the rubber ring over the end of the bat handle only to have it spring back into his hands. David felt uncomfortable. He stared into the bright, honeycomb elements of the gas fire; then he took the resolution.

'Tones . . . can you look me in the eyes and say this isn't some sort of mildly animal demonstration?'

'No,' the boy said, without raising his head. 'But I can always look you in the eyes when I want to.'

'Then for heaven's sake put the bat away and I'll see what I can do with it later!' David was exasperated.

Tony's face became animated as he looked up again. 'I want you to smell it first.'

'*Smell* it?'

'The linseed oil,' Tony explained. He stood up; then sat down quickly again. 'Can't have them hanging skew because of *that.*'

'God's sake! You're winning,' David said, bitterly almost. 'You're winning.' But he went to the bed.

'Now!' Tony exclaimed triumphantly. He reached out carefully with the bat; laying the tip of the cool blade against David's cheek. Then, squaring the blade, he laid it fiat against his chest, following every movement with his eyes. It came obscurely to David that he was being tested for radioactivity with a Geiger counter.

Tony's face was slightly flushed. His loosely sheathed body had the shadow of old pewter. It became brightly polished when he stooped through the white beam of the reading-lamp. He slid the bat under the bed and kissed David. 'Bardot,' he said without much conviction.

David stood back not knowing where the travesty ended and reality began, or what the travesty might be designed to conceal. He looked for words; but the task was impossible. One might as well transpose Beethoven for typewriter. But there was no need for words, because love was a synthetic transmission like music.

He was watching the slow-motion film again. This time there was no fury in the boy's face. Tony turned off the reading-lamp. He lay back. Like the Mayan on the stone he looked for release into immortality. But it was David who must use the knife, and as priest it was his faith, the lead part, which discovered doubt. When he did obey it was with the aggression

of spoiled confidence. He saw Tony pull off one of his shoes.
Then he had thrown it at the ceiling light and there was broken
glass falling into the room.

'They sew them specially strong on boys' things,' Tony
gasped, letting David's hand alone, and licensing the violence
of its down-stroke. David was enraged and his hand continued
down with sudden madness to tear cloth now. Tony's disbelief
convulsed his whole body. He was twice naked. Fantasy had
hidden from him that truth may be unpredictable, a wilderness. He was lost and quite alone there before he discovered
its freedom.

David had passed through hatred, and was equally confused
by its aftermath. For an instant his teeth had touched the boy's
shoulder. Then he had snatched them away, and it was his own
forearm that was bruised.

After that, tentatively, they came together. Their individual
peace, selfish, jealous and sovereign, they found could be one.
An equally strange but deeper peace possessed and bound
them. The sweet water had passed beyond protest to blend
with the salt.

Nearly asleep, David gave expression to the idea. 'We're like
the Otter and your sea.'

'Where I threw my clothes away?'

'I didn't think of that!' Could the boy have read his unconscious? But even Tony's intuitive moment couldn't raise David
far from the threshold of sleep. 'Which of us is which?'

'I'm the Otter,' Tony said practically. 'I'm smaller. Then
coming to you is only coming home.'

'I wonder . . .' Doubt, perhaps, tilted David into the security
of sleep.

'Yes! Your bed is the *sea* bed!' Tony's excitement woke him.

'Okay! Then I'm embracing you, slight stream. You cease to
meander and forfeit your babbling sound. Lose your identity
just now at least and . . . be still, Tones . . . The tide's full, and
the sea's asleep . . .'


The dawn couldn't penetrate the curtain. Instead, it tumbled
beneath it in radiating shafts, and spread out across the floor
to be reflected by the myriad, pearl-like fragments of the shattered light bulb.

David picked his way carefully over the carpet and turned the fire on. He smiled faintly as he remembered an idiotic impression of the night before that Tony was going to ask for a coat-hanger. Now he collected the boy's clothes from the floor and laid them on a chair in front of the fire.

Tony opened his eyes. 'I was only pretending to be asleep! When do we have to get up?'

'About an hour.'

Tony turned on his stomach and lay with his head on his arm. He brought his lips to the back of his hand and blew through them vibrantly, purring like a cat. 'All quick like a rubber-band plane,' he said. 'Does it look like a long trousers day?'

'You have odd waking thoughts.'

'Put them to warm, anyway,' Tony said.

David did so; then settled on the edge of the bed in his dressing- gown. 'Tones, where did you come from?'

The boy shifted his head on his arm. 'A long way away,' he said. 'From a magic place.'

'Tell me.'

'A shore, I think,' Tony seemed to be remembering. 'Perhaps it was an island. Anyway there was sand and it was bright yellow.'

'What did you do there?'

Tony turned to look at David. 'That's where I lived. Under a very tall tree. A special sort. It was called a Storm Tree. Then there was the sea, too, which was blue, and some ordinary green palm trees. But the Storm Tree was my tree. It was always safe there . . . If you were near enough to touch it. It had bright things high up in the branches sometimes. They were babyish, sweet things, like glacé cherries and angelica and something that was silver. I don't think they mattered much though . . . And anyway they weren't always there . . . or else you just couldn't see them.'

'Were there any people?'

Tony was sucking his forearm, and had made a scarlet patch on the skin. He shook his head. 'Just me.'

'Were you lonely?'

'No, never.'

The room was getting warmer, and Tony sat up, resting on his elbow. 'You needn't believe me if you don't want to,' he added confusedly.

'I'm sorry,' David said. 'Tell me what you were like. What did you wear?'

Tony thought for a moment. 'It's hard to remember. Clothes. No . . . nothing. Because I remember piling the sand on my knees and feeling how warm it was. Sometimes I felt I had glass feet . . . You could see the flowers through them where there was grass. I don't know what sort they were. Quite often you could hear music in the Tree.'

'What kind of music?'

'Wind music. And the noise the sea made on the beach. It was real music . . . Only it *wasn't* . . . Tony puckered his brow. 'It was certainly harmonised. I think someone must have done it specially for me.' He smiled archly.

'Oh, and I had a red boat I used to row about in,' Tony said suddenly. 'And lobster pots which I let down into the sea. There were pineapples on a row of bushes above the beach.'

Leaning over, Tony moved his head from side to side; trying to tickle David's chest with his hair. 'It's a secret though . . . Where I lived,' he said.

Tony became restless; bouncing on the bed. 'I hate you, you know, Rogers,' he said after a moment. 'You're very rude to me sometimes. You don't like me enough. I think I'll have to organise you better.'

David smiled at the ceiling, 'What'll that involve?'

Tony didn't answer; but began punching him at close quarters.

'I think I can guess,' David went on, catching hold of his wrists. 'Violent ambivalence.'

Tony struggled to free himself, the colour mounting in his face. 'What does that mean?' David laughed. '*Tell* me!' Tony demanded, butting fiercely with his head.

'No.'

'Right! I'll jump on you,' Tony announced simply. 'No, on second thoughts, I think I'll just snooze a bit.'

He sank back on the pillow. David released his wrists. Tony was on top of him in an instant; kneeling on his stomach, and pinning his shoulders down.

'*David, what does that word mean?*' He began brutally bouncing on his knees, while his eyes searched David's for the first signs of weakening.

David shook his head solemnly between gasps. Tony landed

with particular violence; then, parting his knees, he collapsed on top of David like a crumpled paper-bag. At the same time he drew the sheet over both their heads; pouncing with it like a giant butterfly net.

'Sandel has got you, I think,' he said in the yellow twilight. 'You can't beat me just because you have more words.'

'Tones – for heaven's sake – we're not at war, you and I.'

'That depends on your behaviour,' Tony said.

Still in the opaque world beneath the sheet, Tony cupped his hands about his eyes trying to create a pool of deeper darkness in which to read the luminous figures on David's watch. 'Stop shaking or I can't see!' he demanded unreasonably.

David could feel his concentrated breath stirring the fine hairs on his wrist.

'Still!' Tony said indignantly. 'I've got it . . . Twenty-five to eight. I'd better get up and collect our morning tea.'

Tony crawled to the end of the bed, drawing the sheet with his teeth like a puppy. David sat up. The room wasn't as warm as he'd supposed.

'I don't want you to fall asleep again,' Tony explained. He tore the sheet right off to make sure, then knelt on the end of the bed, laughing, and with his hands clasped between his knees. Suddenly he was back with a shallow dive. David caught him.

'Rogers! . . . B-bully!' Tony protested. 'You're hugging me in *two*'

> *'Godes bones!*
> *It's semi-Tones!*
> *And calls for diatonic!'*

David released him.

'D.i.r.e. t.o.n.i.c., I suppose. Witty,' Tony said, panting. 'You're madder than Schumann.'

Inwardly David checked. Bruce, he thought.

Tony filled his lungs threateningly. 'Shall I do a bit of *Frauenliebe und Leben*?'

'No!' David made a grab to cover his mouth. 'Spare me lieder in bed.'

'Leda wouldn't have you in bed,' Tony said. 'Only swans.' Even at its smuggest his smile was tolerable. Imperiously, he elbowed David in the ribs. 'Rogers, I've been thinking. With you schizoid as Schumann, and me brilliant without complications . . .'

'Yes, Tonimus.'

'Shut up . . . without complications, we ought to . . .'

'Tonimus.'

'. . . to find the pun about Sandel's sandals. But I'm more concerned,' Tony still breathed heavily, his new concentration becoming fierce, 'about those cathedral drips – Christ Church. Some of them have started to wear shorts and suits of that greasy, drab man-made fibre stuff. The rot has set in. It lowers the tone of the university.'

Profoundly David nodded. '*The Times,* Tonimus.'

'Yes, I *will* write.' Tony reached out for his superior shorts. 'I'll expect a cheque for these.' He held up the rent flannel. 'Or d'you want me to ask Miss Poole to mend them?'

'The boiler,' David said.

'They'd never mend well enough to wear,' Tony said, grudgingly.

David was irritated. 'You must bloody well learn to lose some things sometimes, you vain nit.'

'If they were sewn up you could do it again.'

'And if you consciously prepare for that sort of contingency you're revolting – and I opt out.'

'Oh, so? Ho-hum!'

They were silent for some moments.

'The glass,' David said. 'Put my slippers on your feet.'


## 27


S OMEHOW the school worked. Behind the functioning of the choir, whose members marched out two or even three times daily, the school carried on with an improvisation that was only a little less competent than David's jazz band. Education happened. David, moving from class to class largely as the muddled head of Jones directed him, went with it. '*Ex* and *ducere,* Rogers,' Tony said to him one day. 'It means to *lead out*. Your job is to capture the imagination of those drips. There's not much hope for them . . . but you'd better get on with it.'

'Prig,' David said; but he proceeded to lead out with enlightenment. The problem was what to do with the precipitate. Mediaeval noblemen, he learnt from a contemporary of Hunter's, *wore soft leather bots with clocks on top of them;* while von Manz, after some desperate concentration with a dictionary, informed him that *Mercedes had good engines, but the Rolls-Royce the better carcass.* Well, why not? As it stood the English language dealt dully with inanimate bodies. From one of the smallest boys he discovered that *Oliver Twist* was the creation of Dick Chickens.

At the beginning of the second week of term Tony announced his resignation from the choir. The move was accomplished by the simple expedient of calling upon the college organist Sir Vernon Bull and explaining to the astonished man that he proposed to choose his own time for going out to pasture, and that though there was as yet no necessity, he felt it would better suit his dignity to do so now. Imagining the scene later, David suspected it must have been a speech not unlike General McArthur's. When pressed, Tony had apparently confessed that he had a secondary motive, which was to devote himself entirely to recording a work of a fellow Academician, Sir David Rogers.

The truth, David realised, was that the boy was terrified of losing control of his voice suddenly. In fact he never did. His voice, which had always been a freak, slipped half an octave without falter; while its last moments remained true.

Meanwhile Tony officially retired; the opera cloak, which he had chosen to consider his own, going to join the best grey suit in its polythene wardrobe bag. He made it quite clear, however, that he would continue to hold more than nominal control over the choir, as well as the school. Among other official functions he would certainly preside on November the 22nd, which was St Cecilia's Day, when, by a long established tradition, the choir held a beano behind locked doors at High Table, while any resident dons made do with a sandwich in Common Room. In addition, he intimated to the appropriate quarters that he would expect the gold replica of the senior chorister's cup for the second year running; the two plucked capons,

half-score of lampreys, and five crowns, which were now a
personal cheque, from the Steward; and the boxed-games of
Snakes and Ladders and Ludo from the Friends.

As David had expected, Tony's attitude towards himself was
at times oddly ambivalent. His egocentricity was still that of
a child; but was compensated for by a precocious tenderness
which he carried to lyric extremes. The calculated assertions
of Sandel in the first two weeks of term were innumerable,
and David found them exhausting. Invariably, though, they
were followed by counter demonstrations designed to redress
the balance of relationship, so that David, remaining largely
passive, had the impression that he was being tempered like a
piece of steel. At least he seemed alternately to be plunged into
hot and cold waters; or perhaps, as Tony put it, he was being
'organised'. The demonstrations were mostly simple, and their
true intensity hidden from an outsider.

A typical instance was the business of the light bulb. Tony,
straying into the staff room when David was alone there, found
a burnt-out bulb on the mantelpiece. He threw it, David caught
it, and the game continued for some minutes until, inevitably,
the boy turned his back and strolled out of the door leaving
the bulb suspended briefly in mid-air. It hit the floor, like a
royal salute, as Mrs Jones walked into the room. The counter
demonstration to this incident was likewise typical of many
more. While David was talking to a visiting clergyman later
that morning in the break, Tony appeared in the staff room,
dragged David's shoes from his feet without explanation, and
returned to replace them brightly polished just before the bell
went.

Other demonstrations took place in class. For some reason
the top form was reading *Hamlet*. Tony announced that he
proposed to take the part of the Ghost's aide-de-camp. David
protested, scanning the table of Dramatis Personae in vain,
whereupon Tony became indignant. 'The *Marshal,* sir,' he
explained patiently; and turned up the relevant line. Of course
there it was:

> Thus twice before, and jump at this dead hour,
> With martial stalk hath he gone by our watch.

After this he developed a strained facility for punning. There was Theseus' lover's reduced mobility in the Labyrinth: 'Sir, 'Arry 'ad knee trouble;' and brain-child of the same occasion, the proposed 'Mini-minor tour of Crete'.

Related to the same freak of mind was the episode of von Manz and the fire-lighting; a task the boys performed by rota. 'Sir, please,' the Austrian asked, turning from an impressive wigwam of paper and sticks, 'have you fire for me?' Tony was on to the idiom at once. 'Mr Rogers,' he insisted flamboyantly, 'only has *fire* for *me.*' Then, unable to contain himself, he elaborated in German that was fortunately beyond anyone else in the form room, and finished by producing his own box of matches which he kept for the purpose of lighting David's cigarettes.

In these, and a thousand other ways, which included such diverse things as the drafting of cryptic inscriptions and pathetic saucers of stolen chocolate biscuits or meat-paste pots of flowers placed by David's bedside, Tony emphasised his presence, having recourse to a repertoire of provocations whose intensity was the greater or the lesser as opportunity and his mood prompted him. At night he flung away the childish arms, which were the tools of aggression or endearment in his waking hours. Often they had been assumed with an eye to the public gallery, and so could be abandoned when the two of them were alone together.

Tony's intolerance grew to cover all aspects of the school, which he had taken to terming 'this mediaeval institution'. David watched the process with apprehension, curbing its wilder manifestations wherever he could. The most obvious target was Mrs Jones, and Tony began crossing her path with more frequency than was comfortable. The truth, as David defined it to himself, was that the boy had grown out of the school. With his scholarship secured, and his responsibilities in the choir ended, he was at a loss for constructive interests. But more than this, Tony saw himself for the lover he was; as someone entering a new dimension of life. He was jealous of the environment he had outgrown, and of the cardboard conventions that crowded in upon him. He turned at bay, kicking out savagely to knock them down. In an attempt to channel some of the boy's energy David increased his music lessons. Tony made good progress.

David, too, suffered from frustration. From the start he saw

himself as an amateur – a term whose literal derivation Tony
was quick to comment upon. His colleagues would spend an
hour dissecting some character trait in a boy which David,
having grasped intuitively, would deny space to in his conscious
thought. The prominence of the superficial in conversation
made him afraid. Perhaps indeed there *was* nothing behind it.

Jones was no mean offender. He would talk to a boy in
rhetorical periods. Argument might not interrupt their rhythm,
and so logic ceased to have meaning. Witnessing this abnega-
tion of values, David could feel nauseated.

Hayden, Samuel and the curate were honest straightforward
men. For David the flashpoint was Wallace. The boys were
not wrong in calling him pansy. He tickled their chests in the
dormitory and patted their heads in the dining hall. He had
smoking-jackets, hair oil, and lizard-skin shoes. He was small
and frivolous – not a fat, moody being like Amelia Jones, but a
creature effete, and with the pathetic flamboyance that comes
to those who recognise their tottering decadence unconsciously, and are lost and afraid. Flirting with young boys the
way Wallace did was indeed pathetic. It could be hideously
rationalised. David sought some sterner ethic. He left Wallace
well alone, and consorted largely with the rotund Samuel for
whom life held no ambition save to be able to park his car in
a lane at night in order to capture moths in the head-lamps.
Sometimes too he drank lager with the curate who knew an
enormous amount about railway engines.

In all his impressions David realised that the capacity to
create was the virtue won from a genius to destroy. Sometimes
there was a great deal of hate in him. He hadn't needed Lang
to tell him this.

He never discovered what motivated Amelia Jones. Her
mentality was as insipid as a nursery print. There could be no
doubt that she was 'good', and none that she was 'sincere'; but
this reflection was the more appalling to David in discovering
to him the vastly divergent sincerities of different worlds.

The excruciating agony was watching the moral logic
of Mrs Jones at work. The case of the French boy's breakfast was a milder instance of this. Alain resolutely refused to
eat 'a proper', which by definition is an 'English' breakfast.
Amelia Jones' conclusions were immediate, and displayed

an astonishing mental alacrity. Of course he had been eating sweets in the night!

Jones himself, as David early discovered, would retreat whenever he could, and particularly at the first signs of any crisis in the school, to the under-stair cupboard which was known as his office. Here, among a chaos of letters and accounts, he held silent communion with his golfing photographs, and the framed etching of the Gloucestershire church of which he had once been the untroubled incumbent. David's eyes strayed with relief to these things whenever he had to visit Jones there as the decoration of the shabby room stung his sense of harmony unbearably. Among other things there was on the floor a linoleum like blood trampled into butter. Despite this it was, together with the staff bed-sitting rooms, the only corner of the school where Mrs Jones never set foot.

Hayden, the curate, Samuel and Wallace, were all in some degree victims of Tony's tilting. The ladies of the establishment, with the exception of Mrs Jones, he gallantly spared, and even befriended. Jean Poole, in fact, he presented with a small photograph of himself in token of her former complicity in getting him off games.

Tony convinced himself that it was the lack of his photograph which was holding up the appearance of his record. The photographs were processed, he chose a straightforward portrait, and this was despatched. Jean received a naked head, which Tony lovingly decapitated, etherealised, and fixed in sepia, having elicited the various processes from David while his concentration was directed elsewhere. A selection was prepared for Tony's aunt; and David jealously duplicated the entire opus.

David's motor insurance was paid. Its effect was to remind him poignantly of his lost mobility. That night the *Oxford Mail* was scanned, and the next afternoon they inspected a 1934 Austin Seven. Tony took one look and said, '"Frescobaldi", I think. It's just what we want.' And so Frescobaldi, with an impressive cork in lieu of a radiator-cap, and gears whose selector-rods had occasionally to be sorted out by hand subsequent to the removal of the top of the gear-box itself, came into commission. Its previous owner had fixed to the windscreen a boldly printed notice which read: *Help stamp out New Austin*

*Sevens.* The appeal was as mysterious and pathetic as it was uncompromising. The notice was allowed to remain.


The care and maintenance of Frescobaldi replaced a lack in both their lives; but David saw that there was still something wanting in Tony's. He had left his tropical fish behind him in Devon.

One morning fate intervened. Waking early, as he often did, Tony roused David excitedly to announce that there was a bird in the room. Still drugged with sleep David muttered that he was aware there was a bear and would it stop behaving violently, whereupon Tony only shook him harder. When he was sufficiently awake he followed the boy's pointing finger. Sure enough there was a bird; huddled on the inside window-sill. Its eyes were closed and it looked totally depressed.

'It's asleep,' said Tony.

David raised his eyebrows. 'Are you going to wake it?'

'How?'

David sank back and closed his eyes. 'Tones . . .'

The boy ignored him. 'That's funny!' he said. 'It's a swallow.'

'It couldn't be,' David explained patiently, still with his eyes closed, 'it would have migrated by now.'

'I'm off!' Tony said.

'Where?'

'To the public library. It opens at eight.'

David opened his eyes. 'Can't that wait?'

Tony shook his head. 'It might need special food or something . . . Keep me some toast if I'm late for breakfast, and fob off the Major if he misses me.' He still peered curiously at the bird.

'Remember there's no need to cross the road,' said David.

'All right!' The boy laughed, and was gone.

David took another look at the bird when he got up. It had nestled its beak on to its puffed-out breast feathers and was trembling slightly. There was a fine grey streak running down the back of its head; but it certainly looked like a swallow.

'It's a *mutant!*' Tony announced happily when David next saw him in the break. 'I couldn't find a picture of it so I rang up the Edward Grey Institute of Field Ornithology. They usually try and kill them.'

'Who? The Institute?'

'The other *swallows*, you idiot, Rogers!'

'Well, how do we persuade it to fly south? It looks too sleepy to me.'

'They say it never will fly south now,' Tony explained.

David was doubtful. 'We could try pointing authoritatively. But let's go up.'

'We'll have to look after it, so what shall we call it?' Tony said on the stairs.

'*Byrd*,' David suggested. 'Since it's obviously determined to be a native.'

Tony placed a saucer of milk in front of the huddled form on the sill while David looked on feeling rather redundant.

The boy was perplexed, even resentful. 'Why the hell should the others leave it behind? It's more beautiful than ordinary swallows.'

In the succeeding days Byrd showed no inclination either to die, or to become more sociable. As Tony put it, he was unhappy. The boy constructed him a cardboard box filled with cotton wool, and eventually, though with considerable reluctance, Byrd moved in. He was offered all varieties of branded canary seed and large quantities of warm milk, which he consumed gratefully, but without undue demonstration, and his feeding soon became ritual. His comfort, too, was very carefully considered; David being forbidden, among other things, to smoke in his room except when the curtains were drawn in case Byrd didn't like it. So he became a permanence. Tony referred frequently to 'the three of us', and Byrd shared their existence uncritically.

The Argo recording came out at the end of the third week of term; a complimentary copy preceding it by two days. Tony behaved very well; modestly sucking his lip and swinging one foot when it was played to the school. The private celebration was more eventful. Champagne was bought, Byrd was offered, but declined, a silver thimbleful; Frescobaldi had a dash poured into his radiator, before it was again corked up; and Tony got joyfully drunk on approximately the amount offered to them both. In fact he was wholly possessed by a spinning, lyrical joy, and eventually fell asleep in his second best suit. For this he never really forgave himself.

The recording was superb. Tony had acquitted himself with a control which, in its immediacy, was virtually embarrassing. One heard it and held on to one's chair. The volume, intricacy, and precision defining of phrase, formed a combination that was uncanny, and certainly without precedent in any existing recording of a boy soprano.

After a second glass of champagne David went downstairs and bequeathed the remainder of the bottle to the Major. Then, while the boy slept in a crumpled heap beneath a blanket, he went to work on the final stages of his soprano concerto. At 3 a.m. the conclusion was sufficiently assured as to justify a large whisky, and when the first daylight feinted its rectangular halo about the curtain the job was done.

The sense of urgency, though, was far from burned out. In fact it was only just beginning. David marshalled and rehearsed a small orchestra. In the event this was not easy. Ultimately it consisted of a few undergraduates, some boys from the school, and four ladies from the musical sub-section of the Chapel Friends, to whom David made humble approach, and who proved most enthusiastic.

The recording was made, and a dozen copies of the ten-inch disc were privately ordered and struck off.

'That was the end of the road,' Tony announced in a brisk aside, while the musical ladies put away their strings. Later, though, he became petulant and unmanageable, and kneeling on the floor, he talked for a long time to Byrd in strange, esoteric terms.

The records, when they arrived, had faithful chair-creaks and a muttered apology from the choirboy with the cymbals who had nearly decapitated timpani. But the simple, three-movement piece lived despite everything: Tony hovering at height, or else swooping down to taunt the majesty of his alto range like an osprey courting with the face of the sea.

Tony's sadness lifted when one of the musical ladies wrote him a letter asking him to tea with her children. Characteristically the boy took one of his photos with him in case she should want to paste it to the sleeve of her record.

✧

Adrian Crawley appeared. He showed small curiosity about David's affairs, and explained he had come simply to talk about himself.

'God Almighty!' he said dully as, prowling about the room, he came upon a photo of Tony.

'How did Schools go?'

'Fourth. Dons must have smelt the embryo artist . . . Nothing frightens them more – happy, disciplined intellects. Let one into the club and who knows? He may even start writing thrillers. No! The academics' relationship with the artists is about as profound and embarrassed as is the nobility's with the academics. Know what the Duke of Gloucester said when he met *Decline and Fall* Gibbon? "Another damn, thick, square book! Still scribble, scribble, scribble, is it, Mr Gibbon?" Superb judgement, don't you think! Now you've got to smuggle me out of here.'

'Why smuggle?'

'Jean Poole,' Crawley said.

'Good Lord! Is she *your* Jean?'

'Was.' Crawley began wandering round the room again. 'Do you want Jean in a nutshell? She saw through me . . . they all do. D'you know what she calls me? Her second favourite boy – that's *little* boy, you understand. First favourite's someone called Roo or something – big brown eyes, missing tooth, and a croaky voice. Extraordinarily, he's literate. She used to show me his essays . . . I suppose you teach him. Alas, poor Jean! And she wants to marry *a schoolmaster.* She needs constantly to be told she's loved. All the boys bring her their troubles and so forth. Do they? I wonder? When I was at prep school we were scared stiff of matrons – they were girls.'

Crawley had reached the window. He scowled at Byrd. 'That thing looks as if it's possessed by the soul of a doomed traveller, A victim of ballad-magic, perhaps . . .'

Rain soaked Oxford. Sometimes the sun broke through so that, prematurely, it assumed its winter look of a mirage city whose dusty gold spires stood in a shallow bowl of mist. On

other days the air was cold and clear, and autumn seemed to
be guarding her perilous vacuum tunelessly.

The playing fields were flooded. Tony had no need to
cultivate verrucas. In the hollow afternoons they tracked
Oxford's water-ways; or followed the wandering path of the
Scholar-Gipsy around Bagley, Cumnor and Bablock Hythe.
Sometimes they took Frescobaldi, but mostly they went on
foot, through all weathers, when Tony would insist on walking
with his hand in the pocket of David's jacket. David never
discovered the significance of this gesture, or thought to
enquire about it. Once he endeavoured to return the compliment only to find that the pockets of Tony's suit were too small
to comfortably admit his hand, and to be told by the boy that
he would rather they weren't stretched out of shape.

A favourite walk became the towpath out beyond Godstow.
They watched the building of a bridge that would eventually
join the severed arms of the new by-pass. Beyond it, where
the heavy green river and wide fields spread beneath the dark
shape of Wytham Woods, there was solitude. At its banks the
river played a restless game with the reeds. Some were broken,
the greater part of their lengths fallen on the water. Currents,
whose motions were invisible to the eye, would draw an olive
blade beneath the surface and, as mysteriously, relinquish it
again, so that the banks were constantly alive although the
body of the stream seemed barely to flow at all. Down-river
they watched the same water tumbling through a weir and
wondered whether its turmoil was indignation or joy. It was
on the towpath that Tony, forging ahead for once, suddenly
halted, clicked his muddy heels together, and began to sway
regularly from side to side.

'I'm a pendulum,' he said as David came up. 'Hold me a
minute . . . to stop me.'

David laughed. 'If you want to be metaphysical, Tones, then
I'd say you were a grain of sand in the top of an hourglass. The
hell of it is I don't know which.'

Later on the same walk Tony plucked a straw from a ravaged
cornfield. He held it, protruding, in his teeth. 'Clutch!' he said,
as articulately as he could; bubbling over with the ingenuity
of his conceit. The wit went to his head. He laid the straw on
David's back; first instructing him to bend double. 'The last!'
he explained. 'It's called Tony Sandel.' Then he galloped away.

For the rain the boy had a grey plastic cape and sou'wester. Being Tony's they matched. It was dressed like this that he crouched motionless in Wytham Woods when they saw the badger. He was trying to photograph it; holding the Rolleiflex ready in his hands. The rain poured down, lashing his face like silver needles that could only make him smile. David stared wildly at the boy's concentrated expression beneath the turned-up rim of the ridiculous hat. His body seemed crushed by a steel press, and a sudden depression lurched like mercury between his temples. The weight lifted as Tony clicked the shutter. In the same moment David knew how much he had become a part of his own being.

Often Tony became wild. He would intersperse fits of animal joy with passages of tenderness whose lyricism was raised to a degree where it became comic. There was the day he found the pool of mud. Bringing his heels together, as on the occasion when he had been a pendulum, he fell backwards into it with the same lunatic confidence with which he had once leapt from the bath-tub. He was in his waterproof cape, but even so the behaviour struck David as being close to masochism, until he discovered he was wearing games clothes underneath. It had all been a put-up job; which perhaps was worse.

'Elephants!' said Tony inexplicably; then stopped laughing only gradually like a mill-race rejoining its parent stream.

David suffered other moments of pain. The worst was in class. Tony had just finished punctuating a sentence on the blackboard, and had rubbed it off with the duster. He propped one foot on the cross-bar of the easel's front legs, and turned his face to David, waiting. Sunlight filled the head of the room where Tony stood; splashing on the soft silver of his clothes and hard gold of his limbs, it was reflected by the dancing particles of chalk-dust. David watched him as helpless as he had ever been. Suddenly irrational jealousy changed to terror, because the bright gems of dust were touching the boy. He stood there careless; and the effrontery of the chalk-dust was unbearable. David felt sick and afraid.

In his dreams Tony would become confused with the image of the grain of sand in the hour-glass.

✧

One day Tony said, 'Tell me about Italy.'

David told him about the wide-eyed fields of France. Of the traditional route to the south running through the broad belt of vineyards, and the towns with their almost legendary wine names, until it reached the rough landscape of Van Gogh with its gnarled scrub, its hard, broken angles, and bright, grease greens. He told him about the sharp Mediterranean foreground; the haze which distorted distance, and produced perspectives that were alien to northern eyes, and about the blue of the sea and sky. He did his best to describe the hilltop towns of central Italy with their black-eyed, gap-toothed houses, which were dusty clay boxes miraculously defying gravity. He told him of Florence, Siena and Arezzo; and ranged wherever his memory led him from the Lombardy plains and the magic of Venice, to Perugia and Orvieto, and the sinister, inky hills around Rome.

Tony was avid for repositories of statuary. David had to confess he had seen very little. But the boy pressed him repeatedly for details of Italy in the first weeks of term. David began to suspect that he dreamed of it as the Great Good Place.

Meanwhile the fourth week of term came to an end. Tony seemed happy enough. For his own part, David would often pause curiously to review their world.

## 28

THE first paper to arrive was *The Sunday Times,* Tony supposed that he was to receive the attentions of Atticus, or become the subject of Portrait Gallery. In fact the people were in Oxford mainly for another story. Nevertheless a small paragraph did eventually appear.

Throughout the subsequent boom David was constantly to ask himself how one recording should have caused a singer to become the dramatic focus he did. Tony's voice, certainly, was a freak: its unparalleled performance was the coherent core of the business; but even so it was an insufficient cause. Had the boy been appearing live somewhere, in the sort of wild cabaret capacity which he sometimes indulged in an empty room on a wet afternoon, or, alternatively, had this been a Latin country, and his devotional performance become adopted as a stunt by a politic Church, the eruption of Sandel into the public eye might have been more readily explained. But neither of these things were so. Tony had simply made a recording which was as expensive as, patently, it was *square.*

Part of the trouble, David concluded, in as much as it particularly inspired the lower echelons of the press hierarchy, was topographical. Oxford is always good copy; and Tony left his visitors in no doubt that St Cecilia's choir, for all the abuses it suffered, and which he carefully described, was an integral part of the university, A further inflammatory ingredient was the attitude Tony himself adopted on interview. While this might never be described as immodest, it was, as David had often to acknowledge when prowling uneasily outside the prefects' room which Tony had commandeered as a press office, a show, and one of no mean conception. For the rest the boom followed the non-logic of a craze. Inspired reasonably enough by a musical feat, the craze soon acquired its own dynamics. The song was all but forgotten; the singer became a cult.

The two factors most obviously responsible for swelling the issue were both connected with the proximity of Christmas. The first was an opportunist move on the part of the record company, who struck off a forty-five record, comprising only two arias. Another quickly followed it. The success of the new discs was immediate. The public, always amenable to sentiment, and particularly mindful of its place in the approaching season, not only accepted the first record but promoted it in an impulsive moment to the hit-parade. Thus Tony with his square recordings becam.e top of the top twenty pops. People elected avidly for this traditional piece of England. The choice of at least some of the purchasers of the forty-five records, David imagined, was considerably influenced by the new sleeve. This carried his photograph of Tony with one or two conspicuous differences. The portrait had been transposed into colour, with unlikely blue eyes; while in place of the favourite suit, the boy was wearing a surplice and ruff-collar. This last transformation outraged Tony because he supposed they'd somehow had first to undress him. If the sleeve had any distinction it was that a *Tide* packet looked dim beside it.

But what really intensified the limelight was the publicity given to the four-figure offer of a film company who proposed to feature Tony in a special Christmas short. The idea was that he should appear in a three-and-a-half-minute technicolour feature when he would sing the Schubert *Ave Maria* with pathos, and supported, as the letter put it, 'by other photogenic youngsters'. Quietly Tony refused. The company raised their offer; and when Tony refused again the press, unable to announce the payment of perhaps the highest fee per screen minute ever made to a singer, became indignant. Tony, they felt, was their property. He had no right to deny this seasonal benediction to the nation.

David watched helplessly while cuttings collected. Tony's eyes changed arbitrarily from blue to brown, and back to blue again. Not once were they the admittedly indescribable grey or hazel of the reality. For the purposes of the press the domestically attractive boy had blue eyes, and that was that. Grey was unheard of; while hazel suggested the possibility of beauty. David smiled wryly over this. Of all the attributes scattered over the boy, no one had used the most obviously appropriate one. Yet what were they afraid of? Tony's beauty was of a kind that denned itself in even the smudgiest newsprint; while its linear regularity could, and did apparently, survive radio transmission.

The stir caused some consternation both in the school and the college. Mrs Jones found in it reason to crystallise her resentment against the boy. Despite this it was agreed that it would be futile to try and insulate Tony from the press, and that the affair should be allowed to blow itself out. Tony's aunt was dismayed; and David wrote to her early in the boom saying he would do all he could to contain it. For his own part he began to hate the intrusion into their lives the more heartily.

The Master of St Cecilia's also showed consternation. Pilgrims had begun to arrive at the Chapel. All aspects of the college were fringe-news. There was an embarrassed meeting of the Governing Body; and a notice in the lodge announced that Master Sandel no longer sang.

Of the school staff it was the Major who really enjoyed the commotion. Since it was the staff who were ultimately responsible for Sandel's fame, he was convinced that sooner or later some right-headed society would recognise the fact and reward them with unlimited beer.

The choir, too, were not without consciousness of glory. They marched up St Aldate's with their noses just that little bit higher in the air. One or two of the smaller boys were seduced into wandering eyes and smiles when flash-bulbs ambushed them. This though was a serious breach of Tony's discipline, which still overshadowed them. Long ago he had schooled them carefully in the proper conduct to observe when besieged by American tourists.

On the Saturday morning of the fifth week of term Bruce Lang turned up. David had seen him only fleetingly earlier in the term, and was glad to have him to talk to. He unfolded the story of the press campaign. Some of it was familiar to Lang who had, in particular, noted a statement of Tony's where, in a moment of exuberance, and anxious to seize upon what he supposed to be a telling superlative to describe his friend, the boy had referred to one 'Sir David Rogers'. The news desk had apparently failed to check on its information. 'Sir David' was.

'Where does this lead?' Lang asked eventually. 'For you, I mean. I can't imagine for a moment that you've got the makings of a schoolmaster. When the boy leaves . . . what then? He'll grow up . . . stray away from you. He couldn't do otherwise. I can sense something of the intensity of your world . . . I know the sort of critical equipoise that governs it. Get out while you can. Get out now.'

David stood looking out of the window. 'I can't, Bruce. Ridiculous as it may seem to an outsider, he needs me. Ours is an equipoise too.'

'Then answer me one thing,' Lang said. 'Does it never occur to you that the relationship is ludicrous? What beats me is how you can ever see it as whole. For instance, how does this child provide you with intellectual companionship?'

'Easy! His musical genius gives him a certain precocity . . . while for my part, I'm very young. We meet about half-way.'

'I'm unconvinced,' Lang said. 'And you don't believe a word of what you're saying.'

David flicked Lang a cigarette; spinning it over and over across the room.

'It's Glenelgin he's going to, isn't it?' Lang asked.

'In theory . . . He's got a scholarship. The trouble is he doesn't really want to go anywhere. To school, that is . . .'

'Away from you, I suppose,' Lang finished.

David turned his lip down. He lit a cigarette.

'I gather you've made no further contacts with the Church,' Lang said. 'What is it you want? What *do* you believe in?'

Now David smiled playfully. 'Practically all of Beethoven. I'm an artist without definition. Amongst other things that means that my relationship with the real world is tenuous . . . Yet at the same time it's vital. I demand a lot of it, I know. For instance, that it harbour me.'

'And the pixie?'

'I don't know. Since I can't think in patterns that aren't of my own making, I can't see any long-term picture. Sometimes I'm afraid, though, that he may only be a part of my lack of definition. I repeat, I can't see. He's someone I thought I'd always wanted. Now that he is, I must go on. At least, he needs me.'

'You're very sure of that.'

'I have to be.'

'You condemn yourself from your own mouth.'

'No! There'd be no need for defence . . . argument . . . if it weren't for the constant, irrational challenge . . . That can make you doubt your senses. It magnifies doubts, but proves nothing. Then I came through a lot to arrive on the life side – as you might say. I want Tony to get there . . . is it stay there? . . . with less pain. And perhaps there's more life to find . . . somewhere else.'

Lang touched his fingers together and nodded towards the bed. 'Meanwhile . . .?'

'Sorry, Bruce! I'm not being drawn. Well, perhaps I am. There was one night. There couldn't not have been . . . I see that now . . . But not since then . . .'

'Guilt?'

'No. I don't think so. It was simply premature . . . And then possibly only because of my position here . . .'

'I can't see any future – '

'But there *must* be. We live into tomorrow . . . Then, we can usually shape it somehow.'

They talked of other things. David played Lang an excerpt from the fatal record, and showed him his photos of Tony. Lang leant back with his head on one side. Returning to his usual circumlocution he said:

'I'm forced to concede that this little boy is a remarkably beautiful creature. That is all, though,' he added heavily. 'Now cease being so desperately anxious to impress me with lewd snaps of someone else's child and get me a drink.'

Remembering the hospitality extended to the ice-cream man on the occasion of his first visit to the school, David found Jones and asked him whether Lang might stay to lunch. He considered the crowded dining hall carefully; then, finding what he wanted, he weeded out one boy, slid the bottoms of Hunter and Crockett a little wider apart on the shiny bench, and ushered Lang in between them. He left him. The chorus began. Later Tony sidled over to rescue Lang and routed out Hunter. Meals were like that. David would have given a lot to have overheard their conversation.

After lunch David went up to his room, signalling to Lang that he would find him there. He had become involved with the Major, who had proudly drawn him a glass of beer.

At two o'clock Tony was due to give what David fervently hoped would be his last interview, and he felt he could safely leave him to it.

When Lang came into the room David instantly sensed that something was wrong. 'The boy seems to be beating up the press,' he said with unusual simplicity. 'I think you'd better go and investigate.'

David looked at him quickly, and was out of the room before he had finished speaking.

When he opened the door of the small prefects' study the scene that greeted him stamped itself on his memory. What was strange about it was its incongruity. The familiar, panelled room, with its few worn armchairs and desks, was somehow the wrong set for the trio that stood within it. The dramatic posture of the actors, too, was the more enigmatic for the lack of any apparent explanation.

Tony stood where he had evidently risen from the seat in the bay-window. His face was flushed, and he was quivering all over, though from what proportions of anger and fear David could not be sure. The uncertainty made him intensely uneasy. The boy looked like a trapped animal that might do anything. One of the men present was just lowering a large press camera, and Tony's eyes were fixed on this as if it constituted a live threat that held them mesmerised. The other man was also standing. Now he put a scratch-pad in his pocket, and they both began to move away from the window.

David closed the door behind him, leaning on it. 'Just a minute,' he said. 'What the hell do you think you're doing?'

The man with the pad saw him for the first time. He pulled his lower lip down with the stub of a pencil and his eyelids creased into leathery folds. It was a lizard's face.

'You Rogers?'

David stared into the liquid slits of his eyes. 'I am.'

The man gestured faintly with his head, but the other had already raised the camera.

There was a flash. The camera had a blitz device which didn't need reloading with bulbs.

A change came over David which later he was to try and analyse with some embarrassment. Whether the weird scene fired some latent sense of melodrama in him, or whether the shock of the outraged boy tensed him so much as to produce a state of hyper-cunning where his normal responses were momentarily reversed, he never quite discovered; in fact he didn't like to recall the episode at all.

At any rate something like meekness overcame him. He went towards the cameraman like a pupil called before the headmaster. Nodding at Tony, he asked, 'What did you do to him?' His eyes met the man's. Then his left fist was in his stomach, and his open, right hand cut down with a release of vicious, wholly animal fury. It was unfortunate that this was allied to the timing sense of a skilled musician. The man looked as if he might never get up off the floor. He could be dead.

David felt weak. The upsurge of violence had surprised him. His right hand ached abominably. He slid the holder off the back of the press camera and exposed the plate to the light. Then he exposed some others that were scattered on the floor before tossing them to the photographer who was, after all, getting to his knees.

The other man said, 'You shouldn't have done that.'

The threat, if it was one, sounded unconvincing.

'No? And why not?' David replied, equally meaninglessly.

The man said nothing. He squashed a felt hat on to his head, which instantly reduced his role to comedy. The photographer was on his feet now; collecting his scattered equipment, and blowing through his nose. He looked the sort of man who might go in daily expectation of being slapped down. Possibly it was an occupational hazard he had grown accustomed to.

'Now get out, both of you!' David said. He crossed the room and held the door open. To his surprise the pair shuffled out.

He went back to Tony in the bay-window. For a moment he looked at him in puzzlement; then he put his hand on the boy's head. 'Not like you to refuse a photograph.'

Tony smiled faintly, but said nothing. He was clearly still very shaken. They sat down on the cushions of the window seat.

'Tell me,' David said.

Tony rested his chin in his cupped hand. 'I thought they were nice at first . . . then they were rude.' He faltered. It wasn't like him to fall back on childish terms.

'How?'

Tony jerked his chin out of his hand. 'I told them about us.' he said with quick resolution. 'Oh, how we got on, though we had fights, and how I only really sang for you. I said I loved you and would have run away if you weren't here . . .'

Slowly David nodded. Tony broke off, frowning at a memory. Then suddenly he shrugged his shoulders.

'They got rude and asked private questions . . . They got on to the choirboy joke.' Tony had been picking at the cuff of his jacket. He began to make swooping motions with his hand, like a duck or a seaplane landing on David's forearm. 'There was more son stuff: "Now, careful, son, you mean this *master* . . ." As if you were just a master! But I warned you, didn't I! Anyway . . . Then I knew they didn't understand – though I tried to explain. I got very angry, I'm afraid.'

David smiled. 'I could see that. I heard your voice, too, before I came in. But what was happening before I did come in?'

The combination of exuberance and resentment left the boy. His body tensed as if the recollection had assumed a physical

presence in the room and he was poised against it with the
resilience of a hair-spring. Instinctively David moved nearer to
him. At the same moment Peter stirred in his memory.

'I hated them,' Tony said slowly. He put the palms of his
hands together, crushing them between his thighs. 'You see
. . . I sensed they were *dangerous*. Then when they wanted
to take the photos . . .' He broke off to straighten one of his
socks. 'Well, just suddenly, I didn't want those men to have
pictures of me.'

The boy looked up. 'Another thing. One said: "You ought to
have longs, or is there a school rule against it?" Then the other
said: "Rules don't count for much round here," and they both
sneered. They were talking without me. Well, you remember
how that morning I asked you to look at the day, and you put
my long trousers to warm by the fire? That was my thing . . .
and our thing. It was as if they were trying to spoil it. I should
have hit them like you did . . . I kicked that dirty rat Hunter in
the balls once.'

Tony turned to look out of the window, pressing his nose
against the glass. 'You don't think I told them anything I
shouldn't have done?'

'No, Tones. You only told them the truth, and what you
wanted to tell them.' David smiled as the boy's composure
returned. Feed Byrd,' he said. 'Bruce is up there with him.'


'There's blackmail,' Lang suggested as they walked down the
drive between the gnomes. 'I should say they were unlikely to
print a scoop on the strength of the boy's lyrical claims alone.'

David stared at him. 'You must be nuts! Anyway,' he went
on more thoughtfully, 'the blackmailed may get nasty. I think I
hit that slimy bloke insanely enough to alarm him.'

'I'd never really associated you with physical violence, you
know,' Lang said, pausing to poke the belly of a particularly
repulsive gnome with the ferrule of his umbrella.

'Nor me,' David confessed. He was still nursing the blade of
his right hand. 'I was shown the trick by a drunken Irishman
in Algiers. It never occurred to me it would *work*. But then the
animal's a funny thing. The gambit must have been lurking at
his disposal all this time.'

They had arrived at the gates. 'No,' David went on, 'it's Tony

– and perhaps the animal in him – I'm worried about. I'd no
idea some lousy gutter gang might rub him up like that, or I'd
have put a stop to the interviews long ago. I've seen him like
that before . . . Twice. He seems to become possessed by an
absolute terror. A hare in a trap doesn't touch it. It's horrible
. . .'

David put his foot on one of the wrought-iron gates. 'Well,
no more press conferences, and that's for sure,' he said,
relieving the guilt he felt in the alien idiom. 'God, how I hate
bloody England sometimes!'

'Your old genius for generalising from a personal affront
– even an imagined one,' Lang said. 'And Tony's an equally
hypothetical antidote – though to *what,* heaven knows.'

'Maybe. Let's not start on that.'

'Don't blame yourself; and do,' Lang said at his most enigmatic, 'come and see me.'

David smiled rather wanly. 'Yep!' he said.


'It's me,' Tony announced unnecessarily, closing the door
behind him. 'I've come to pack my case secretly in here . . .
No!' He ran the few remaining steps across the room and
clapped his hand over David's mouth. 'No questions! Sandel is
at the helm and he knows best.' He relaxed his hand cautiously,
testing the efficacy of his command. 'Promise?'

David mumbled and the hand instantly tightened again.

Tony brought a knee unscrupulously into action. *'Promise!'*
David nodded, choking.

'Okay!' Tony breathed. He took his hand away.

Then he spun joyously across the room and threw open the
wardrobe. Without warning he stood on his hands; his feet
crashing to against the wall. 'Three cheers for the telephone!'
he said. 'Do you know who invented it? It was Alexander
Graham Bell in 1876.' Tony's feet hit the floor again but he
didn't pause. 'Bet you don't know what the first thing he
said on his telephone was? No, you don't, see! He said: "Mr
Watson, come here; I want you".'

## 29

' S ir,' Tony whispered, 'go out to the pub quickly.'
His voice held a mixture of irony and urgency as he
bent over David in the staff room. Its only other occupant was
the Major who was reading a paper. The word 'pub', however,
had been of sufficient significance to penetrate his concentration. He said :

'Get along with you, Sandel. Can't you see Mr Rogers is
busy marking? He doesn't need you to tell him when it's time
for a drink – eh, David?'

'Rather!' David said with enthusiasm. He often found that
the best way of answering Hayden.

Tony's only reply was to square his behind more deliberately
towards the Major, leaving no doubt as to how he regarded the
intrusion. He pinned David's wrists to the arms of his chair.
All but touching his face, he moved his eyes in a stage gesture
towards the door. *'David!'* he said very quietly.

As David got up a small boy appeared in the half-open
doorway.

'Mr Rogers, sir, Mrs Jones wants to see you, sir,' he said
breathlessly.

'Knock!' Tony exploded with uncontrolled fury. 'Goddam it,
boy, this is the Staff Common Room!'

'But, sir, Mrs –'

'You *knock*.' Tony advanced menacingly. 'Now, once round
the whole playing field.'

'It's dark!' the child complained indignantly, startled by the
imposition. 'I can't!'

'Then you can do fifty press-ups in the hall, can't you?' Tony
said, placing his hands on the small boy's shoulders.

David, who was standing near the door, became conscious
of the fragility of Tony's hands as they lay patronisingly, yet an
unspoken threat on the child's shoulders.

'But, Sandel, Mrs Jones . . .' the small boy began.

'We've got your message, Cox. Now go!' Tony said softly, without releasing him from the hypnotic lock of his eyes.

'Do I still have to do the press-ups?' Cox pleaded.

'Yes,' Tony said. 'On your Cub's honour. And I'd stand over you myself with a cricket bat if I could spare the time.'

'Big bully Sandel!' Cox blurted out.

'Little boy,' Tony said with a contemptuous toughening in his voice, 'if you haven't gone when I open my eyes, I'll do you!'

It was uncompromising. Desperately David looked over towards the Major, but no sympathy was forthcoming. In fact the battle-hardened man hadn't looked up from his paper. Then, ridiculously, Tony closed his eyes and suffered an expression of martyrdom to illumine his face. Cox scuttled away.

'He won't do them anyway,' Tony said in the hall, as if answering David's unspoken protest. 'A rule is a rule; besides, I had to protect you.'

He took David's college scarf from the hallstand and disposed it dashingly about his neck.

'All comrades are equal but some are more equal than others, I know,' David muttered through the convolutions. 'What do you think you're doing with me now, anyway?'

But Tony, with the palms of his hands firmly established over his kidneys, had already propelled him out into the darkened porch. 'Listen,' he said. 'Mrs Jones wants to see you. But you've got to avoid her until four o'clock tomorrow afternoon. Will you do that?'

'No,' said David. 'I can't happily ignore the instructions of the management the way you seem to.'

Tony sighed. But there was no suggestion that anything other than his own will would triumph. It was a formal sigh. 'That's the attitude I was afraid of. It's been the root of the whole trouble too. I've got it organised now though . . . Oh, brother!'

Suddenly, in the faint light that came through the opaque glass of the front door, Tony smiled. It was not a formal smile; but the full effect, to which the silver wire had never been more than an unnecessary ornament. David weakened.

'I don't suppose you'll reveal this "organisation" any more than you've revealed the reason for your packing yesterday.

But why this specific trysting hour with the lady? Why four o'clock tomorrow?'

For the first time the boy's resolution seemed to waver. Absentmindedly almost, he endeavoured to knot David's third and index fingers together.

'Well,' he said, deliberating, 'for one thing she'll be eating.'

'And?'

'So she'll be in a good mood,' Tony said. The pronoun carried the ghost of a capital.

'Is that all?'

Tony looked at him sideways; then shook his head. 'No . . . Not exactly. But will you do it? It really is important.'

David stared out at the winter night into which he was being driven. Some imaginative child had given one of the gnomes luminous eyes and a prominent luminous navel in the days before radiation scares when you could still buy small tins of the paint. 'All right,' he said. 'It's my half-day, so I've no call to be here.'

'Then I'll fix it with the Joneses,' Tony said confidently. He reached into the pocket of his jacket. 'There's a letter for you . . . A messenger brought it.'

David opened the unstamped envelope in the dim light. It was a note from Ricks. The college, it seemed, were prepared to take him back into residence at once. They must have his decision the next day.

'Is it important?'

'I don't think so,' David said.

'Have you enough money for the pub?'

David smiled faintly to himself. 'Yes.'

Tony said, 'Don't be too late. And don't come back drunk.' He found a loose end of the St Cecilia's scarf, and pinned it to his ears like a veil so that only his eyes showed. 'I'll wait up.'

Then he swung open the veil like the hinged door of a henhouse, and pecked David on the cheek.


Mrs Jones was in fact eating. She put down a scone as David entered the room. However, despite Tony's suppositions about her tea-time moods, she didn't now seem disposed to resume the scone. She looked embarrassed.

David had spent the morning with his usual classes, but, in

the interim periods particularly, had gained the impression that Tony was playing the role of fleet escort, and was steaming guardian circles about his person. Once he had been abruptly manoeuvred into the lavatory, while he was forbidden the staff room altogether during the break. At four o'clock exactly, though on the retarded authority of Tony's watch alone, he had been released from his room. 'Now God save Sandel and King David!' he said simply, and relapsed into an attitude of unsubtle devotion in the best armchair.

Mrs Jones cleared her throat of crumbs as David explained his presence.

'Yes, we did rather want to see you, Mr Rogers,' she said; then appeared to be waiting for something.

Sure enough Jones got up and made his way out of the room with mumbled excuses. Royal, or simply courteous, the plural pronoun was no longer valid. Jones had closed the door behind him, and now they both remained standing.

'Mr Rogers,' Mrs Jones said, 'I will come straight to the point.' She let her head sink into her shoulders, producing a third chin, while her eyes swam back and forth across the floor like the diseased carp in the St Cecilia's pond. 'We are not very happy about you.'

'I'm sorry,' David said.

'The headmaster thinks you are a very good teacher,' Mrs Jones went on, 'but that can't make up for other things, can it now?'

David waited. Mrs Jones' face had begun to quiver. Then she took the plunge.

'We mean your morals, Mr Rogers.'

David continued steadily to look at her; feeling no dismay, or any involvement at all, as if he were watching a bad play. Still avoiding his eyes, Mrs Jones burst out suddenly:

'Oh, Mr *Rogers*, how can you stand there! How can you stand there when you've been having that horrible sexual inter-course with Miss Poole!'

She had found the words with difficulty. For David the spell was broken. He stared at her now wildly. There was silence for a moment while Mrs Jones recovered. Then she said:

'And I hope you are even more ashamed of making the head-boy sleep in your bed in order to do it. Yes,' she went on, 'you made the head-boy use your room so that you could use his with Miss Poole.'

David opened his mouth. It was getting too much for him. But Mrs Jones cut his words short.

'Please don't lie, Mr Rogers. The head-boy was seen coming out of your room early in the morning and his own room was at the same time found to be locked.'

David wanted badly to light a cigarette. He said, 'Mrs Jones, if only for Jean's sake, I must tell you that this is quite untruc. I can't conceive where you can have got such an idea.'

'There are little birds in the trees,' Mrs Jones said primly,

'I know there are. But that doesn't answer my question, does it?'

'Can you think of any other reason why the head-boy should have been sleeping in your bed, Mr Rogers?'

Now David did light a cigarette. Mrs Jones nodded her permission, but her face contrived to make it clear how she felt about what, after all, was only another vice. David said:

'I must insist once and for all that I have had no intimacy of any sort with Jean Poole. As for Tony . . .' He was never allowed to finish the sentence.

'I don't want to hear your excuses and reasons,' Mrs Jones cut in abruptly. 'The other thing that upset us, Mr Rogers, is your *rudeness*.'

David suspected it was the child's connotation, and adapted his mind patiently.

'You were very rude to me personally the other day.'

'Then I am sorry,' David said, genuinely enough. 'This isn't a hotel, Mr Rogers, you know. It's a private house!'

David's head began swimming again.

'You can't just ask anyone to lunch!'

For the first time indignation stirred seriously in David. 'If you mean Lang,' he said, 'I found the headmaster and asked him whether he might stay. I should have liked to have asked yourself, but you weren't available.'

Mrs Jones was silent for a moment. Then: 'Well, really, Mr Rogers, it wasn't quite the act of a gentleman, was it? Your friend was *embarrassed* by being asked to stay uninvited.'

'Lang and I have known each other since we were nine,' David said evenly. 'I think I would know if I had placed him in an embarrassing situation. Incidentally,' he added, more pointedly than he had intended, 'Bruce Lang is the only real Christian that I have ever met.'

Mrs Jones ignored this; maintaining her mentality unruffled. 'If you weren't properly brought up, Mr Rogers, and don't know how a gentleman should behave, we can't teach you now.'

Suddenly there it was; a blazing anger. But in the same moment David knew that it would be both pointless and unkind to release it. Unsure, as so often in his life, where real feeling ended, and histrionics took over, he swung on his heel towards the door.

There was a knock, and a small boy opened the door, timidly holding it aside. David realised even before she spoke that the woman who now entered the room could not be other than Prudence Laying.

'I've caught you, Amelia!' she boomed. 'Stuffing yourself too, I see. Jones is in hiding, I suppose?'

Prudence Laying strode across the room after glancing at Mrs Jones' interrupted scones. She was the sort of woman who, at sixty, would still look right in climbing boots. Now she turned to David.

'I know it,' she stated. 'You're David!'

David shook her hand.

Prudence Laying took what was almost a deliberate step backwards and David had the impression of being scrutinised like a tricky escarpment. At last he seemed to have been sufficiently measured.

'Good!' Prudence Laying announced enigmatically.

David was relieved when she turned again to the obviously flustered Mrs Jones.

'Amelia,' she said, 'I'm taking the boy away at once.'

David recalled that Tony's aunt wasn't a woman who wasted words.

'But first things first. I'm not normally one to interfere with school discipline on a boy's behalf, but confiscating that book of statues was ridiculous. Hand it over! Does it have any of the Etruscan phallic stuff?' She turned to David conversationally.

'I really don't know,' he confessed. 'I've only seen what Tony subsequently showed me.'

Mrs Jones produced his present, which he had no idea had been confiscated.

'Are you all ready and packed, David?' Prudence Laying asked.

'He very soon will be!' Mrs Jones said bravely, rallying a little.

Miss Laying ignored her. It was borne in upon David that they must be old, if not happily assorted, school friends.

'*Tony's* packed,' he said.

'But you *have* agreed to take him to Italy?' Miss Laying was earnest.

'Why, I will,' David said, groping for comprehension. 'I'd heard nothing to that effect.'

Suddenly Prudence Laying laughed. 'Gracious me! Whatever can Ant think he's up to. He didn't talk to you at all about this?'

David shook his head and smiled. 'No . . . Though there have been curious signs that some scheme was afoot.'

'Then that's settled.' Miss Laying looked relieved. 'I've got plane bookings for tomorrow, and the boy's passport. The rest is up to you.'

Two years ago David would have shifted his feet, but now he found himself simply nibbling his lip. After a second he stopped that too, although the trust had moved him quite as much as the amateur performance of his first symphony in an asbestos shed in Slough. It had been raining then, whereas the room he stood in now was red with the November sunset.

'I'll look after him,' he said.

Throughout this conversation Mrs Jones had maintained the air of someone who had successfully insulated herself from kitchen smells. Now Prudence Laying turned to her again. At the same moment there was a knock on the door and Tony came in.

'You'd better stay now, Ant,' Miss Laying commanded.

Tony said, 'Yes, Aunt,' rather as if one of the nursery prints had spoken aloud. He sat down by the door, but didn't take his eyes off the carpet.

'You'll understand why I'm taking him away, Amelia,' Miss Laying went on. 'You can see for yourself he's outgrown a prep school, and this nonsense in the press finally decided me.'

Mrs Jones produced a third chin and looked secretly pleased.

✧

The lounge of the Mitre was full, but David was as little aware of the other people as Crawley might have been. Prudence Laying put down her coffee cup. For a second David thought she was going to ask for a cigar.

Despite the latitude he had been allowed in planning the holiday, Prudence's orders for Tony's welfare were explicit. The temptation to regard her as an alarming crank had been modified by her obvious dedication to her nephew's upbringing. Superficially David knew he was committed to a trust against which he would find no cause to rebel. His real feelings went deeper.

'The boy should expand,' Prudence Laying said. 'Southern sunshine will see to that. You've ten weeks before term starts. But it may be we'll cheat the public schools yet. He wants instrumental training. I've arranged for an audition with a small school in London. That's in January.'

'He wants to train as a concert pianist?' David was astonished. 'You didn't know?'

'I'd no idea.'

'There may be a lot you've still to learn,' Prudence Laying said. 'Both of you.'

'Of course he's old to begin instrumental training,' David said, getting up. 'But then I don't know what his potential may be.'

He escorted Prudence Laying to her car. It was as old as Frescobaldi, but had many yards of bonnet. Then he returned to the school for the last time, where he packed the majority of his worldly possessions, and made arrangements for the remainder. By the time he had finished St Cecilia's clock was booming two, sadly, across the Great Park.


Frescobaldi's radiator cork was turned towards London Airport. The idea was that he should be left to die there. Out of consideration for his age they had loaded only hand luggage.

'I think you'd better confess,' David said.

Tony looked up brightly. 'What?' Then he added, 'Oh yes!'

'To start at the beginning, why did you put on a show, anyway? Why didn't you just ask me about the Italian plans?'

Tony considered a cardboard shoe-box he held in his hands.
'I thought you wouldn't like to leave the school suddenly
because you're expected to give a term's warning,' he
explained.

'So you arranged to have me sacked?'

Tony said nothing. David looked up at the reversed image
of the notice on the windscreen: *Help stamp out New Austin
Sevens.*

'What about Jean Poole?'

'That was *hardly* me, honestly!' Tony said. 'There was a
rumour going about that you liked her, though.'

'But locking your door was no accident. . . You knew Mrs
Jones pried around?'

'Yes, I knew that,' Tony said slowly. He was cornered.

'Then you *did* try to get me sacked!'

'I suppose so . . . But only to make it easy for you.'

'Funny sort of logic.'

'Well, it worked, didn't it?'

'Demonstrably,' David admitted. 'That's the wardrobe wool
you're wearing, isn't it?' he asked after a moment.

'Yes,' Tony was running his knuckles down the new creases,
'Did you know they're making some of our best shorts with
*zips?*'

'So?'

'Nothing . . . Just they don't hang right in front.'

'It'll be quite a day when such finer aesthetic considera-
tions halt progress,' David said after a while, because the boy
seemed to have gone into sulks at the idea.

'Actually, I bought six new pairs yesterday,' Tony said,
looking away. 'Three with, and three ordinary.'

'Six!' To have torn his hair David would have had to jeop-
ardise their safety.

Tony brightened again. 'We're escaping!'

'Thanks to your folly.'

Tony turned to look at him. 'You don't sound very
enthusiastic!'

'Oh, I am. We've rather been tumbled into it though. I've
hardly had time to think.'

'But we're getting away! Isn't that all that matters?'

'Yes, I think it may be. At least it's the first step. And the
right one.'

'No more rules!' Tony began to bounce and the car swayed. He subsided again; counting off his fingers. 'Let's see — no more school, *choice* of food, statues, large sand castles, white shorts all day, and no comments, if I feel like it . . . then, where are we . . . no insults from newspapers, and of course breakfast in bed, because after all I *am* practically a millionaire . . .'

David laughed. 'Okay! But everywhere life has to have some rules.'

'Not the old ones,' Tony said. Adopting a former trick, he slid down the seat on to his shoulders. David reached out compulsively and squeezed his stomach. Tony had evidently been hoarding a new pullover to go with the ultimate outfit. Quietening, he said: 'I don't think I'm ever going to read a newspaper again.'

David continued playfully bullying handfuls of wool and surprisingly the boy made no protest. Then he saw that Tony was far away. The shadow of the incident with the press still hung over him.

'We must find a good beach — perhaps we can find a *private* one,' Tony said. 'Then we might find the pun about bear and bare and Sandel and sandals — remember?'

'Now wait a minute! We're going to a Catholic country, you know! Perfect decorum.'

'Like Bruce's?'

'I hope not! That's something quite peculiar.'

'You'll miss him, won't you?' Tony said.

David looked at him quickly. 'Yes . . . I will.'

'D'you know what he said to me the other day at lunch?'

'What was that?'

'He said to look after you because you were a bit crazy, and not really *sinful*.'

'Did he indeed! Darned handsome of him!'

Tony laughed. 'You know, I once built a huge sand castle at Budleigh — near the Otter . . . you know about that. It was supposed to last a year . . . But the sea got it after all. So in Italy we'll build one above the tideline.'

'No problem,' David said. 'The Mediterranean has no tide.'

'Really? Then we *are* going to the right place!' Tony's voice contrived to suggest that the ultimate justification had now confirmed his choice of country, and his devious way of achieving it.

Frescobaldi entered the Airport tunnel as boldly as the many sleeker cars. David held his steady thirty-five in the left-hand stream.

'Whatever have you got in that box on your knee?'

'Byrd,' Tony said. 'He'll wake up in Italy.'

'Hope he won't make trouble with the officials.'

'Why?' Tony was indignant. 'He would normally be flying south anyway. I told him it just so happened we were going that way.'

The Airport was a sea of colour; swirling with elegant people. David experienced new wonder at the neat figure of the boy, which seemed to stand out amid the concourse as the brightest, most compelling thing. Tony's face was radiant with happiness. Throughout the rush of paper formalities David followed behind him feeling that there could be no possible connection between them, or that if there were, then he was shadowing a phantom through the last moments of a dream.

'A bird called Byrd,' Tony explained.

'What kind is it?'

'A grey swallow.'

'Keep it out of sight then,' the officer said.

There was little time to lose. Loud-speakers muttered sooth-ingly. Then came the announcement of their own departure: 'Viscount flight one-zero-seven-nine: passengers for Rome.' The reassuring voice was almost bored.

'Us!' Tony said.

They stepped from the bus into freak November sunshine. Tony placed his right hand firmly in David's jacket pocket as they walked.

'Tones, for goodness' sake!' David exclaimed, though he knew the protest to be useless.

A few yards from the foot of the steps the boy stopped abruptly. David felt the tension in his body from the light contact of the hand in his pocket, and turned to look at him.

'It's those men,' Tony said. David had no need to follow his gaze. The meaning was apparent in his face, and in his eyes, which were like those of a young colt which is about to be branded. Now David did turn his head. The two familiar pressmen were approaching from a small knot of people who had been standing beneath the wing of the Viscount. The leading one raised his camera as he advanced. He never used it.

David heard the boy shout: 'I'm going round the other side!' Simultaneously Tony wrenched his hand from his pocket. The voice held the unnerving tremulousness of panic; but at the same time there was in it a note of inspiration and defiance.

David heard the cry and turned round. There was a patch of oil where Tony had slipped. His arm had cradled his face as he fell. Slowly David moved forward.

Byrd stepped out of his spilt box indignantly. He blinked in the unaccustomed sunlight; then, unsteadily, he took flight.

From where he crouched beside the boy David raised his eyes to meet those of the pressman, who was lowering his camera. He looked about him at the gathering people, and down again at the boy.

'It's broken . . . my leg's broken!' Tony said hysterically. Tears came to his eyes; but then he passed into a heaving unconsciousness with bitter fury twisting his lips.

Perhaps his groaning sleep was a blessing. Minutes later it occurred to a keen doctor in the first-aid station to slit both best sock and shorts with a scalpel. Through his numbness David sensed the particular expertise as stemming entirely from a private emotional state existing between the young man and his admiring nurse. Power was being demonstrated, though for no medically apparent reason.

Hysteria snatched at David's own breathing. It was too funny. But he drove his nails into the palm of his hand and walked quickly away into the crowd.

*Book Three*

## 30

T HREE days later David left for Spain. He stayed there six
months absorbing music and physically playing with gold.
From a nursing home in Budleigh Salterton Tony cabled him
fifty pounds. He described this as his *special* agent's fee. The
goldsmith to whom David had unofficially apprenticed himself
was delighted. They had, as it were, more Plasticine between
them. The outcome of David's training was an exact copy of
Tony's snake-clasp belt buckle – in the purest refinement in
the world. He airmailed this ironic gift to Glenelgin. London
Customs didn't so much as open the envelope.

After the burnt browns of Spain England looked tenderly
green. The trees and hedgerows seemed edible as lettuce
hearts. The sunlight came filtered through pastel gauzes, and
the fields were pale as new butter. In Scotland the contrast was
worse. Grey and pink people matched the heather in watery
sleep. Air filled the lungs like a scent-spray blown over ice.

Once more David ate with his brother. Half-seen vapours
found out bare skin in the baronial hotel. There was no smiling
or laughter. People ate with unfocused eyes. Had Dracula
shrieked in the turrets it must have gone unremarked by the
diners. A paralysed waiter limped among the tables with horse-
radish sauce in a silver boat. He brought cold quantities of beer
in grossly moulded tankards. If only, David thought, some
Bertie Wooster would begin chucking rolls. None did. They
themselves were a frivolity grudgingly suffered, and they kept
their voices down.

All that had been an hour ago. Now at least they were alone.
The sun's impartiality was more benevolent; the air washed
free from other people, and from memory. Like all new things
the laundered afternoon was not without sadness.

Tony was totally blue. He'd contrived to look only a little less woolly in navy. There was an explanation for this.

'They're Dragon – from Oxford,' the boy said. 'The uniform ones don't have pockets – I *ask* you!'

'Can't have Glenelgin boys slouching round like Mods, I suppose. Where do the others keep their hankies?'

'Bugger the inconvenience and insult – it's the *looks*,' Tony said impatiently. 'But they haven't forbidden these yet.'

David sat in Frescobaldi. Standing outside, Tony rocked the car dangerously.

'Oh, I've hair – some!' Tony said suddenly: the voice, the enthusiasm, the quick movement of his body was the St Cecilia's child's again.

David turned away. 'Splendid . . . splendid, dear boy! Tones, I must go now.'

'It was a bloody good lunch anyway.'

'Anyway – I must go.'

'One of our maids!' Tony said, pointing suddenly. His expression had become uncertain, yet aggressive.

'We had fun with ours – I remember,' David said. Frescobaldi seemed at that moment a ridiculous car. 'These really are new and woolly *and* blue.' With some mechanical disinterest driving him, he squeezed the boy's behind. But angrily.

Tony arched his hips away in mock ecstasy and horror. 'Not my day,' he said inexplicably.

'You've a long way to go,' David said. 'Home? For the holidays?'

'That too. Or anywhere that's . . .'

'There's the little . . . well, ah-hem . . . *tart!*' Tony interrupted. 'The one I lent your gold belt to.'

David smiled. Somewhere something was absurd. 'He isn't even pretty,' he said with genuine amusement.

'Well, shit it, Rogers – you can't get up a maid every night!'

'Up?'

'To the dormitories,' Tony said, half-listening.

'You're being bloody silly, Tones. The hell of it is you'll have to live it, know it, regret it . . .'

'Philosophy!' Tony said, bowing, and smiling happily.

'If you like.'

'And I've only been done once in two terms.'

'Shut up!' David said. The boy's loneliness rather than jealousy made him bitter.

'Forbes has a maid or a boy *every* night,' Tony said excitedly. 'And he says crazy, *disgusting* things! Oh, "Don't get the wrong 'ole – there are three, you know," about the maids; and, "Good fun ripping new shorts off a Kid-boy" . . .'

'Tones – this bloke never said that last bit. You *thought* it.'

Under the cheek-bones the blood springing up; the eyes dropping away, discovered. Tony's fingers, gripping the window, slid apart and together again, leaving a smear on the glass. David stooped to check his hand-brake. Tony recovered the more quickly.

'Did you ever do a little boy *properly?* When you were in Arabia?'

'Algeria.'

'Well, they're Arabs.'

'Berbers,' David said. He didn't know why he had become pedantic and remote at the same time.

'Did you *bugger* one?' Tony asked with a guilt-filled smirk. 'Did you? Hayward says it bursts them.'

'Who – who's Hayward?'

'Oh, sorry – a prefect. But *tell* me!'

David laid an unlit cigarette carefully down the length of the boy's nose. 'Tonimus,' he said.

Tony frowned. He looked about him at the trees, the drive and buried buildings. 'I still love you,' he said. 'One night I'll let you do what you want to me. All right?'

'It was what *you* wanted before.'

'*And* you!'

'True. It was *with*, though – not *to*,' David said.

'Only . . . properly.' Tony was looking intense. Then his thought scattered. 'Anyway, I'm going to do one of the maids – soon, anyway,' he said. Petulantly, his fingers explored mute chords on the lowered window. 'G minor,' he explained, dreaming. 'D'you want to kiss me now no one's looking?'

David clasped Tony, though the steel door divided them. It was disinterestedly violent, mushy, without taste – like biting into a water-melon with white marble pips.

'Strewth!' Tony said. He drew the back of his hand across his lips.

David pulled the self-starter. It whined tiredly. 'I'll give you a push down the hill.'

'The broad and primrose,' David said. The engine started. Tony didn't hear.

'Be good!' David called cheerfully. He was alone now. Nothing dramatic. And perhaps only for a bit. Then probably one often uttered inanities from loneliness.

'Write!' Tony yelled.

'Rather . . . Surely!' David called happily.

The Austin Seven was gathering speed. He'd started to race in a Seven-Fifty. But that had had a torsion bar, special rear springing . . . You could feel the road beneath it. Now David could not even feel his own body. There was strength in his wrists and he knew some live thing in his mind must keep him locked to the road. It was like an aircraft's blind-landing equipment perhaps.